OWEN NORTH

NINA LEVINE

ISBN: 9780994585851

Cover Design by Letitia at Romantic Book Affair Designs

Cover Image by Wander Aguiar

Proofreading provided by Read by Rose

This one is for Jodie & Tamara.
If you put us together, you create Charlize <3

1

Charlize

I'm going to kill Poppy.

It's her fault I'm currently sitting in a hotel toilet cubicle half-naked with welts the size of I-don't-know-what under my breasts and on my back, caused by the tiniest strapless lacy bra known to womankind. I had to pull my dress down and rip that sucker off so I could have a good scratch, and now I have scratch marks all over me that make it look like I've been tackled by a grizzly bear.

It's also her fault that when I finally get up the courage to put said bra back on and fasten the tightest red dress I've ever worn back in place, I'm going to have to walk out of this public bathroom wearing only one shoe. The heel on the other one snapped when I skidded on the shiny tiles in the bathroom. The shoe broke and I went flying, landing on my ass.

Damn my cousin for making me wear a bra, dress, and shoes I would never choose to wear to her wedding. "The society wedding of the year, Charlize" as my mother has taken every opportunity to tell me over the last few months.

Insert eye roll.

Kill me now.

No, seriously, do it.

I love girl stuff just as much as the next woman, but honestly, when did it become mandatory to put ourselves in so much pain just to attend social functions? I can do heels, just not the kind of heels that cause arthritis, back pain, heel deformity, ugly toes, overstretched Achilles, and bunions. Yes, I've read the data on heels.

And dresses? I'd rather not be squeezed into one that is so tight my breasts and my lungs want to take out a restraining order on it.

And that strapless bra with that allergy-causing stuff on it? As soon as I get home, I'm burning it.

My phone buzzes with a text and I reach down to grab it out of my purse that I unceremoniously dumped on the floor of the cubicle. Yes, disgusting, I know. All those germs down there, but I was desperate to get that bra off.

As I reach for the phone, the sound a woman never, ever, *ever* wants to hear comes from behind me.

My. Dress. Rips.

I freeze, willing it not to be true.

Holding my breath, I twist my arm around to the back of my dress to feel for a rip, and sure enough, I find it.

"Oh, my God, why does this shit always have to happen to me?" I mutter as I stand. "I told Poppy I had a dress I could wear, but no, she wants me to wear this damn dress."

"It'll help you meet a man," she'd said, as if meeting a man was the highest thing on my agenda. To be clear, it isn't. No, my current priority in life is to meet someone who can print bank notes that no one would ever suspect of being counterfeit.

I kid.

Kind of.

Actually, I just need a job. One that will *pay* me in bank notes.

My mother's voice rings loud in my head—*"You need to find a man, Charlize!"*

Ugh.

My mother.

I grab my bra and put it back on, ignoring the itchy welts I'm covering. I then wiggle my dress up and into place. It has a zip at the back that I carefully attempt to pull up. It plays nice; however, I can feel what the problem is. When I stretched to reach for my phone, the fabric has ripped on one side of the zip, right down to my bottom.

Opening the door of the cubicle, I peer out and find no one else in the bathroom. As carefully as I can, I make my way to the mirror and turn to see how bad the dress looks from behind.

Oh. God.

It's gaping open.

Anyone who walks behind me will be subjected to my back, half my ass, and a flash of my red thong.

All this at the society wedding of the year.

I do the only thing worth doing right now.

I scream to let my frustration out.

It feels so good that I continue screaming until it kind of turns into a wail. No tears or anything, just a good old-fashioned release of the disappointment, resentment, and irritation filling me. This is something I should do more often. Hell, everyone should do this more often. Between screaming, wailing, and having sex, I think humans could probably resolve a lot of issues without resorting to violence.

A deep voice cuts through the air. "Jesus, are you okay?"

My mouth snaps shut as I catch sight of a man entering the bathroom. My body fills with anticipation while my knees threaten to give way.

This man is hot.

Really hot.

Like, on a scale of *I'd throw myself off a cliff to avoid ever having to look at you* to *I'd take all my clothes off right now if it meant you'd just talk to me*, he has to be at the level of *I'm never wearing clothes again*.

He's probably the best-looking man I've ever come across.

I'm even ignoring the way everything about him screams money. I'm not usually attracted to wealthy men in suits anymore, but *damn*, this guy knows how to wear one. He also has just the right amount of beard. And don't get me started on the way his dark brown hair falls effortlessly into place. I'd bet all the money in my bank account—a huge risk because I don't have much in there

—that he's had it styled, even though it looks like he simply dried it with a towel and let it do its own thing.

I grip the sink and throw out the first thing that comes to mind. "Do you always wander into women's bathrooms?" I mean, I'm all for him doing that, just not when I'm in the middle of the kind of personal crisis that is threatening to send me to the brink. My dress is gaping open, and my ass is hanging out. That's a crisis with a capital fucking "c".

His brows arch as his gaze drops to my back, clearly taking in everything on display. When his eyes meet mine again, he says, "Only when I think a woman is in that bathroom possibly dying. You do realize you were screaming like a woman on her deathbed, right?"

I grip the sink harder. "That's because I am!"

His lips twitch as if he's trying not to smile. If he smiles or laughs, I swear I'll turn around and clock him. He doesn't, though. He's smart as well as hot. "So, now that we've established you're close to death, do you want a hand with that?"

My brain scrambles fast to come to a decision. I figure things could be worse. Poppy's mother and mine could have walked in on me. The Winters sisters would not be as cool about this situation as Mr I-Could-Blow-Your-Damn-Mind is being.

I nod. "Thanks. I'll just grab my purse." My emergency kit for these kinds of crises is in there. I'm choosing to ignore the nagging feeling deep in my gut that there isn't any kit that can fix this problem.

I make my way back into the stall where I left my purse on the floor, at which point I see the flaw in this plan. If I bend to retrieve it, my dress will probably rip some more.

"I hate today. Why can't anything ever be easy?"

"Problem?"

I spin to find Mr I-Could-Blow-Your-Damn-Mind standing directly behind me. Well, in front of me now. "What's your name?" It comes out like a demand. It is, really. I don't have time to keep referring to him as Mr I-Could-Blow-Your-Damn-Mind every time I reference him in my head.

"We're dealing with your death and you want my name?"

I pull a face. "Funny." He is, but this is not the time to be funny. I click my fingers to convey the urgency I feel. "Give me your name."

His lips twitch again. "Owen. And you are?"

I want to spend time drooling over his name. It's a good strong name, and I briefly imagine it falling from my lips while he gives me the kind of orgasm I bet a man like Owen can give. But I power on instead. This is no time for orgasm dreaming.

"Charlize." I step back, over my purse so that it's in between us, and nod at it. "I need you to please pick that up so we can get my emergency kit out of it."

"Your emergency kit? You really think this dress can be fixed?"

My eyes widen in horror. "Don't you say that! Now is not the time to give up, Owen. If I have to walk in front of my mother again tonight, she will *not* be seeing my ass swinging in the wind."

He cocks his head. "Are you Seth's or Poppy's? I'm guessing if your mother is here, you must be family."

"Poppy's. You?"

"Seth's. We met in college."

He passes me my purse. *Finally*. However, my run of shitastic luck continues, and I fumble as his hand brushes mine, resulting in me dropping it. Tampons, condoms, and cash scatter across the floor. None of those things catch Owen's attention. No, it's my Motley Crue vibe and my small notebook that draw his gaze. The notebook that has a penis drawn on its cover. I mean, blink, and you might not realize it's a penis because it's been drawn in an abstract way, but a penis it is.

His lips pull up in a smile as he turns to face me again. "Motley Crue, huh?" He bends to retrieve the notebook. "This looks interesting."

I snatch it from him as he straightens. Really, the only thing worse that could happen right now would be my mother walking in and finding me with this notebook full of drawings of dicks and sex acts. That I'm standing next to the hottest man on earth, in a toilet cubicle, holding said book, is mortifying. It's the kind of book a teenager would own, not a twenty-seven-year-old woman. And why the hell are we still smooshed together in this cubicle?

"My bestie gave it to me. And for your information, the Motley Crue vibe was a joke between Poppy and me." I hold the bullet up. "And also for your information, you'd be surprised what I can do to a man with this."

Poppy is deader than dead after this fiasco. And Dylan, my bestie, is, too. They will now have to spend the rest of their lives listening to me complain about the night I met the man who could have given me the best orgasms of life, only to watch him walk away laughing because he thinks my vagina has a thing for Motley Crue.

His eyes twinkle. "I bet I would."

I try to ignore the butterflies that just whooshed through my tummy. Owen is way too close for my comfort. I mean, if we were about to get it on, sure, this would be awesome. But we're not, so he needs to take a step back because I'm concerned I might throw myself at him if he doesn't. And that would be all kinds of embarrassing.

It's his eyes.

I have a thing for eyes.

They're the bluest of blue. Like, I want to swim in them, they're so blue. And I want him to come swimming with me. Naked. We should have no clothes on while we do all that swimming together.

"I can't say I did," he says.

His deep voice snaps me back to attention, and my heart stutters when I realize my hand is clutching his shirt. I blink and quickly remove my hand. "What?"

What, exactly!

What was I thinking when I touched him? And how did I not even know I was doing that? This man has some kind of voodoo magic power over me. And I just met him. I'm losing my damn mind.

"You asked me if I realized my eyes looked like the ocean at Shipwreck Beach. And then you said something about going swimming with me there. Where is it?"

"Holy mother of... shit.... No, just ignore me." Words fall out of my mouth at a horrifying pace. I'm helpless to control them.

He chuckles, and the lines around his eyes etch themselves deeper into his skin. I could stare at those lines for hours. I'm always fascinated by the lives people live, and to me, the lines on someone's face tell a story.

"Are you always this intriguing?"

I still.

No one has ever called me intriguing before. Quirky on numerous occasions. But never intriguing. My body fills with a warmth that almost takes away all my mortification over everything that has transpired tonight.

Smiling up at him, I give him my truth—something I don't usually give this easily. Owen has managed to catch me off guard and since we'll never see each other again, I feel safe doing this. "That's not a word used when referring to me. People are more likely to call me quirky or weird. I'm going to take intriguing as a compliment."

He smiles big again and good Lord above, it's a movie-star smile if ever I saw one. Nodding, he murmurs, "Yes, intriguing is a compliment." His gaze roams my face as he speaks. It's like he's trying to get a read on me, in much the same way I'm trying to get one on him.

"Shipwreck Beach is also called Navagio Beach. It's in Greece. You should go there sometime. The water is so blue. It's one of my favorite places in the world."

"I'll check it out."

We fall into silence, each watching the other. I don't know about him, but I could stay like this for a long time. Even with my ass hanging out the back of my dress. He's managed to calm me in a way not many people do.

However, Poppy has other ideas. Or, should we say, other *needs* that prove far more important than us gazing at each other.

"Charlize! Where are you, girl? I neeeeed you!"

The sound of her heels clicking on the tiles fills the bathroom, coming closer to the cubicle at the end where Owen and I are. Always the last cubicle—I never choose any other than that one. Even if I have to wait in line longer for it to become free. There's just something safe about the last cubicle.

Poppy comes to a stop in front of us, holding the tulle ballgown skirt of her wedding dress up. "Oh, good, there you are." She pauses. "Ummm, why are you standing in a toilet cubicle with Owen?"

I regretfully drag my eyes from Owen to glance at my cousin. "He was, ah, helping me with something."

Her face scrunches into a frown. "Is that code for like, sex?"

I figure it's easier to show her than to tell her what happened. I turn so she can see my back. "I ripped my dress. Owen came to my rescue. We were just in the middle of getting my emergency kit out of my bag." Well, kind of.

Poppy retrieves my purse and its contents from the floor and passes it to me. "Hate to break it to you, Charles, but I don't think even *your* emergency kit can fix that dress."

My kit is world-renowned. In my world, that is. Whenever I'm out with friends, it's me they come to for any little emergency. I've never once failed to fix a situation. "I am not a quitter," I declare loudly as I rummage for something to save my ass from my mother's eyes.

"Aunt Joan is going to have a conniption when she sees your dress."

I stop what I'm doing momentarily and hit Poppy

with a glare. "I know! Why do you think I'm losing my shit over here?"

She returns my glare while she pushes her shoulder-length red hair off her face. "Don't snap at me. I'm just the messenger. And besides, we don't have time for this. I need you to come work your magic."

My eyes bulge. "Do I look like I'm in any state to go anywhere with you?" It's a good thing Poppy and I are as close as sisters, otherwise our relationship would disintegrate quickly with the way we snap and snarl at each other sometimes.

"I don't care what state you're in. My shares are going to crash! I need you to tell me what to do."

Poppy has millions tied up in shares. I've always helped her with her investments, but about three months ago, Seth insisted she hire his friend to take over her portfolio. Something about me not being qualified enough for him. Whatever. I told her to keep the peace and let the guy take over while I watched from the sidelines. About a month ago, he insisted she invest in a company I didn't think she should. Seth stepped in and told her to listen to the professional. I get it, she was between a rock and a hard place, but now it seems that maybe the advice was bad.

"Duttons?" I ask to clarify what I'm already guessing.

She nods. "Yes." Her shoulders slump. "I should never have stopped listening to you."

My mind swings into action. "Okay, there has to be a way up to my room without anyone seeing my ass. You can walk behind me and shield me."

Owen shrugs out of his jacket and hands it to me. "Here, wear this. It'll cover everything you need it to."

I want to kiss him.

Well, let's be real, I already wanted that.

Now, I want to kiss him and hump his leg.

Okay, okay, I wanted that before, too.

I grab the jacket before he changes his mind. "Thank you."

He confuses me when he exits the stall we've been squashed in and says to Poppy, "Good luck with your shares. Yell out if you need help."

"Wait," I call out. "You're not coming with us so you can get your jacket back?" I cringe at how desperate I must sound. I'm just not ready to let him go yet. I want more time in his company. I want to stare into those eyes of his and imagine swimming some more.

His baby blues sparkle as they take me in again. "Keep the jacket. I have a feeling you need it more than I do tonight."

With that, he turns and leaves Poppy and me alone in the bathroom. I'm ready to sag against the wall and run a play-by-play in my head of the entire interaction I just had with Owen, but Poppy grabs my arm and demands, "We need to go!"

She drags me out of the cubicle before I can collect myself. I stumble because I'm only wearing one of those heels she's trying to kill me with. "Geez, Pop, give me a moment."

Letting me go, she drops her gaze to my feet. "Where is your other shoe? Goodness, Charles, what's gotten into you tonight? You're a mess."

I make my way to where my other shoe landed in the corner of the bathroom when it broke. Snatching it up off the ground, I mutter, "*You* got into me tonight! You made me wear things I would never usually wear. And being in this hotel for the entire weekend with my mother is enough to put me off my game for months. You're lucky I love you as much as I do."

She takes a deep breath and allows some of the tension in her body to seep out. "You really must love me. Who else would put up with all my shit? Especially when I didn't even ask you to be one of my bridesmaids. I'm sorry I'm such a bad cousin."

I put my arm around her waist as we exit the bathroom. "You're not a bad cousin. And for the record, I do not do the bridesmaid thing. You know that. And can I just say, this jacket is the best jacket I've ever worn in my life." It really is. Mostly because it smells all manly and sexy.

"That's because it belongs to Owen. I'm not sure how you managed to get him into that stall with you, but girl, he's the guy every woman at this wedding wants to score."

I don't doubt her. When it comes to gossip, and scandal, and all the juicy society things, Poppy knows everything.

I fled New York a year ago to escape a broken engagement and travel the world, and only arrived home eleven days ago. Besides not having a clue about any of the New York gossip, I've missed Poppy's entire relationship with Seth except for Zooming with him. I also missed the pre-wedding dinner and brunch her mother insisted she hold two weeks ago.

I sniff Owen's jacket again. "It's his eyes."

She looks at me. "He might have great eyes, but you

know what else he has? An ex-wife no woman needs in her life. I recommend you stay far away."

"Ah, Pop, this is me we're talking about. You know I now stay far away from men who wear suits that cost more than some people's annual salary."

He might be hot.

And I might want to go swimming with him.

But there's no way Owen and I would ever be a match.

I don't do men from this world anymore.

"True," she says.

"What the hell made you look up your shares at your wedding, anyway?" I ask as we head toward the elevators.

"Don't give me hell about my devotion to my shares, Charles. A girl has to make sure she's able to take care of herself at all times. Even if she is married now."

She's absolutely right.

Our mothers may have taught us a lot of useless stuff about how to act in public, how to host a dinner party, and how to walk in heels, but *we* made sure we know how to fend for ourselves in life. Poppy and I are not the kind of women who will ever rely on a man to take care of us.

I hook my arm through hers. "Right. Let's get your shares sorted. And then I'm taking this dress off, putting my pajamas on, and perusing the room service menu to plan what I'm going to eat for breakfast."

Poppy rolls her eyes. "You and your breakfast." She shakes her head. "Charles, there's no way I'm allowing you to leave the reception yet. Put those pajama ideas away."

I silently sigh.

If there's one thing I know for sure it's this: Poppy is

the bossiest person I know and I allow her to boss me around because there's no one I love more in this world than her. There's no way I'll be planning my breakfast in the next few hours.

2

Charlize

"What happened to the red dress?" Nate asks as he leans back in his seat at the reception an hour after my bathroom fiasco. "I could have sworn you were in love with it."

Nate's sarcasm is duly noted. My brother knows how much I detested that dress. He's the one who's been subjected to all my complaints about it today. "It's dead."

He looks at me, amused. "Dead? How does a dress become dead?"

I reach for my wine and take a sip. "When it rips down to one's ass it becomes dead." I glance down at the little black dress I'm now wearing. "This one looks better, don't you think?"

He eyes it before meeting my gaze again. "This one is sure to be a crowd pleaser."

I smack him. "I thought you loved me, Nate Cohen."

He grins. "I'm sitting with you, aren't I? I'll protect you when Mom comes over to tell you what she thinks of that dress."

My mother will hate this dress simply because I chose it. Also, because it's too sparkly for her taste. And far too short. Joan Cohen prefers conservative clothes, especially for her daughter. I truly feel sorry for her some days that she was gifted me as a child. We couldn't be more opposite if we tried.

"How much longer do you think we have to sit here?" I ask.

Nate shifts his attention to a woman at the next table. "I'm giving it another five minutes."

"I'm surprised you're still sitting with me to be honest." My brother isn't known for not making the most of a wedding. He may hate them as much as I do, but he never fails to use them to his advantage when it comes to sex.

He drains his glass of whiskey and stands, eyes still on the blonde at the next table. His interest is recipro- cated. "I've changed my mind. I'll see you next weekend."

I frown. "Next weekend?"

"Yeah, family dinner, Sunday."

I groan. "Oh, God. Really? That's a thing again?"

"I'm surprised Mom hasn't already made it clear that she expects you every Sunday night."

I haven't really given her a chance to do so. Since I arrived back in New York, I've holed up at my bestie's Brooklyn Heights condo and done everything in my power to avoid my mother. I love her, but she's intent on harassing me about getting married, and that is something I have zero interest in.

"The only thing she's made clear is how much she still thinks Benjamin and I are the perfect couple." I roll my eyes. "Honestly, she's like a broken record over this, messaging me constantly about him." I shoo him. "Go. That blonde can't keep her eyes off you."

He gives me a knowing look. "I'll see you next Sunday."

"Ugh," I grumble to myself as I watch him leave.

I sip some more wine as I glance around the ballroom.

It has to be said that not much changes in Manhattan. I may not keep up with the gossip, but the people never change. My mother and Poppy love it here, but I don't do well with the shallow. The fake. The emptiness.

And the men.

Don't get me started on the men of New York.

I've dated a lot of them. And I was engaged to one for six months after a two-year relationship.

They're nothing but suits, money, and power.

And arrogance.

God, the fucking arrogance of them blows my mind.

"Charlize."

I turn to my left to find Owen looking down at me with a smile. "Owen." I jerk in my seat, uncrossing my legs and knocking the table with my knee. It sends my drink flying, spilling wine all over my dress and legs. "Shit. Jesus."

Honestly, my lips should be taped together while out in public.

I stand. At the same time, Owen steps forward and

reaches toward the table. All we manage to achieve is a collision that involves his hand almost groping my breast, my hand almost groping his dick, and then, our lips almost smooshed together.

His hands settle on my hips, steadying me. His eyes meet mine, a smile filling them. "I imagine being your friend would never get boring."

I place my hands to his abs. It's unintentional; they move of their own accord. I don't blame them. He has great abs. I mean, I haven't seen them, but feeling them now.... These are the abs of a man who dedicates good time to them.

And that smile he's giving me? Along with the way his eyes crinkle? He means what he just said in the very best way.

I return his smile. "Really, you have no idea. You should try it." Someone absolutely needs to tape my mouth now. Stat. Before I start talking about swimming naked with him. Because that's where my mind has already gone. Naked swimming with Owen.

If I thought his smile of a moment ago was something of great beauty, I had no idea what he's capable of. Now, he adds sexy to the mix, and I'm unsure if I'll be able to keep all my thoughts to myself much longer.

"I'm willing if you are."

Why does it suddenly feel like my heart has decided to take part in a 100m sprint? It's beating fast enough to win.

When I don't respond to what he said—because my thoughts and heart are far too tangled for me to form words that make any sense—Owen glances down at my dress. "I suspect this dress is about to go the way of the red dress. Have you got a third one?" He meets my eyes again. "If not, my shirt is all yours."

I look at his shirt.

I mean, it would be remiss of me if I didn't inspect what he's offering.

His shirt, that is.

I'm absolutely not imagining the abs I'll get my eyes on if I accept his offer.

I'm still staring at his shirt when he says, "You want the shirt, don't you?"

I find his eyes again. "Well, I do like this color."

"It's a good, strong color, white."

"My thoughts exactly."

"I imagine white suits you beautifully."

"It really does. Far more than this black I'm wearing."

"I find that hard to believe. Black looks great on you. I'll need to see it to believe it."

"There's only one tiny problem with this plan."

"What?"

"My underwear."

His eyes flash with the amusement I know he's been working hard to conceal. "Underwear is often a problem in my experience. Tell me more."

"Come on, Owen. You've seen the color of my underwear. It won't be a good look for me to flounce around this reception in a white shirt with red underwear."

"Do you tend to flounce around a lot?"

"Oh, you have no idea."

"I'd like to see that too."

"The flouncing? Or the sinful red underwear worn under white?"

"Both."

Poppy takes this moment to interrupt us. "Charles, did you wet yourself?"

Owen and I are still standing together with his hands on my hips and my hands on his abs. Sadly, he lets me go and takes a step back when Poppy joins us. I miss the contact instantly and fight to keep this from my face. If the way Owen watches me is anything to go by, I fail. I think he's very aware of the fact I wish his hands were still on me.

I look at my cousin. "I spilled my drink."

"It was my fault," Owen volunteers. "I snuck up on her."

Poppy frowns at my dress. "Do you have another dress? I don't think this can be salvaged."

"No. I'm all out of dresses now, but Owen has offered his shirt. I think it's a good option."

"I bet you do. The fit Aunt Joan would have over that would be fun to witness." She throws a glance around the room, looking for what, I'm unsure. "Jessa is your size. She might have something you can borrow."

"Did you lose your brain the minute you said 'I do' to Seth?" Poppy knows I'd never ask Jessa for anything, let alone a dress. She and I may have been friends years ago, but I cut those ties when she made a move on my ex just after I got engaged to him. The only reason she's at this wedding is because she's a plus-one. Poppy would never invite her to anything.

She ignores my smart remark. "Well, we don't have a lot of options." She continues searching the room. "What about Faith? Or Marta? They're about the same size."

"Seriously, Pop, I think this is a sign that I'm done for the night. My pajamas are looking great right about now."

Her eyes widen. "This is not a sign to swap a dress for pajamas. I will help you clean this dress."

"No. You have a husband to dance with and guests to talk to. And I have a date with my room service menu."

"You can't leave," she blurts getting a wild look in her eyes. "I can't do this without you."

I frown. "Do what without me?"

Her arms flap as she gestures to the room around us. "*This*."

"What? Get married? You've already done that. And it's not like I've been with you every step of the way today, Pop. You haven't needed me to help get you through it." I knew Poppy was nervous about today. However, it's not like her to be anxious over anything, so she's confusing me now.

"I don't need you *right* by my side, Charles. But I need to know you're here. With me. You know this. I can't get through life without you. I may have let you run off for a year without me, but I refuse to let you run off on my wedding day. I just won't stand for it."

My strong, beautiful Poppy.

She's five feet of fierce but under that she's vulnerable and uncertain at times. We've been by each other's side our entire lives, lending our strength when needed. I know she struggled while I was away, and I hated that, but I needed to put space between New York and me more than I needed anything. Tonight, I can give her what she needs.

I squeeze her hand. "My room service menu can wait."

She exhales a breath. "Good." Then, she's all fierce

business again. "Do you need me to find you a dress? Or help you clean this one?"

"No. I've got this. Don't worry about me. If worse comes to worst, Owen's giving me his shirt. You just go and be married."

She hits Owen with a stern look. "Please make sure she doesn't flounce around my reception in your shirt. I do not need to hear about that from Aunt Joan for the next decade."

He chuckles. "Got it. No flouncing. No white shirts."

More of her stern look. "I'm being deadly serious, Owen. I will hurt you if you don't step up."

He shifts his expression to mirror her serious one. "I understand the assignment. You can count on me."

"Good." With that, she leaves us, striding toward her husband like she's on a mission. But then, my cousin is always on a mission.

Owen leans in close. "I now believe that you do a lot of flouncing. And let the record show, I want to see it at some point."

"That would imply you intend on seeing me after tonight since I'm not allowed to do it here."

"You understood me correctly, Charlize," he confirms in that sexy tone of his that I'm beginning to think he's trademarked because I've never heard it from another man.

My heart starts that 100m sprint again.

It sends me into a fluster and causes words to trip over themselves in their haste to leave my mouth. "Right, you should make yourself useful while I go and clean this dress. I'd like another wine. Maybe an entire bottle. No, scratch that, it'll only get me into trouble." I release a breath as I reach for my purse. Without waiting for a response from him, I turn and make my way to the bathroom.

I spend longer in there than is necessary.

In fact, I take so long that I don't expect to find Owen still waiting for me when I return to my table. But there he is, waiting with the glass of wine I requested.

He takes in my dress before giving me an amused look. "Did you make a trip to the dry cleaner instead of the bathroom?"

I sit next to him. "I'm surprised you're still here." I mean, I was gone for almost thirty minutes. Time which I spent doing mental acrobatics over coming back to Owen. I don't trust myself with him. I told myself no more New York men when I came home. I'm here for a year to make some money before leaving to do more travel. I'm not here to get involved with anyone, and something tells me that Owen isn't a man a girl spends just one night with.

"You and I have a flouncing date to plan, remember?"

I take a sip of my drink. "I don't date."

"You're married?"

"No."

"You're too busy washing your hair every night?"

My lips quirk.

I enjoy bantering with this man far too much.

"I never bother with my hair." I point at it. "This cleanliness is highly unusual."

"The upkeep dating requires turns you off it?"

"What upkeep? I am not a woman who bothers with any upkeep."

"You've been burned one too many times?"

"Try a hundred times too many."

He narrows his eyes at me. "You've swapped men for cats?"

"I knew you were smart the minute I met you, Owen. It only took you five guesses to figure me out."

He drinks some of his whiskey. "I need to have a word with the universe and find out what I did to ruin my chance with you."

I smile at him. "It wasn't you; it was me."

"Fuck. The words a man never wants to hear."

My smile turns into a grin at his playful tone. I angle my body so I'm facing him. "You seriously think I believe *you've* heard those words before?"

"You think I haven't?"

I sip some more wine. "Okay, tell me who and when, because no, I can't imagine any woman saying that to you."

"You just did."

"That's not quite accurate."

"That's how I took it."

"Are you going to prove your 'me, not you' claims or was I right to think you were making up stories?"

Those blue eyes of his twinkle. "Right. Amanda Cleary broke up with me when I was seventeen. She told me it was her, not me."

I roll my eyes. "Teen heartbreak doesn't count."

"It absolutely does. Amanda was my first love. We were together for two years before she broke up with me. You can't tell me you don't have a high school broken heart story."

"I didn't have a boyfriend in high school."

That appears to stun him. "What? Bullshit."

I shake my head. "Not bullshit. I was eighteen when I had my first boyfriend."

"Did you date before that though?"

"No." I take a moment while I consider being fully honest with him. Normally I wouldn't share something so personal, but since I don't plan on seeing Owen again, and since I feel a connection with him, I decide to be more vulnerable than I ever am when I first meet a guy. "I was filled with too much anxiety to even talk to guys in high school. I mean, you've seen me in action. I get myself into all kinds of trouble just being out in the world, let alone when I talk to guys I like. I was a hot mess whenever I tried to talk to my crush."

"So, I should interpret you spilling your drink all over yourself as a sign you like me?"

I take another sip of wine, doing my best to slow this all down. To shift us away from the direction he keeps trying to take us. "Was Amanda the only girl who's used the 'me, not you' line on you?"

"No. Danika Jackson told me that when I was twenty, and Heather Martin did too when I was twenty-two. And now, you've said it to me before I've even had the opportunity to show you what you'd be missing. I think this may be my worst dating moment."

I laugh.

I can't help myself.

Owen is fun, and as much as I'm trying not to flirt with him, he brings it out in me.

"This is hardly a dating moment."

He drinks some whiskey before flashing a sexy smile at me and doing his best to wipe my memory so I can't remember my plan to never see him again. "This could be a dating moment if you let it."

"I don't date, remember?"

More of that sexy smile. "Give me the chance to change your mind."

I assess him for a moment. I have no intention of dating Owen, but I am enjoying talking with him. There's no harm in spending the rest of this night having a conversation with him. "Tell me something about you that no one knows."

Surprise flickers across his face. The kind that lets me know he likes this question. "I detest small talk even though I'm good at it and people probably think I like it."

"Oh God, yes. It's the worst. I'd rather sit in silence than engage in polite conversation. My mother raised me to excel at it. She'd die if she knew I've stopped doing it over the last year while I've been away."

"You just ignore people now?"

"I try not to be rude, but if someone is intent on talking with me, I'll throw in some big talk. That'll either scare them off or lead to some great conversation."

"Big talk. I like that." He eyes me over the rim of his glass as he drinks more whiskey. "What's something about *you* that no one knows?"

"Well, that's hard because Poppy knows everything about me."

"Absolutely everything?" He says this like he doesn't quite believe me. But then, women are different to men, so I guess this may seem hard to believe.

"Yes. There's nothing we don't discuss. But if we remove her from the equation, no one knows I count things." At his look of confusion, I elaborate. "I count stairs as I take them. I count the cracks in the sidewalk. I count the things in front of me. I count the clouds. Anything and everything. I mean, I'm not counting all day, every day, but it can help calm my anxiety."

"Have you always done this?"

I nod. "For as long as I can remember. It's often how I get to sleep too." I reach for my drink. "Okay, your turn. What's something else others don't know about you?"

"I'm a great cook."

It's my turn to experience disbelief. "No one knows this about you? Really?" I mean, Poppy told me Owen was married. Surely a wife would know that about her husband.

"No one."

"Okay, so full disclosure; Poppy told me you have an ex-wife. How does she not know you can cook?"

A smile touches the corners of his mouth and eyes. "You asked Poppy about me?"

"She volunteered that information without my prompting."

This doesn't wipe the smile from his face. He still seems pleased to know we discussed him. "Jill and I didn't eat in often. And when we did, she cooked. It was her thing she enjoyed. I didn't take over."

Jesus, I need to stop with the big talk. I'm only discovering more things to like about Owen.

Before I can switch to small talk, he angles his body more toward mine and asks, "Why did you leave New York for a year?"

"Why does any woman run away from their life?"

He nods knowingly. "Did it work?"

"It was the best thing I've ever done, and yes, it worked, but not in the way I thought it would."

This catches all his attention. Well, I already had it all, but everything about him becomes more attentive and it feels like he's listening even more intently. "In what way did it work?"

"Instead of forgetting him, I've started to find me, which has helped me move past him. Forgetting him was my goal, but it was the wrong goal. We don't forget those we loved. It's just not possible. But I learned that healing is possible so long as I'm good with the lines that loving well carved into my heart."

It's like the room and all the people in it fall away from us as Owen listens to every word I say. It's just him and me, and this big talk that's doing big things to me that I don't want it to be doing.

This was supposed to be a wedding reception I had to just get through because I don't like wedding receptions. Instead, it's turning into a party for two. A party I'm actually enjoying.

Owen nods slowly. Thoughtfully. "Loving well does carve lines, doesn't it?"

"Yes. Some good and some bad. I thought I had to rid myself of the bad ones, but I realized those lines are the currency love trades in. They're permanent. And while I wanted nothing but to remove them from my heart, getting intimate with them helped me learn so much about myself. I thought I'd made a mistake by loving him. I hadn't. Loving others is how we learn to love ourselves."

"I've never thought of it like that. I think I agree with you."

I finish my drink. "Finally. A man who agrees with me

without too much encouragement." I hold my glass out to him. "And now, you should get me another drink."

He takes my glass and stands. "The same?"

I nod. "Thank you."

My eyes don't leave his ass while he walks away from me. It's a good ass. God, it's a great ass. One I should not spend time with.

I'm in the middle of pondering just how many hours a week Owen spends maintaining that ass when my bestie texts me.

Dylan: How's the wedding?

Charlize: Well, I'm two dresses in, nearly three, and I'm having big talk with a guy I shouldn't be. I may need rescuing. Oh wait, you're busy tonight and can't do any rescuing because you're the worst best friend of life. I forgot that for a moment.

Dylan: I'm not going to touch the dress situation, but a guy who can do big talk? That's not someone you need rescuing from.

Charlize: Oh, trust me, he is.

Dylan: Babe. It's time.

Charlize: Don't you "babe" me. It may be time but it's far from the right city.

He switches to a call which I answer immediately. "You should not be calling me right now. You have art to show." Dylan is an artist and is in the middle of a traveling exhibition. He's showing his art in Chicago tonight.

"I've got ten minutes to kill. Talk to me. Tell me again why you can't date the men in New York."

"You know why."

"No, I know some bullshit story about arrogant New

York assholes, but may I just remind you I'm not an arrogant asshole. Not all New York men are."

"You can be arrogant. And an asshole. Just FYI."

"And yet, here we are twelve years later. I can't be that bad."

Dylan has been my bestie since I was fifteen and he was seventeen. He took me under his wing at school when I was being picked on. When I was awkward and anxious and cared too much about what others thought of me. He's never given any fucks what people think of him and has taught me to do the same.

"You know my history of dating bad guys here. I'm not falling in love in New York again."

His voice drops into the low tone he uses only with me. The tone that is filled with the kind of care and love a twelve-year friendship cultivates. "Char, bad guys and shitty relationships can be found in every city. You're being irrational."

He's right. I know he is. But still, just the thought of letting my guard down now makes me nervous. I've spent twelve months leaving hurt and anger and disappointment behind. And before that there were many years of the same from all the guys I've dated and had relationships with. All here, in New York. I can't help but feel skittish about hooking up with another man here.

"I know, but I can't change how I feel."

"We're talking dating. Nothing else. Just have some fun and maybe some sex. No feelings need to get involved."

I catch sight of Owen coming back to me and run my gaze over him.

He's tall.

Maybe six foot three.

Tanned skin.

Athletic body.

Well, I haven't actually seen his body, but the way that white shirt fits him, and the way his ass and legs fill out his trousers, he's got muscles.

And his hands.

Owen has good strong hands.

With veins I'm struggling not to stare at.

What is it about the veins in a man's hands?

Maybe Dylan is onto something.

I could have fun with Owen.

I could definitely have sex with him.

That wouldn't be a hardship.

I could check out his arms. I imagine they'd steal my attention the same way his hands are.

And those blue eyes of his.

I could think a lot about naked swimming with him while staring into them.

"No feelings," I say to Dylan while watching Owen's confident stride.

"Yeah. No love. Just fun."

I smile at Owen as he gets closer. "Okay. I can do that. And now, I have to go. I'll see you when you get home tomorrow."

"Don't forget the condoms. We don't need a repeat of that time you decided your eggs had magical powers and you were incapable of getting pregnant."

"Hush. No eggs were harmed in the making of that. And no babies were made." And besides, I'm now on birth control.

"That may be the case, but it was a long, stressful wait for those results."

"Honestly, it's a good thing you were born a male. You would not survive as a woman."

I end my call with Dylan and watch Owen take the last few steps to me. I decide that athletic really is the perfect way to describe his body. Unless, of course, one prefers the words "fucking hot", which, let the record show, I can get behind.

"You must not sleep much," I say as he hands me the glass of wine he got me and sits. The words are out of my mouth before I can stop them. Jesus. Where's the tape I need for said mouth?

"I'm fascinated to know where you're taking this." He sips some of the whiskey he got himself before placing the glass on the table and waiting for my reply.

I wave him off. "No, I'm not taking that anywhere. I don't know where those words came from."

He laughs. Goodness, even Owen's laugh is sexy. I wonder if I could convince him to alternate swimming naked with me, laughing with me, and having long big-talk conversations with me? I mean, he did say we could share a dating moment.

"You can't make a statement like that and leave me hanging," he says.

"You're not going to let this go, are you?"

"Not a chance."

I take a sip of wine, enjoying the way he's watching me like I'm the only woman in this room. "You have the body of a god, so I was thinking that in between eating, cooking, working, having your dating moments, spending time with your friends and family, getting to and from all the things you do, and working out, you mustn't have a lot of time for sleeping."

The look he gives me lets me know he's here for this conversation. "There's a lot to unpack there."

"There really isn't."

"Eating is first on your list. Does that mean you're a foodie?"

"No, it means I like to eat. I'm not fussy about what food that is."

His mouth kicks up at the ends. "That's good for our future dating moments. I know some great places to take you."

"Did you forget I don't date?"

"Surely you'll make an exception for me. I do have the body of a god after all."

"There is that, but honestly, I'm a high expectations kind of girl, Owen. I look for men who are willing to make a strong emotional commitment. With all the time you spend in the gym, you wouldn't have time for that with me."

"I think you're being presumptuous about the hours I spend in the gym. You might be surprised to know it's not that many."

My eyes drop to his chest. "I think your idea of not that many must be different to mine."

"Let's just say that I have plenty of time for sleep, right alongside plenty of time for dating moments with a woman who has high expectations of the men she lets into her life."

We're interrupted when Poppy yells my name out from the dance floor. "Charles! It's time to dance!"

My conversation with Owen has drowned out the

music. It comes back into focus now and Poppy's right. It really is time to dance when "Shut Up and Dance" is playing.

I look at Owen as I push my chair back. "This is one of Poppy's and my songs. I'll be back. Unless, of course, you want to come and dance with us."

He leans back in his seat, all sexy eyes and interest. "I think I'd rather watch."

Oh, this man has it all going on.

And not an ounce of arrogance detected yet.

I drag my eyes from him and make my way to the dance floor where Poppy's letting loose. She's arms and hips everywhere, having the time of her life. When I reach her, she throws her arms around my neck. "I fucking love weddings."

I laugh and dance with her. "On a scale of one to ten, how much are you loving *your* wedding?"

The happiness that's written all over her only intensifies, telling me everything I need to know. "My love for my wedding is off the scale. I think Seth and I will renew our vows every year. Maybe every six months if I can convince him."

"That man would give you a wedding every month if that was what you wanted."

She sighs happily. "He would, wouldn't he?"

I've spent barely any time with Seth, but I've talked with him a lot over Zoom, and even from a country away I could see how much he adores Poppy.

"He would, but I'm out. I'm not made for weddings."

She pulls a face at me. "We both know you love me enough to come to all my weddings. And Dylan's not getting out of the rest of them. I'll set up a recurring event on his calendar so he doesn't double book again."

"Good luck getting anywhere near his calendar."

"You underestimate my abilities, Charles."

I don't, but I also don't underestimate Dylan's assistant. She's hardcore when it comes to running his life. Okay, so that may be exaggerating a little, but she annoys me with the way she won't let me have anything to do with his schedule. I hold this against her even though I know her reasons have something to do with the fact *Dylan* won't let me anywhere near his business. I may be an executive assistant with some of the best references in New York, but years ago when I tried to help him, he'd said, "We're not fucking our friendship up by working together, Char." Ugh. The man drives me crazy at times. And so does his assistant.

We stop talking and devote all our attention to dancing. Our second favorite thing to do together. Well, Poppy would say it's our third favorite, with talking and people watching coming in before dancing. I'm not a huge people watcher, though, so dancing is an easy second favorite for me.

When "Shut Up and Dance" fades into "I Wanna Dance With Somebody", we really get down to business. Whitney never fails to get our hips going. "24K Magic" by Bruno Mars comes on after that, at which point Seth steals my girl from me. I only put up a tiny argument with him before turning to find my way back to my seat.

I run smack bang into Owen's hard chest as I turn.

He catches me in his arms, and they slide around me easily. His dazzling smile is all mine when he says, "Dance with me."

My hands go to his chest as I process everything happening. My brain doesn't do well with this much sensory overload. It tends to malfunction in situations like this, which leads to me saying or doing things I wish I didn't.

Those eyes of his.

His hands on me.

Those muscles everywhere.

And his scent.

It's hitting every pleasure button I have.

It's salty ocean air, hot sand, lazy afternoons in the sun.

It's woody and musky and masculine in all the ways I like, and it's taking everything in me not to lean into his chest and live there for the rest of the night.

"You smell like my favorite candle." Good God, my mouth thinks it's in charge tonight. I grip his shirt. "Just pretend I didn't say that."

More of that sexy smile from him. "I'd rather not."

It's his voice.

Out of everything he's throwing my way, it's his voice that will be my downfall.

"Stop talking and just move those hips," I order. At his grin, I add, "And stop doing anything with your mouth."

Owen shows me he's bad at following directives when he brings his mouth to my ear and says, "I'm just getting started with my mouth, Charlize."

He then lets me go and shows me how well he can move his body.

I dance with him, and by the end of the song I'm convinced sex with Owen would be great sex. The man can move. Holy hell, he can move.

"Crazy In Love" by Beyonce and JAY-Z comes on and we keep dancing.

The dance floor fills up and we're pushed closer together. By the end of this song, our bodies are almost fused. When "Want to Want Me" by Jason Derulo starts playing, Owen's hands slide around me, and I fully accept my fate.

I'm so turned on right now.

I can't deny it a second longer.

I am not in charge of myself anymore.

Owen assumes control when this song bleeds into "Earned It" by The Weeknd. He turns me, bringing my back against his chest. His hands start at my hips as we move together. When I grip his right forearm, he dips his mouth to kiss my neck.

My core loses herself at the press of his lips.

When his hand glides around my body to rest against my stomach, *I* lose myself.

There's being turned on, and then there's being turned on by Owen. They're two completely different things.

I can't stop myself; I arch against him. His growl of approval against my ear as my ass connects with his dick is unlike any sound I've ever heard from a man, and good God, I like it.

Owen's fingers splay across my stomach, and I moan when they tease the edge of my breast.

"I'm trying to be a gentleman here," he rasps against my ear. "But if you keep making noises like that, I may fail."

I turn in his arms and meet his gaze while his arms

circle me. "If this is your idea of being a gentleman, I think I need to see what filthy looks like with you."

"Fuck." He looks like he's in actual pain. "I was trying, but you don't make it easy to keep things clean."

I curve my hand up over his chest to his neck, enjoying the feel of my fingers on his skin. My gaze drops to his neck. "I think we should grab a bottle of wine and get out of here."

"I think you should keep your eyes on me exactly how they are right now. I'll take care of everything else."

I do as he says, keeping my eyes exactly where they are.

That is, until Poppy cuts in on my time with his body. "I approve," she says, drawing our attention when she joins us. "But Aunt Joan will not if you two start losing clothes on this dance floor."

"Owen was just about to make sure that doesn't happen," I say.

She eyes him. "Good man." Then, pasting a stern look on her face, she adds, "Don't fuck this up, Owen. You're part of my family now, and since Charles is joint head of my family, I can't have issues between the two of you. Have some fun and treat her good, 'k?"

His lips twitch. "You are the absolute right woman for Seth, Poppy. And I will do my best not to fuck this up."

She arches her brows for a good ten seconds, making her point. "I'm being deadly serious here. She's my person. I will not have her messed around."

Owen's amused expression disappears. "If there's one thing I'm fast learning tonight, it's that where Charlize is concerned, you're deadly serious. And I should not fuck anything up if it concerns her."

Poppy relaxes her brows. "I like that you're a fast learner. Now, go. Aunt Joan is busy in the corner with Bobby Young. She won't see you leave if you hurry."

"She's a good cousin," he says after she leaves us.

"The best." I resume getting acquainted with his neck, wishing his throat wasn't covered with that bow tie.

"Right, let's get that bottle of wine." He takes hold of my hand and leads me off the dancefloor back to my table where we collect my purse. He then heads to the bar, where he gets what we're after before guiding us out of the ballroom to the elevators.

I don't even hesitate to follow him.

In the space of four songs, Owen has managed to get me from not wanting anything to do with another New York man to being all in on a night with him. And since it will be our only night together, I intend on making the most of it.

3

Charlize

"Your room or mine?" Owen asks as we step into the elevator.

"Yours." Mine looks like a tornado hit it. I can't allow him to see that tornado. Not even if he's only going to be a one-night stand.

He selects his floor and then looks at me. The heat in his eyes matches mine. "It's your turn."

"My turn for what?"

"To tell me another thing about you that no one else knows."

"I feel like it's your turn. I told you about what I learned in my year away."

He moves into me, backing me up against the elevator wall, looking down at me with all that heat. "You did, and then I told you about my gym habits. It's your turn."

"Okay, but I imagine your gym habits aren't a guarded secret. I don't think that information counts. And honestly, I'm still in the dark as to just how many hours you dedicate to this body. You say you have enough time to work out, to sleep, and to date, but—"

Owen's mouth silences all the words tumbling out of my mouth.

It also silences all the rambling thoughts in my mind.

Not to mention his hand that's sliding into my hair while his other hand is getting intimate with my waist again. The man is a magician, juggling the bottle of wine and my body.

I grasp his shirt while I lose myself in his lips, easily forgetting anything and everything that came before this moment in my life.

Owen knows his way around a kiss.

He's sure about what he's doing. Confident in a way I like.

When he deepens the kiss, his tongue moving over mine, I'm helpless but to moan into him.

I actually think I'm only one moment away from just giving up on anything *but* moaning.

At the sound I make, Owen tightens his hold of me and growls while kissing me even more thoroughly.

If I thought I was turned on while dancing with him, I had no idea he has the power to make me want him more. Right now, I want nothing more than to spend every second of my life with his hands and mouth on me. And Jesus, I know that's ridiculous, because we just met, and because this is one night only, but a girl can't tell her body how to feel or what to want.

I kiss him back just as thoroughly. When the elevator

sounds to alert us that we've arrived at our destination, we're so consumed with each other that we ignore the alert.

It's not until a couple join us in the elevator that Owen lets me go with a growly curse.

I meet the woman's eyes as I attempt to regain control of my thoughts, my body, my life. She reminds me of my mother by the way she's dressed uber conservatively and the look of judgment in her eyes. The only difference between them from the outside is their age. This woman looks to be no more than thirty-five. How sad for her that she's so stiff.

"Darling," I say to Owen as I note the fact we missed our floor and are now on our way back down to a lower floor. "You really need to stop trying to fuck me in elevators. We missed our floor."

The amusement in his eyes beats the shock in the woman's. I said it to play with her, but I'm here for the way it's entertained him.

The elevator stops and the couple exit.

Owen presses the button for his floor again. "Feel free to call me darling again. Particularly if you're trying to stir up trouble."

I pull him back to me. "I feel like you should be made aware that I'm always trying to stir up trouble."

I've got my hands and mouth on him again before he can reply to that. I've also got a leg curled around his.

When the elevator reaches his floor, neither of us move fast to untangle our bodies. When Owen does make a move to let me go, I grip his neck and keep his mouth on mine. I really don't want him to stop what he's doing to me.

When the elevator doors close and it starts another descent, he smiles into the kiss and finally finds a way out of my hold. "You think we should just stay in here for the rest of the night?" He presses the button for his floor. Again.

Damn I like his eyes.

Yes, we've established that more than once tonight, but I don't think I'll ever get enough of them. Especially when they're conveying his enchantment with me like they are right now.

I settle a hand on his waist. "I have a freckle between my big toe and my second toe on my right foot."

He takes a moment, processing that, his smile never leaving his face. After he dips his face back to mine so he can brush another kiss across my lips, he asks, "How does no one know that?"

I shrug. "No one's taken the time to discover it."

"You've been with amateurs." He slides a hand into my hair and kisses me slowly, deliberately, like he's exploring, learning, pursuing. When he's finished, he lets me go and says, "You should never give your time to amateurs."

The elevator stops and we're met by Poppy who frowns at us before entering. She selects her floor. "I'm not even going to ask why you two are in here looking like you do."

"Like what?" I ask before taking a good look at Owen and seeing what she's referring to.

Owen's hair is a hot mess.

Well, it would be if it wasn't just hot. I think this man could brush his hair flat and part it down the middle and still look good.

I catch sight of my hair in the mirror. It *is* a hot mess.

Poppy doesn't reply to my question. She just lifts her brows in answer.

"I've been trying to have sex with Owen in here but he's far too much of a gentleman for that."

More lifting of her brows. "Honestly, Charles, you go away a good girl and you return a hussy. Normally, I would commend you on this, but please refrain from this behavior at my wedding. I do not need our mothers to get wind of this."

We reach her floor, and with one last shake of her head, she gathers her dress and steps out of the elevator.

We continue up to Owen's floor and I do my best not to throw myself at him again. Instead, I say, "It's your turn."

I can tell he's struggling not to put his hands all over me in the same way I am. Whereas I succeed, he fails.

He pulls me close and drops his mouth to my neck. Kissing me there, he murmurs, "You're the very best kind of trouble, aren't you?"

There's something about him saying that to me that gets me in the feels. I know what it is: it's the fact that my ex-fiancé and almost every guy I dated before him thought I was too much. Benjamin told me I was more than a handful. That was right before he told me he loved me, but that we would be having a sit down to discuss how I needed to act a little differently for our marriage to succeed.

"I know many men who would disagree with you."

"Amateurs." His lips graze my throat, and he continues his exploration of my skin.

When we reach his floor this time, he takes hold of

my hand and leads me out of the elevator and down the corridor to his room.

He ushers me into his suite, a luxurious and expansive space with views out over Central Park. I pad across the plush carpet into the living room and drop my purse on a sofa.

Eyeing the eight-seater oval dining table in another area off the living room, I look at Owen who has placed the bottle of wine down and is removing his bow tie. "Are you planning a dinner party while you're here?" I'm suddenly feeling nervous now that we're alone in his suite, and random things always fall out of my mouth when I'm nervous. God knows what I'll say next.

His eyes hold a mixture of heat and a smile when he moves into me and snakes his arm around my waist. Dropping his mouth to my neck, he kisses me before saying, "I always make it a point to be prepared for anything." He kisses his way up to my mouth, his eyes finding mine. "It turns out I'm hosting a dinner party for two."

Before I know what's happening, he lifts me into his arms and carries me to the table. Placing me on it, he moves between my legs and slides one of the thin straps of my dress off my shoulder. Bending to kiss my skin there, he says, "I can't recall the last time I was this hungry."

I grip his hips.

I'm now feeling out of my depth right alongside feeling nervous.

Owen has been flirty and sexy since the minute I met him.

Now, he's something else entirely.

Now, he's all masculine energy, power, and command. Those blue eyes of his are filled with determination.

His strong hands feel like confidence and expertise.

And his voice? It's turned to the kind of gravel I find hard to resist.

"Charlize." He traces a finger along my jaw as he watches me closely. "Where did you just go?"

I try to swallow my nerves. I didn't intend on getting this close to Owen tonight when I opened up to him and shared the personal things I did, but here we are, very close. And since I feel safe with him after the things we've talked about so far, I continue in that vulnerable vein. "I was just thinking how you changed from fun, flirty Owen to this whole new Owen."

"Is this new Owen a version you like?"

God, I like that he doesn't discount what I said. And that he's looking at me like he's genuinely interested in my answer.

"Yes."

He takes a moment considering that. "I'm sensing a but here."

I exhale the breath I've been holding without realizing it. "You've got me all nervous. I can't remember the last time I felt like this with a guy."

His smile is slow, and it just may be the sexiest smile he's given me so far. "Good," he murmurs, taking hold of my hand and threading his fingers through mine. "Because you've got me feeling the same way."

"You really expect me to believe a man like you ever feels nervous with a woman?"

"Why do you think men do half the dumb things they do? Because a woman has them all up in their head, overthinking things they never thought they'd overthink." He keeps hold of my hand while putting his other arm around me and pressing gently against the small of my back, so it forces my body against his. "You should know you have every ounce of my attention and that I'm completely captivated by you." He pauses. "And since it's my turn to tell you something about me, you are now the only person alive who knows I lied on a Truth or Dare when I was fifteen and told everyone at a party that I'd lost my virginity to a girl I met on a summer vacation."

I laugh, the vibrations of it in my body calming me. Or maybe it's Owen who calmed me. "So, you hadn't lost your virginity then?"

His fingers that are threaded with mine tighten. "No. I could tell you when I did lose it, but it's not my turn to share something."

My nerves are now a shadow of themselves. "You play a mean game, Owen."

"I'm hoping you'll play it right back." He watches me expectantly, waiting.

Instead of giving him anything, I unthread my fingers from his and reach for the top button of his shirt. The white shirt I can't wait to get off him. Undoing that button, I say, "Are you planning on this game lasting all night, or do you think at some point you may get serious about taking my clothes off?"

The determination in his eyes of a moment ago returns. "If you don't think I'm already serious about that, I'm doing something very wrong here."

I'm unsure if it's the look in his eyes, the rasp in his voice, or what he says that does it, but I move past any nerves I had and all the way into *just get my clothes off already* territory.

I work my way down his buttons.

Owen watches every move my fingers make before meeting my gaze again. The silence between us is charged with the kind of electricity that sends anticipation racing through my veins.

"See, these abs I'm looking at now are very indicative of many hours spent in the gym," I say because, holy hell, I've never laid eyes on abs like his before. Not in the flesh, anyway. "I think I was right that you don't have much time for sleep."

He slides the other strap of my dress off my shoulder. "It's a good thing I took today off from the gym. It means I have all the energy I need for you."

I run my hands up over his shoulders and slide his shirt off. I then reach for the button on his trousers and make quick work of undoing it. I'm about to slide his zip down when he stops me.

He places his hands on my bare thighs and slowly inches them toward the hem of my dress. "We're going to take our time, Charlize. Or I should say, *I'm* going to take my time." He slips one hand under my dress and wraps it around my leg. His other hand moves to my waist and then up to my breast. His eyes never leave mine. "Tell me something else."

If Owen thinks my brain has the capacity to think of things about myself right now, he's dreaming. The only thing that comes to mind tumbles out of my mouth before I can stop it. "I have never been this wet in my life. At this point, I'm beginning to think you have magical powers right alongside everything else you've got going on."

His fingers dig into my thigh and a growly "Fuck" falls from his lips. He brings his hand to my neck, grasping it while his mouth crashes down onto mine.

If Owen is as skilled at sex as he is at kissing and dancing and flirting, I'm in for the best sex of my life.

These kisses he's giving me are next level.

Owen immerses himself in them in the exact same way he's immersed himself in our conversation tonight.

Every piece of him is here with me and he's paying attention to every response I give him. I know this because the things I've liked the most are the things he's making sure to give me again.

The slide of his fingers in my hair.

The amount of tongue I prefer.

The way he bites my lip.

Not to mention everything else he's doing with his body while kissing me.

I am here for all of it.

He drags his mouth from mine and trails kisses down to my throat. He spends time there, driving me wild with how achingly slow he's taking this. I both love how unhurried he is—because, hello, can I get an Amen for a man who knows how to turn a woman all the way on—and just wish he'd get to his destination already.

I grip his hair and arch my body into him.

A moan escapes my lips, which earns me a deeply male sound that only turns me on more.

Owen's hands move to the back of my dress, and he unzips it. He lifts his head so he can take in my body while he peels the dress from me.

I wiggle my ass from side to side to help him remove it and enjoy the look in his eyes when I'm sitting almost naked in front of him.

He places the dress on one of the chairs before moving between my legs again. Eyeing my red bra, he traces a finger over the skin just above it. "Red is my favorite color on a woman."

"And here I was thinking the next thing you were going to share with me was the age you lost your virginity," I murmur, lost in the way he's looking at me.

He undoes my bra and I'm almost certain we both skip a breath as it falls away from my body.

Silence fills the room while Owen devotes time to looking at my breasts. It only lasts for mere seconds before he does that growly thing of his that I wish all men did and drops his mouth to them.

I wrap my legs around him and clutch a handful of his hair again.

I thought kissing Owen was next level.

I change my mind.

Owen kissing my breasts is next level.

I mean, I'm beginning to think the levels I'd set for myself in life were all wrong.

I'm beginning to think I have no idea how many levels there actually are.

Owen spends an exorbitant amount of time with my breasts.

He also spends time kissing the welts that god-awful bra caused.

I'm taking it he's a breast man.

It's a little sad for him that I don't have much in that department.

"Those veins in your hands are doing so many good things to me right now." My words trip over themselves in their haste to leave my mouth, and it has to be said that Owen's gotten me to the point where I don't even care. I no longer require tape for my mouth. I'll happily share all my random thoughts with him and not worry that he'll judge me.

He slowly lifts his head, almost like he's more than regretful to be dragging his attention from my breasts. I expect him to say something about what I just said, but he doesn't. Instead, he brings his lips to mine and bruises me with a scorching kiss I don't ever want to end. Well, except I kinda do because I really want that mouth somewhere else.

When he finally ends the kiss, he says, "I fucking like the way you just say whatever's on your mind."

This inspires me to attempt gaining control of our situation.

I reach for his trousers.

I want that zip down and these pants off.

Owen's eyes heat more than they already were.

His hand wraps around mine, halting my progress. "We've got all night, and there's no fucking way I'm rushing even a second of it." He kisses me again while keeping hold of my hand. He then moves his mouth to my ear. "I'm going to teach you some patience, Charlize. You're going to be a good girl and lie back on this table, and you're going to stop trying to distract me from what I want."

Holy. Fuck.

I've never been called a good girl during sex.

Not once.

Not ever ever ever.

It turns out I like it.

A *lot*.

This inspires me to do what he says.

I lie back and rest on my elbows. "Like this?"

Owen's gaze sweeps down my body and I see the moment his determination strengthens. And goodness if it doesn't cause him to assume even more dominance than he already has.

He takes hold of my waist with both hands and slides me back further, positioning me so I'm lying down with my legs bent and my feet resting on the edge of the table.

"You are so fucking beautiful," he says, grasping my right ankle. He curves his hand around it so he's holding the back of it. Then, slowly, and gently, he brings his other hand to the back of my shoe. Bending, he kisses the top of my foot before removing my heel. He repeats this on my other foot and removes that shoe too.

I've never been more about a man taking charge of undressing me.

If Owen wants to take my shoes off every night, he can go right ahead.

"You also have the tiniest of freckles right here," he says, tracing a circle around the outside of my left ankle.

The inside of my stomach is suddenly a menagerie of butterflies, butterflies, and more butterflies.

Unable to stop myself, I sit up and reach for Owen's neck. Gripping it, I pull myself back to the end of the table, bringing our bodies together again, and kiss him.

I give him what I've worked out *he* likes: a little more tongue than I do, me leaning right into him, and my arms around him with my fingers threaded up into his hair.

I kiss him so deeply we could drown in each other.

He kisses me back just as deeply.

We're both breathless when we come up for air.

Owen's hands are in my hair as he stares down at me. "You make it hard on a man, Charlize."

"Hard for what?" My thoughts are disordered from all this kissing and touching. I've no clue what he means.

He tugs a handful of my hair, pulling my head back so he can lick my throat. "You have no idea, do you?"

I really am drowning here.

Drowning in Owen and his intoxicating ways.

"It's like you're speaking in riddles to me. All I know is that I may die if you don't fuck me soon."

He lets go of my hair. "Lie back."

He says only two words, but his tone says everything he's not saying.

I really like flirty, sexy Owen, but I think I like take-charge, commanding Owen more. I imagine this Owen is single-minded, driven, unstoppable. All traits I like in a man.

I comply with his directive and lie back.

He watches me while I settle myself on the table before shifting his attention to my panties. Hooking his fingers in them, he slides them down my legs. He is neither fast nor slow in how he does this. He's deliberate and focused. Something I'm learning about this man is that when he's got a goal in mind, it takes a lot to distract him from it.

He pockets my underwear and it's disturbing to me how hot I find this. I mean, is he actually a stalker who likes to keep women's panties? How many pairs would I find in his dresser if I were to take a peek? Will he maybe try to choke me with them later? Jesus, who really is Owen? I hope Poppy will seek revenge for my murder if that's where this is leading.

"Charlize." Owen's husky voice cuts through all my weird thoughts as he takes hold of my legs and places them up over his shoulders. "Don't disappear on me now."

"I was just wondering if you're secretly a serial killer who strangles women with their own panties."

His lips quirk in amusement. "It makes perfect sense for you to be wondering that, but I want you to stop thinking about that and start thinking about the fact I'm going to give you my tongue now."

Oh. God. Yes.

I don't even care if he's a serial killer.

He can strangle me with my panties if he wants.

Or he can take them home and add them to his stash.

But he must give me his tongue first.

"That's my only condition." I say this out loud even though I meant for it to stay inside. Again, I don't care. I have no doubt Owen will run with it.

More of that lip quirking, and yes, he runs with it. "You're only condition for what?"

"You can strangle me with my panties, but only after you give me your tongue."

"And here I was thinking you were a girl with high expectations. You should up your conditions for agreeing to be strangled."

"You think I should add dick to my conditions, don't you?"

"Absolutely." I have no idea how, but he manages to keep a straight face.

"Okay, you drive a hard bargain, Owen. I'm adding that. You can strangle me after you give me your tongue and your dick. But you should be aware that Poppy will come for you if you go through with that."

This coaxes a smile out of him. "I have no doubt. You *are* joint head of her family, after all." He runs his gaze down my body, his eyes settling on my pussy. I know by the way his nostrils flare and the way his breath quickens that he's done with our conversation. That all he can think about now is tasting me.

I watch him taking me in, and every inch of my skin blazes with anticipation and desire more than it already was.

I don't know if my vagina has ever felt so ready for a man.

Owen is far too good at foreplay.

I never imagined the day I'd think that about any man, but here I am.

When he finally bends to give me his tongue, it's like I'm watching in slow motion.

My breaths stall.

My pussy clenches.

My need intensifies to all new levels.

Owen doesn't disappoint.

He gives me his lips first, kissing my clit.

It's a closed-mouth kiss that slowly turns into an open-mouthed one that he adds tongue to. He sucks my clit so perfectly that I know for sure he's got magical powers. And he does this for long enough that it makes me think he's as much a clit man as he is a breast man.

By the time he shares the love with the rest of my pussy, licking and sucking his way down me, I'm halfway to an orgasm. I mean, who am I kidding, though? I've been halfway to an orgasm since he started flirting with me. I'm more like three quarters of the way there now.

When he gets to my entrance, he makes a deep growly noise and buries his face in me, his tongue in me, his everything in me, and eats me with so much skill I may find it hard not to demand he does this over and over tonight.

I rock my pussy against his mouth, tightening my legs around his neck and arching up off the table.

I reach for his hair and grab it. "Oh God, Owen.... *Yes.*"

His fingers dig into my ass when I continue chanting incoherent words at him that let him know how much I like what he's doing.

And then, he rocks my world completely.

He pushes two fingers inside me while sucking my clit back into his mouth and giving me his tongue in all the ways I really like.

My orgasm is the best orgasm I've ever had.

It reaches the tips of my fingers, toes, head, everywhere.

It bursts into bright colors behind my eyes.

It touches deep inside in places an orgasm has never touched.

I'm not sure, because I forget I'm even living, but I think it lasts and lasts and lasts.

By the time I open my eyes and come down from it, Owen's kissing the inside of my thighs and looking at me like he's ready to ravage me completely.

And good God, *I'm* ready for that too.

I've never been so greedy for another orgasm so quickly.

I sit up and slide down the table to Owen in such a rush I catch him by surprise.

This time when I reach for his zip, he doesn't stop me.

Instead, he rasps, "Fuck," and allows me to unzip him, push his trousers down, and take hold of his cock.

"Have you got a condom?" I ask while I stroke him.

"No." His breaths are ragged. "But I know you do in that emergency kit of yours."

"And I thought all you saw was my Motley Crue vibe."

Owen has been good at keeping up with my conversation all night, but it seems he's reached his limit. He stops what I'm doing with his dick and takes a step away from the table. "You need to go and get one of those condoms."

I don't drag this out. The man has given me the best orgasm of my life; the least I can do is get a condom for him.

I retrieve one from my purse and come back to him. He makes a move to take it from me, but I shake my head and give him a sexy smile before taking hold of his cock and rolling it on.

Once I've got it in place, I pull his face down to mine so I can whisper in his ear, "I want you to fuck me hard, but be careful. I don't think I've ever been fucked by such a big dick."

"Fuck," he growls, his hand coming to my waist so he can spin me to face the table. Bending me over it, he says, "You've got a filthy mouth, Charlize. One I really fucking like." With that, he thrusts inside me, filling me so well I know I'll wish tomorrow that he wasn't only a one-night stand.

Owen gives me what I asked for.

He keeps one hand gripping my hip while pounding into me and bringing his other hand around to my pussy so he can give my clit what it needs.

He fucks me hard and so damn well that by the time we both come, I'm boneless and practically unable to hold myself up.

"Are you okay?" he asks, pressing a kiss to my shoulder and pulling out of me.

I lean on my elbows, breathless and spent, but completely and absolutely feeling more than okay. "Yes. I just need a minute to find my legs again."

"Wait there. I'll be back to get you." He leaves me for less than a minute before coming back to carry me into the bedroom.

After he deposits me on the floor, I eye the bathroom. "I'm going to clean up."

He nods. "I'm going to crack that bottle of wine. Do you want a drink?"

I smile. "Yes, please."

I turn to go into the bathroom, but Owen reaches for my hand and pulls me to him. Circling one arm around me, he rests his hand on my ass while he kisses me. He steals more of my breath and a whole lot of my attention when he lets my lips go, presses a finger to the skin behind my left ear, and murmurs, "You also have a tiny birthmark here."

"I didn't know that."

"Now you do." He brings his mouth to my ear. "And it's sexy as hell."

I'm still processing all this when he lets me go and exits the bedroom to get the wine.

I did not come home to New York to look for a man.

I didn't, I didn't, I didn't.

But this energy between us is fire and it's undeniable.

I take a deep breath.

This is one night only.

Some sex and some fun.

I refuse for it to be anything more than that.

4

_____

Charlize

Pancakes.

That's what I wake thinking about.

Blueberry and lemon pancakes to be specific because that's what I'm ordering for breakfast. Well, it's one of the things. When I insisted on perusing the in-room dining menu at two a.m. after Owen fucked me for the third time, I had trouble choosing between the pancakes, the eggs benedict, and the avocado sourdough toast. I spent a good ten minutes going over the options before Owen took the menu from me and announced we'd be ordering all three plus the smoked salmon bagel for him. That was right before he pulled me into his arms, kissed my shoulder, and told me to get some sleep.

I'm not sure I intended on spending the entire night with him. But here I am, our bodies pressed together with one of my legs over his, an arm draped over his chest, and my thoughts running wild about pancakes and the sex we had last night.

It was the best sex of my life, and I'm both happy about that and annoyed.

I mean, once a girl's had such great sex, how is she supposed to go on without it again?

Last night may have been a monumental error in judgment.

"Good morning," Owen murmurs, bringing his hand to rest on my arm and cutting in on all my thoughts.

"How do you still smell so good?" I look up at him, mapping his morning face and storing it for future reference. I may not plan on sleeping with him again, but a girl can save memories for later use. "Did you get up during the night and put on more cologne?"

His lips pull up at the ends. "I didn't leave this bed once. I wasn't game to."

"Why not?"

"I got the distinct impression from you last night that convincing you to see me again may prove difficult. Once I had you in my arms, I didn't want to let you go in case you make good on that."

"So, what, you just plan on not letting me go?"

"I haven't devised a solid strategy yet, but that one's tempting."

"I hate to break it to you, but you're going to have to let me go when breakfast arrives. And speaking of breakfast, you need to order it. I'm famished."

"Are you as dedicated to lunch and dinner as you are to breakfast?"

"I'm dedicated to food, full stop, but breakfast is my

favorite meal of the day. I don't know how it's not everyone's favorite meal."

Owen's cell sounds with a text that he ignores. "Do you still want what you decided on last night or have you changed your mind?"

"I haven't changed my mind."

Two more texts arrive for him, at which point he says, "Sorry, I have to check these. And then I'll order breakfast."

He leaves the bed and uses the bathroom before exiting the bedroom to check his messages.

I take the opportunity to go to the bathroom while he's on his phone. I also take the opportunity to calm the nerves that are making themselves known.

This is the part I hate about one-night stands.

The morning after.

Not that I've had that many one-night stands, but when I do, I don't find them like they seem to be in the movies and books. I'm not as able to just wake up and pick up where we left off the night before. Not even if the sex was as amazing as it was with Owen. I tend to wake feeling a little awkward.

I mean, sure, Owen's had his face up close to my vagina. He's fucked me on a table, in a bed, and on my hands and knees on the floor. He's said filthy, filthy things to me. He knows secrets of mine that no one besides Poppy knows. But prior to that all happening last night, we were strangers. I really don't know the guy, so there's a lot of overthinking happening right now.

Should I shower?

Should I not?

I'm naked and we're going to have breakfast. That requires clothes. Or does it?

Where did I leave my dress?

And my bra?

And let's not forget that Owen pocketed my thong. I'm going to need that back.

And good God, my hair.

I stare at it in the mirror, assessing the bird's nest it is. How am I going to fix that without tools?

Not to mention my face.

I peer closer.

Is that a pimple coming up?

Jesus, no.

See, *this* is why one-night stands are the worst in my opinion.

The freaking morning after.

I take a deep breath and comb my fingers through my hair before splashing my face with water. I then spy Owen's toothpaste and swipe some over my teeth.

I can't have breakfast with Owen.

I might love breakfast, and I might really like Owen, and he might have given me the best sex I've ever had, and he might be a thoughtful and attentive guy (sexy and charismatic too), but I can't stay.

I need the safety of my room.

I can eat all the breakfast I want in my room without all this overthinking.

Also, my attraction to him needs to be kept in check.

He's making it clear he wants this to be more than one night, and while I don't think he's a New York asshole I should avoid, I didn't come home for anything more than to refill my bank account so I can see more of the world.

Owen is a decent guy. I don't want to mislead him. I'm here for twelve months only. It wouldn't be fair to him to begin something that can't go anywhere.

I spend a good amount of time on these thoughts. By the time I step out of the bathroom, wrapped in a robe, I've managed to get all my thoughts into a knotted mess while my nerves have gotten my body into the same. This isn't an unusual thing for me, but I've reached a whole new level this morning. This *all-new level* thing seems to be an Owen specialty.

I silently count every step I take from the bathroom into the bedroom. Owen is nowhere in sight, but I can hear him out in the suite talking.

I count more steps as I walk from the bedroom to the sitting room, and through to the living room where Owen's standing in front of one of the floor-to-ceiling windows on his phone, looking out over the city.

He's wearing his trousers but no shirt, and I stare at his back. At the muscles moving under his skin as he lifts his arm to run his fingers through his hair.

Fragments of memories from last night flash through my mind.

Kissing his back.

Digging my nails into his back.

Holding onto his back while he fucked me.

I squeeze my thighs together.

This is not the moment to be thinking about these things.

I divert my gaze to the left, to the dining room. When I spot my dress on one of the chairs, I quickly dart toward it.

Must get dressed.

Must grab my phone and purse.

Must get out of here.

"Charlize." I've just seized my dress when Owen's deep voice cuts through the air.

I stop and turn to face him.

He strides my way, his eyes greedy for me, tracing my curves before meeting my gaze. "You know," he murmurs as he slides his arm around my waist and pulls me close, "I liked your bed head." He brushes his lips over mine, sending my pulse racing. "It was sexy as hell and reminded me of all the things we did last night."

Could his voice be any sexier?

It does things to me.

Delicious things that make thinking hard.

Like, *really* hard.

Particularly when the nervousness I'm experiencing is already making that difficult.

I hold up my dress. "I'm going to get dressed and go."

A slight frown creases his forehead. "You haven't eaten yet."

"I'm not hungry anymore," I blurt.

Jesus, is that the best I can come up with?

I mean, I told him I was famished.

I pretty much forced him into ordering breakfast for me.

In my next life, I'm coming back as a put-together, ass-kicking woman whose brain works at all hours of the day, one-night stands be damned.

Owen's frown disappears, replaced by a look of understanding. "Don't go. Let me order you breakfast."

I step out of his hold, willing my brain to kick into

gear so I can give him a plausible reason for why I must leave this very minute.

My brain does not save me, but my phone does.

A succession of texts bombard it. Texts I rush to check with an apologetic look at Owen and a "Sorry, let me just check these."

I bend to retrieve my shoes that I've just spied and take them with me into the living room. I locate my purse on the sofa where I left it last night and grab my cell. The texts are from my mother. I've never been so happy to see a message from her.

Mom: Are you still asleep or have you already checked out?

Mom: I just stopped by your room.

Mom: If you're still here, your father and I would like to have breakfast with you.

Mom: Nate isn't answering his door either, or his phone.

Mom: Charlize?

Charlize: Where are you now?

Mom: Back in my suite. Are you still at the hotel?

Charlize: Yes, but I can't have breakfast. I have things to do this morning.

Mom: What things?

"Everything okay?" Owen asks, joining me.

My head snaps up and I look at him.

He really needs to finish dressing because I really need to stop being bombarded with those muscles of his.

"Yes, but I have to go. My mother needs me for something."

Thank goodness I'm not Catholic. I'd have a lot of lies to confess after this morning.

Mom: Can you delay whatever you have to do? I've invited Benjamin for breakfast. He'll be here in half an hour.

Holy. Fuck. No.

I don't even bother replying to her last text.

There's no time.

I need to get out of this hotel within the next half hour.

There's no way I'm having breakfast with my ex. I will do absolutely anything to avoid running into him this morning. It's not that I don't ever want to see him again. It's that I'm not prepared for that first meeting to be *today*. And since I don't trust that my mother won't organize a key to my room just to confirm I'm not still in there, I'll be checking out before he arrives.

I shove my cell in my purse and eye Owen. "I'm sorry to rush out like this, but I really have to get dressed and go. Some family stuff has come up."

I then hurry into the bathroom, get dressed, take a deep breath, and go back out to say goodbye to Owen. I catch a glimpse of my hair on the way out. Owen must be blind. My bed head was not sexy as hell. It looks much better without that bird's nest.

He watches me come back out into the living room. I like that he's not forcing himself on me, that he's giving me the space to do what I need to do.

I slow down as I watch him watch me.

My brain might be imploring me to hurry up and leave, but my body and soul are drawn to Owen. I move into him and place a hand to his chest. Smiling up at him, I say, "Thank you for last night. I don't like weddings, but I won't ever forget Poppy's wedding. And not just because it was Poppy's." I pull his mouth down to mine so I can brush my lips over his one last time.

I know I've made a mistake the second our mouths come together. That connection between us that was undeniable last night is still very much the same today. I only intended on a quick kiss. A goodbye kiss. However, this chemistry between us demands more than quick. It won't settle for fast.

Owen slides one hand into my hair and one around my waist, growling deeply into the kiss, and waking my desire up all over again.

I lose myself in him.

I forget my mission to escape the hotel as fast as possible.

I kiss him back with the same passion he's kissing me.

It's the elevator from last night all over again.

For these moments, we exist in a world that only the two of us are in.

A world I don't want to leave.

When he ends the kiss, I stare at him breathlessly. I have so many words for him, but none find their way out of my mouth.

"Have dinner with me tonight," he says, not letting me go.

"I can't. I already have dinner plans." It's the truth. Dylan and I have plans.

Owen's eyes search mine. "Tomorrow night, then."

Kissing him goodbye was a *big* mistake.

"I told you last night I don't date, and I meant it, Owen."

He keeps me in his arms. "I'm not the kind of man who walks away from what I want, Charlize."

I stand firm even though Owen's determination and confidence is working against that. "I imagine you aren't, but that doesn't change the fact I'm not looking for a relationship."

He watches me thoughtfully for a few moments before finally bringing his mouth to my ear and murmuring, "This isn't finished between us. I've still got a million things to discover about you."

With that, he lets me go.

He has no idea what his words do to me. He simply steps back and watches as I gather my wits. He stands in front of me, still half freaking naked, and looks at me with intent and desire that sends chaos through my veins. Chaos that causes me to clutch my shoes and purse close before exiting his hotel suite without another word.

On my way out, I swipe the hotel key card that Owen placed on the entryway table last night. It's not weird at all that I'm stealing it. I mean, I'm leaving my underwear behind in my haste to leave. I feel like this is a fair swap.

Owen does not have a million things still to discover about me, but if he wants to know one more thing, then it can be this: I do odd things like swiping the hotel key cards of men I want to remember.

This is *most definitely* finished between us.

However, Owen will be the one-night stand I never forget.

5

Owen

I rake my fingers through my hair and stare at Julian, my Co-Chief Investment Officer. "You're fucking kidding, right?"

His lips flatten and he pulls a face. The kind of face that tells me he's not fucking kidding. "Sorry, Owen. I wish I were. But he's effectively wiped twenty mil off our bottom line."

I don't waste time mulling over my choices. As far as I'm concerned, there's only one to be made here. "Get rid of him and find us a new analyst. And have Maxwell take over his work in the meantime."

Julian nods and I exhale, trying to force the angry energy from my body.

It's not so much the money that's angered me; we'll make that up without a problem. It's Graham, one of my analysts. He's been sloppy for months now. I've given him space and time to fix whatever the hell he's been dealing with, but he's continued to make mistake after mistake, and hasn't taken advantage of the passes I've given him. I can't tolerate people who waste opportunities.

A knock on the glass wall of my office draws my attention. My assistant, Tahlia, waits expectantly on the other side of the glass, entering when I motion for her to come in.

"Sorry to interrupt, but Jill just called." A pained expression fills her face. "I wanted to warn you both that she's about five minutes out and she's worked up about something."

"Fuck," Julian mutters, echoing my exact thought. He looks at me after Tahlia exits the office. "You have to do something about her."

I blow out another long breath. "I know."

"I know you know, Owen, but you've been saying this for months now, and I'm telling you that if you don't act soon, she's going to cause us the kind of problems we'll take hit after hit from." He pauses, giving me that look of his that says he's weighing up whether to share what's on his mind.

"What?" I ask. "Just say it. We're way past the point of not getting stuff off our chest when we need to." Seven years working together has ensured this, and it's something I know we both value. Neither of us like operating without the full facts.

"It appears that Jill's getting extra friendly with the staff."

I frown, unsure if I've understood him correctly. "As in she's sleeping with them?"

He nods. "From what I'm hearing, yes."

That *yes* is still working its way through my brain when my office door is pushed open by my ex-wife.

"I see you two started without me again," she says, her voice filled with the snappy tone that's become her norm over the last few months.

I met Jill when I was twenty-five. I barely knew myself back then. I certainly didn't know what kind of woman I wanted to spend the rest of my life with. It's taken a marriage, a divorce, and a year of navigating post-divorce life while still working together to show me exactly what kind of woman I'd choose to spend the rest of my life with. It's not a woman like Jill.

She refused to let me buy her out of the company when we divorced, and I didn't force her hand because I understood what this company means to her. During our marriage, we built North Management into one of the most successful hedge funds in the United States with more than $40 billion in assets under management. I'd hoped that her fight to keep half of it would mean she'd put our differences aside for the sake of the company's success. That was a year ago, and since then she's let her anger and bitterness over our divorce get in the way of her work. North Management might be doing well financially, but behind closed doors we're a mess of bad decisions and battles for control. I'm close to losing my patience with her. The only thing keeping me in check is the fact I once loved and respected her.

"You're late," I throw back, unwilling to put up with her bullshit today. It might only be eight a.m., but I've already put four hours in this morning, and those four hours have been filled with fixing a handful of problems she's caused. If she continues on this path of butting heads with me today, she may live to regret it.

She presses her lips together. "Hardly. Besides, it's impossible to be late to work when it's your own damn company, Owen."

I glance at Julian. "Can you give us a minute?"

The look that crosses his face can only be described as relief. With a nod, he exits my office, leaving Jill and I alone. Something I'm detesting more and more each day.

I undo the top button of my shirt. I suddenly feel suffocated by it.

"You're off your game," Jill says before I've decided how to broach what we need to discuss. At my frown, she elaborates, motioning at my shirt. "I can't recall the last time you wore a tie to the office. And is that the only suit you own? I could swear it's all you wear these days. If you need help at home, I can come and take care of these things for you."

I run my hand down my face. Is it really only eight o'clock? It feels like this day has lasted a week already.

I ignore the tie and suit comments. She knows I don't love wearing ties. How I survived six years of wearing them at her insistence is beyond me. If I can get away without one now, I do. "Graham's out," I start with. "I know that will likely not sit well with you, but I'm done with tolerating his fuck ups. Maxwell will take over his work until Julian finds someone to replace him."

Jill has a soft spot for Graham, which is why I'm expecting an argument over this decision. Also, Jill is our COO, so it likely won't impress her that I've taken point on this. However, she surprises me. "I agree with you on this."

"Good." I take a moment to consider how I'll say the next thing on my list of topics to cover with her. Jill has become difficult in almost every way possible. She argues over things she never cared about before our divorce. I'm unsure if she actually cares about them now or if she's determined to make my life hell. I can't read her mind any better than I could when we were married, so I can't be sure which it is. "I took a call from Ron yesterday. He's not happy."

She knows exactly what I'm referring to and she doesn't take even a second to come out swinging with her argument. "He's an asshole, Owen. You know this, so I'd appreciate it if you'd skip the lecture I'm sure you have planned for me and just move straight onto the next item of business."

I arch a brow. "You finished?"

She presses her lips together again; a signature Jill move with me lately. "I was, but I can see you're not."

"No, I'm not. Not when his business pays for the three homes you own, the body your expensive surgeon is building, the vacations you take around the world, the trainer who practically lives with you, the chef who does live with you, and all the fucking clothes and shoes you buy." I exhale harshly, frustrated with her and the headaches she's causing me. I don't give a fuck about all the shit she buys, but I give a lot of fucks about the business I've spent years building. I'll be damned if I'll let anyone destroy it.

Venom pools in her eyes. "You can be a real bastard when you want to be. Some days I wonder how I ever made it through six years of marriage with you."

I ignore that. Getting into the weeds of our marriage won't be productive this morning. "You slept with him?"

She stares at me, her perfectly-put-together face losing some of its beauty as acid spills through the cracks. "I can't believe you just asked me that."

I clench my jaw, working hard to remain in control of my anger. "Believe it because I'm going to ask you again. Did you fuck Ron?" I already know the answer to this question, but I need to hear it from her. I need her to own what she's done so we can move forward with an understanding that she can never do it again.

"Is that what he told you?"

"Jill, answer the question."

"We don't need his business. I'll find us ten new Rons today if I have to."

My chest tightens, my forehead tightens, my mouth tightens, and my patience snaps. "There aren't ten more fucking Rons to find. And if you think we don't need his business, I don't know who I'm talking to anymore." I pause. "Why?"

"Why what?"

My anger finally explodes out of me as I yell, "Why the hell would you pull that stunt with him? And stop acting like you don't know what I'm talking about. You know very fucking well what you've done." I was hoping we'd be able to have this conversation like civilized adults. I should have known better.

Ron Johansen is our top client. Has been for four years. Apparently, he and Jill were having an affair for a couple of months until recently, at which point he ended it with her. In his words, "she's turned psycho, Owen." Knowing Jill as well as I do, I find *psycho* a little difficult to believe, but I do know that when her heart has been broken, she tends to operate from hurt emotions rather than the intelligence she possesses.

She inhales a long breath before turning away from me and pacing the length of my office. Standing in front of the floor-to-ceiling window that overlooks Manhattan, she keeps her back to me as she says, "He's very persuasive when he wants something, and I'm not going to apologize for sleeping with him." She turns to look at me, her face twisted with a combination of defiance and hurt. "He made me feel wanted, and that's something I hadn't felt in a very long time."

One of the reasons our marriage fell apart was because I worked too much. I fully acknowledged that during the marriage counseling we had, and I pulled back on my hours while we tried to salvage our marriage. It's not the only reason the marriage failed, far from it, but Jill never lets me forget my contribution.

"It's not so much the sex that I have an issue with—" I start, but she quickly cuts me off.

"Good, because you don't get to have an issue with any sex I choose to have."

Christ, this morning is going to hell in a handbasket faster than any morning with Jill has recently. I take a steadying breath. "You tried to hit him with extra fees when you know that's a bullshit move that will never hold up. And for fucks sake, Jill, he's married. What I can't wrap my head around is how someone as intelligent as you does something as dumb as this." I jab my finger at her. "*That's* why you don't fuck your clients. Sex gets in the way of good judgment."

She glares at me. "Can you please stop using foul language with me?"

"You want a seat at the table, Jill? You want me and Julian to treat you the same way we treat each other? Let me assure you that when he or I fuck up to this magnitude, we don't fucking watch our language with each other." Now, I *am* being a bastard, which isn't something I like about myself. And yet, I'm unable to alter course. Not when I'm this angry.

"No, but that doesn't mean I'll accept you speaking to me this way."

"Can we get back to the point? Ron was ready to walk yesterday. To pull everything from us. And that was solely because of what you did." My chest rises and falls with a heavy thud. "You won't be handling him anymore. I'll take over. And if you ever do something like that again, so help me fucking God, you won't like how I deal with it a second time."

Jill's fury matches mine. "We're equals here, Owen, even though you and Julian like to pretend you two run the show. As such, you don't get to boss me around. There's no way I'm handing Ron over to you. Not after I had to fight you tooth and nail for my seat at your table. We agreed that I'd look after the top clients, and I intend for that agreement to stay in place."

"Yes, we're equals, but when your good sense has been fucked out of you, it's time for me to step in."

She slaps me, her hand stinging my cheek hard when they connect. "Fuck you." With that, she stalks out of my office in the direction of hers, leaving me in the kind of mood that's no good for anyone or anything.

It's not often I get worked up like this. I'm the guy who

generally gets on with most people. Even when I think someone's an idiot, I can tolerate them longer than most can. This is why I've indulged Jill while she's worked her way through her resentment at me during the last year. While it was directed my way, no harm came to the business. Now that it's affecting the company, I won't stand for it. And if I know anything, I know that my refusal to tolerate it a second longer is going to cause an enormous problem for me, for Julian, and for the company.

I undo another button on my shirt as I take a seat behind my desk.

Fuck.

I glance to my right, to Julian's office. We're separated by glass and since I didn't lower the blinds while I argued with Jill, he was able to witness every moment of it. He meets my gaze, reading me as expertly as he can after all these years together, and stands to come into my office.

"I take it that didn't go well," he says, dropping down into the chair across from me.

"Whatever the extreme opposite of well is, that's how it went."

"You told her you'll take over Ron?"

I nod. "She's not going to make it easy."

"Well, neither of us expected she would, so that's no shock."

Both our phones buzz with a text notification.

Jill: Since I didn't get a word in this morning, Owen, I want to alert you both to the fact I've brought our 10am meeting forward to 9am. Don't be late. We have many issues to discuss.

Julian looks at me after he reads the message. "Fuck me, I hate Mondays. And I quit."

Our Monday morning meeting with Jill is not the highlight of either of our weeks. "Your resignation is no good here." I spot our head analyst striding toward my office. "You spoke with Maxwell already?"

"Yeah. He wants to discuss a merger he's heard rumors of."

I meet Max's gaze and motion for him to come in. The three of us spend the next fifteen minutes evaluating some of our positions before moving onto the merger he's heard about. After making a plan for Max and Julian to get more solid facts and information on it, the two of them leave me. I fill the time before the meeting with Jill calling some clients to check in on them.

Ten minutes before the meeting, I head to Jill's office. It's the furthest from mine on our firm's third floor. She had the office next to mine until our divorce. She then made it clear she didn't want to be that close to me. I didn't care either way, but lately I'm grateful for the distance between us.

I want these ten minutes to ask her whether she's getting close to our staff. It'll be a tricky conversation, though, so I'm not looking forward to it.

Jill didn't want our divorce. Initially, I didn't either. However, after six months of counseling and working on the marriage, I faced the difficult truth that we probably should have never married in the first place.

Jill and I are not compatible. Not in any way, shape, or form. Sex was our glue, and the thing I've learned the hard way is that sex can never be the glue for me. Maybe it can be for other people, but I need a strong emotional connection right alongside the sex.

Because our lives are still so intertwined, with us

seeing each other almost every day at work, I've tried to be discreet in the way I've approached dating since our divorce. I've been sensitive to the fact Jill has struggled to let our marriage go.

She didn't put herself out there again for a good six months. And when she did, she appeared dedicated to making sure I knew. After that first date, she threw herself into more dates like it was a project she'd taken on. I was happy for her and took it as a sign I didn't have to be so delicate with the whole situation.

That was a mistake.

As was taking a date to an industry function a month after Jill began dating. She didn't hesitate to let me know that I should have been more thoughtful.

Any kind of dating or sex life talk between us is a land mine guaranteed to cause me damage. I avoid it at all costs. Today is shaping up to be the day I'm going down because I can't avoid any of it now. Not if I want our company to remain strong.

I'm halfway to Jill's office when my mother calls.

"Hi," I answer immediately. My mother will generally keep calling until I answer if I don't. "I only have a minute. What's up?"

"I was calling to let you know I spoke with Marcia Montgomery. She told me that John says you're looking good for the Bluestone Award. I thought you might like to know." Her tone is a little cool. Mary North doesn't like being rushed, however it's not the first time I've done it, and it won't be the last.

"Thanks, Mom." She's right; this is good information. The Bluestone Best in Business program honors businesses and professionals in every industry in America.

The top award is the Bluestone Award and I made it a goal to win it this year after being nominated. John Montgomery is an old family friend and one of the judges, so any information he has is solid.

"Oh, Owen, one other thing. Jill. You need to keep her on your side. If she rocks the boat, that award may go to someone else."

This isn't news to me. The Bluestone Award not only recognizes excellence in business, but also personal excellence. Every aspect of my life will be looked at. Winners of this award are highly esteemed. Personal problems within my company won't look good.

"I have to go." Getting into yet another discussion with my mother about my ex isn't something I want to do this morning.

"I told you that you needed to force her out, Owen. She—"

"I'm handling her." I'm almost at Jill's office. "I appreciate you calling with this information. I'll talk to you later."

We end the call right before Jill comes into view through the glass door separating us. She glances up, her features soft before she spots me. Her face turns to stone fast, and she stands, letting me know I can enter.

"We're meeting in the conference room," she says with more chill than a winters day.

"I know, but you and I have some things I want to discuss in private."

She crosses her arms, ready for battle. "What things?"

I get straight to the point. "Are you sleeping with any of the staff? Or considering it?"

Her breaths come a little quicker as her face and

shoulders harden more than they already had. "If I was, it would be none of your business."

"Everything you and I do with any of the staff is each other's business, Jill. Just like anything either of us do with the clients is also each other's business. That's what owning a company together means."

"I'm not an idiot, Owen. I don't need you to mansplain business to me. And fuck you for coming in here and asking me that question."

Jill doesn't swear and doesn't appreciate it from anyone else. The fact she's sworn at me twice today already tells me where our relationship is at. It's not in a place that's good for either of us.

I'm about to ask her for a do-over of the conversation, *of the entire morning*, so I can tell her I don't care who she sleeps with. That what I care about is our company and that maybe sleeping with the staff isn't such a great idea. However, as I open my mouth to say all this, she looks toward the office door behind me and motions at someone to come in.

"I'll just be a minute," she says.

I turn and lay eyes on the woman I met at Seth's wedding two nights ago. The woman I spent one of the best nights of my life with. The woman I haven't been able to get out of my head.

Charlize.

Our eyes lock. "Okay," she says slowly to Jill like she's having trouble getting the word to leave her mouth. "Umm, do you want...." She gestures toward the door, her beautiful blue eyes widening as she takes me in. "Should I.... Do you want me to wait outside?"

"No," Jill says. "We're just finishing up here."

I struggle to draw my gaze from Charlize, but somehow manage it so I can say to Jill, "Actually, we're not."

Jill looks at me. "Actually, Owen, we *are*. I'm not having this conversation with you."

"I'll just wait outside," Charlize says.

I glance back at her as Jill says quite fiercely, "No, Charlize. You stay. Owen's leaving."

Charlize's eyes meet mine again. They flare like she's highly perplexed with this situation.

I don't blame her.

I too am confused as to why she's here, but at least I'm not also dealing with the fact I walked in on the person I slept with two nights ago in the middle of an argument with their ex.

I glance between them. "How do you two know each other?"

Jill frowns like I've asked her the strangest question. "Marla is sick. The agency sent Charlize over."

Charlize and I didn't discuss what we do for work the other night. It was refreshing to meet a woman who was more interested in me as a person than me as a CEO.

I eye her. "You're filling in for the day?" Marla is Jill's assistant and has been sick a lot lately.

Before she can answer, Jill snaps, "Yes, she is, and we have a lot to go over before you and Julian try to screw me over yet again in our weekly meeting. I'd appreciate it if you leave so I have time to do that."

My brain is still trying to process the fact Charlize is here. That she's *working* here.

I'm slow to respond to Jill's request for me to leave. So slow that she snaps at me again.

"Owen!"

I look at Jill. She's glaring at me like she wants to slap me again.

I gather my thoughts and give her a pointed look. "This conversation isn't finished." I turn to leave, slowing my departure as much as possible so I can run my gaze over Charlize.

She's the most beautiful woman I've ever met. And the most genuine. She left in such a hurry yesterday morning that I missed out on time with her. Time I wanted, because one night with her was far from enough.

Today, her long blonde hair is in a bun, and it's the sexiest bun I've ever had the pleasure of looking at. She's wearing make-up, but it's subtle enough that her natural beauty shines through in ways I like. Her curves are covered by a dark gray skirt that ends just below her knees, and a white blouse that she's teamed with flat shoes.

I can't drag my gaze from her.

Her eyes are glued to mine just as much as mine are to hers.

I know she feels this too. She was up in her head yesterday morning when she left my hotel suite. Anxious about something. I let her go without a fight because I could tell that was what she needed me to do, but I meant every word when I told her I don't give up when I want something.

Her scent fills me as I walk past her, instantly reminding me of our night together.

Of hanging off every word she uttered.

Of touching her.

Of kissing her.

Of being inside her.

I may have entered Jill's office with a million thoughts in my head, but I'm leaving with only one: I want more time with Charlize, and I fully intend on making that happen.

If there's one thing I know for sure, it's that she wants the same thing even though she couldn't stop telling me she doesn't date. She kept my hotel key card after all. A woman doesn't keep something if it doesn't have any meaning to her.

6

Charlize

Naked swimming with Owen.

That's what I'm thinking about right now.

In between counting the items on Jill's desk.

I'm also thinking I need to find some brown contact lenses for him. If I'm going to spend two days working for his ex-wife in the same building he works, the chances are high we're going to run into each other again. I need those blue eyes of his to be brown so I can think of muddy water that's not fit for any kind of swimming.

Also, I have a mind to reach out and quickly do up those top two buttons of his shirt as he walks past me. I know what's under that shirt and even just that little hint of skin is enough to force my thighs together.

Good God, how do I get myself into these situations?

I've been searching for work since I returned home, and because there's a shortage of assistant work in New York I signed up with an employment agency at my mother's suggestion. I will never take a suggestion from her again.

I'm just over here trying not to get attached to my attraction to Owen, and there's the Universe over there doing everything in its power to force him on me.

I've barely stopped thinking about him since I scurried out of his hotel suite yesterday morning. I learned so many things I like about him. We talked a lot in between all the sex we had, sharing things no one knows about us, sharing some of our dreams in life, and sharing funny stories about our teen years.

Among other things, I know that Owen lost his virginity at sixteen; that the most embarrassing moment in his teen years was when he was fourteen and got an erection while standing in front of his class (directly in front of his crush) giving a speech; that he's inspired by athletes who push themselves further than they ever imagined they could; and that he doesn't like Nutella. I gave him a little hell over the Nutella thing. I mean, who doesn't like Nutella?

He learned that I lost my virginity at nineteen; that my first time was a horrific night of calamity after calamity and that I'm still not sure to this day why the guy I was with even bothered to keep pursuing me (Owen seemed quite sure he understood why, but since I'm still mortified by that experience, I didn't get into that with him); that I'm inspired by people who go their own way; and that I don't like carrots or green beans. He gave me some hell over that. He told me that for a person who loves food, I'm not well rounded. I shut him up when I mentioned how much I prefer sucking dick to eating a carrot. He seemed quite okay with my dismissal of certain vegetables at that point.

And now, here we are.

Him looking at me like he wants to eat me.

And me trying hard not to think about just how well he does that, and just how much I really do want him to do that again even though I'm busy telling myself I don't.

Spoiler alert: I'm failing epically.

"Charlize," Jill says as Owen strides away from her office. "I've set you up with an email and sent through the tasks I need you to work through today. I've also included a list for tomorrow, but that may change, depending on the meeting I'm about to have with Owen."

The way she says his name tells me a lot about her current relationship with him. As did the way they conversed while I was in the office with them. And let's just say, I'm not sensing any good vibes here.

When I first arrived at Jill's office this morning, she seemed lovely. The only thing I knew about her is that she's the COO of North Management. The minute I laid eyes on Owen and heard them arguing, I put two and two together from his brief mention of his ex-wife's name the other night and guessed who she is. The rest of their conversation left me quite sure of who she is. It surprised me that they still work together, especially since she doesn't seem happy with him. She might have been lovely to me, but she was far from lovely to Owen. However, I'm not one to form an opinion based on how a person interacts with an ex. God knows, I probably don't come across as lovely when I speak to any of my exes.

After Jill gives me the email login, we spend ten minutes discussing the tasks on her lists. She supplies me with most of the information I need to complete them, promising to email through any other information I'll require.

She appears very efficient, capable, and intelligent.

The other thing about her? She's just as beautiful as she is smart.

Looking at Jill, I wonder if Owen usually has a type. If he does, he deviated when he met me. Physically, that is. We look nothing alike. Jill is taller than me with long, brunette hair, paler skin than mine, and boobs for days. She also looks like she works out a lot. I can see definition all over her. Me? My body doesn't even know what a gym is.

I'm thinking about this when Jill says, "Charlize? Are you good with all that?"

I shift my thoughts back to the job at hand and nod. "Yes, I'm good."

"Okay, great. Just let me know if you need anything. I'll be in this meeting for about an hour and then I'll be here for the rest of the day. Marla is also available on email if you get stuck."

At this point, the plan is for me to work two days with Jill while her assistant is sick. However, the agency made it clear this could turn into extra days if Marla doesn't recover as fast as Jill hopes.

Before Owen became part of the picture, I was secretly hoping Marla develops some kind of tropical disease that necessitates her quitting her job so I can be hired full-time. Now that I know who Jill's ex-husband is,

I'm aware that wishing tropical diseases on people only leads to sticky situations best avoided.

If working for the ex-wife of the guy who had his face in your vagina on the weekend is not classified as a sticky situation, then I don't know what is.

I take up residence at Marla's desk and log into the email account Jill directed me to. I'm just about to open the email she's sent when my cell buzzes with a text. I ignore it because I'm at work and Jill strikes me as the kind of boss who sees everything even when it appears she's not watching. It's probably my mother, anyway, and I'm not in the mood to deal with her incessant requests for dinner with her, Dad, and Benjamin. Apparently, Ben mentioned yesterday when they had breakfast together that he'd love to see me.

Another spoiler alert: *I* would not love to see him.

A few minutes after I get to work, Jill leaves her office to go to the meeting she mentioned. I keep working for half an hour, losing myself in the jobs she's assigned me, until another text comes through. This time, I check my phone.

Mom: Don't forget we've got the charity gala next week and that I want you and Nate to be involved this time.

Mom: And please wear something appropriate.

Shoot me now.

After being away for a year, I'd almost forgotten about the family duty she lumps on me and my brother at times. Almost.

I send her a reply.

Charlize: I haven't forgotten. Dylan's coming with me.

A call comes through on the office line. After I finish with that call, I google North Management on my phone. I didn't have time to research the company after I received this job this morning, which is what I would usually do. I like to know who I'm working for. Naturally, the only time I don't do my research is the time I get caught out and presented with a totally unexpected situation.

Of course, I know of the Norths. Not Owen and Jill, but having grown up in New York, I've heard of Owen's family. Everyone has. However, since I don't make it a point to keep up with society, I don't know much about them.

I learn that Owen and Jill founded this company seven years ago and have built it into a huge company. I learn that Owen is one of the most successful hedge fund managers ever. And I learn that since they divorced a year ago, Owen has become one of the most eligible bachelors of New York. It's at this point that I put my phone away. I don't like reading gossip and I don't want to know anything about Owen that comes from people who probably don't even know him.

I spend the next hour working through Jill's tasks. She returns from her meeting looking furious. I take it by that and by the way she barely acknowledges me that I should do my best to avoid her.

"Charlize," Jill says just after noon, "I'm heading out for an appointment. I should be back in about two hours. Call me if you need me but try not to need me."

I nod my understanding.

Once she's gone and I finish the current job I'm working on, I head into the break room to grab the lunch I stored in the fridge. I'm pleasantly surprised to discover the break room has a high-end coffee maker, so I make myself a coffee and then take it and my lunch back to my desk. An email that just came in catches my eye while I eat.

FROM: **Owen North**
   To: Jill's Assistant
   Date: May 17, 2021, 1:13 PM
   Subject: My office

CHARLIZE,

CAN **you please come to my office? We have some things to discuss.**

OWEN NORTH
   CEO, North Management

THE FACT I'm sitting with my thighs pressed together while reading this email does not escape me.

Also, I really am going to require those brown contact lenses. Stat.

A thought suddenly comes to me and I'm not sure why it hasn't already come to me.

If Owen is the CEO, does this mean *he's* my boss?

Also, no, I can't go to his office.

I have work to do.

And when he says "we have things to discuss", I'm pretty sure he doesn't mean work things. I'm pretty sure he means "I'm putting your red thong in my pocket" kind of things, and that isn't a conversation I should get involved in. Not if I have any hope of keeping my attraction to him under control.

I send him a reply.

From: Jill's Assistant
　　To: Owen North
　　Date: May 17, 2021, 1:16 PM
　　Subject: Re: My office

Mr. North,

I'm rather busy at the moment. Could you possibly email me about the things you want to discuss?

Charlize Cohen
　　Assistant to Jill North

His reply comes back in a couple of minutes.

From: Owen North
　　To: Jill's Assistant
　　Date: May 17, 2021, 1:18 PM

Subject: Re: My office

CHARLIZE,

THIS CAN'T BE COVERED in an email. It requires a face-to-face conversation.

OWEN NORTH
CEO, North Management

I EMAIL STRAIGHT BACK.

FROM: Jill's Assistant
To: Owen North
Date: May 17, 2021, 1:19 PM
Subject: Re: My office

MR. NORTH,

IT'S my experience that emails are far more efficient than in-person meetings.

CHARLIZE COHEN
Assistant to Jill North

. . .

OWEN'S REPLY is almost instantaneous.

FROM: Owen North
    To: Jill's Assistant
    Date: May 17, 2021, 1:19 PM
    Subject: Re: My office

CHARLIZE,

MY OFFICE.
    Now.

OWEN NORTH
    CEO, North Management

AND WITH THAT, I think I have an answer to my earlier thought.

I think Owen *is* my boss.

He certainly feels very bossy right now.

I push my chair back and stand. I have no idea where his office is, but I figure it's somewhere in this building, so I begin my search.

It doesn't take me long to locate him. The glass surrounding him helps. Most of the offices here have walls and doors that give privacy, but Jill's office and the three offices that are the furthest from hers are made completely of glass. As soon as Owen's office comes into view, I meet his gaze.

He watches me walk his way.

And when I say watch, I mean his eyes do not leave mine for even a second.

The twenty steps I take to get to him might be some of the hottest steps of my life. I mean, there he is sitting behind his large desk, with those undone buttons of his, that sexy beard of his, those blue eyes I can't get enough of, and those strong hands I've thought far too much about. Owen is the actual sexiest man I have ever met, and he doesn't have to do a thing but watch me to get me hot.

He stands as I draw closer and opens his door. He says something to his assistant, and she nods before going back to her computer. He then gives all his attention to me again, stepping back and ushering me in when I reach him.

The office door gliding shut is the last sound I hear before Owen and I are enclosed in his office, alone.

His hand comes to the small of my back. "Take a seat." It's a deep murmur, and while he only says three words, it's like his eyes are saying a million as he looks at me.

I sit, watching as he rounds the desk and sits across from me. I can still feel his hand on my back. "Do you order all your new employees to your office?"

"Only the ones who are insubordinate."

"I would argue I was trying to be efficient."

"I would counter that arguing with me repeatedly means you're being defiant. And while I have my preferred ways of handling defiance, none of them are suitable for the workplace."

If I thought I was hot before, I knew nothing.

I cross my legs. It turns out to be an incorrect move because it draws Owen's attention, and let's just say his eyes on my legs are the last thing I need right now.

It's all too much and it causes me to throw out, "Do you always walk around your workplace with those buttons undone?"

He doesn't answer my question, but his heated gaze tells me he likes that I asked it. Instead, he says, "So, I can check one thing off my list of things I still have to learn about you. You're an executive assistant."

"I am. And you're a hedge fund guy."

"I am."

I narrow my eyes at him. "Are you not that good at it? I mean, why didn't Seth ask for your advice with Poppy's shares?"

"I follow your line of thinking there. Very analytical, but you made an assumption that was wrong."

"Which was what?"

"You assumed that Seth made his choice based on the best man for the job when that wasn't a factor in his decision."

I frown. "Why not? That makes no sense."

"I agree. Seth chose based on family connections."

"See, this is why I detest family connections. They fuck you up at the best of times."

"Not always, but on this, yes. However, the good news is that Seth has now asked me to help."

"I already advised Poppy which shares I think she

should sell and which she should buy. I hope you're not going to mess with that."

It does not escape me that Owen is the CEO of a company that manages billions for their clients. *Billions.* He clearly is not bad at his job. But still, Poppy is my girl, and I am nothing if not protective of my people.

"That was your advice?"

"The Bliss and Fira Industry shares? Yes."

He's impressed by this. I see that in his eyes. "I spoke with her an hour ago and told her to double down on those Fira shares. That was a smart move."

His praise works its way through me. I'm not trained to do the work he does, but my grandfather taught me all about shares and money when I was a kid. It's because of him that I love investing and am good at predicting the market. However, I'm not good with money once I make it. I tend to give money to friends when they need it and lend it to boyfriends who end up screwing me over and not paying me back. My parents only seem to see the mess my finances are in and ignore the fact I know about investing. I feel like they dismiss me during any family conversation about money. Owen's recognition means a lot.

"Thank you," I say softly.

His phone rings. When he doesn't make a move to answer it or even check who it is, I say, "I can come back if you need to take that call."

"No, you're not leaving yet."

The way his voice drops deeper as he says that, coupled with all the masculine energy radiating from him, sends a rush of desire through me and causes my brain to stop sending words to my mouth.

We both turn silent, watching each other until Owen says, "You missed out on a delicious breakfast yesterday."

The word *delicious* should be banned from Owen's mouth.

Actually, all words should be banned from his mouth.

He could be telling me all about the features on a new vacuum cleaner, and I would even want those words banned.

"I have no doubt," I say.

"I meant it when I said this isn't finished between us, Charlize."

"And I meant it when I said I'm not looking for a date."

His eyes search mine. "You can't tell me you're not feeling this."

Oh boy.

Whyyyy?

Why must this man have those blue eyes I want to get lost in?

Why must he have that body, that voice, that magnetism?

Why must he not be an asshole?

"I like you, Owen. A lot. But we can't start something. The timing isn't right."

"Why not?"

"Because I'm only back in New York for a year at the most while I save to travel again."

He appears confused about this. "Why does that mean we can't see each other?"

"Well, assuming our dating moments don't end up on your list of *Worst Dating Moments of Life*, it wouldn't be cool for me to use you for sex for a year and then just leave."

Amusement flashes across his face but he remains serious when he says, "I would be more than okay with you using me for sex for a year. However, I'd also like the opportunity to get to know you better."

And now I'm having flashbacks of all the things he did to me on Saturday night.

Using Owen for sex for twelve months? That would *not* be a hardship. Breaking up with him at the end of those twelve months, though, would be. "What if I somehow convince you to really like me? I don't want to be the kind of person who makes someone really like them while having no intention of sticking around."

His eyes search mine for a long moment. "How about you let me worry about that? I know where I stand, and I still want to stand there. And Charlize?" He pauses, his eyes boring into mine. "You've already convinced me that I really like you."

7

Charlize

"I'm never coming home," Poppy says over Zoom on Monday night. She's in Rome on her honeymoon and I've managed to catch her even though it's just after midnight there.

"You have to come home. I need you."

"Charles, you are the most independent woman I know. You went away for a year by yourself. Sadly, you do not need me."

"Why don't you want to come home?"

"Seth works too much when we're in New York. Italy is inspiring him to work far less and spend more time fucking me. I'm in no hurry to leave."

"Well, I think that's very selfish of you. Contrary to what you think, I do need you. Right now, I need you a lot."

She frowns and leans into the camera, inspecting me more closely. "Why? What's going on? Did you run into Benjamin? I swear, I will choke the life out of that asshole if he's trying to convince you to get back together."

"No, it's not him." I take a sip of the wine I poured myself as soon as I got home. "It's Owen."

More frowning. "I thought you'd decided not to see him again."

"I *did* decide that. The Universe decided something very different."

"Stop drawing this out, Charles, and just tell me. I'm on a time schedule here. Seth is about to make good on his promise to do dirty things to me before we go to sleep."

"I'm temping for Jill North for two days. Today was my first day."

She stares at me, blinking slowly for dramatic effect. "How is that going?"

"Well, Jill was nice to me, but I walked in on an argument she was having with Owen first thing this morning, so that was awkward."

"Jill was nice to you?" She's shocked. "Jill isn't nice to anyone."

"I definitely got the impression she and Owen don't get on, but she was okay with me. I only saw her for half the day, though. She was out of the office all afternoon." She ended up getting a migraine and going home for the rest of the day.

"Well, all I can say is tread carefully there. Especially if she catches wind of the fact you slept with her husband."

It's my turn to frown. "Her ex, right? They're divorced, aren't they?"

"They may be divorced, but everyone knows she never wanted the divorce and still thinks of him as hers. I witnessed it for myself about three months ago when I was out with Seth and Owen one night. Owen met a woman while we were drinking and was chatting with her at the bar when Jill showed up. She wasn't happy with him and practically drove the woman away with her jealous outburst. And let me just say, she can be *mean*. The kind of mean that draws blood. Do everything you can to stay off her radar when it comes to Owen."

"Right, got it. Tomorrow I won't even look at him, because let me tell you, if she catches me looking at him, she'll know I've done filthy things to him." I gulp some wine down.

Poppy watches me drink. "As in, you've done filthy things to him at work? Or are we talking about the filthy things you did in the elevator at my wedding?"

"I did no such things to him in that elevator. I wanted to, but he's got more class than me and made me wait until we had privacy in his suite."

She arches her brows, waiting for me to answer her question.

"I haven't laid a hand on him in the office. I'm trying to never lay a hand on him again."

"Why not? You said the sex was the best you've ever had. Get yourself some more of that."

I groan. "I really want some more of that, but this can't go anywhere between us, Pop. I'm not staying in New York for more than a year. I may even leave earlier than that if I can save what I need sooner."

Her eyes widen. "Ah, no, you're not leaving sooner than that. You told me a year, and you're giving me a year. End of story. And as far as Owen's concerned, just have some fun. Not every relationship has to go somewhere."

"Ugh, you sound like Dylan." I pause. "I don't want to hurt Owen if he wants more than I can give."

Poppy's face softens. "This doesn't have anything to do with Owen, though, does it? Not if you're honest with yourself. Benjamin hurt you. Sampson hurt you before him. And Tim hurt you before that. You're avoiding Owen because *you* don't want to get hurt again."

The way my chest and stomach are reacting to what she says tells me she's right even though I don't want to acknowledge this. Why must she be so good at understanding me?

"Some days, my life would be much easier if you were more clueless and self-absorbed," I mutter.

"I *am* self-absorbed, so clearly you don't do as good a job at hiding yourself as you think you do."

I smile at her. Poppy might be a little self-absorbed, but she loves me so well that nothing sneaks by her. She sees me like no one sees me. "I can't get hurt again, Pop," I say softly. "I don't know if I'll survive it. I think I might be all hurt out, you know?"

"Oh, my darling, what is life if not to get all hurt out a few times in the pursuit of love and happiness and great sex? And where's the Charles I know and love? She would never let a little hurt keep her down."

"What's this about the pursuit of great sex?" Seth asks, slipping behind Poppy on the sofa and wrapping his arms around her while looking at me through the computer.

Poppy places her hands over his and turns to kiss his cheek before looking at me again. "Charles and Owen. She's temping at his office for two days. Working for Jill."

He gives me a knowing look. "He texted me yesterday and asked for your number."

My heart makes herself known. "He did?"

Seth smiles and nods. "Yeah. I haven't given it to him yet. I told him I'd check in with you first."

"Well," Poppy says, "I don't think he needs that clearance anymore. He'd have access to it through work now."

"He's not the kind of guy to abuse that, though," Seth says to me. "He might look it up, but he won't use it unless you tell him you're okay with that."

I'm not so sure about this. Not after the way he bossed me into his office today. "He's already had a conversation with me about us seeing each other,' I say.

"And?" Poppy asks.

"And I've been trying hard to tell myself no, but you've just stomped all over that, thank you very much."

She smiles triumphantly. "Good." Then, softer, she says, "I like Owen for you. I know you both and I think you'd be a good match. And I think that even if it's just a fling, it could be what you need to help you see that not every guy is going to hurt you."

My heart continues making herself known.

She seems to agree with Poppy.

And the more she carries on, and the more I think about it, the more I wonder if Poppy might be right.

Maybe I should run with this.

Maybe I should use Owen for sex for a year.

Maybe it's time to figure out how to be okay with getting all hurt out a few times in life.

8

Owen

I arrive at work later than usual on Tuesday, striding into the break room to make coffee just after 6:30 a.m. I've been up since four running on my treadmill while reviewing our current positions, reading overnight news, and going over new opportunities. I called Julian at five thirty and got into a lengthy discussion over our positions which caused me to be later into the office than I prefer.

The office is already alive and busy, but the break room is quiet. There's only one employee in here, and if I thought I was fully awake already, I'm proved wrong when I realize it's Charlize. My body wakes right the hell up at the sight of her.

She has her head in the fridge when I walk in and straightens at the sound of company. Her gaze comes to me, a smile instantly kissing her lips and fast reaching her eyes. "Owen."

Fuck, my name on her lips is the best kind of way to start a day. "Good morning." I briefly wonder why she's so early, but that thought is quickly discarded with her next move.

She runs her eyes over my body before bringing them back to my face. "You wear jeans as well as you wear a suit."

Fuck me.

She appears to have moved past her concerns over dating me.

"They're my preference."

She gives me a sexy look. "Mine too."

If we keep this up, I'll have no hope of not kissing her here in the office. After the clusterfuck that was yesterday with Jill, kissing Charlize while she works for us is the last thing I should do.

She's got one more day of work here.

I can last one day of not touching her.

After that, we're going all in on a date.

In an effort to shift the conversation to safer topics, I say, "Would you like a coffee?"

She moves closer to me, stopping about two feet away. Nowhere near close enough, but actually far too close while I'm effectively her boss and unable to do any of the things I want to do. Looking at me with what can only be described as trouble in her eyes, she says, "Are you offering to go and get me a coffee? Or is this the part where I become *your* assistant and go get you coffee?"

Jesus, we should not be in the same room today. "While the idea of you being my assistant is more appealing than it should be, that's not what I had in mind."

"What did you have in mind?"

"I was going to offer to make you coffee."

She rests her hip against the countertop. "I know you said you're a great cook, but has that been verified by anyone? And if so, do those skills extend to coffee making, because I have to tell you, I'm fussy when it comes to my coffee."

"My mother and brother can verify my coffee-making skills for you, but I'd prefer to show you myself. I make the best coffee."

"Ahh no, Owen, *I* make the best coffee."

"I see we're going to have to fight this out. Just so you know, I've never had coffee better than mine."

"Well, I'll never say no to a man offering to make me coffee. Even if he is a little cocky about his skills."

"It's not cocky when the thing he's confident about is proven."

"Trust me, cocky is cocky regardless. I hope you can live up to this promise of yours because I won't let you forget it if you can't."

"I'll make the coffee today. You'll make it next time. Then we'll compare." I close the distance between us and bring my mouth to her ear. "Prepare to lose this fight, beautiful."

I'm instantly aware of the mistake I've made.

I'm too close to her now, too consumed by her scent, too affected by her.

"Way too cocky," she says, her breathy reply showing me she's just as affected.

I take a step back, but I don't get to work on the coffee

just yet. I'm too busy taking in everything about her. She's just as busy doing the same. Almost as if we're looking at each other for the first time today.

Charlize is wearing a red skirt, a black top, and leopard print sneakers. My brain is stuck on the fact I told her that red is my favorite color on a woman and I'm wondering whether she chose the red for me. It's an arrogant thought but one I can't shift. I fucking want that to have been her reason.

I'm stuck in a loop of that thought when Tahlia comes into the break room. "Owen, Julian is looking for you. He said something about finishing a discussion with you from this morning."

I look at her. "Let him know I'll be in my office in about five minutes."

"Will do."

After she leaves us, I get to work on the coffee. Charlize watches me silently, but I'm more than aware her eyes are all over me. If I wasn't trying my damnedest to keep my hands off her, I'd have them all over her in the same way. This day can't go by fast enough.

"Here," she says, passing me the milk from the fridge.

Our hands brush as I take it from her, sparking desire through me.

I shift my attention back to the coffee and finish making our drinks before looking at her again. "You ready to be blown away?"

She rolls her eyes as she takes the mug I offer her. "Calm down. The only one of us who is going to be blown away is you when you drink my coffee next time."

I arch my brows. "Who's cocky now?"

She takes a sip, and I see the surprise in her eyes, but

she doesn't give me anything else to go on. After the fourth sip, she caves. "Okay, so you weren't kidding when you said you make good coffee."

"And?"

"I may just call it now. I'm not sure even my coffee can stand up to this."

"And here I was thinking you weren't a quitter. You were very adamant about that the other night. Where's that fighting spirit?"

"Right, so, cocky *and* competitive. I see."

"What do you see?"

"That we're going to fight this out after all."

Fuck, I like this with her too much.

We're interrupted when Jill joins us and snaps, "I need a minute of your precious time, Owen. In my office." She doesn't wait for my response; she simply turns and stalks from the break room toward her office.

Christ, it looks like Jill's mood has not improved since yesterday.

I meet Charlize's gaze again. "We need to talk. Later."

"I'm sure you'll email when you're ready to start bossing me around."

She has no idea just how much I want to boss her around.

I throw all good judgment out the window and bend my mouth to her ear again. "I only boss people around when I want something as much as I want you."

I'm rewarded with her hand to my chest as she steadies herself. And a flash of heat in her eyes that will keep me going for hours until I can find a way to see her again.

With that, I take my coffee and head to Jill's office, my mind in overdrive about Charlize the entire way there.

I struggled to stop thinking about her yesterday and last night. Hell, I've barely stopped thinking about her since I met her. I need to find a way to focus today. Jill and I have an interview with a journalist from *The New York Times* later today. It's an interview that will help me with the Bluestone Award if it goes well. The fact Jill will be sitting in on it means I need to give it all my concentration. Thinking about Charlize will be a distraction I can't afford.

"What's up?" I ask after I step into Jill's office.

She stops scrolling her phone and looks at me. "I had to shift some meetings around today, so I've moved our interview to ten this morning. I hope that works for you."

That doesn't work for me and she's more than aware of that fact. I never schedule anything before eleven. All my time before then is dedicated to monitoring the markets and working with my leadership team.

"It doesn't," I say. "You'll have to reschedule it."

She presses her lips together. "I'm not rescheduling it, Owen. My time is just as important as yours, and I don't have a spare minute this week."

"I never said your time isn't as important." Fuck, she likes to try and put words in my mouth that were never anywhere near it.

"You didn't need to. Your actions convey it."

I exhale a long breath. "Is this how we're going to play every day now?"

"I was not the one who started this. Just remember that every time you want to throw blame my way."

"Jesus, Jill. You're talking like we're in the middle of a war."

She gives me a long, pointed look. "Possibly because we are."

Jill was not happy with the conversation I forced her to have during our meeting with Julian yesterday. The conversation about whether she's sleeping with the staff. She neither confirmed nor denied the rumors Julian has heard. Instead, she fumed over the fact I'd dared to ask her about it. We didn't resolve anything, but I made it clear that if her actions come back to bite us in the ass, I won't hesitate to make changes to the way we run the company together.

For the first time, I wonder if my mother and brother were right when they encouraged me to find a way to pay Jill out and remove her from the company.

A text comes through on my phone and I quickly check it.

Julian: Where are you? The shit has hit the fan.

I look at Jill. "I can't make that time. If you can't reschedule to sometime after lunch today, shift it to next week."

I stalk to my office as my temper flares.

It'll be a fucking miracle if Jill and I don't end up in outright battle soon. My patience with her has never been as low.

I SPEND hours with Julian and some other members of our leadership team in an emergency meeting to strate-gize a change we need to make to a Manhattan property investment we've been working on for six months. The entire investment turned bad this morning after an announcement from the New York governor that she's no longer proceeding with a planned project in Manhattan that was the reason we pursued our initial strategy.

Tahlia lets me know just after nine that Jill has changed our interview to four this afternoon. She also lets me know that Jill's mood has worsened.

I take a call from Ron Johansen after my meeting is finished.

"Ron," I answer, leaning back in my chair and looking out over Manhattan while hoping like fuck that Jill hasn't been in contact with him. "What can I do for you?"

"I'm calling to see if you've dealt with Jill."

I sit up straight. "I've spoken with her. You won't hear from her again. I'll be handling your account now." I've already discussed this with him, so I'm unsure why he's bringing it up again.

"Owen, I want more than to never hear from her again."

"I'm not following." I am, though, and if I'm following correctly, this is going to turn into a difficult conversation soon.

"I want her gone."

I stare out at the city, contemplating my next move. Contemplating the last seven years of building this company to the level of having this view. Contemplating losing it from a misstep.

"Jill's not going anywhere, Ron."

He's quiet for a moment. "It's either her or me, Owen."

"I know she fucked up, but I've fixed the issue and I assure you it won't happen again."

"That's not enough. I don't trust your company so long as she's still the COO. You need to get rid of her. I'm sure you have other clients who wouldn't appreciate knowing what she's capable of."

Fuck.

"Are you making a threat, Ron?" He's our biggest client. We can't afford to lose him. And we can't afford for him to spread this story around.

"I'm simply stating a fact. Look, I like working with you, Owen, and I want to continue working with North Management, but I don't want a thing to do with Jill. I want her out."

"You're putting me in a hard place here."

"Yeah, just like Jill's put me in a hard place." He pauses. "Let me know once you've gotten rid of her."

The line goes silent, and I drop my phone down on the desk.

I push up out of my chair and stalk to the window.

I look at the street sixty-three floors down.

Jill and I clawed our way to the top and I'll be damned if we don't stay here.

She might be at war with me currently, and she might have fucked with the wrong client, and she might be causing me enough headaches to rip my skull apart some days, but I loved her for years and I refuse to throw her under the bus to keep an asshole client happy.

I'll find another way before I'll ruin the woman I thought I'd spend my life with at one point.

$\sim$

I SPEND the next couple of hours working uninterrupted before eating lunch at 2:00 p.m. and sending Charlize an email.

FROM: Owen North
    To: Jill's Assistant
    Date: May 18, 2021, 2:09 PM
    Subject: Conference Room

CHARLIZE,

I'LL BE in the conference room in ten minutes and require your help with something.

OWEN NORTH
    CEO, North Management

I RECEIVE a reply within five minutes.

FROM: Jill's Assistant
    To: Owen North
    Date: May 18, 2021, 2:13 PM
    Subject: Re: Conference Room

MR. NORTH,

. . .

I'M RATHER busy for the next half hour checking jobs off my boss's list. If you're able to not activate your demanding and bossy trait, and wait half an hour, I'd be quite happy to help you then.

CHARLIZE COHEN
Assistant to Jill North

I'VE NEVER REPLIED to an email faster.

FROM: Owen North
To: Jill's Assistant
Date: May 18, 2021, 2:14 PM
Subject: Re: Conference Room

CHARLIZE,

YOU'RE RATHER busy a lot and I'm not good at waiting.

OWEN NORTH
CEO, North Management

SHE COMES BACK WITH:

. . .

FROM: Jill's Assistant
   To: Owen North
   Date: May 18, 2021, 2:16 PM
   Subject: Re: Conference Room

MR. NORTH,

I'M GOING to teach you some patience. Now, be a good boy and wait.

CHARLIZE COHEN
   Assistant to Jill North

FUCK. Me.

FROM: Owen North
   To: Jill's Assistant
   Date: May 18, 2021, 2:16 PM
   Subject: Re: Conference Room

CHARLIZE,

I'LL EXPECT you at 2:43 p.m.

. . .

OWEN NORTH
  CEO, North Management

WHY THE FUCK is it not five p.m. yet?

I'm beginning to doubt my ability to wait until she's finished working for North Management to put my hands on her.

9

Charlize

It has to be said that emailing your boss is hot foreplay.

By the time I slip into the conference room at 2:42 p.m., I'm ready to get up on that boardroom table and beg Owen to do what he's good at.

He's already waiting for me and locks the door after I join him.

"For the record," he says, moving closer to me, backing me up against the table, but stopping short of bringing his body against mine. "I want to kiss you." His eyes drop to my throat. "But I can't do that while you work for me."

I didn't expect that, but it has to be said that I respect it.

"You have a no-fraternization policy that restricts relationships?"

"Between managers and their direct reports, yes. So, technically I could have a relationship with you. However, Jill and I now have our own agreement and I can't go there with you."

"The more I get to know you, Owen, the more I find to like." He could easily kiss me right now. I've got just over two hours left at North Management. No one would ever know he touched me, and yet, he's honoring his agreement with his ex.

His eyes roam my face. "Are you free for dinner tonight?"

"Yes."

He pulls his phone out of his pocket and hands it to me. "I need your number."

I smile, remembering what Seth said last night. "Seth was right about you." I take his phone and key my number in.

"How?" he asks, taking his phone when I pass it back.

"He said you wouldn't abuse your role in the company to get my number. I thought you would. I mean, you had that kind of look in your eyes yesterday when you were trying to boss me around."

He sends me a text so that I have his number. "Don't be so sure you were wrong."

And suddenly, I really want to kiss him.

Like, *really*.

Damn that agreement he has, and damn him for being such an honest guy. Well, just this once. I'm here for honest men.

I think Owen can tell I'm struggling with this. I think he is too.

"Send me your address," he says, taking a step away from me. "I'll pick you up at eight. Is there anything you don't like to eat besides carrots or green beans?"

I smile remembering our conversation the other night. "Nothing I've found so far. You get extra points if you find a place that has Nutella on the menu."

"Consider it done." His tone leaves me with no doubt he'll move mountains to do this.

"I'm thinking this competitive streak of yours can be used to my advantage."

His eyes bore into mine and I *really* get the impression it's taking everything in him not to pull me into his arms. "Charlize, everything can be used to your advantage. I'm not just going for extra points here."

I stare after him as he leaves the conference room, his last statement working its way through me.

I text him my address while processing it.

Holy Jesus.

Owen wants me.

Like, *wants* me.

And he's not playing games with me.

He's being honest.

He's letting me know exactly where he stands and exactly what he wants.

This is a refreshing change for me and my dating life.

I've never dated a guy like him.

And goodness if I'm not looking forward to our first date more than I've ever looked forward to a date.

∼

THE AFTERNOON quickly goes downhill after I leave the boardroom.

And when I say downhill, it should be spelled *shitshow*.

It begins when Jill leaves for the interview she's giving with Owen. She's on edge before she even sets foot outside her office.

"Are you nearly finished with those jobs I gave you?"

Her tone catches me by surprise. It's quite tart and very impatient. Like she's been waiting forever for me to finish these jobs when that's not the case at all. The jobs she's referring to are new items on my list that only appeared an hour ago.

"I should be by five," I say.

She doesn't appear pleased by this. "Make sure you are."

Ok, wow.

She leaves me and I mentally thank the Universe for making this a two-day-only job. Jill started yesterday with being nice to me, but she's slowly become more difficult as time has gone on. I don't think I could work for her full-time.

She's gone for forty-five minutes, and when she returns, she's in a bad mood.

And when I say bad, it should be spelled *foul*.

She storms into her office and commences throwing things.

At first, because my back is to her, I don't know what the noise is that I'm hearing. When I hear it again, I turn to make sure she's okay. A picture frame comes flying my way, hitting the glass wall that divides us, and smashing to the ground.

I've literally got less than fifteen minutes left before I officially finish working here. I'm inclined to turn back to my computer and see those fifteen minutes out without getting involved in whatever Jill's dealing with. However, when I realize she's crying, I can't stop myself from going to her to make sure she's okay.

"Jill," I say as I enter her office. "Are you okay?"

Tears track down her cheeks as she looks at me. "Whatever you do, Charlize, don't ever give up your entire life for a man. They're not worth it."

Right, so I think my boss is maybe having a moment. Like, a big moment. One I may not be equipped to help her with.

I glance around at the mess of broken glass from the items she's thrown. "Would you like me to clean up?"

She shakes her head and waves me off. "No, I'll do it." She reaches for a tissue and blows her nose. "I'm sorry I was awful to you this afternoon. I'm having the week from hell, and I took it out on you. That wasn't fair when you've worked exceptionally hard for me."

Poppy tells me often that I'm a bleeding heart. She's right and I stand proud knowing that I care for people even though I know the term is usually used to disparage people. That heart of mine opens right up for Jill now.

"I get it," I say. "And I appreciate your apology."

She stares at me through her tears.

She does this for what feels like forever.

Then, she says, "*I* appreciate that you didn't pretend it didn't happen. Most of the staff here pander to me. I never know what they're really thinking about me. They fucking love Owen, like actually, truly like him and want him to like them, but with me, I think they just act as if they like me so they can get something out of me."

I think my bleeding heart may have gotten me into a situation I don't want to be in.

I feel for Jill. I really do. However, that doesn't mean I want to get into this with her.

I'm saved by Tahlia, Owen's assistant, who knocks on her office door. "Jill, I've got those documents from Owen for you to sign."

Jill motions for her to come in.

I excuse myself, glad to go back to my desk.

I eye the time on my computer.

I've got eight minutes to go.

I've never watched the clock in any job like I am this afternoon.

I count down as Tahlia leaves and I quickly send through the final few things Jill has asked me to do for her.

Five minutes.

Three.

One.

At five p.m., I wonder if it would be wrong to leave without checking on her again.

I'm in the middle of warring with myself over this when she comes out at 5:06 p.m. and says, "Go home, Charlize. And thank you for getting everything done."

I look at her.

Never in my life have I seen a woman compose herself so quickly and so well after breaking down. To look at her, you wouldn't know she was throwing things and crying and bleeding her heart out about her week from hell fifteen minutes ago.

"You're okay?" I just can't help myself.

She pushes her shoulders back and nods like she was never not okay. "Yes." With one last look at me, she turns and goes back into her office, closing the door behind her. I get the impression she intends on working late tonight.

I switch the computer off and tidy up the desk that was mine for two days. I then grab my purse and leave North Management.

Excitement fills me as I push through the front doors of the Lexington Avenue building. In three hours, I'll be with Owen, and whereas this time yesterday I was trying to deny my attraction to him, today I can't.

I want Owen just as much as he wants me.

10

Charlize

I wear a red satin dress for our first date.

The dress barely reaches my knees, hugs all my curves, and drops low in the front with its slash neckline. The thin spaghetti straps are a little loose and I know they'll likely annoy me later because at least one of them always slides off my shoulder repeatedly. But it is one of my favorites, and since I know Owen loves red too, I don't hesitate to wear it.

I don't bother with a bra tonight. The only reason I wore one to Poppy's wedding was because my mother insisted. "Bras were created for a reason, Charlize." Honestly, I can get away without one if needed, and tonight I am. It's taken until today for my skin to fully recover from that god-awful bra I wore to the wedding. It wouldn't be too soon if I never had to wear a bra again.

I'm still getting ready when Johnathon, Dylan's doorman, calls to let me know Owen has arrived. I've gotten friendly with Johnathon since I've been staying here and have found him helpful in a variety of situations. "You can let him in," I say, "but maybe can you stall him a little? I'm still getting ready for our date."

"Got you," he says.

He does a good job, but I'm the kind of girl who's always running late, so I'm still not ready when Owen comes up.

"You're early," I say when I open the door to him.

He gives me a pointed look. "I was five minutes late thanks to traffic, and your doorman delayed me another five minutes. I am far from early."

I barely hear a word he says. And I have no idea how I manage to keep my eyes glued to his when all I want to do is check out his body.

"Trust me, you're early."

Unable to stop myself, I move closer to him, almost completely closing the entire distance between us, and drop my gaze to look at him.

Owen has swapped the dark blue jeans he wore to work today for black jeans that fit themselves over his leg muscles so perfectly I may never be able to drag my eyes from them. He's paired them with a white button down that he hasn't tucked in, a black sweater, and brown boots.

My hand makes its way to his body all by itself, grasping a handful of his sweater. I lean in closer, inhaling that scent he wears that reminds me of my favorite candle. "You smell good. And you look good. I'm not sure it's safe for you to wear these kinds of clothes around me. You should invest in some baggy attire. I think that'd be a safer option."

He pulls me close and slides his hand through my hair. "Two days of not touching you has been hell," he growls. His mouth crashes down onto mine and he reminds me of how skilled he is at kissing.

If I never kiss another man, it won't matter because I've had Owen's kisses. They are the absolute best in the world. I don't even need to test that. All I need is to get lost in them to know they're everything.

He kisses me for a long time. When he finally ends the kiss, he keeps hold of me and says, "You look beautiful. And I'm never investing in baggy attire if this attire gets that kind of reaction out of you."

I snake my arm around him. "Is it bad that I'm not sure I can make it to dinner before ripping those jeans off you?"

"Fuck," he rasps, bringing his mouth back to mine.

I kiss him while pulling him into the condo and closing the door behind us. I make quick work of getting his sweater off and then begin working on the buttons of his shirt. I'm not thinking about anything but getting him naked. Well, that, and getting his mouth on me in more ways than it already is.

Owen seems to have other ideas, though.

He pulls his mouth from mine as I begin work on his fourth button. His eyes are filled with raw desire as he says, "You really want to skip dinner?"

I finish with his fourth button. "Does that question even need answering?"

He takes hold of my hand, halting my progress down his shirt. "Once I start, I'm not stopping, Charlize.

There may not be any food for a while if we skip dinner now." His voice is filled with the same raw need as his eyes.

I place both hands to his chest and glide them up his body, looping them around his neck. "I don't want you to stop, Owen."

His nostrils flare. "You can finish with my shirt and then I'm getting started with your dress."

I press myself against his hard cock while threading my fingers up into the back of his hair where I know he likes them. "I want you in my mouth first."

One of his hands comes to my ass and he pushes me even harder against his cock. "No."

With one word, uttered in that deep, gravelly voice I can't get enough of, he owns me and everything I do tonight.

I finish unbuttoning his shirt and discard it, eyeing every inch of his skin that I can now see. I also eye the jewelry he wears. A silver box chain necklace and a thick silver bracelet. He also wears a solid plain silver ring on his left pinky. I've never been with a guy who wears jewelry. I'm into all of it.

He traces a finger over my lips before saying, "Be a good girl and take a step back so I can look at you."

God yes.

I do as he says.

He keeps his eyes on mine for a few more moments before letting them drop to my body, and goodness if his attention there doesn't get me wetter than I already am.

He takes his time, looking at every inch of me before finally moving closer again. "Do you know how hard it was for me not to take you on my boardroom table today?" he asks as he runs a finger along my skin just above the neckline of my dress.

"As hard as it was for me not to beg for that?"

My breaths come a lot faster as Owen teases me with that finger on my skin. Can he just take my dress off already?

He keeps up the teasing while sliding one of my straps off my shoulder. Doing so reveals half a breast, and I am more than sure I just stole a breath from him.

"You've given up on the bras that cause you problems?" He keeps his eyes glued to my body while he asks this.

"I'm thinking about giving up on clothes altogether. Especially if you're going to insist on taking so long to get them off me."

He cups my breast, pushing the material of my dress down so he can see everything he wants to see. Tweaking my nipple, he bends to suck it into his mouth.

I arch into him, gripping his waist, needing more than he's giving.

"I told you I'm teaching you patience," he says.

"I'd like to make it known I don't like being patient."

"You will learn to." He keeps his hand on my breast while his lips move to my throat. He then kisses his way up to my mouth, his eyes meeting mine. "You'll like the payoff."

I place my hands to his stomach. "Has anyone ever told you you're bossy?"

"I recall you may have mentioned something to that effect."

"Well, in case you weren't aware, you're turning out to be very bossy."

He kisses my neck. "Are we going to have a problem with that?"

I want to tell him yes.

I want to tell him we're going to have all kinds of problems with his bossy ways.

But I don't.

Because it turns out we're not going to have a problem at all.

It turns out I like bossy.

"No," I say.

Approval and lust blaze in his eyes. "Good girl."

If being a good girl makes Owen look at me the way he is right now, then my only goal in life from here on out is to be a good girl.

His good girl.

He lifts me into his arms, "Where's your bedroom?"

I direct him, and a few moments later, he places me down in front of my bed. Taking hold of my face, he kisses me. Long and deep, and with the kind of attention that I'm learning is his signature move.

He slides my other strap off my shoulder while he kisses me. The dress slips to my waist and Owen pulls his face from mine to study my body.

I wiggle out of the dress and push it to the side after it drops to the floor.

As I do this, Owen slides his hand into my panties and finds my clit. He circles it before running his finger down my pussy.

He meets my gaze as he pushes his finger inside me. "You are so fucking wet for me."

I grip both his arms, my fingers digging into his skin, my eyes closing.

"Oh, God," I moan. "Yes."

I rock myself into his hand, practically begging him to make me come.

He finger fucks me for a few moments before stopping and crouching in front of me. He slowly peels my panties down, taking his time and getting his fill of my pussy; kissing, licking, and sucking me.

I grip his hair, steadying myself while he brings me closer to the orgasm he's been teasing all day.

He doesn't make me come.

Instead, he stands and says, "I want you on the bed, on your back."

They might be my favorite nine words of today.

I instantly comply.

Owen unzips himself and strokes his cock. "Spread your legs for me."

I do that, struggling not to touch myself as I watch him.

He continues stroking himself for a few moments before toeing off his boots and stripping out of the rest of his clothes.

He then moves onto the bed.

I run my eyes over the perfection that is his body. I still don't know how many hours he works out each day, but I quickly let that thought go because all I can think about right now is how big his dick is and how much I want it inside me.

Owen leans over me so he can kiss me, placing one hand to the mattress and one on my breast while grinding his cock against my pussy.

This kiss is bruising. As is his hand moving over my breast. The roughness in his moves only gets me hotter for him because I can tell he's really fucking turned on. It's like he can't kiss me hard enough, or deep enough, or for long enough.

When he ends our kiss, he says, "You're going to show me what you want me to do to you."

A moment later, he's got his face between my legs and his eyes on mine while he waits for me to show him.

Holy fuck, this is hot.

Bringing my knees up, I put my feet to the bed while reaching down to circle my clit. Owen watches like nothing else exists in the world for him right now. Like this is the only thing he ever wants to watch.

I start slow with my clit. Owen only watches to begin with, but when I reach my other hand down so I can touch the rest of my pussy, he takes hold of my ass and bends his face to me. His tongue joins my finger at my clit and together we circle it.

He looks at me while he does this.

His eyes are filled with so much desire for me.

My back arches up off the bed at that desire and I slide a finger inside myself.

"Fuck...Owen," I moan. "I need you."

He keeps working his tongue on my clit for a few moments before saying, "Tell me where you need me."

"I want your fingers inside me. And your tongue."

He lets go of my ass and presses my thighs out to the bed. He then brings one finger to my clit while kissing the lips of my pussy.

His pressure mirrors the pressure I was using and it's so fucking perfect that it's giving me pleasure everywhere.

I've always had a love/hate affair with oral sex. Some guys eat a little too enthusiastically for me. And some rub my clit like they're actually trying to rub it right off me. Owen does neither of those things.

I grip his hair as he uses both hands to spread my lips and push his tongue inside me. He slowly works his way in, the sensation light and teasing.

"Oh my God." I writhe on the bed, my pleasure building to the level of *can I just get it already*.

Owen's eyes meet mine. He circles his tongue inside me before easing it out and licking my taint.

Pleasure explodes through me.

Between what he's doing with his mouth, his hands, and his tongue, along with the way he looks at me while he does it, every nerve ending in my body is alive.

My back arches up off the bed and my eyes close.

My orgasm is so close.

When Owen pushes two fingers inside me, I squeeze them.

So close.

"Fuck." The word drops from his lips right before he sits back on his heels, takes hold of both my legs, pulls me up to bring my pussy closer to his mouth, and bends his face to it.

I hook my legs over his shoulders. "Oh my God...oh God...yes..." I grip the sheet as he eats me.

His mouth.

His tongue.

His beard.

His fingers digging into my skin.

That growl of his while he brings me to orgasm.

It all sends me over the edge, and I swear I now know more pleasure than I've ever known.

I think I'm chanting, but who knows.

I may be imagining that.

All I know is that I know nothing.

Not a thing.

Except that I want more.

And I want it from Owen.

The next thing I know is that he's stopped giving me his mouth.

He leaves the bed.

But only for a few moments.

I open my eyes to find him rolling a condom on, and then he's on top of me and finally giving me his dick.

"So fucking beautiful," he rasps before kissing me roughly.

I wrap my arms and legs around him and hold on while he thrusts inside.

Yes.

He pulls out and thrusts back in.

God yes.

I grip him harder while he pounds into me.

Owen has some stamina.

I've long orgasmed again by the time he comes.

And after he orgasms, he doesn't collapse onto the bed to recover. He looks down at me, searches my eyes, kisses me, and pulls out before moving off the bed to dispose of the condom.

I watch him leave the bedroom and then come back. I'm so thoroughly fucked that I'm having trouble focusing on him.

I feel the bed dip when he lies next to me, but again, *really fucked*, and still lost in the pleasure.

His lips brush my cheek. "You good?"

I turn my face to him and smile while keeping my

eyes closed. "I am more than good, but you fucked me so well that I don't know if I'll ever be able to open my eyes again."

He chuckles. "Is this a thing I don't know about women yet?"

I nod, my smile lingering on my lips. "It really is."

"I hope not. Your eyes are too beautiful not to see again."

I open my eyes and roll to face him. When I drape my arm across his chest, he takes hold of it in a way that feels like he doesn't want to let me go. "Where did you learn to have sex?" I ask. "Like, did you go to school for it?"

He smiles and then kisses me. "I can never anticipate what you're going to say next."

I curve a leg over his. God, I love his legs. And I really like having them in my bed. "That's a good thing, right?"

"A very good thing."

I lie silently for a minute, tracing lines over his chest before looking up at him again. "You know how I told you I was good with not eating for hours?"

"You're not, are you?"

I shake my head. "No. And I'm not even a little bit sorry I lied to you. I mean, it's all your fault that I did."

"Because?"

"Because you have the body of a god, remember? Honestly, Owen, you can't carry that body around and expect women not to throw themselves at you."

His lips twitch. "This is why I need you. To remind me of this fact."

"Oh, I don't believe you're not reminded of this fact often. I imagine women are lining up to let you know."

"I have no idea. The only woman I'm paying attention to is you, Charlize."

The thing about Owen? When other guys have said stuff like this to me, I learned not to believe them. When Owen says it, I believe every word.

I'm not sure if that's a good thing or not.

All I know is I want him to say more things like that to me and I really want to be right in thinking that he means every word.

11

Owen

Charlize stares at the nine boxes sitting on her kitchen island. She does this for a long time. She then meets my gaze, and the look in her eyes hits me deep in my gut. It's the kind of look I want to inspire in her often. "Holy shit, you found some Nutella places."

I did.

I found nine to be exact and that was the result of only a short time dedicated to the search. I was only able to find half an hour in total today for that search. I've added it to my mental list to find more time in the future and locate more Nutella places for her.

When I decided on a restaurant for dinner, I allowed for the fact we might not make it out the door once I got my hands on Charlize. With that contingency in mind, I emailed Tahlia the list of the nine restaurants I found this afternoon that have Nutella dishes on their menu along with a list of items to order if requested.

After Charlize told me she was hungry and wanted to eat now, I texted Tahlia and asked her to have the food delivered.

"Who knew there are restaurants out there who serve so much Nutella?" I ask.

She opens one of the boxes. "Who knew there are people out there who didn't know this?" She eyes me. "What are you eating for dinner? I mean, you told me you don't like Nutella, so I'm guessing this is all mine." She gives me a look that says I better give her the right answer here. "I'm hoping this is all mine."

I chuckle. "Yes, this is all yours. I've got some food coming for me."

She grabs a fork from the drawer. "Good, but I'm not waiting for you."

I can't wipe the smile off my face. "Far be it from me to keep a girl from her Nutella."

With one last pointed look at me, she takes a bite of the Fried Nutella Pizza from the first box.

Watching Charlize eat something she likes may fast become a hobby of mine. It may be one of the most sexual activities that doesn't involve sex that I've ever seen.

She drops her head back ever so slightly as she chews, her throat becoming a focal point for me right before I realize she's closed her eyes and is making a noise that sounds like a soft moan.

When she does moan, I comprehend the fact that I

now know there's such a sound as a pre-moan. I wonder how I never knew this before the age I am now.

"Oh my God, Owen." I'm unsure if I'd call this voice she's using a purr, a hum, a murmur, or something else entirely. Whatever it is, I hope to fuck she uses it a lot with me. "This is to die for." Her eyes open. "If all the food in these boxes tastes this good, I don't think you're getting any more sex tonight. I'll be in the kind of food coma I've never experienced."

I'll forego sex for this.

Hell, I'd give it up for days if she keeps looking at me the way she is.

We're interrupted when her doorman calls to let her know my dinner has arrived. A few minutes later, I carry all our food to the dining table while Charlize brings plates and cutlery.

I look out at the river and the Brooklyn Bridge as I sit. "Dylan has a great view." She told me a little about her friend the other night while telling me she's only staying with him temporarily. He's got a great place here in Brooklyn Heights. Spacious and a few blocks back from the river.

"Oh, shit!" She goes back to the kitchen and grabs her phone before coming back to me. "I just have to remind him about something." She madly taps out a text, placing her phone on the table once she's done. Bringing her legs up to sit cross-legged on the chair, she says, "Dylan's in flow with new art he's making at the moment. If I don't remind him every day about the gala we're attending next week, he'll forget, and I really can't have him forget."

"Because?"

She makes wide eyes. "Because if I have to go alone, I

may hurt my mother. Dylan will keep my hands away from her neck."

I cut some of the steak I had delivered. "Tell me about your mother." We only spoke briefly about her family the other night, and while I know of the Cohens, I want to hear about them in her words.

She opens another box of Nutella goodies and takes a bite of the Nutella Dumpling in it. Her eyes light up as she eats, and she makes more of those noises I like. After swallowing her food, she says, "Joan Cohen is your perfect WASP with her old money, perfect manners, deeply embedded sense of entitlement, disdain for new money and excess of style, pointless discipline, and an insane ability to sit still for long periods of time."

She's just described half the women I know. Her description tells me everything while telling me nothing. "Who is she besides all that?"

This catches her by surprise, causing her to still and consider the question. While she thinks about that, she opens box number three and then looks at me. "Seriously, I'm not sure how you're ever going to beat this dinner. I feel like a man shouldn't bring out the big guns on the first date. Where does he go after that?"

I reach for her chair and drag her closer to me. "Firstly, I like that what I'm hearing in all this is that there'll be a second date." Fuck, she's beautiful sitting there wearing only my shirt. "And second, this isn't the big guns, Charlize. Trust me on that."

Her breaths become uneven as she takes all this in. She doesn't respond at first, which is unusual for her. Charlize usually has a lot to say on most topics. It's one of my favorite things about her so far, the way words just fall out of her mouth. Like I told her earlier, I never know what's coming next. I like that kind of unpredictability in a woman.

She's silent for a little while before finally saying, "My mom wears the pants in her marriage and cares way too much about keeping up appearances. She married my father because he comes from old money too and she liked the idea of their union more than she liked the idea of love. In fact, I'm not sure she's ever been in love, which is sad if true. We're not the kind of close, though, that would let me ask her about this, and I find that sad too. If I ever have a daughter, I'll make sure we're that kind of close. I want her to ask me all about love and hate and sex and boys and dreams and disappointments and hope. And if I have a son, I'll make sure he knows that the pants should be shared. Like, cut them in half and wear half each, you know?" She stops talking and takes a deep breath. "And just so you know, you should never make me a promise and then not keep it. Now that you've said this wasn't the big guns, there better actually be bigger ones. I don't do well with disappointment."

Fuck me, where did this woman come from and why did I take so long to meet her?

Before I can stop myself—not that I'd want to—I've got my mouth on hers and am kissing her with everything I've got. She kisses me right back, giving me the same. Then, not letting my mouth go, she's crawling into my lap and hugging her arms around my neck and kissing me with even more.

By the time we come up for air, we're wrapped in each other's arms and both breathless.

"I don't do well with disappointment either," I say,

pushing a strand of her hair off her face and trying like hell to get all my thoughts back into a straight line. A fruitless endeavor when I've got Charlize in my lap. "There are absolutely bigger guns. And I agree that pants should be cut in half and shared."

She takes a moment with that before relaxing into me. "Tell me about your mom."

"You don't want to eat your dinner before it goes cold?" Hell, I'm more than good with keeping her in my arms and talking with her, but I don't want her to miss out on her food.

"I might be into food, Owen, but right now, I'm into you, and I want to know all the things I don't know about you."

I tighten my arms around her. "Mary North didn't wear the pants in her marriage, but she tried hard. It sounds like our mothers could be best friends. I hadn't thought about it before, but I wonder now after you mentioned it whether my mother has ever been in love. She—"

"Wait. You've never wondered that about your parents? Like, how?"

"I'm a guy, Charlize. I think about work, sex, finances, and sports. I don't think about whether my mother was in love when she married my father."

She narrows her eyes at me. "Do you think about those things in that order? And how is food not on that list? Honestly, I don't think I'll ever understand men. I have no idea how you can only think about four things while I'm over here finding new things to think about every hour of my life."

"Obviously, I think about more things than I listed. The point is that we think differently."

"I can share some new things with you that you can start thinking about. Maybe if I get them into your head, I can get them out of mine." She wiggles around on my lap like she's settling right in. "Okay, keep going about your mom. And are your parents divorced?"

"No, my father passed away when I was nineteen. He had a heart attack."

Charlize's expression softens. "I'm sorry. That must have been hard for you."

"It was. But my older brother was there for me."

"How old is he?"

"Ryan's thirty-six, three years older than me." I smile as I think about him. "You'd like him, I think. He's more like you than me."

"In what way?"

"Ryan is the kind of guy who probably does think about whether Mom was in love when she got married. He's also the kind of guy who'd travel the world after having his heart broken."

"You're right. I like him already." She pauses. "Tell me something about your mom that most people don't know."

I think for a few moments, with nothing coming straight to mind. And then, a long-forgotten memory comes. Something that seemed insignificant at the time, but with the way Charlize is shuffling my thoughts, seems very different now. "I think she had a love affair about three months after my father died that she never told anyone about."

"It didn't last?"

"I don't think so, and I don't know for sure what the relationship was. I saw her at lunch one day with a man and while I didn't think a lot on it, I recall thinking the way she looked at him was a way I'd never seen her look at anyone."

She smiles. "I hope it was a love affair."

I eye her dinner. "You need to eat."

She doesn't move. "You don't like to talk about this?"

"There's no point. Whatever it was for Mom, it's in the past. Why go over the past?"

Her expression leads me to believe she doesn't agree with me, but she doesn't say anything further. Instead, her fingers weave their way through my hair while she brings her mouth to mine. This kiss isn't as deep and all-consuming as our last one, but it's not quick either. When she ends it, she says, "I understand that."

She doesn't try to push me.

She doesn't try to change my mind.

And she doesn't try to tell me I'm wrong.

She simply tells me she understands me, climbs off my lap, and moves back to her seat.

She then works her way through the rest of the boxes, trying everything, killing me with her sounds of pleasure while talking with me about random things from our lives.

We discuss our senior proms and I learn that Charlize refused to go with a date.

We talk about our grandparents, and I learn she loved spending time with her grandfather in the same way I like spending time with mine.

She brings up the topic of Nutella and digs around in my head for a bit trying to figure out why I don't like it. I find this entire conversation amusing. I've never met a woman who can carry on a discussion about food like Charlize can. The fact she could keep my attention for hours on a topic as simple as Nutella if she wanted to astounds me.

The truth is that I'm fucking captivated by this woman and everything about her.

12

Charlize

I wake early on Wednesday morning thanks to Owen staying the night and getting up at some ungodly hour to go home.

"What time is it?" I mumble into my pillow. I do not want to open my eyes or lift my head because that will mean I am in fact awake. However, I desperately want to do both those things so I can catch a glimpse of him before he leaves. Why must life be so full of conflicting desires? I feel like we should be born as a set of clones so that these situations don't occur.

Owen's hand comes to the back of my head right before his lips do. He kisses me and says, "It's just before five. Go back to sleep."

"I'm not awake." I keep my face firmly smooshed into my pillow, willing this statement to be true.

"I agree. You're absolutely not awake."

"I will hurt you if you're laughing at me, Owen North."

"Fuck." He says that with the kind of growly sound that could encourage me to wake up for real. His hand on my back after he says it goes a little more toward waking me up. "I like my name on your lips," he murmurs before kissing my shoulder.

"Oh my God, stop it," I grumble as I roll onto my side and crack my eyes open. "Stop waking me up. Who even gets up at this time of the day?" I stare at him. "And who looks that good at five fucking a.m.?"

Owen is sitting on the edge of my bed, dressed, and looking as good as he did when he arrived last night. He bends so he can press a kiss to my lips. "I take it you're awake now?"

"Yes, and you should take this as your one and only warning that I don't do well before seven in the morning on days off."

"I'll try to remember that."

"That makes me think you're maybe not going to pay any attention to it, though."

He smiles. "I like the speed with which you catch onto things, Charlize."

I try to send him a death stare. "You won't like the speed with which I inflict bodily harm if you continue waking me up at this time."

The way he's still smiling makes me think I failed at my death stare. "All I'm hearing is that you still intend on using me for sex for a year, and that's all I'm interested in." He checks his phone at the sound of a message and then eyes me again. "How do you feel about having coffee with me this morning?"

My eyes widen. "What, now?"

"No, later. Seven thirty at the coffee shop around the corner from my office?"

Usually, I'd say no because me being even close to presentable at that time for a coffee date isn't something I'd usually be. For Owen, though, I'm beginning to think I'd run there to have that date with him.

Jesus.

Did he put drugs in the sex we had?

"You're buying," I say.

He stands. "I'll see you then."

I try to go back to sleep after he leaves.

Half an hour later, I give up and stomp out to the kitchen in search of coffee.

Dylan's sitting at the kitchen island, halfway through a coffee. "There she is," he says. "The girl who kept me up half the fucking night."

"Well, it's only fair. I mean, the number of nights you've kept me awake over the years is well into *I can't count it on two hands anymore*." I locate a mug. "What time did you get home? I didn't hear you come in."

He lifts a brow. "Yeah, because you were making enough noise to not hear anything. It was around one."

I roll my eyes. "Calm down. I'm not that loud during sex."

That draws a laugh from him. "Record yourself next time, Char. You fucking are. And so is that bed. If you guys put a hole in my wall, you're paying for it."

He's right, the bed did hit the wall a few times. Owen doesn't know what quiet, sedate sex is. I'm not complaining even though I've discovered muscles I didn't know I have.

I make coffee and sit on the stool next to him.

"So, what's on the list for today?" he asks. "You're finished with that job, right?"

"Yes. I'm hopeful I'll get a good reference from it so more work will come in. Today, I plan on seeing what's new to apply for and then I thought I might get a haircut."

"Didn't you just get one last week?"

"I appreciate that you are not like other boys, Dylan Hale, and actually remember things about me, but you can stop now, okay? So I wanna get another haircut?" I shrug. "I'm a girl. That's what girls do. We get lots of haircuts."

He shakes his head at me again, with that look of his that says he really doesn't understand me half the time. "I like that you're giving him a chance. I've heard good things about him."

"When? How?"

"You forget how many people I know in this city, babe. They only say good things about Owen."

Dylan does know a lot of people. He comes from an influential family with connections everywhere.

I gently nudge my shoulder against his. "You love me, Dyl."

"You somehow convinced me to."

"That's my specialty in life, convincing boys to like me. But you're the one who stayed, and you're the one who looks out for me. Thank you." I take a sip of my drink. "Owen and I have a coffee date this morning."

"Good."

I give him one last smile before going to get ready for my date. "I'll try to be quiet next time. And I'll tell him not to put a hole in your wall."

"Or maybe you can just fuck him at his place."

"Yeah, maybe, but where would the fun be in that?"

I laugh as he shakes his head at me again.

Friends really are the family we give ourselves.

I WEAR a black leather-look pencil skirt, a white tee that says *But First Coffee*, and white sneakers when I meet Owen for coffee. His eyes are all over the *But First Coffee* the minute he spots me. Or maybe it's my breasts that catch his attention. My T-shirt does hug them.

In return, my eyes are all over his dark blue suit. Yesterday, I told him jeans were my preference. Today, I'm not so sure. This suit is something else. Or maybe it's the body that I know is under it.

He's waiting outside the coffee shop for me in the sun. When I reach him, his arm comes around me easily and his lips meet mine without hesitation. I like that we don't have to keep our hands to ourselves anymore.

"Hey," I say.

He kisses me again before brushing his mouth against my ear so I can hear him over the crowded shop. "What do you want me to order for you?"

I ask for a cappuccino and an almond croissant, and while he orders, I find us a table.

It's busy this morning so it takes almost ten minutes for Owen to come back to me. My phone sounds with a text as I spot him coming my way. I quickly check the message in case it's my employment agency letting me know I have a job to go to. I brought a change of clothes with me in case.

I read the text twice.

And then I read it again.

I seriously don't know what I did to the Universe today, but she's not happy with me over something.

When Owen moves the chair from across the table to sit next to me and stretches his arm across the back of my seat before leaning in to kiss me, I place a hand to his chest and stop him. "You might not want to do that."

He allows me to stop him, but he stays right where he is. "You are very wrong. This is exactly what I want to do."

I show him the message on my phone.

NYC Employment: Charlize, Jill North has asked for you again today. The job has turned into a three-week contract. Can you confirm with me in the next ten minutes that you can do this? And that you can start at eight thirty this morning?

Owen curses but remains where he is. "Are you going to confirm?"

See, clones. They really are the answer to all of life's dilemmas.

"I don't know. I have like eight minutes to decide, and trust me when I tell you, this is one of the worst decisions I've had to make this year."

He likes that. Not that he smiles. I mean, I think the only thing that will make Owen smile right now is if I say I'm not going to confirm. However, it's clear in his eyes that he likes how affected I am by him.

"If you want the work, you should take it," he says, removing his arm from around me and sitting back.

"I do want the work, but I'm sure there are other jobs out there." I already miss his arm around me.

"It's only three weeks. They'll fly by."

I drop my gaze to his undone shirt buttons. "Ah, not if you keep walking around with those kinds of buttons, they won't."

His lips quirk. "I'll make it a point not to."

I exhale a breath. "Could you also make it a point to invest in that baggy attire we discussed last night?"

He turns serious. "Take the job, Charlize."

"You know I'm not good at being patient."

He doesn't respond to that, but he doesn't need to. I see everything he's thinking in his heated gaze.

He's right; it's only three weeks. We can wait that long.

"Okay," I say. "I'll take it." I start tapping out a confirmation to my agency, but then stop and look back up at Owen who is watching me intently. "Tell me what that means for us."

"It means no contact besides seeing each other at work when necessary."

"We can't see each other at all?"

"No."

"Texting? Calling? Anything?"

He looks torn, like he's trying to redefine his own rules. "I had strong words with Jill on this topic two days ago. I can't see you in any way while you're working for the company. It would be detrimental to my working relationship with her."

I nod slowly. "Okay." I send the confirmation text. "Does this mean we can't drink this coffee together now?"

"Don't you dare move your ass. You don't start work until eight thirty. You're mine until then."

I place my hand on his thigh and lean toward him. "Well, technically I'm yours after then, too, but please give me one last kiss before my three-week ban."

He gives me what I want, and he gives it to me so well that I'm not sure I should have requested it. This is now what will be on repeat in my head for the next few weeks.

13

Owen

Charlize has swapped the *But Coffee First* T-shirt for a white blouse that buttons all the way up to her throat. Pleats line the front while the sleeves puff out like balloons. The thing that draws all my attention, though, is the long red ribbon sitting under the collar that she's tied in a bow. A lot of white material makes up that blouse, but all I'm seeing is the red ribbon that falls fucking beautifully down between her breasts. I don't think I've ever dedicated as much brain space to ribbon in my life.

"Owen," Jill says sharply from the right of me where I sit at the head of the boardroom table. "The report?"

I drag my gaze from Charlize who's sitting to the right of Jill and find my ex-wife scrutinizing me. We're halfway through a meeting with Julian and Wesley, our Head of Commodities. To say the meeting is not going well is a gross understatement.

Jill is barely talking to me after our *New York Times* interview yesterday. I've no idea why she's angry with me. I thought the interview went well. The reporter seemed engrossed with the story of how we built North Management to the size it is today. She spent an inordinate amount of time asking how we spend our days, what we attribute our success to, what our vision is, what advice we would give others, and where we see ourselves in ten years. Jill was pleasant to her to begin with, but by the end, she'd grown hostile. She stalked out of the room before the reporter left, leaving me to extricate myself politely when the woman mentioned something about having a drink sometime.

I glance down at the report in front of me. The one I was about to lead a discussion on until I looked up and caught sight of that red ribbon.

"Right," I say, forcing all thoughts of Charlize's wardrobe from my head and launching into the discussion.

At Jill's request, Charlize is sitting in on the meeting to take notes. I usually have Tahlia do this, but for some reason that I'm unaware of, Jill insisted her assistant do it today. She's never once asked for Marla to take notes, so I find it puzzling that she was insistent on this.

I also find it highly distracting.

In both the best and worst kind of way.

My concentration is not where it needs to be with Charlize so close.

Case in point: red ribbon.

I make it through the meeting at which point Jill speaks with Charlize while Julian pulls me aside to quickly go over some stock news he just heard. By the time I'm finished with him, Charlize has left the room and Jill is waiting to talk with me. The animosity in her eyes doesn't give me hope that our conversation will be productive.

"The next time you want a spotlight piece in The Times, don't expect me to have anything to do with it," she says once we're alone.

I frown. "I didn't arrange that interview. The reporter came to me."

"Of course she did." Her catty tone confuses me.

"I don't have time to figure out your point here, Jill, so can you please just enlighten me?"

She glowers at me, but somewhere in that look is hurt too. I know that look well, even if I don't under-stand where it comes from half the time. "You made me feel beneath you yesterday, Owen. You sat there laughing and flirting with that reporter, talking about all your accomplishments while barely acknowledging mine." She pauses, swallowing like she does when she's close to tears. "I gave up my life to help you build this company. It would be nice if you at least acknowledged that."

Before I can respond, she turns and walks out of the conference room.

I file through my memory of the interview, trying to pinpoint the behavior of mine that Jill thinks was flirting. I know damn well I didn't intend for anything to be construed as flirting. Not when the only woman I'm interested in doing that with is Charlize. And sure as hell not when the only woman I'm actually looking at is Charlize.

I didn't flirt with that reporter.

I engaged with her.

I laughed with her.

I shared stories with her.

But not once did I make advances on her.

However, the important part of what Jill said is that she doesn't believe I've acknowledged what she gave up to help me build our company.

Fuck.

I run my hand down my face.

This isn't something new between us, but I thought we'd covered it in therapy. The fact we haven't is troubling. And hell if I know how to fix it.

"Owen." Charlize's voice instantly registers in my body as she enters the conference room and comes my way. "Jill asked me to give you this." She hands me a folder.

I quickly glance at the contents, noting signed documents. Looking back up at her, I say, "These three weeks are going to be some of the longest weeks of my life."

She nods and I wish I could see her throat because I know that when she nods it causes a delicate ripple of skin there. I've watched it enough times now for it to be lodged in my memory. "Mine too."

Fuck, I want her.

Even just one touch would suffice.

"How's your day going?" I don't want to let her go yet.

"Let's just say that I don't understand Jill's moods. My day is as up and down as those moods. And I'm totally about to break my rule of no caffeine after two p.m."

"Rules are meant to be broken."

"I don't know you well enough yet to know for sure, but I feel like you might be a rule-following kind of guy."

I drop my gaze to the red ribbon. "I have only one rule and that is to make my own decisions as to which rules to follow and which to break." I find her eyes again. "Most rules are bullshit, and I think I've found a kindred spirit in you on that."

"You're right. You have." She moves a step closer to me. "I was getting rules mixed up with values. I think you're a values kind of guy."

A text hits my phone, and then another, interrupting our conversation.

"Sorry." I eye my phone. "I have an appointment to get to." I pause and run my eyes over her face again, my mind circling on her assessment that values are important to me. They are. "Jill's moods don't have anything to do with you. She's impressed with your work." I take a step toward the door before stopping and adding, "This blouse is hell on a man, Charlize. I'll do up all my buttons for three weeks if you refrain from wearing it again."

BRADFORD: What's this dinner for tomorrow night that your assistant emailed me about?

Owen: A client of mine. Just be there.

Bradford: Jesus. They must be an asshole if you're arranging a last-minute dinner.

Owen: He's got cash to burn.

Bradford: The only kind of asshole I like. I'll bring the scotch.

My friend may regret his decision when he learns just how much of an asshole Ron can be. But I want him at that dinner. And I wasn't wrong that Ron has cash to invest. Bradford is always open to meeting investors.

I put my phone down and stretch my neck to one side and then the other.

I glance at the time.

6:43 p.m.

It's been a long day and I've still got at least a couple of hours work ahead of me.

My focus tonight is putting together a proposal for Ron to present to him at dinner tomorrow night. I intend on offering him a new contract that lowers his fees. Something I've never done for any other client. In exchange, he'll let go of his demand for me to remove Jill as COO. It should be a no-brainer for him, but that's only if he considers it from the angle of making money. If Jill's wedged herself in his brain emotionally, I won't have a hope in hell of moving him past that demand.

A text lights up my phone, letting me know the takeout I ordered has arrived.

I make my way out to the elevators and meet the delivery guy.

"Thanks, Terry," I say as I take the food from the guy who almost always delivers when I work late and order dinner in.

"Two nights already this week, Owen. You gotta get yourself a woman."

"I agree."

He grins. "I know a few if you ever need me to hook you up. Although, they might be a little rowdy for you."

I return his smile. "You might be surprised at just how much I like rowdy. But I'm good for now."

"Good to hear, man. Good to hear." He points at me. "I hope I don't see you again this week."

He steps back into the elevator, and I head into the break room to find cutlery.

The office is quiet at this time of day, something I appreciate. I find the solitude between the hours of 4:00 a.m. and 6:00 a.m., and after 7:00 p.m. to be the best for getting work done. Tonight, I note only a few other employees still here.

As I turn to enter the break room, I catch sight of Charlize sitting at her desk outside Jill's office which is at the far end of this floor.

I stop and watch her for a moment. She's quite a distance away, so I can't see her in great detail, but she appears to be hunched over staring at her computer screen. As I'm watching, she starts shaking her head and throws her arms in the air before leaning back in her chair, looking at the ceiling, and muttering something to herself.

My feet are moving in her direction before I can stop them.

A voice in the back of my head is telling me not to do this.

That I'll regret it.

But everything in me is driving me toward Charlize, and there's not a force in this world that could stop me.

"It's a good thing you're not a quitter," I say when I reach her.

She was so absorbed in what she was doing that I catch her by surprise. Her head jerks to look at me.

"Jesus, Owen, how do you not know that sneaking up on a woman is something you should never do? For future reference, you may be harmed in the making of these situations. And for the record, I am definitely not a quitter. If this computer"—she stabs her finger at her computer—"ends up smashed against a wall, it did that all by itself, okay?"

It's mind-boggling how okay I'd be with having to replace that computer.

"What's it doing?"

"Everything it should not be doing. Like, for real, how old is this thing? It's so slow I want to take a nap."

I am absolutely having Tahlia conduct an audit on the age of our computers tomorrow.

"Would you like help?"

That slows her down and causes a breathtaking smile to fill her face. She stands and motions for me to take a look.

As she moves away from the desk and I move to sit at it, her body brushes against mine and our faces come closer than I know what to do with. Charlize continues giving me that smile I never want to see removed from her face.

I allow my hand to brush hers. Hell, I curl my fingers around hers for at least a moment as I say, "Why am I being blessed with this smile?" Not for the first time in my life, I wish that I could read women's minds. Whatever I did to earn her smile, I need to repeat often.

"You didn't just take over. You asked if you could help."

Fuck, is that a thing women prefer when a man can help them?

I make a mental note to remember that.

"Good to know," I murmur as I sit.

I place my takeout on the only spare spot I can find on her cluttered desk and eye the computer.

Charlize has a million tabs open.

"Do you need all these tabs?" I ask.

She rests her ass against the desk and looks at me like I've asked the dumbest question she's ever heard. "That's a question you never need to ask a woman. Of course, I need all those tabs."

I click through them, my brows furrowing at most of them. Besides the tabs she needs for work, she's searched some random things. The weather forecast, the best coffee in Manhattan this year, the best hiking places nearby, Jon Bon Jovi's marriage, do mermaids exist, should you swim in winter, how bad is it to sunbake, why is my computer so fucking slow, and how hard is it really to birth a baby. There are a lot of question marks in her search term for that last question.

My lips curl up as I read them. "Are these the things you thought of to think about in the last hour?"

She gives me a strong look of warning. "I will hurt you if you close any of them."

"You're still in the research phase?"

"Yes, just like I'm still in the research phase with you."

"How close are you to drawing conclusions?"

"It's hard to say. I'm still collecting data."

"Let me know when you're ready to analyze it. I can help with that."

She turns silent for a moment and then looks at the computer screen. "I feel like you should get to work or else we're going to be breaking a rule you shouldn't break."

I eye the red ribbon I haven't stopped thinking about all day. "I feel like you should help me eat all this food I had delivered."

"I don't think that's a great idea."

"You're an employee, Charlize. One who's working late. I can't have you starve."

She considers that before finally saying, "I *am* hungry. I mean, it's been a good hour since I've had a snack."

I lift my chin at the takeout. "Go and start without me. I'll take a look at the computer and then join you."

"I'm not eating without you."

"It'll go cold. I won't be long."

She only argues with me once more after that before I convince her to eat.

I then spend a little time going through her computer, deciding it does need to be replaced due to its age. It would also help if she didn't open so many tabs, but I got the distinct impression I've no hope of convincing her of this.

When I meet her in the break room, I say, "I'll have a new computer for you in the morning."

She's got two plates and cutlery on the table for us and has started serving her food. Looking up at me, she says, "That was the exact right thing to say. Thank you."

I sit across from her and reach for one of the dishes. "The lobster noodles are the best I've ever tasted."

"I already tasted them. I agree." She points at the crispy baby back ribs I'm holding. "But those ribs? They're heaven. And I'm dying to try the chicken satay and whatever is in that other dish there. I appreciate the fact you order up big. I mean, why only order one dish when you can order the entire menu, right?"

I laugh as I finish with the dish containing the ribs. "I do have this body to feed, after all."

She stops serving food and looks at me. "You had to go there, didn't you? That's just mean, Owen. Reminding a girl of what she's missing out on. I'm filing that data away for deep analysis later."

Fuck, this was perhaps not my best decision today. I could do this with Charlize for hours. I could also do many other things with her for hours. I need to steer the conversation in another direction.

I hold my hands up in defense. "I'll keep the conversation clean from here on out." I motion at the dish she's holding, indicating I want it when she's done. "Did your father share his love of the stock market with you? Is that how you know about investing?"

She hands me the noodles. "How do you know my father loves the stock market?" I detect the surprise in her voice. If she knew me well, she wouldn't be surprised to learn that I've taken the time to discover what I can about her.

"I make it a point to learn everything about the people I want in my life."

"I knew you had stalker vibes that very first night." She eats some chicken, her eyes lighting up. "Oh wow, this is good," she says before answering my question. "Yes, my father does love the stock market, but he's never shared that love with me. He was always too busy working. 'A lawyer has to stay on top of his game' he always told me. It was his father who made me fall in love with numbers, shares, and the thrill of predicting the market.

My grandfather spent hours teaching me everything he knew. He never made me feel like I was taking up too much of his time. I never felt as loved by anyone as I did by him. It stunned my mother when he died and left me some of his money with a letter that said he wanted me to invest it. She had no idea I knew so much about investing. Neither of my parents did. They still think I'm useless with money." She stops talking suddenly and pulls a face. "God, I don't know why I just told you that. I hate it when people talk about their money."

I frown. "Why do they think you're not good with money?"

She sighs as she eats some of the lobster. "I have a stock portfolio that I don't touch, but when it comes to accessible cash, I tend to give too much of it away or lend it to friends who either don't pay me back or take forever to do that. And I do like to spend it on travel and fun. I can be a little frivolous at times. And impulsive, which I'm sure you will find hard to believe."

She says this like people have told her this is a bad thing. And like she expects me to think that.

"I get told often that I'm too deliberate, too cautious, and not spontaneous enough. That might all be true, but it doesn't mean I should change just because others think I should." I keep my gaze firmly on hers. "I like your impulsivity. I liked it from the minute I met you."

She gives me another one of those breathtaking smiles I'll do almost anything to earn before going back to her food.

We settle into a conversation about investing after that. Charlize is animated, sharing some predictions she has about the market and asking for my thoughts. I've never dated a woman with as much knowledge about the stock market as she has. Getting this glimpse into how her mind works is fascinating, and to say she's smart is a fucking understatement. I could sit here for hours discussing this with her.

At 8:15 p.m., I realize we've been talking for over an hour. "You should go home. It's late."

Charlize leans back in her seat. "Have you got much work to do?"

My eyes have dropped to that red ribbon again. All I want to do is take her home and find other ways to use that ribbon. "Yeah, I've got a couple of hours still to go."

"I know I'm not your assistant, but is there anything I can do to help?"

I look at her hair, at the strands of it cascading down over her shoulder in a ponytail. I've thought about that ponytail more than I care to admit today. I could find many things for Charlize to help me with tonight but having her anywhere in this building will only distract me.

I stand and reach for the food to clear it away. "No, go home. I won't get any work done if you stay to help."

She helps me clear the dishes, not arguing that I'm wrong.

We're entirely too close while cleaning up, our hands and bodies enjoying too much contact as we brush against each other.

"Thank you for dinner," she says once we're finished, looking as affected as I'm feeling. "I really enjoyed it, but I don't think we should do this again in a hurry. I'm almost certain that if we do, I'll make it so none of those buttons on your shirt ever see another day."

My eyes are glued to her ass while she leaves the break room.

She's right that we should not do this again.

That red ribbon wouldn't survive another night like this.

14

Charlize

I barely see Owen at the office on Thursday. I'm both disappointed by this and relieved. But mostly disappointed.

When I do catch sight of him walking from his office to the boardroom, deep in conversation with Julian, I stare for at least five hundred minutes too long.

Okay, slight exaggeration, but everything feels exaggerated. Heightened. More intense.

How I made it through that dinner with him last night without throwing myself across the table and demanding he fuck me is beyond me. Honestly, good sex should not exist because once you've had it, it's all you can think about.

Owen's wearing a dark gray suit today. With a black shirt. And a tie.

I haven't seen him wear a tie this week, and I can't help wondering if he's wearing it for me. So that he isn't tempted to undo those top two buttons.

"Charlize," Tahlia says when she finds me in the break room making a coffee just after lunch. "Can you help me with something this afternoon? It'll probably take about an hour."

I mentally run through the jobs I have to get done for Jill today and quickly decide I can make some time for Tahlia. "Sure. What is it?"

"Owen's attending a conference in London next week and I need to arrange a couple of dinners he's holding for clients. I also need some documents prepared. I'll email it all through to you in about ten minutes." She looks a little stressed. "Thank you for this. I'm run off my feet with other stuff for this trip that came up this morning."

"No worries. I'm happy to help with anything you need."

She leaves and I go back to making coffee. I'm in the middle of thinking about Owen's tie again when his deep voice sounds from behind me. From *right* behind me. Like, so close that when he speaks, I feel his warm breath on my neck.

"You owe me a coffee."

Dear God, does thinking about him conjure him into existence?

I must cease all thinking about him.

I place my hands on the counter and grip the edge while taking a steadying breath. How have I lived for twenty-seven years and never known that a man has the power to make you come without even trying? Not that he has, but I have no doubt he could with the way my body just screamed to life.

"You owe me an orgasm."

"Fuck." That one word growls itself all the way through my veins.

I turn to face him. "No coffee for three weeks. Then, I'm all about the coffee war."

He's all heat and a little amusement when he asks, "The coffee war?"

"Ah, yeah, we're fighting this out. I've decided I was wrong about your coffee. It's nowhere near as good as mine. I was just under the Owen sex spell that day."

More amusement flashes across his face. "I don't recall us having sex that day."

"We didn't. You have superpowers that last long after I sleep with you."

I really need to stop talking because it's only encouraging him to become more entertained by me. "Good to know."

I look at his tie. "One of us needs to leave this room and it needs to be you." I meet his gaze again. "I'd go, but I haven't finished making my coffee yet."

He stays for another minute, taking his sweet time looking at me, before finally saying, "This dress needs to be added to your list of clothes not to wear while you're working here."

With that, he turns and walks that fine ass of his out the door, leaving me in a hot mess of lust and bewilderment.

I'm pretty sure that by the end of my time here, Owen will have decreed that none of my clothes are to be worn again, and that I will have tried to throw myself at him at least fifteen times.

I WORK like a maniac to complete all of Jill's tasks this afternoon as well as get through the jobs Tahlia requested help with. I'm grateful for the new computer Owen had delivered. I would have surely thrown that old one at the wall today if he hadn't.

I outdo myself with the dinners I arrange for Owen in London next week. That's in part thanks to the time I've spent in that city. I know where all the best restaurants are, and since Tahlia mentioned I could choose the restaurants if I knew of any worth eating at, I chose based on my favorites. I, of course, didn't base my decisions on whether they have Nutella dishes on the menu. Owen really has no idea what he's missing out on there.

I also email Tahlia some suggestions for extra touches his clients might appreciate based on my knowledge of London and previous work I've done for bosses. Not wanting to step on her toes, though, I make sure to mention in my email that I realize she likely has this handled but that I wanted to be diligent and highlight them in case. She emails back to thank me, telling me that work is so hectic for her this week that some of these ideas had slipped her mind and she's grateful I included them.

After completing that work, I make a start on the jobs that are on Jill's less important list of tasks. I'm so busy checking jobs off, feeling accomplished, that I lose track of time. When I glance at the computer to check, it's almost 7:30 p.m.

"Jesus," I mutter to myself. "No wonder I'm hungry."

I shut down my computer and tidy my desk. Well, *tidy* might be embellishing. That word and my name don't really go together, but my desk is orderly as far as I'm concerned by the time I leave.

I'm about to step into the elevator when Tahlia calls out, "Charlize! Wait!"

I eye her running my way. She appears frazzled.

"Can I beg one last favor of you today? Please?"

"So long as it doesn't involve me doing anything that will stop me from eating. I have a hot date with pizza and it's not a date I want to give up."

She laughs. "I totally get it, and no, you won't have to give up your hot date." She shoves a bottle of whiskey at me. "Can you please take this to Owen? I was on my way out to do it, but my mom just called and asked me to look after my niece tonight because my sister has been taken to the hospital."

"Oh my gosh, is she okay?"

"She's pregnant and has been experiencing heavy bleeding. They're monitoring her. She's okay at the moment."

I glance at the whiskey while every part of my body blazes alive at the thought of seeing Owen tonight. "Where do I have to take it?"

"To his place. He's having a client over for dinner. This whiskey is the client's wife's favorite, and since the guy's an asshole who Owen's trying to placate, I promised Owen I'd get it to him for the dinner."

I like Tahlia a lot. Not that I've spent much time with

her, but she's not formal or rigid like some women I've worked with.

She rattles off an address on West 57th Street and I assure her I'll get this to Owen straight away. A few minutes later, I'm in a taxi on my way.

Owen lives in one of the tallest residential towers in New York. I stare up at it as I step out of the cab. Just looking up makes my stomach drop a little. I'm okay with heights, but this building is *tall*. I can't imagine living on any of the top floors and looking out over the city. I think that would be too much for me.

I walk into the lobby, taking in the waterfall at the entrance and the pure luxury inside. It's dripping in gilded details. There's gold and sparkle everywhere from the chandelier to the luxurious carpet to the marble throughout. My mother would approve of all of this.

I'm sent up to the 90th floor and met by Owen's butler as I step out of the elevator into his foyer. He welcomes me and leads me through a series of galleries to the open floor living area that showcases the glittering lights of Manhattan thanks to floor-to-ceiling windows and tall ceilings.

Laughter and voices grow louder as we walk into the living area. And then someone starts playing a piano near a window just as it comes into view. A blonde woman sits at it, her fingers moving over the keys with very little skill. Three men are standing around her talking. One of them is trying his best to get her to stop playing, but she just laughs at him, telling him, "Darling, let me be. You know I love playing the piano, and since you refuse to have one, I need to make the most of Owen's."

Owen strides into view, moving to stand next to the

man who's trying to stop the woman playing. "Yes, let her be, Ron." Then, to the woman, he says, "Crystal, feel free to come over and make the most of this piano whenever you want."

Crystal blows an air kiss at Owen and carries on.

"Sir." Owen's butler gains his attention which is quickly then drawn to me.

He excuses himself from his guests and comes my way, bringing all that black he's wearing with him.

Black trousers.

Black dress shirt.

Black shoes.

I'm not even looking at the skin I can see at the top of that shirt.

Except, I am, and I really wish I wasn't.

I hold the whiskey out to him. "Tahlia asked me to drop this by."

He takes the bottle, looking at me in such a way that it makes me think he wishes it was only us here tonight. "Thank you."

We take a moment.

A long moment.

No words are exchanged, but then, none are needed. Our bodies are doing all the speaking.

I'm about to make a move to leave when a waiter appears at my side with a tray of canapés.

When I give a quick shake of my head and start to decline, Owen says, "You're going to want to try that one," while pointing at a shrimp canapé.

His eyes spark with encouragement and warmth like he really wants me to try it.

"I should go," I murmur.

Owen takes one of the shrimp canapés and places it on a napkin before passing it to me. "Not before you try this."

A woman joins us as I take the canapé. She would have to be one of the most beautiful women I've ever seen. Smiling at me, she says, "He's right. You need to try that."

My nerves make themselves known as she says this. I stopped by to drop a bottle of whiskey off. I didn't stop by to join a party. And while I love a good party, I also like to be prepared for it and for the people I'm going to have to talk to. I wasn't prepared for any of this.

I shove the canapé in my mouth.

All of it.

In one go.

I need to eat this and then get out of here.

But, oh my goodness. Owen was right. It's an explosion of yummy goodness in my mouth.

Unable to stop myself, I make a noise that expresses my delight. And it just keeps on going while I eat because this canapé is one of the best things I've ever tasted.

Owen watches me like he can't get enough of me.

His friend watches me with a nod and a knowing look.

When I finally get it all down, I say, "Holy fuck, that was amazing!" I throw a glance around the room looking for the waiter. "You need to get that waiter back here, Owen. I need to try all those canapés."

It's only when the woman eyes Owen's shirt that I realize I've reached out and grasped a handful of it.

Her eyes twinkle as she says, "A girl after my own

heart. You must stay for dinner so we can try all the food together and compare notes."

I let go of Owen's shirt. "No, I have to go."

Before I have a chance to leave, and before Owen has a chance to help me do that, she's got her arm hooked through mine and is dragging me to the sofa. "How do you know Owen? I'm the long-suffering wife of one of his best friends."

A dark-haired man walks over from the piano and sits with her on the sofa across from me. "I hardly think six months of marriage qualifies you as a long-suffering wife, Adeline," he says as he spreads an arm along the sofa behind her.

I don't miss the affection all over her face when she eyes him. "Well, I may not have been your wife for long, but I have been suffering." She looks back at me and introduces us. "My husband, Jameson."

My attention is divided between Adeline and Owen who's watching from where I stood with him a moment ago. I'm trying to figure out how to leave, but his expression says he's more than happy for me to stay.

I've never found myself in a bigger potential-wreck of a situation.

Three weeks.

We only have to make it through *three weeks,* and yet with each passing minute, I'm becoming more convinced we're not going to.

I know nothing of the agreement he has with his ex on this, but I shudder to think what she'll do if she finds out about us while I'm working for her. Poppy has mentioned Jill's jealous tendencies more than once, and my cousin never exaggerates when it comes to this kind of thing. If she's told me to be careful, I need to be careful. The last thing I need is for my boss to unleash her jealousy on me at work.

Owen moves back to the piano, leaving me to deal with Adeline and her husband on my own. I concur with this decision. The less he and I are together, the better.

I smile at Adeline, thinking again how beautiful she is with her flawless skin, long dark hair, and perfectly put together features. How God decides who gets this level of perfection and who doesn't is a question I've often pondered. She and I will be having a little conference on this when I get to heaven, because I'd like to point out that she could make it all a little more equal.

"I'm Charlize. Owen and I met at my cousin's wedding on Saturday."

Adeline seems surprised by that but doesn't show it for long. Her surprise soon eases into excitement. "You've only known each other for five days?"

"Yes."

Another dark-haired man joins us, sitting next to me. He's movie-star handsome with his chiseled jaw, high cheekbones, and striking brown eyes. Taking a sip of his drink, he says, "No wonder you're looking at Owen like he's a god. It's still early days."

Adeline laughs. "You're just jealous, Bradford."

"Well, when the only woman who gets close to me is Cecelia, can you blame me?" he says.

"Have you two announced a date for the wedding yet?" Adeline asks.

"Fuck, no. Although, she'd have announced it three months ago if I'd given her the go-ahead." He throws more whiskey down his throat before glancing at me. "We've met before. I'm sure of it."

I reach back into my memory trying to figure out when, but nothing comes to mind. "I don't think so."

He clicks his fingers. "I've got it. You're friends with Dylan Hale. I met you at a party the Hales held a few years ago."

It comes back to me now and it's not surprising that I've blocked that night from my mind. I was at a party at Dylan's uncle's home with Benjamin that night. We had the kind of fight just before I met Bradford that ensures anything and everything before or after the fight is forgotten.

"I remember now," I say, "and you'll have to forgive me for anything I might have said or done that night. I'd just had a god-awful fight with my ex-fiancé before we met."

"It didn't show. In fact, I wondered how you even had the time of day for Ben. I can't stand the asshole." He nods at Owen who's deep in conversation with the man at the piano. "You've found a much better guy in Owen."

"Oh, I work for Owen." I've no idea what his friends know about us, but I don't want to say anything I shouldn't. "Well, I work for Jill. I'm filling in for her assistant while she's sick. Just for three weeks. It started as two days only, but it's changed into three weeks now. I've no idea what's wrong with her assistant, but I hope to God she doesn't have the kind of ailment that'll mean she needs months off." I snap my mouth shut and stare at Bradford, smoothing my dress while willing my mouth to never open again.

I should have never agreed to deliver that bottle of

whiskey to Owen.

Bradford smiles at me and leans in close. "Your secret is safe with me. And I hope for your sake that Jill's assistant is back in three weeks. There's no fucking way I could work for that woman. I've no idea how you're managing it."

This is why I never allow people to tell me their secrets.

I am bad at keeping them.

I abruptly stand and throw out, "I need the powder room." My eyes latch onto Adeline. "Any idea where it is?"

"I've got you," she says, giving me directions to a room that's near a library not far from the sofa.

I don't really need the bathroom. I just need a moment. Or a thousand.

I lock myself away in the room that may just be the most elegant powder room I've ever been in with its glossy black marble tiles, gold accents, black and gray damask wallpaper, and muted lighting. Resting my hands on the vanity, I draw a long breath and exhale it. While I do this, I look in the mirror and am instantly horrified at the mess my hair is in.

I chose a simple chic black dress for work today. One that reaches my knees, has cap sleeves, and a high neck-line. I wore my hair up in a bun and applied minimal make-up while matching the dress with flat black shoes. Buns usually ensure my hair doesn't get in the way and that it stays where it should all day. This bun has let me down.

I've got flyaway strands of hair everywhere and the back is a loose mess of hair that's making it look more like a messy bun than the perfect art I created this morning. I like a good messy bun, but not for work.

I quickly try to fix it, but all I end up doing is making it worse. In the end, I give up and just let my hair down while muttering about the fact I need to excuse myself and leave this dinner party far behind.

All I can think about is Owen's bedroom.

Like, where is it?

How has he decorated it?

Does he have a bath I could get lost in?

How many pillows does he have?

Does he have something he can tie me to in there?

I squeeze my eyes closed.

Right, I'm going to go out there, find that waiter, steal a tray full of canapés, say my goodbyes, and get the hell out of here before I go in search of that bedroom.

I have a date with pizza to get to, and I'm also now scheduling in a date with my vibrator.

I take one last deep breath before opening the door to leave.

Owen is standing on the other side of the door, leaning against the wall, waiting for me. I stop myself from taking the step I was about to, and say, "One of us needs to go and steal a tray of canapés and that needs to be you. And then I'm leaving."

His lips pull up at the ends and he pushes off the wall. "Stay for dinner."

I hold my hand up to slow his roll. "That is a very bad idea, and you know it. Your friend has already figured us out. The last thing we need to do is share a meal together and have your client work it out too. And don't say I'm your employee and you can't let me starve. Let me starve,

Owen. I'll be less inclined to force my way into your bedroom and demand filthy things from you later."

"Fuck," he growls, only just stopping himself from moving into me. "The word *filthy* is not to leave your mouth while I can't do anything with it." He takes a moment. Probably trying to talk himself out of what he fails not to say next. "I want you to stay. You can sit at the other end of the table from me. We don't need to talk." His eyes search mine. "Five minutes in the break room was nowhere near enough for me today."

I read somewhere once that when a person is turned on, all good sense flies out the window. That they do things they would never normally do. I'm here to tell the world it's true. All of it. True, true, true.

"Okay." *Why must he have those blue eyes?* "I'll stay."

"DID you tell Owen that Crème Brûlée is my favorite dessert?" Crystal asks her husband when dessert is served.

Ron shakes his head. "No."

I eye him. I don't think much of Ron, but then, I've only just met him tonight and I haven't had a proper conversation with him. Still, he strikes me as the kind of man who has an inflated sense of self-importance from the things he's said.

"Oh, to have a husband who shares those kinds of secrets," Adeline says with a teasing look at her husband.

"That would require a wife who doesn't have a new favorite each week," Jameson says. These two banter like pros but it's obvious they adore each other.

Adeline grins. "Well, just in case you spring another dinner party on me this week before I fly back to London, I'd love to see chocolate mousse on the menu with perhaps a little Nutella on the side."

"I am one hundred percent in agreement with that suggestion," I say.

Owen's eyes find mine, a smile hiding in them. "If I'd known you were coming, Nutella would have been served."

Bradford gives me a knowing look from beside Owen at the other end of the table before raising his glass at me.

"Girl," Adeline says as she eats her dessert, "If you love Nutella, you need to check out that new coffee shop around the corner from here on Seventh Avenue. They have this to-die-for Nutella slice."

Thank goodness for Adeline. She's managed to keep me distracted from Owen for most of this dinner. It helped that the men have been engrossed in business conversation, leaving Adeline, Crystal, and me to our own devices. Owen did try to steer the conversation to one we could all engage in, but Crystal made it clear she'd rather talk about something else with Adeline and me.

It turns out that Adeline was a fashion model and now runs her own über-successful fashion brand. I bet Poppy has heard of her before, but I never have. I love clothes and make-up and all things girly, but I don't follow brands. I just buy what I'm drawn to at the time.

The three of us have talked non-stop all night about clothes, make-up, travel, food, and yoga. Adeline and Crystal are yoga devotees. They've tried to convince me to give it a go, but I'm standing strong on my desire to only move my body for sex and dancing. Maybe if I hadn't found a man who wants me to use him for sex for a year, I'd be more inclined to consider yoga, but since I know Owen can get my body into positions that will work all my muscles, I don't need it in my life.

"Oh," Crystal says, "I know the coffee shop you mean. A friend told me about that place last week. She recommended it too."

Owen's completely committed to this conversation even though he's not involved in it. Ron and Bradford are discussing something with Jameson, but Owen is paying them no attention. He and I need to discuss what "no contact besides seeing each other at work when necessary" actually means because he clearly has no idea.

I'm suddenly feeling hot. Bothered. Flustered. In the kind of way that necessitates putting some distance between Owen, that attention of his, and me.

I stand and excuse myself to go to the powder room again.

I spend way longer in there than is necessary, although I would argue that putting out the volcano-level of heat raging through me requires even longer than I take.

Owen is nowhere to be seen when I emerge from the powder room, and I take this as my opportunity to leave. I say goodbye to everyone, resisting Adeline when she encourages me to stay for more dessert. I also resist Crystal when she practically begs me to stay and drink some of the whiskey I brought over.

I'm waiting for the elevator when Owen's deep voice sounds from behind me. "You were going to leave without saying goodbye?"

I turn to face him. "Considering we're not supposed to

be having any contact except when necessary for work, I shouldn't have even stayed for dinner. You're a bad influence."

He moves closer. "I would argue this dinner was necessary for work."

I arch my brows. "Really?"

"Really. Crystal is charmed by you, and since she is the key to keeping her husband happy, which is my reason for this dinner party, your presence here was required."

I search his face. God, I really like his face. "I hope I helped."

"You did." He smooths a wisp of hair off my cheek and murmurs, "You took your hair down."

My breaths come faster. "It was a mess."

He gives a slow shake of his head. "No, it was sexy as hell."

"You like messy buns." It's not a question but rather an observation I'm filing away for later use.

He trails a finger down my neck, sliding my hair back over my shoulder, his eyes following the line his finger takes. "I like to see your neck." He finds my eyes again. "I like your hair however you have it, but any hint of untidiness makes me think about you waking up in my arms that first morning after we met. It makes me think about everything I did to you that night."

My breaths are now in a state of *what even is breathing?*

"Thank you for dinner, Owen," I say, trying to find some oxygen to fill my lungs with.

My ruin is complete when he gives me a sexy smile. "Good night, Charlize."

15

Owen

Bradford: I like Charlize. It's about time you stopped letting Jill dictate your dating life.

Owen: Says the guy whose family is dictating his.

He calls me, asking, "What's with keeping her a secret, though?"

I stop reading my emails and lean back in my chair. I've been in the office for three hours this morning, since four a.m. I worked late last night after the dinner party ended and didn't get a lot of sleep. I can usually function on little sleep, but I'm feeling it today. Or maybe it's the tension my body's holding because it can't get the release it needs. Either way, I sense a long day ahead.

"Jill slept with a client and caused issues there. Julian has also heard talk that she's getting close to the staff. She and I had words about all this." I exhale a long breath. "I can't be that asshole who sleeps with an employee after telling her she can't. And if I do, and she finds out, it'll ruin the relationship we've got hanging by a thread."

"Didn't you meet Charlize before she started working for you?"

"Yes, but Jill wouldn't be interested in that detail."

"So, what, she won't be okay if you date Charlize now, but she'll magically be okay with it if you wait a couple of weeks?"

"No, but I don't need to give her any ammunition to go to war with me over at work."

"You see what you're doing here, don't you?"

I've known Bradford since we were five. He's my oldest friend and the one who never fails to call me on my bullshit. Jameson does that too, but Bradford's been doing it for longer. He's spent the last six months trying to set me up with women, telling me to remove Jill's claws. I've no doubt this conversation is leading back there somehow.

"I'm sure you're about to enlighten me."

"You've spent the last year trying like fuck to minimize Jill's pain because you feel guilty over the divorce. You're still doing that with this situation. You've met a woman you're interested in and you're letting this bullshit be the reason why you won't let Jill see you with someone else."

"Jill has seen me with other women. That's not with this is."

"Yes, but those were women you saw once or twice. Women you slept with and moved on from after. You weren't interested in them. There's a vast difference between those women and Charlize, Owen. Everyone at that dinner saw that last night, my friend."

Julian appears at my door, motioning to let me know he needs to discuss something.

My brain is processing what Bradford's saying because he usually isn't wrong in his assessments of people. He hasn't studied psychology, but I'd swear he had if I didn't know better. However, Julian and I have a lot to go over today, so I push those thoughts to the side and signal for him to come in. "I have to go," I say to Bradford. "Thanks for coming last night."

"I can't say I thought much of Ron, but I enjoyed meeting Charlize. One other thing, we're golfing at Bayonne this Saturday and don't try to get out of it. I need you to help me win Senator Bailey over. We fly out at seven. Tee time is eight."

"I'll be there."

"Good."

We end the call and I look at Julian who is now sitting across from me. "Ron declined the new contract. He did, however, appear to appreciate the dinner and the things we discussed for the future. He's given me two weeks to decide on Jill. He's on vacation, off grid until then."

"So, Ron thinks he's now the fucking CEO here?"

I feel him on this. "His return last quarter should make him think twice about walking. I've emailed him a reminder of that and what this quarter is shaping up to be."

"He's not going to leave. He knows he won't get better anywhere else. This is all a fucking power trip."

"I don't disagree, but we need to tread carefully. The last thing I want is to be fucking blindsided."

"You're meeting with Saul next week. And Mathius. We bring them on board, it won't hurt as much if we lose Ron."

It'd still fucking hurt, though, so it's high on my priority list to not lose him.

We spend ten minutes going over our game plan for my discussions with Saul, Mathius, and a couple of other potential investors I'll be meeting with while I'm in London for a conference next week. Julian is sharing his thoughts on Saul when I see Charlize walking toward my office. My eyes are immediately drawn to the black bow around her neck. She's wearing another white blouse and that bow is a feature of it, so large that it takes up most of the space between her throat and her breasts. She and I need to have words about her love of fabric that clings to her neck. I barely notice the black skirt she's wearing because I can't stop imagining untying that damn bow.

She doesn't come to my office. She makes her way to Tahlia's desk and places a folder on it before turning and leaving. She doesn't look at me once but after talking with her last night, I suspect that wasn't easy for her.

Charlize wanted to force me into my bedroom last night.

It took everything in me not to demand she do that.

Charlize passes Jill on her way, and after they talk for a minute, Jill joins Julian and me. She and I haven't spoken a lot over the last two days since she expressed her anger after the *New York Times* interview. Because of this, I don't have a feel for her current mood.

Her attention is squarely on me. "Is Tahlia going to be in today?"

I shake my head. "I doubt it."

Concern etches Jill's face. "Is she going to be available for the conference next week?"

Tahlia is working from home while looking after her sister's two-year-old daughter. I've no idea when she'll be back in the office. Usually, this wouldn't be an issue since Tahlia can do her job remotely, but I'll need her in London with me next week while I meet with potential investors. She plays a key role in making the things happen that need to.

"I believe she will be," I say.

Jill doesn't appear convinced. "What if she's not, Owen? Do you have a plan for that?"

"No, but I don't think we'll require one. Tahlia has never let me down."

"This may prove to be the kind of situation in which she has no other option but to put her family first. And if so, we need to make alternative arrangements."

Jill has exceptional organizational skills. When she's on her game, she's good at managing people and finding the best ways to achieve goals. I'm good at managing myself only. I don't always look outward, which is where Jill has always come in. She's right; we need to go over our options for next week. There's no way I can manage everything in London by myself.

"You're right," I say. "How about Lisa? She might be able to help."

Jill screws up her face and shakes her head. "No, she didn't leave on good terms."

I frown, recalling Lisa's resignation differently. She was Julian's assistant until six months ago when she quit to go to college. I turn to him questioningly. "I thought everything was okay when she left?"

He glances between Jill and me. "It was, but I can think of one reason this won't work."

"She wanted to sleep with you," Jill snaps impatiently. "You're not taking her to London. She'll be far from efficient."

Jesus.

I scrub a hand over my face.

I miss half the shit that goes on around here.

"Okay, well, do you have any suggestions? Perhaps someone from the agency Charlize is with?"

Jill nods slowly. Thoughtfully. "You could take Charlize."

Those are four words every cell in my body likes, but there's no way I can take Charlize. If Jill thinks Lisa wouldn't be efficient, she has no idea just how inefficient it would be to send me away with Charlize.

"You need her here," I say. It's not far from the truth. While I'm busy bringing in new business next week, Jill will be busy working on client retention here. She has a packed schedule of her own and will need Charlize.

She thinks about that for a moment. "Tahlia can help me." When I pull a face, she says, "No, it makes sense, Owen. You need someone sitting in on the meetings with you. I can get my stuff done with the help of someone virtually. You should take Charlize. She's efficient and capable. It won't take her long to figure out your needs."

If only she knew how quickly Charlize has figured out my needs.

"I agree with Jill," Julian says as he stands. "We've got a lot riding on next week. You want to make sure whoever you take is ready to run with it all, and from what I've seen, Charlize picks things up quickly."

"I'll talk with Tahlia today and figure out where we stand," I say, not wanting to commit to anything yet.

"Do that ASAP," Jill says. "We'll want to prepare Charlize if we decide to send her."

After the three of us finish discussing everything we need to, I call Tahlia. Deep in my gut, I believe it'll be Charlize on that plane with me next week, and I don't know what to make of that.

I suspect Bradford was right about one thing he said.

There's a vast difference in the women I've dated since my divorce and Charlize.

Not one of them has entered my mind since the last time I saw them while Charlize hasn't left it since the minute I discovered her wailing in that bathroom.

My mother's words come back to me about the Bluestone Award. *You need to keep Jill on your side. If she rocks the boat, that award may go to someone else.*

That award is another high priority of mine. I don't need to give Jill any reason to rock the boat.

16

Charlize

I re-read the email Jill sent me half an hour ago. There's no need to, though, because I've already read it a million times. Or maybe a million and one times. I'm not sure if I'm hoping something will change in the email or if I'm secretly excited by the contents of it.

I have to fly to London on Monday afternoon with Owen and spend three nights there with him. Jill asked me about an hour ago if I would be okay with doing this. After I said yes, she sent this email with all the details about the trip. The email feels like the closing of the deal, the thing that says I can't back out now.

I should quit my job.

Right now.

Yes, that's exactly what I should do.

I immediately open a new email and draft a letter to Jill.

FROM: Jill's Assistant
    To: Jill North
    Date: May 21, 2021, 10:05 AM
    Subject: Resignation

MS. NORTH,

I'M regretful to advise I must resign as your assistant. I can't possibly continue in this position. Not when I want to break the agreement you have with the CEO that states he won't fuck a staff member. I mean, while we have had sex outside of company time, if you send me to London with him, I am very sure we will have sex *on* company time.

I HOPE YOU CAN UNDERSTAND. I'm more than happy to service the needs of your CEO, but I do think in this instance that you should find another assistant to service the actual needs he'll have in London.

CHARLIZE COHEN
    Assistant to Jill North

. . .

I'M STARING at this email when Tahlia calls me.

I snatch up my phone while hitting delete on the email. "Tahlia."

She laughs and I realize I must have sounded needy or desperate. I *feel* those things. I feel completely bewildered over my London assignment and it's scrambling all my thoughts. "Are you okay, Charlize?"

I grip the phone harder. "Yes. Sorry, just having a moment there. What's up?"

"Jill asked me to call and go over everything you'll need to know for next week. Is now a good time? It'll take a little while."

I take a deep breath and center myself. "Yes, shoot."

We spend the next hour covering everything in detail. Tahlia emails me copious documents and information I'll require while I take just as many notes. Owen has a conference to attend which I'll be sitting in on with him so I can follow up on any action items for him. He'll also be holding meetings with potential investors that I'll be in charge of making sure go ahead without a hitch.

"Owen's generally good at time management," Tahlia says, "but he needs someone to keep him on track when he's surrounded by people. He's a little too good at networking and will get sidetracked if someone engages him in a discussion that he finds interesting. A lot of your job will be to manage him and his time in respect to his priorities and goals, so please make sure you familiarize yourself with the expected outcomes of this trip."

I make a big note about that: *MANAGE OWEN.*

"I will."

"Thank you for this. I've never left him hanging like

this, so it puts me at ease to know you'll be there to help him."

I smile at what I hear in her voice. Tahlia genuinely cares about Owen and his success. "I hope your sister is okay. And please know I've got this. I'm going to spend this weekend making sure I have all the information I need."

"Just call, text, or email if you have any questions. I'm always available."

We end the call and I get to work. Jill has made it clear her list of jobs comes second now. She's switched a lot of my work to Tahlia and vice versa so I can prepare for the trip. I haven't spoken with Owen about any of this yet and can't help wondering his thoughts. I don't dedicate too much time to that today, though. There's far too much for me to do that I'm completely focused on work.

At four thirty, Tahlia calls me again. We've been in touch throughout the day whenever either of us thought of something I need to know for next week. This time, she says, "I need to ask Owen something, but he's got his phone switched to silent. Can you go and interrupt him and ask him to call me?"

"Sure." I push my chair back to stand.

"Thanks. He's in the gym."

"Oh, okay. Is that close by?"

"Yes, it's our gym."

I frown. "Owen owns a gym?"

She laughs. "No, it's the company gym. It's down on the next floor."

Oh, God, of course the company has a gym. This place is filled with people that have more muscles than I've ever seen.

"Right. Got you. I'll head down there now."

I make my way down to the next floor and locate the gym. Owen is the only person in there. Well, besides the guy who's training him, but I barely see that guy because all I see is Owen.

Holy God, I need to acquaint myself with the gym if this is what's to be found in it.

Owen's wearing black shorts and a black tee and is currently lying on a machine with his legs up pushing a metal plate that lifts what looks to be a lot of weights.

All his muscles are flexing.

His leg muscles.

His arm muscles.

His face muscles.

I move closer while my brain tries to figure out how I can persuade him to let me work in here whenever he trains.

His trainer spots me before Owen does. "Hi."

"Hi." I point at Owen. "I just need him for a minute."

Owen looks at me. Sadly, his muscles stop working, and he pulls himself up off the machine. Reaching for a towel, he wipes his face and comes my way.

"What's up?"

What's up?

Everything.

All the things.

Nothing is not up right now.

I feel like I've been presented with something that I never knew existed, and now, my entire world has been tilted.

I'm coming back as a gym bunny in my next life.

My eyes drop to his chest, and I throw out, "This shirt

needs to be removed from your wardrobe for the next two weeks."

Heat flares in his eyes. "Do you intend on spending time in here during the next two weeks?"

I've told Owen that I don't care for the gym. I like that he remembers the things I tell him.

"I intend on joining a gym now that I've seen what happens in them."

"I have one at my place. You're welcome to join me there at any time."

I stare into those blue eyes that now feature in my dreams and I think about the next twelve months. Once we get through these few weeks of not being able to touch each other, he's not going to know what hit him. I don't think I'll keep my hands off him.

"Right," I say, trying to stick to the reason I'm here. "Tahlia needs to speak with you for a minute. She asked me to get you to call her. And now that I've completed my mission, I shall immediately leave."

I spin on my heel to do just that, however, Owen's hand curls around my bicep and he stops me. When our eyes meet again, he asks, "Are you okay about next week?"

I look at his fingers that are still wrapped around my arm.

I feel them everywhere.

Everywhere.

He lets me go and I look at his face again, trying hard not to wish he hadn't let me go.

"Yes. I'm going to spend all weekend preparing. I can do this."

"That's not what I'm asking, Charlize."

"I know." I smooth my skirt. "I'm okay."

He takes that in for a moment before saying, "I'll call Tahlia. Thanks."

I do my best to ignore the apprehension flooding my body as I go back up to my desk.

Owen told me it would be detrimental to his working relationship with Jill if we become involved while I'm working for him. I don't want to be the cause of any problems in their relationship, and I'm very concerned that flying to London and working that closely together won't make it easy for me to stay away from him.

I'm not coming back as a gym bunny in my next life. I'm coming back as a cat.

Surely there are far less opportunities to get myself into this kind of situation as a cat.

THE WEEKEND FLIES by in a blur of research and denial.

I have a haircut, a full body laser hair removal session, a manicure and pedicure, and a facial.

I research the conference Owen's attending and the investors he's meeting. I also research the hedge fund industry in general, giving myself a crash course in the major players, the history of the industry and returns over the last ten years, future predictions, and a range of other information that I'm sure I'll never need. If there's one thing I like to be with my work, it's prepared.

By the time I arrive at my parent's home for Sunday night dinner, I feel ready for the London trip.

I've fully embraced denial.

Owen and I can absolutely make it through a few days together.

We're grown adults.

I can keep my hands to myself.

Besides, we'll be too busy with work to even look at each other.

I really only had all those beauty treatments this weekend to pamper myself.

"Charlize." My brother's voice draws me from my thoughts as I walk into Mom's kitchen. "What's with the pajama pants?"

I look down at the baggy, floral print pants I've teamed with a white T-shirt that says *Sorry I'm Late, I Didn't Want To Come.* "You don't like them?"

He grins. "I fucking love them. That shirt, too. Mom is sure to as well."

I return his grin. "My thoughts exactly."

He shakes his head while continuing to smile. "I've missed you. Tell me you're done with travel for a while."

"For a year or so. I want to go back to Europe at some point."

He rests against the kitchen island, crossing his arms. "When are you going to stop running?"

This is an old conversation between us. Nate thinks I'm a runner. That I never stay and deal with my shit. I don't agree. I prefer to think of myself as a free spirit with wanderlust.

"You know, travel is a great way to connect with yourself. You should try it sometime."

"I connect with myself just fine here."

My brother is such an arrogant ass sometimes. I love

him to death, but he likes to give me advice without ever listening when I try to give him some back.

Before I can get into this any further with him, Mom comes into the kitchen. She frowns as she takes in my outfit, but she doesn't mention it. Instead, she says, "You're late, Charlize."

"Ten minutes is hardly late."

"It is in my world. I've got a lot to do tonight after dinner, and now we're running ten minutes behind."

I try not to laugh but fail. "Mom, it's a family dinner, not one of your galas. We can leave ten minutes early if need be."

She gives me a stern look. One I know not to even bother arguing with. "Your father is waiting in the dining room for us."

Ten minutes later, the four of us are sitting around the dining table that I have many memories of sitting around in silence while our parents taught us that children should be seen and not heard.

Dad and Nate discuss their work for a good fifteen minutes. My brother followed our father into the law. To say our parents are proud of this is downplaying it. I could take an actual nap, and no one would notice.

Nate gives Dad his fifteen minutes before eyeing me and saying, "How's your job hunting going?"

I finish eating the chicken I've decided Mom needs to serve at every family dinner. "I picked up some work for a few weeks at North Management. I've been working there this week."

"Any chance it might turn into full-time work?" Nate asks. "That'd be a great company to work for."

"I don't think so." I look at Mom. "I've just realized I

won't be able to make the gala next week. I have to go to London for work."

This news doesn't make her happy. "I wanted you and Nate to help me."

"I know, but I can't get out of this."

She presses her lips together. "If you'd taken my advice and asked Benjamin for a job, you wouldn't have to go to London."

Lord, give me strength.

"I did take your advice. I signed up with an employment agency. They found this job for me."

"I know Benjamin would give you a job in a heartbeat," she says.

"I don't want to work for Benjamin's company."

"Goodness knows why not," she says. "You know how successful his company is."

My mother would pee herself if she knew I'm having dating moments with Owen. Benjamin is a property developer and, yes, his company is successful. It's nowhere near as successful as Owen's, though.

"Goodness knows why you choose to forget he broke my heart, Mom."

She dismisses this in the way only a woman who believes in uniting families rather than marrying for love can. "I am sure there were many misunderstandings on both sides, Charlize."

She will go on and on about this if I don't find a way to stop her. It's because of this that I blurt, "I met someone."

I'm met by silence from the entire table.

And then, Nate grins, leans back in his seat, and

extends his arm across the back of the empty seat next to him. "Who?"

Shit.

Damn.

Why did I run with *that*?

Mom waits expectantly for my reply.

Dad appears interested.

My parents act like the only way I'll make it through life is by standing behind a man. They don't think I'm capable of providing for myself. The way they're both looking at me now is how they look at Nate when they ask him about his work. Besides checking in on my employment status, they never inquire about my work. The only thing they ask me about is my dating life.

"It's still new," I say.

"Well," Mom says with a hint of impatience, "who is it?"

"I don't want to say yet. Not until I decide if I'm going to continue seeing him."

Nate eyes me with amusement. His expression says *good luck with that*.

"Why tell us you've met someone if you've no plans to tell us who?" Mom says.

"I thought you'd be interested to know."

"We are," she says. "I'm even more interested to know who. Please tell me it's someone we know."

My mother is nothing if not a snob.

"I imagine it's someone you know."

Mom's impatience grows, but she doesn't grill me any further. I can read her mind though. She's already making plans to investigate. She'll drag her sister in on the search. The two of them will do their best to uncover the name of the man she'll pin all her fresh hopes of marriage on.

Poor Owen if either of them figure it out.

But yay for me (hopefully) hearing the end of all this Benjamin talk.

Nate comes to my rescue, changing the subject when he asks Mom, "So, what do you need me to help you with at the gala?"

They spend almost ten minutes discussing the gala.

I tune out, but am pulled back into the discussion when Mom asks Nate if he can help bring some of the people he knows through work to another gala she's helping plan for an Inner-City Scholarship Fund that provides scholarships for disadvantaged children in New York.

I stare at her, wondering why she never asks me to help her in this way. This isn't the first time she's asked Nate to help her attract donors. It hurts that she's never asked me once. It's a completely irrational feeling because I've never shown an interest in her galas, yet I'm feeling it. I wish my mother saw me as more than just a daughter who needs to be married off.

"I could help." The words are out of my mouth before I can slow them down.

Mom stops talking and looks at me, blinking like she doesn't know what to say. Then, she dismisses me. "You're busy with your job and your new boyfriend. Let's leave this with Nate."

My mother needs to be dragged into the twenty-first century and I need to be the one to do that.

"I'm not too busy, Mom, and I know a lot of people who I can put you in contact with."

What are these words leaving my mouth?

"Oh, Charlize, I don't think—"

"No, I'm helping. Can you please email me all the information on the gala?"

Nate looks at me. "We can put our heads together."

I smile at my brother. While he *can* be an arrogant ass at times, I know he thinks I can do anything I put my mind to. I also know he doesn't believe I need a man to help me make it through life. Nate is firmly in the *cut the damn pants in half* camp.

"I would love that," I say.

He nods and looks at Mom. "Leave it with us. We'll have some names for you soon."

"And don't forget to email me that information," I say, making a note to hound Mom until she sends it.

I arrive home just after 9:00 p.m. to a text from Poppy. She's been messaging me every night while on her honeymoon.

Poppy: I miss you.

I smile as I curl up on Dylan's sofa and reply to her.

Charlize: Of course, you do. I'm very missable. But tell me you're getting all the sex still.

Poppy: Of course, I am. My husband knows what's good for him.

Charlize: How many more centuries do you think it will take for full equality to exist between men and women?

Poppy: Charles, you know I live for your questions, but that's the kind of question that requires at least a night and a few bottles of wine to get into. Also, I'm three orgasms into this night. I don't want to ruin my happy buzz by thinking about inequality.

Charlize: I took a massive step back in life tonight, Pop.

Poppy: How?

Charlize: I offered to help my mother with one of her galas.

Poppy: How is that a step back?

Charlize: Ugh, you know how I feel about these galas and the socialite ladder Mom climbs with them.

Poppy: I've told you, think about it as philanthropy. We need philanthropists.

Charlize: I know, but still. There's a certain amount of "look at me" she does with her friends. She's always so fucking concerned about her social standing.

Poppy: You need to get laid. How many more days until your ban is lifted?

Charlize: TOO MANY. And now we have London to get through.

Poppy: Maybe his dick will just accidentally fall in you. Accidents happen, you know.

Poppy: Oh, I have to go. Seth is giving me the eye.

Charlize: OMG since when do you speak like that?

Poppy: I'm now a married woman. We speak differently. Goodnight, Charles x

Charlize: Night, Pop x

I love seeing my cousin so happy. She's had to wade through a lot of men to find her happy every after. I can't count on two hands the number of times we've devoured ice-cream late at night while crying our way through her messy breakups.

I'm remembering some of these nights while brushing my teeth fifteen minutes later when another text comes through. Figuring it's probably Dylan telling me he's staying late at his studio, I snatch my phone up to send a reply. The name blaring from my phone stops me in my tracks.

Owen: I'll pick you up at eleven tomorrow morning.

I stare at his message for what feels like forever.

We haven't texted since I agreed to stay on at North Management four days ago. I've thought about sending him a message so many times, even tapping a few out before deleting them.

My body comes alive with anticipation as I read the message over and over. It's crazy that a text like this, one without even a hint of anything personal or sexy or suggestive, can make me feel the way I am.

I type a reply and then delete it and re-write it.

I do this no less than five times.

Jesus, he's going to see the dots going up and down all over the place like they're confused.

The truth is they *are* confused, just like I'm confused.

I think about the space Owen and I are in. That space where I feel like I know him because we've shared a lot of personal things, but where I really don't know him at all.

I don't know how his brain works yet.

How he connects dots, or how the train tracks in his mind work, or how he sees the world.

I don't know how much space he needs in between spending time with a woman.

Is he the kind of guy who texts a lot, or does he like silence, or does it all depend on the things he's dealing with at the time?

I don't know if he feels things as deeply as I do.

Does he feel a connection fast, or is he purely physical to begin with?

Another text comes through while my mind thinks all these thoughts.

Owen: One of my favorite memories from childhood is the first time I went out on a boat with my grandfather. I was six and he let me help him sail. My parents had never let me help them do anything. I'll never forget that feeling of having contributed to something. I think that was the day I learned about challenging myself. About the thrill of learning new skills and competing with myself to do better.

My fingers stop typing as a new rush of thoughts and feelings flood me.

And then I'm madly tapping out a message that I don't think five times about deleting.

Charlize: It's my turn now, right?

Owen: Yes.

Charlize: One of my worst childhood memories is of getting caught in a lie by my mother. I shoplifted a cheap ring when I was twelve, and when she saw me wearing the ring, she asked me where I'd gotten it. I lied and told her a friend had given it to me. After confirming that was not the case, she told me she was taking me to the store the next morning to confess what I'd done. It was awful. The store came to an agreement with Mom that I would work off the cost of the ring with interest. I had to face those people twice a week for six weeks.

Owen: Did you ever steal again?

Charlize: Never. I also never lied to my mother again. Well, I mean little white lies for sure, but nothing of significance. I actually can't lie to save myself. My face always screams "she's lying right now!"

Charlize: I told my mother about you tonight.

Charlize: Oh God. See: open book.

Charlize: I don't mean that the way it sounded. I mean, I told her I met someone.

Charlize: Just ignore all that. None of it came out right. I'm going to bed now. Goodnight, Owen.

He calls me.

"I don't think phone calls are on your list of acceptable behavior to engage in with staff members outside of work," I answer as I lie on my bed.

"We do have a work trip we need to discuss."

"That is true. I'll be ready at eleven tomorrow morning, Mr. North."

"Fuck," he rasps, "if you keep calling me that, we won't get through this trip without me making unacceptable demands."

"I will do some research tonight to ascertain what constitutes an unacceptable demand from a boss. I've been told it's my job on this trip to manage you, so I need to be fully abreast of what I should be managing."

"Whoever told you to manage me needs a pay raise."

"Is it bad that I want to touch myself right now?" My hand is already making its way down my body.

Owen takes a moment to come back to me on that question and when he does, his voice is so guttural it unleashes a whole new level of need in me. "I've fought myself over calling you all weekend, Charlize. My dick has been in my hand far more than I care to admit."

Holy mother of all things dirty.

I really want to have phone sex with Owen right now. More than I've ever wanted phone sex with any man. But that is the last thing we should do.

"I'm sure you've been to London," I say, shifting the conversation completely, "but I always like to ensure my boss is well prepared. Make sure you take an umbrella and clothes for layering."

It turns out that Owen is as good at shifting conversations as I am. "What did you tell your mother about me?"

"Not your name."

"That's disappointing."

"You won't feel disappointed when she figures out who I'm seeing. You'll feel all kinds of frustrated when she starts harassing you into doing things you don't want to do."

"What kinds of things?"

"You think I should prepare you?"

"It's the right thing to do since I'm the man who'll be by your side for at least twelve months."

Oh. My.

"Do your five-year plans come together as fast as your one-year plans?"

"I've never had a one-year plan come together this fast. But then, I had some help with it. I do recall you being the one who first discussed using me for sex for a year. A woman can't make a suggestion like that and expect the man not to run with it."

"My job is to manage you, after all."

"Then, how about you do some managing and get me ready for your mother?"

"No," I smile into the phone, "I think I'll see where the wind blows us on this. You did mention you like my impulsive ways."

"Trouble," he murmurs, and I swear I hear *his* smile. "You're the very best kind."

"Goodnight, Owen. I'll see you at eleven in the morning."

"Goodnight, Charlize." He's saying goodnight, but everything in his voice is telling me he would stay on this call with me all night if that was what I wanted.

If only he knew how much I want that.

I've never been the kind of girl to make a five-year plan, let alone a one-year plan. Well, that's not exactly true. I've made plans before, the kind that involved travel and forgetting heartbreak.

With Owen, though, I'm already making a one-year plan.

I want lots of sex and lots of late-night conversations with this man.

17

Charlize

Owen has his own jet.

It's as luxurious as what I saw of his home the other night.

He follows me onto the plane and as we step into the cabin, he puts his hand to the small of my back and says, "I have to make a call before we leave, but then I want to go over some things with you in the office."

I look down the length of the plane, noting the doorways that lead into different sections. "You have an office in here?" I'm blown-away by that, but also finding it hard to focus due to his hand on my back.

"Yes. It's through that first door. If you want to set yourself up in there, I'll be in in a few minutes."

When I travel, I fly in comfort, but I have never flown in this level of comfort.

I leave Owen and walk through the first section that has single armchairs on one side and a long sofa that runs down the other side with its back to the windows. The jet is made of plush creams with black accents. The carpet feels like I could sink into it. The space feels like I could stretch out and still never fill it. I never want to travel on a commercial plane again.

The office has a sofa down one side and a table on the other. Four people can sit at the table, and I set myself up there. I then investigate the rest of the plane, finding a bedroom in the last section with a double bed. It's so spacious that there's even a sitting area in one corner. The bathroom is in between the office and the bedroom.

Again, I never want to fly on anything but a private jet.

I set my laptop up at the table and get to work, checking emails and actioning the jobs that Tahlia and Jill have sent through. Owen takes longer than a few minutes to finish his call, joining me ten minutes later.

I glance up from my computer as he takes one of the seats across from me. He's opted for casual attire today with beige chinos and a navy polo. Those chinos are a little too fitted to be worn during our ban period as far as I'm concerned. They attract way more of my attention than is appropriate. So much so, that when I finally drag my gaze to his face after he joins me, I find him watching me with heat.

Right.

Work.

Stat.

I look at my emails. "I'm all yours in a minute. I just have to finish something Jill's asked me to do."

"Take your time. I've got plenty I can be doing while I wait."

The task Jill sent me takes longer than I thought it would. By the time I complete it, we're in the air and Owen's immersed in reading something on his laptop.

"I'm ready whenever you are," I say.

We spend the next couple of hours talking about the conference and the people Owen will be meeting with. I've already researched all of this, but Owen gives me further insights that help prepare me better. He goes into detail about the outcomes he's aiming for this week, and by the time he stops speaking so we can take a break, I feel like I know a whole new layer of him.

I see why Owen's as successful as he is. Not only is he smart and strategic, he also appears to understand people. I already know he reads people well. The way he reads me and seems able to figure out how to go with my flow is proof of that. I imagine these skills help him in his business.

We break for half an hour to eat and stretch, and then spend half an hour going over tomorrow's schedule. Owen has an early breakfast meeting at 6:30 a.m. before giving the opening keynote address at 8:30 a.m. After that, the day is packed with conference sessions, a lunchtime meeting, more sessions, a pre-dinner meeting, a cocktail party, and then dinner with some of the conference attendees.

After we discuss all this, I lean back in my seat feeling exhausted just at the thought of it and say, "I imagine you'll be hitting the gym early." I'm joking, of course. We won't get to the hotel tonight until after midnight. Owen needs to sleep, not lift weights.

Owen doesn't miss my teasing. His mouth pulls up in a smile. "I'll be in there at five."

I slow blink. "You're not kidding, are you?"

He shakes his head and reaches for his glass of water. "No."

I'm so relaxed that I momentarily forget I'm here for work. I stretch my legs out and lift them to rest on the seat next to him. As I do so, my ankle brushes Owen's hand that's resting on that seat.

I feel that touch deep inside, and I quickly pull my leg back.

Owen wraps his hand around my ankle and stops me. "Leave it up here."

If I thought the mere brush of my skin against his was enough to start a fire, having his entire hand around my ankle might start an actual inferno.

I leave my foot on the seat.

Owen loosens his grip but doesn't let my foot go completely.

He then proceeds to shift all my thoughts into a disordered state by lightly caressing my ankle while we talk for the next half hour.

I learn more about Owen's love of sailing and he learns about my love of Italy. He's only been to Italy once, so I tell him about my top three favorite places. He listens like he's hanging off every word, but then, my perception could be off due to the chaos going on in my brain with every stroke of his thumb on my skin.

When I can't possibly take another second of his attention, I say quite forcefully, "You have work to do."

He looks at me, amused. "Do I?"

I pull my foot out of his hold and bring my legs back to my side of the table. "Yes."

"This is you managing me?"

I give him what I consider to be a bossy look. "Absolutely."

He reaches for his laptop. "I think I'm going to enjoy your style of management, Charlize."

The last thing I think before he stops looking at me and gets to work is that I should have insisted on him wearing those brown contact lenses I forgot to find.

"No," Owen says to the hotel receptionist in London, "We've got two suites booked."

It's just after 1:00 a.m. London time and the receptionist looks like she wishes this day didn't exist. We arrived ten minutes ago, and it's been nothing but problems since we got to her.

I was handling the check-in while Owen worked through some emails that just came in. The receptionist was rude to me from the second we began talking. When she told me she only had us booked for one suite, I produced our booking confirmation email. She investigated and came back with the verdict that she didn't know how it happened, but that one of our suites was given to another guest a few hours ago. She wasn't apologetic at all.

Apparently, because of the conference, the hotel is fully booked.

I watch Owen take over and think about how calm he

is. I'm ready to tell this woman exactly what I think of her rudeness, but he's still in pleasant mode.

He goes back and forth with her for a good five minutes, at which point, I have to walk away. I'm tired after our flight and don't have the patience Owen does for rudeness.

When he finally joins me, he looks apologetic. "They only have one suite for us."

"It will be a true hardship sharing with you." When he doesn't respond straight away, and continues looking regretful, I say, "It's okay, Owen."

"I've made it clear we're to be top of her list if a room becomes available."

I release a long breath. "Let's just go up and settle in. We've got a long day tomorrow and you need sleep so you can be at your best."

He nods and we find the elevator to take us up to our suite.

There's something to be said for exhaustion: it helps distract a girl from sex.

However, that's not the case when said girl is presented with the view of a king bed while standing next to the man she's going to have to share it with.

"I'll take the sofa," Owen says.

I look at him. "You're the one who needs to get good sleep this week. You take the bed."

He doesn't even entertain that. With a firm shake of his head, he says, "No."

I'm far too tired for this.

And now I'm also really turned on because Owen's looking at me like he's a starved man who's trying desperately to never want to eat again.

I jab my finger at his chest. "I'm in charge of you this week, and I've just decided we're both sleeping in the bed because I know there's no way you're letting me sleep on the sofa and there's no way I'm letting you sleep there." I walk past him and claim the left side of the bed, dropping my purse on it. "I'm going to take a quick shower before passing out. If I try to hug you during the night, you should probably just go with it rather than waking me up to get me to stop because a tired Charlize tomorrow won't be fun for either of us." I look at him expectantly. "Are we good?"

His lips quirk. "We're good."

"Good."

He's halfway out the door of the bedroom when he turns back. "There was never any chance of me not running with it if you try to hug me during the night."

Holy mother of *I don't know what*.

Is it hot in here?

18

Charlize

I slept like a baby.

I have no idea if I tried to hug Owen in my sleep, but I made it through the night without his dick accidentally falling in me. Poppy was wrong: accidents do not happen.

Owen's in the gym when my alarm wakes me at 5:30 a.m. and thank goodness for that. It gives me the chance to wake up and center myself for the day without his presence causing my thoughts to jumble.

When I emerge from the bathroom at 5:50 a.m., wrapped in a towel, I hear Owen in the suite talking on his phone. I dress in the white blouse and black pencil skirt I selected for today, and then dry my hair. I'm halfway through doing that when it occurs to me that Owen needs to shower, so I unplug the hairdryer and take it out into the suite to finish this there.

"The bathroom is all yours," I say when I find him in the living room.

He's sitting on a sofa, dressed in his gym clothes, reading something on his laptop. When he glances up at me, a soft curse falls from his lips. Standing, he comes toward me. "How many blouses do you own with bows?"

I look down at my blouse. It has a collar that becomes two long ribbons of fabric that tie into a prominent bow at my throat. The bow then drapes down the center of the blouse. I meet his gaze again, and suddenly realize why he told me a blouse I wore last week was hell on him. The red ribbon. "You have a thing for bows?"

His eyes are all over my body, but mostly on the bow. "I have a thing for *you* wearing them."

And there goes all that centering I did while he was in the gym.

There's not a calm breath to be found in me anymore.

While I scurry through my brain trying to find words to manage him, *because that's my one and only job here and I'm seriously about to fail at it*, there's a knock on the door of the suite.

"Are you expecting someone?" I ask.

He nods and strides to answer the door.

A minute later, I'm looking at a selection of breakfast food Owen has had delivered.

I frown. "Don't we have a breakfast meeting?"

"Yes, but I didn't want you to starve if you woke hungry. I would have asked you what to order, but since you passed out quickly last night, I took the liberty and selected what I thought you might enjoy."

And I'm lost for words again.

Owen was as exhausted as I was last night. Possibly more so. He stayed out of my way while I showered and got ready for bed. When I said goodnight to him, he told me he was going to do some work while I fell asleep. He mentioned something about giving me space. I thought that was considerate of him, but there he was being even more thoughtful, ordering me breakfast in case I needed to eat before our actual breakfast.

"Thank you," I say softly as I survey the bacon, eggs, and waffles he ordered. "I appreciate it." I have zero shame when it comes to food. I will happily eat two breakfasts today.

"I'm going to take a shower," he says. "Do you need anything from the bathroom?"

"No, I'm good."

I fail spectacularly at keeping my eyes off him while he walks to the bedroom. Owen has a thing for bows; I think I might have a thing for gym clothes. I mean, if a man must be clothed, wearing things that don't cover his arms or legs is my preferred option.

I take a deep breath when he disappears from sight.

Sharing space with Owen for two days isn't going to be easy.

He's *right* there.

In touching distance.

In kissing distance.

In *I'm putting your red thong in my pocket* distance.

But more than that, he's right there showing me his thoughtful, attentive side.

Two nights ago, I wondered whether Owen is the kind of man who feels a connection fast. I'm not sure why

I even questioned that. He's been connecting with me from the very first night we met. And not just on a surface level.

It's that side of him that will make it hard for me to keep my hands to myself over the next few days.

Sex for me is so much more than the physical.

It's also how we spend our time before the actual sex. The time spent talking, the going deeper, the lingering looks, the care taken, the respect shown, the little things that no one else thinks of.

Great sex isn't just a physical act for me.

It's emotional.

It's how I express my feelings over all the little things a man does for me and with me.

Owen can undo his shirt buttons, he can wear gym clothes I die for, he can look at me with those blue eyes I want to get naked in, and he can kill me with that growly voice of his. I can survive all that and keep my hands to myself.

What I know I *can't* survive are all the little things.

Being in close proximity with Owen like we are will give him the chance to do so many of those little things I already know he's good at.

My hands won't have a hope in hell of staying by my side if that happens.

Owen and I work our asses off today. And we do it in sync.

There's only one boss I've ever had who I worked better with than Owen. It's exhilarating. To move through a workday, achieving everything you set out to, with ease, and doing that by someone's side who you know is feeling everything you are. It's been many years since I've felt like this in my work, and I find it hard to contain the energy it gives.

Owen kicked the conference off with a keynote address that had every attendee on their feet applauding him at the end. Keynote speakers have a goal of setting the tone and dictating the energy of an event, and Owen showed why he was the one asked to give this address. The conference is abuzz with excitement for what's to come.

The meetings he had with potential investors also went well. I was impressed with how he communicates and gets his ideas across. Owen has the kind of charisma that could convince most people to do whatever he wants them to, and I've seen it up close all day.

Tahlia was right when she told me he's a little too good at networking and needs managing at times. I've had to step in twice today and redirect his attention. Both times, he gave me a look of gratitude that was tinged with some heat when he glanced down at my hand on his arm.

"That seemed to go well," Owen says after he closes the door to our suite at 5:30 p.m. He just met with a potential investor who I didn't really care for, but who he appeared to get on well with.

I cock my head. "Did you like him as much as you looked like you did?"

He smiles, reaching for his phone that has just sounded with a text. Before he checks the message, he answers my question. "If I liked all my clients, I wouldn't have a business."

"Is that a no, then?"

"That's a no," he confirms, glancing at his phone. "Fuck," he mutters as he reads the text. Then, he says, "I'll have to meet you at the cocktail party. Something's come up that Julian needs me to take care of."

"Okay." I paste my best stern expression on my face. "But if this is your way of getting out of the party, there will be hell to pay." He's told me at least twice today that he finds these cocktail parties at conferences a chore.

"What kind of hell are we talking?"

I arch my brows. "You think I'm joking?"

"I wouldn't dare think that. Not when you've shown me all day how bossy you can be. I just need to know whether this hell you're threatening is the kind of hell I'd like to experience with you or not."

"I'll make sure it isn't."

"Trust me when I tell you that I'm very open to encountering all sorts of hell with you."

His words scorch their way into my body, at which point I decide it's time to manage him again. It turns out that Owen takes a *lot* of managing. "You should go. And when I see you next, please ensure there are only clean ideas racing through that brain of yours. It's getting a little out of control in there."

He looks suitably chastised at that and I can only hope that we course-correct in between now and the cocktail party.

Except, I'm torn.

I really love bantering with him like this.

You have ten sleeps, honey, and then you can do all the bantering you like.

I really dislike that voice of reason in my head some days.

Owen leaves to do whatever it is Julian needs him to do, and I get ready for the cocktail party. I wear a sleeveless black dress with a fishtail hem that covers my knees. It's classy and demure, perfect for a business function. I keep my hair down. Owen does not need the distraction of my neck tonight.

Jill emails me three times and calls me twice while I'm dressing. I've been receiving emails from her all day while she fusses over Owen all the way from New York.

She wanted to ensure that *I* ensure he wears a tie at all times.

She wanted to tell me that he doesn't eat enough during conferences. That he's often too busy to remember food exists, and that I should make sure he eats.

She wanted to warn me that when he gets tired, he can become a little short with people. She told me not to take it personally if this happens.

Besides these things, there were a myriad of work things she wanted to remind me of for the meetings Owen's holding.

I can't decide if Jill thinks Owen's a fucking idiot, or if she thinks I am.

I patiently talk with her when she calls, answering every question she has, and listening to everything she advises. Two of the men Owen's holding meetings with tomorrow are the two she and Owen are most interested in signing as clients. Jill has some great suggestions, so I note them all down and thank her for them. I then assure her Owen is eating, wearing a tie, and sleeping. I can only hope she doesn't go on social media and spot any photos taken after he removed the tie he started the day with. I don't think Jill would appreciate being lied to.

I arrive at the cocktail party fifteen minutes after it started. Owen is nowhere to be seen, so I try to locate a waiter for a glass of champagne. I'm on the hunt when one of the men Owen met with today stops me.

"Charlize," he says with a smile. "How has your day been?"

"Hi, Joss. It's been a great day. How about you?"

I liked Joss the most out of all the people I met today. He spent a little time talking with me about his wife and the interior decorating business she runs. He also showed me photos of his sons. I liked that when I look into his eyes, I see the same kind of thing I see in Owen's eyes. genuine care and interest in me as a human.

He tells me his highlights from the conference today and then we get into a discussion about stocks. We've been talking for ten minutes when I spot Owen.

He's dressed in a tuxedo with his hair styled into that almost-messy sexy look I've fallen hard for.

And he's staring at me with hungry eyes.

If his looks aren't enough to turn me on, the way he's watching me will do it.

He takes a step in my direction but is interrupted by a woman who wants to talk with him. She's got her eyes all over him, and when I say all over, I mean she's eye-fucking him. It turns out I am *not* okay with this.

I forget the fact I'm talking to Joss because all I can think about now is the fact another woman is talking to my man.

My man.

Uh, no.

Where did that thought come from?

But also, *honey take your eyes off those buttons.* They're mine.

I need champagne.

Now.

I excuse myself from Joss and make my way to the bar.

Owen watches every step I take. He might be talking with that woman who is throwing herself at him, but he doesn't take his eyes off me. By the time I reach the bar, my legs are weak and butterflies have taken over my stomach.

The way Owen watches a woman he wants to fuck should be banned if he can't follow through.

I try to find my legs again while I wait for the bartender. Not an easy thing to do when Owen has made it so my legs don't even know what their function is anymore.

"Charlize." Warm breath whispers across my neck and I jump.

"Shit," I mutter. "I've told you that you need to give a girl warning when you're thinking about sneaking up on her."

"You couldn't see the warning in my eyes as I watched you?" His voice is so damn growly and sexy. "I've undressed you five times over. Just like every man here tonight has. When you're mine, we're going to have to negotiate the dresses you wear."

I grip the counter of the bar as I do my best to calm the sensations his words cause.

When you're mine.

I've never felt so wanted.

Twisting, I face him. "I'm not good at negotiating, Owen."

"Then it's a skill you're going to need to learn."

My breaths come a little faster. "I've never let a man into my life who wanted to control what I wear, and I'm not about to now." I might be saying these words, but I can't deny I'm so turned on by the thought of battling Owen for control. And by the possessiveness blazing from him.

His gaze drops to my neck, my throat, my chest, and the entire room falls away.

It's just us.

And a steady hum of need that we've been trying to silence for days.

Unable to stop myself, I move my hand to his jacket.

To his stomach.

To *him*.

He finds my eyes again. "I'm not interested in taking control of you. I'd just like to keep dresses like this one between us."

Silence descends on us again as we watch each other. I don't think we even need words right now. The electricity between us speaks volumes.

Our silence is interrupted by Joss who wants to continue an earlier conversation he had with Owen.

I excuse myself so I can go to the restroom.

I stay in there for a great deal of time.

I begin to make plans to stay all night because that would be safer for both of us.

By the time I exit the bathroom, there are three thoughts on a permanent loop in my brain.

One: Owen's expectation that he can negotiate a dress with me should be classified as an unacceptable demand from a boss.

Two: I will never negotiate the dresses I wear, but hot damn, I'll enjoy the foreplay of it all.

And three: I hope Jill doesn't think murder is a reasonable response if she ever learns her CEO made an unacceptable demand of a staff member.

19

Owen

I undo my bow tie and the top two buttons of my shirt as I follow Charlize into the suite we're sharing. My eyes are glued to her ass. This dress she's wearing is something else and I'm not sure what to make of my reaction to it.

I've never reacted to any woman's clothing the way I'm responding to Charlize's. Tonight's response, though, was extreme.

I meant every word I said.

I would like to keep dresses like this one just between us.

It's a level of possessiveness I don't understand.

I don't expect Charlize to pay any attention to my demands, but that doesn't mean I'll be able to stop myself issuing them.

"Do you need anything before I take a shower and go to bed?" Charlize asks as she walks toward the bedroom, kicking her heels off.

My eyes are drawn to her legs. "No."

She stops and turns to me. "Are you sure? I know there are still a few things you want to work on before your meetings tomorrow. I could help so you can get through it faster."

I search her face, noting the tiredness in her eyes. "You go to bed. This work won't take me long."

The expression on her face says she wants to argue with me but in the end, she says, "Okay."

With that, she goes into the bedroom, and I find a spot on the sofa to complete my work.

After opening my laptop, I spend far longer than I should staring at the screen while thinking about Charlize. She's one of the most capable assistants I've worked with, which ensured today ran smoothly. The way she manages and directs appears effortless, like she was born to do what she does. Having this opportunity to see her work has pulled me further under her spell. I almost demanded she leave the cocktail party and allow me to tear that dress off her.

I finally open my emails and am immersed in a report Julian sent through when Charlize comes out of the bedroom.

"Owen," she says, standing near the sofa across from where I'm sitting, frowning at me with concern. "It's almost one a.m."

I glance at the time on my laptop, unaware that more than an hour has passed since I opened my computer. "I'm almost done."

"Please tell me you're skipping the gym in four hours."

I smile. It's a barely-there smile, a tired one, but it can't help but push its way onto my face. I like the way Charlize cares about me. It feels good in a way I haven't felt in a long time. "I was thinking of it."

"I imagine your muscles will thank you for the sleep."

I narrow my eyes at her, noting that she doesn't look like she's just woken up. "Are you having trouble sleeping?"

She nods. "My brain is wired. It's nowhere near ready for sleep."

"Would it help to talk your thoughts out? You could try to get them in my head so they're out of yours."

She's amused by my use of her words, her frown shifting into a smile. "I like that you're willing to take one for the team, but I'm not interrupting your work. You need to finish that and get some sleep."

Truth be told, I was done with my work a while ago. I've been stalling on going to bed because all I can think about is pulling Charlize into my arms in that bed. I barely slept last night. I spent more of the night out of bed than in it. Thank fuck she was exhausted enough to sleep through all that. We likely wouldn't have made it through the night without me touching her if she hadn't.

I close my laptop and place it on the side table. "I'm finished."

"Okay, well then, you should go to bed."

"Sit and talk with me, Charlize."

She stares at me like I've just ordered her to do something very objectionable. "Is this another one of your unacceptable demands?"

My eyes bore into hers, remembering my last demand. "Yes." Fuck, I could stay up all night with her.

She looks torn, unable to decide which way to go with this. Just when I think she'll tell me no, she joins me on the sofa, sitting as far from me as she can. After she curls her legs up under her, she says, "If you're going to force me into this, I'm going to force you into absolutely skipping the gym."

I've never enjoyed being bossed by a woman so much. "Done."

She opens her mouth to say something but snaps it closed just as fast. Her flustered state is endearing as fuck. I want so much more of this with her.

I extend an arm across the top of the sofa and lean toward her. "Tell me one thing you've been thinking about."

Her gaze drifts to my arm on the sofa, staying there for long enough to cause my gut to tighten. When she gives me her eyes again, she says, "Do you play the piano?"

If I was asked to write a list of things I imagined Charlize to have been contemplating, that thought wouldn't have been anywhere near my list.

"Yes. I started lessons when I was four."

"Do you play it often?"

"Not anymore."

She wiggles around for a moment getting comfortable, bringing an arm up to rest on the top of the sofa. "So, you have a piano that just sits there looking pretty?"

Now I'm the one who's distracted. I look at her arm and extend my fingers so I can touch her hand. Then, keeping my fingers resting there, I look back at her. "I don't have the time or reason to play it."

Her brows pull together. "Why do you need a reason to play? Isn't the joy of playing it enough?"

I stroke her hand lightly, the feel of her skin irresistible. "I'm not certain I ever thought of playing the piano as joyful."

She sits with that statement for a long moment before softly saying, "Because you only ever did it for your parents, and their expectations suffocated any chance of joy being discovered?"

Fuck, if anyone has ever nailed something about me, it is this.

"I had a piano lesson weekly and was expected to practice for half an hour every day until the day I turned ten, at which point that daily half hour became one hour."

She looks at my fingers that are still ghosting across her skin. "What else did you take lessons in?"

"Polo, tennis, Chinese, French, philosophy." I curve my fingers around her wrist. "You name it, I took lessons in it. My mother ran our household and her sons like a company, always with an eye to destroying the competition and gaining market share. I had tutors around the clock, six days a week."

"Wow," she says, her eyes widening, "I thought my mother was the boss of bosses, but now I think that was your mother. What was your father like?"

"*He* was the boss of bosses. My mother was the COO, but my father wore the pants, and he didn't cut them in half and share. Any expectation Mom held was tripled in his eyes."

"Were you two close?"

"Not in an emotional way, but he was always around teaching me what my place in the world was to be."

"And what was that?"

"To carry on the North name. To ensure our family held its place in the world."

As I unlink my fingers from her wrist, Charlize threads hers into them. It's everything I need right now. "That's a heavy load to carry, Owen."

"I'm not sure I carry it."

"What do you mean?"

"I'm not my father and never will be. I don't play the game as well as he did."

"Are you trying to, though? Or are you trying to figure out your own way to live your life? One that doesn't require you to keep carrying all that weight?"

I search her face. It's so damn beautiful, just like the inside of her. "Some days, it feels like that weight is all I know," I say honestly, sharing myself in a way I've never shared myself.

"I know that feeling." She pauses. "I hope you never learn to play the game well."

I want to kiss her.

Charlize is the only woman I've been with who hasn't wanted me to play the game. I want to show her how I feel about that.

Somehow, I manage to keep my mouth to myself. Instead, I find my brain and say, "You should go to bed."

She nods. "I should." She doesn't move, though. "Do you still speak French?"

"It's rusty, but yes."

"I'm going to need to hear something in French. I

mean, you can't tell a girl you speak that language and not speak to her in it."

With our fingers still linked, I rub my thumb across the palm of her hand. "Fais de beaux rêves, belle fille."

Her breaths come a little faster as she stares at me with the kind of desire that will get us into trouble if I let it. "I have no idea what you just said, but I'd really like you to say that to me a *lot*. And if it has anything to do with your stalker tendencies, let's just pretend it doesn't."

Fuck.

"Go to bed before I take you there," I rasp, letting her fingers go.

Charlize goes to bed.

I give her half an hour to fall asleep before I make my way into the bedroom. That's after contemplating sleeping on the sofa because fuck knows how I'm going to stay on my side of the bed tonight.

She's lying on her side, all the way to the edge of the bed with her legs pulled up to her stomach. The room is dark, but I spend long enough looking at her to see this.

When I've almost talked myself into going back out to the sofa, she looks at me and says, "I promise I won't hug you in my sleep."

I scrub a hand down my face, wishing like fuck that I'd never spoken to Jill about sleeping with staff members. I also wish I was more like my father who would never have honored any agreement in this way.

"It's not you I'm concerned about," I say.

Ten minutes later, I'm on my side of the bed, staring at the ceiling, figuring I'm in for another restless night, when Charlize says, "I've never met a man like you, Owen. I'm glad I convinced you to really like me."

How anyone can not like Charlize is unfathomable to me. That she thinks anyone would need convincing is also puzzling.

I want to point all this out to her, but what I want more is for her to go to sleep. She worked hard today, and I saw her exhaustion during dinner and then after while I worked the room. So, instead of getting into another conversation with her, I simply say, "There was no chance of that not happening."

She embraces silence for five minutes before saying, "Goodnight, Owen."

"Goodnight, beautiful."

I WAKE with Charlize in my arms.

I'm spooning her, holding her tightly, my erection pressed firmly against her ass.

I should let her go, but I don't.

Fuck, I don't want to.

I've no idea what the time is, but since neither of our alarms have gone off, I keep her in my arms and think about the things I want to do with her when we're able to spend time together.

I want to take her out on my boat.

I want to take her hiking at Breakneck Ridge.

I want to spend long nights talking with her, dancing with her, laughing with her, making her blush, and kissing the soft skin of her throat before discovering all the ways I can make her body sing.

There's not one thing I don't want to experience with Charlize.

Her phone vibrates on the nightstand. It does this a few times, at which point she stirs and grumbles something I can't make out as she reaches for it.

"That's my cue to let you go, isn't it?" I murmur against her ear.

"I really want to say no, but yes, it is."

It takes everything in me to do so, but I loosen my hold on her and roll onto my back. "What time is it?"

"It's almost six." She turns silent for a moment, reading her message before muttering, "Oh my God, my mother will be the death of me."

"Why?"

She rolls over to face me, eyes wide in a dramatic fashion. "I made the mistake of offering to help her with one of the galas she's planning. Honestly, I think aliens took over my head that night, but here we are and there's no way I'll try to get out of it. She just texted me to ask me to take charge of some of the suggestions I've made that I think might help her get more donors." Her eyes widen more. "I'm not sure in which universe she thinks I want anything to do with helping run a gala."

"But you made the suggestions, right?"

"Yes." She looks at me with confusion. "But that doesn't mean I want anything to do with them."

"Why not?"

"Because I am not a gala girl, Owen."

I laugh. "What the fuck is a gala girl?"

"You know, those society women who immerse themselves in galas and charity work so they can climb the social ladder."

"They also do a lot of good work for the world. What were your suggestions?"

She tries to wave me off with, "Honestly, they're not even worth discussing. I don't know why I sent them to Mom."

"I can't imagine any suggestion you make not worth discussing. Tell me."

Charlize is a beautiful contradiction of strength and vulnerability. I've seen hints of this from the beginning, but right now, I'm seeing it in vivid color. I can tell she's hesitant about sharing her ideas with me. Guarded, like she's unsure she can trust my response.

But then, her fierce side takes over and she says, "Well, I'm not an expert on attracting donors, but I read through the planning committee's ideas, and I thought they could do so much more than relying on an elevator pitch and a boring dinner that doesn't engage the right kind of people. I see so much more potential in the time before and after the gala. It's like sex. There has to be the right amount of foreplay that speaks individually to the heart of the person. Then, the act itself has to engage all the senses rather than just relying on one or two. And after, follow up with the person. Especially if you want to build a relationship with them. Show them the impact they made and do that from the heart." She shrugs like she hasn't just fucking nailed this. "I don't know, it just seemed like there wasn't enough heart in the plan they have. I always want to see more heart. I suggested ways for them to do this."

Both our phones sound with the six-a.m. alarms we set. Charlize turns hers off, asking, "Do you want the shower first?"

"No, you go." As she makes a move to leave the bed, I

reach for her arm to stop her. "I would like to hear the suggestions you made to your mom at some point."

She processes that for a moment before blessing me with a smile and moving off the bed. Right before she disappears into the bathroom, she turns back to look at me, that smile still firmly in place. "I can't wait until you are no longer my boss. I need so many more of your three-a.m. hugs."

Fuck me.

WE SOMEHOW MAKE it through the day without me tearing Charlize's clothes off. Today's outfit that I had to deal with was a black and white polka dot blouse and black skirt. My eyes were almost glued to the thin belt she wore. I learned that not only do I have a thing for bows on Charlize, I have a thing for belts too.

On top of distracting me with her beauty, Charlize gained all my attention with the way she had potential investors eating out of her hand.

I ran late most of the day thanks to an issue that came up in New York that I had to fix. That left Charlize to start my meetings for me. After seeing her in action yesterday, I believed her capable of this, but I couldn't have imagined just how well she'd do it. Her intelligence and quick thinking, along with her people skills, helped me sign the two men I didn't want to leave London without signing.

Something shifted between us last night. I'm not sure what it was, but I've felt it all day.

Charlize's eyes have lingered on me for longer.

Her hand has brushed mine repeatedly.

She hasn't managed me every time I flirted with her.

And now, she's moving around our hotel suite, getting ready for dinner in a way that wouldn't convince one person that we aren't involved.

First, she showered and emerged from the bathroom wearing a towel.

Then, she proceeded to stand in the living room, wearing that towel, while resting a foot up on the arm of the sofa, applying cream to her legs.

After that, she told me she'd dry her hair in the living room while I showered. I was still finishing up some work on the sofa and sat through a good five minutes of her flipping her hair before finally closing my laptop and escaping to the shower.

The bathroom looks like a bomb hit it.

Charlize's polka dot blouse and skirt from today are strewn across the floor.

Her hair and beauty products are strewn across the vanity.

Her essence is strewn across the entire room.

My gut tightens at the sight of it all.

I want this with her.

All of this.

Mornings waking up with her, days spent thinking about her, nights together, long conversations, deep conversations, laughter, flirting.

I want her driving me wild in her unawareness of how she affects me simply with a foot up on the sofa.

I want her driving me crazy with her mess of beauty products and clothes everywhere.

I want her to thread her fingers through mine at the

end of a day and tell me she likes me exactly how I am. That she never wants me to change.

I close the bathroom door and take a shower.

I only just stop myself from jerking off.

After, I dry off, wrap the towel around my waist, and walk into the bedroom in search of something to wear to dinner.

I'm zipping my trousers when Charlize comes into the bedroom.

"Shit," she says from the doorway. "Sorry, I should have knocked."

I'm standing in front of the wardrobe that's near the door. When I look up at her, I find her eyes all over my body.

"We're not going to make it to dinner if you keep looking at me like that," I growl.

Her gaze finds mine. "I'll come back when you're dressed."

She's saying she'll come back but everything I'm seeing in her says she wants everything I want.

I reach out and wrap my hand around her wrist as she begins to turn to leave. "What did you come in here for?"

Her breaths deepen. "I need help with my dress."

My eyes drop to the knee-length, navy dress she's wearing. Thankfully, there's not a bow in sight, or a belt. "Turn around."

She hesitates like she's reconsidering her request.

"I've managed to keep my hands to myself for almost a week," I say. "I can manage this." I lift my chin. "Turn around."

She only hesitates for another couple of seconds before turning.

Fuck.

While there's no bow or belt in sight, there's a whole lot of skin in sight at the back of this dress. Skin I'm going to think about for the entirety of dinner.

"Do you have any other dresses to choose from?" I ask as I brush her hair to the side so I can access the two buttons at the top of the dress.

She twists her body and neck just enough so she can look at me. "We are not negotiating this dress."

"I'd very much like to attempt a negotiation."

"Okay then." She turns to face me, her gaze traveling down my body. "Let's negotiate these trousers as part of the deal."

Christ, we're in dangerous territory now if she's going where I assume she is.

"What's your request?" I ask.

"I don't ever want to see them on you again." Her eyes meet mine again. "And unlike you, I don't care who sees your cock so long as *I* see it."

My hand is in her hair before I can stop it, and my mouth is on hers, claiming the kiss I've spent a week thinking about.

Charlize's whole body sinks into mine.

Her arms are around me.

Her hands reach for parts of me that never want to know denial again.

Her tongue demands everything I want to give her.

I can't think straight.

I'm *not* thinking straight.

All I know is that I can't go another second without knowing her touch again.

I lose myself in this kiss, and yet I know I'm finding myself in the only way that matters.

I'll go through hell for this if I have to.

From the moment Charlize told me she wanted to go swimming with me at Shipwreck Beach, I'd have gone through hell for this. She mesmerized me in that bathroom, and I now know I'll do anything to make her mine.

I back her against the wardrobe and cup one of her breasts before pulling my mouth from hers so I can kiss my way down her neck to her throat.

Charlize arches her back and angles her head back while sliding her fingers into my hair.

Fuck, there's something about her fingers in my hair that gets me every time she does it. I grind my dick against her and suck her neck harder, tasting the perfume that has caused me no end of hardship since the moment I followed her onto my jet.

"Fuck," I rasp, coming up for air. "We're skipping dinner."

Charlize's hands come to my chest as she shakes her head. Lust is written so damn sexily all over her that it takes everything in me to hear her out when she opens her mouth to speak. "We're not skipping dinner," she says. "You're not undoing all your hard work by not showing up."

I press myself against her and drop my mouth to her neck again.

She moans when I bite her, giving me her fingers in my hair again.

However, when I reach up to slide her dress off her shoulders, she stops me. "Owen, no." She puts her hands to my chest and pushes me away. "We're not having sex.

We're getting dressed and we're going to dinner. And then, when we've finished dinner, we're coming back here and you're sleeping on the sofa. I mean, I would, but I already know you'll boss me into taking the bed, so I'm just saving us that discussion which would be extra time together in which your dick might accidentally fall in me." She takes a deep breath, looking so fucking sexy in her bewildered, turned-on state. She then smooths her dress and adds, "I'll do up my own buttons even if it means I have to figure out how to become a contortionist. You go"—she waves her hands at me like she's shooing me away—"and put some damn clothes on."

I don't go.

I don't even begin to move.

Instead, I say, "If you think my dick will ever accidentally fall in you, you have no idea how fucking much I want you, Charlize. I spend my days thinking about how I can get you alone, about how I can convince you to spend time with me, about how I can persuade you that I'll meet all your high expectations and give you the emotional commitment you need. I think about the fact that I'd skip time in the gym for you, that I'd put work aside for you, that I'd do things for you that I've never contemplated doing for any woman." My eyes bore into hers. "Nothing I do with you will ever be accidental. Not when I'm deliberately going out of my way to make you mine."

Charlize looks like she's momentarily forgotten how to breathe.

She also appears lost for words.

Then, she shows me why I'm deliberately going out of my way to make her mine.

She inhales a breath and says, "I knew you were going to be trouble from the moment you said I was intriguing that night we met. And then, when you knew exactly how to ease my nerves later in your hotel room by sharing your Truth or Dare confession with me, *that* was the moment I really grasped it." She pauses and when she speaks again, her voice is quieter, less sure. "I've only ever been with men who didn't know a thing about vulnerability. No one has ever been willing to get as naked with me as you have, Owen. And that's in just a week. I'm not sure I'll be any good at this with you."

I will never get enough of Charlize's honesty. It blazes from her in ways I don't think she's even aware of.

"You're already good at it. Trust me on that."

She breathes another long breath in. "This was just supposed to be me using you for sex for a year. I think you've gone and ruined that now."

"I fucking hope so."

Another breath makes its way into her lungs before she finally relaxes and gives me one of her fake stern looks I like far too much. "This doesn't change anything. We're still going to dinner. And also, if you think any of this means I'm going to start negotiating dresses with you, you are very mistaken."

My lips quirk. "Turn around so I can do this dress up. The last thing I want is you hurting yourself while trying to do it."

She allows me to do the dress up.

I then finish dressing and we go to dinner.

I sit through two hours of excruciating business talk.

Not once in my life have I thought any kind of business discussion was torturous, but that was before I met Charlize.

There's not one minute of this dinner that I don't imagine her dress falling to the floor, my lips brushing across the insides of her thighs, her legs around my neck.

She's more than a distraction and I can no longer resist her.

20

Charlize

I drink three glasses of champagne during dinner and do inappropriate things to Owen under the table. In my defense, waking up with his arms around me and his erection pressing against me started all this. I blame him for all the things I did today that weren't in line with *managing* him.

Also, if he ever wants me to keep my hands off him again, he should stop sharing his heart with me like he did last night when he told me about the expectations his parents have of him.

Holy mother of lust, I've never been with a man who is so open to slicing into his heart and showing me what's in there. I never knew just how much a guy doing that could affect me. To say it makes me want to demand he never wear clothes again is putting it mildly.

We have dinner with Mathius Boehme and his wife, Tina. He's one of the investors Owen signed today. The one I actually liked. I also like his wife. I think these facts go a long way to helping me relax so much during dinner that my brain somehow convinces my body to make obscene advances to Owen under the table.

It started with our feet when we first arrived.

I kicked a heel off and ran my foot up his leg after a few sips of champagne.

He eyed me with a look I couldn't quite decipher, so I took it as encouragement to continue.

With my second glass of champagne, I put my hand on his thigh and nudged it closer and closer to his cock until he stopped me when I stroked him. His big hand curling over my small one and staying there was enough to short-circuit the only part of my brain still working.

I can't put into words what Owen's skin against mine does to me. Suffice it to say, it has the ability to make me do very bad things.

When Tina goes to the restroom and Mathius steps away from the table to take a call, Owen leans in close and says, "Do you want to play, Charlize? Because we can if you want to."

I blink in the way only a girl can when a man says something like that to her.

When I don't answer him right away, because my brain is currently trying to un-short-circuit itself, he removes his hand from mine and places it on my thigh. He then slips it under my dress and makes his way up to my panties.

My heart gallops.

Desire pulses through every vein in my body.

My legs part all by themselves.

I look at Owen as his fingers brush over my panties.

A moment later, he slides his hand inside them and finds my clit.

I spread my legs a little further and do my best not to moan out loud.

Owen brings his mouth to my ear again when he pushes a finger inside me. "We need to get out of here because I need my tongue inside you rather than my finger."

I grip his thigh. "If you don't stop, I'm going to come."

His eyes blaze with fire. "I'm not stopping."

Tina comes back to the table. Smiling at me, she says, "Champagne does wonders for you, Charlize. You're glowing. We should have another."

Owen's finger reaches deeper inside me.

My fingers dig into his leg, squeezing him hard.

If only Tina knew why I'm glowing.

"Yes," I breathe out to Tina. "More champagne would be lovely."

She motions to the waiter and orders our drinks before looking at me again. "Mathius and I will be in New York at the end of next month. I'd love to spend some time with you."

Because I can barely form a thought, I nod and say, "Yes, let's. We could go bowling."

Bowling?

Jesus, where did that come from?

I do love bowling, but I'm not sure Tina strikes me as a bowling kind of woman.

Owen's mouth lifts at the end.

"Or to the spa," I throw out, wondering just how I'm going to make it through this conversation.

Can Owen either hurry up and get this done or stop altogether? I'm a hot mess of need here and I'm not certain I can keep all my moans on the inside for much longer.

Oh God, Dylan told me I'm loud when I'm having sex. Does that mean actual sex with a dick inside me and a man who's working hard to make all kinds of noises with me? Or does that mean I'm noisy any time I'm having an orgasm?

I really hope we're not about to find out.

Tina's face breaks out in a grin right as Owen hits my G-spot, my A-spot, my B-spot, all my spots. "I love bowling," she says. "Please don't make me go to the spa."

My pussy clenches and I swear Owen makes one of his growly noises, but then, see: hot mess. He could be over there making all kinds of noises right now while also getting himself off and I'd have no idea.

I'm. Going. To. Come.

Mathius arrives back at the table, eyeing Owen and saying something to him.

I try to listen but fail because all the muscles I have inside are contracting and every inch of my skin is flushing with heat.

My nipples are desperate for Owen's touch.

The center of my body explodes with pleasure and then it's like a wave of never-ending bliss outward to my toes, my fingertips, my everything.

My brain goes completely blank.

I grasp Owen's thigh.

It's taking everything in me not to utter a sound, but

I'm unable not to sink back into the chair and just let the waves of pleasure take over.

Owen removes his hand from under my dress and carries on a conversation with Tina and Mathius.

When I finally recover from my orgasm, I sit up and reach for the glass of champagne Tina ordered, thankful that she did.

Owen turns to watch me as I take a gulp. The look in his eyes tells me it might have been harder for him to restrain himself from actually fucking me on this table than it was for me not to announce to the restaurant that he had his fingers inside me.

Tina frowns. "Are you feeling okay, Charlize? You just looked like you might pass out."

See: hot mess, hot mess, hot mess.

This is what orgasms in the middle of a restaurant do to a girl.

"I'm okay," I say. "I'm just tired."

"Yes," Owen agrees. "It's been a long day." He checks his watch and looks at Mathius. "We've got an early flight tomorrow, so we might say goodnight. Tina mentioned you'll be in New York next month. We'll plan on dinner while you're there."

We say our goodbyes. I promise Tina we'll absolutely go bowling next month. Owen and Mathius agree on dinner. Then, Mathius and Tina head for the hotel bar while Owen guides me to the elevator. I think he's aware I'm in no state to guide myself anywhere.

When we reach the elevators, Owen keeps a respectful distance.

He stands next to me, not touching me.

I don't look at him.

I stare straight ahead.

We don't talk, but everything between us is loud.

The elevator arrives and we step inside.

Owen's hand comes to the small of my back and just that brief amount of contact is enough to cause my breath to hitch.

We stand at the back of the elevator as another couple stand at the front. They're arguing over something. I have no idea what because my focus is completely on Owen.

Whereas he didn't touch me while we waited for the elevator, he now stands so close to me that I'm practically combusting over here.

I watch the numbers highlighting the floors as we ascend.

The couple in here with us selected the tenth floor. Time passes so slowly that it feels like it takes ten years to get to their floor.

When we reach it, the elevator stops.

They continue bickering about something.

The woman doesn't move when the doors open; she continues berating the man.

I want to scream at her to *hurry up and get out*.

Owen's fingers thread through mine as the man exits.

I squeeze his hand when the woman finally leaves.

He turns into me when the doors close, bringing my hand up to rest on the elevator wall above my head. His other hand reaches for the hem of my dress and then my panties. His fingers slide through my pussy as his mouth crashes down onto mine.

My body curves into his and I kiss him while stroking his dick through his trousers.

That indecent sound he makes while I do this is my new favorite sound.

When the elevator reaches our floor, we don't have a reenactment of our first time in an elevator. Owen drags his mouth from mine, his hand from my panties, and directs me to our suite.

When we're inside, he closes the door behind us and reaches for me. Pushing me up against the wall, he kisses me roughly while undoing the buttons of my dress. I kiss him back, just as wildly, reaching for his trouser button and zip.

There's nothing classy, refined, or smooth in the way we undress each other. We're both unapologetically filthy.

Owen forces my dress from me, taking hold of my breast, squeezing it, and pushing my bra cup down so he can suck my nipple into his mouth.

I get his shirt off before shoving his trousers and boxer briefs down and reaching for his dick.

"Fuck," he growls as my hand wraps around it.

He stops what he's doing to my breast and lets his head fall back while I stroke him. When I drop to my knees to take him in my mouth, he grips my hair in a ponytail and makes more of those indecent noises I think I could survive on.

I look up at him, taking in his shoulders, his neck, his strong jaw. I feel there's not enough appreciation for these parts of men. Asses, thighs, and chests tend to get all the love. I, for one, am here for a good strong neck and jaw. I think I could curl up in Owen's neck and live my life out there happily.

I suck him and stroke him while cupping his balls

and gently squeezing them with my other hand. I alternate all this with licking the length of him, sucking his balls into my mouth, and touching his legs and ass.

Owen lets go of my hair and places that hand to the wall while bringing his other hand to the top of my head.

I find his eyes. He's watching me like he wants nothing more than to stay in my mouth for the rest of his life. Like he would do anything for this. *I* would do anything to have him always look at me with this much hunger.

I slide him out of my mouth but continue stroking him. "I love how your dick feels in my mouth."

His fingers grip my hair as he fucks his dick into my hand. "I fucking love how your mouth feels around it."

"I think the next time we play at dinner, I should get on my knees under the table and do this." I slowly lick the length of his shaft before circling my tongue around the tip and sucking the crown into my mouth.

He groans. "There's that filthy side I like." He takes hold of his dick and pulls it out of my mouth. Tracing my lips with the tip, he says, "Do you like to swallow?"

I reach for his balls as I lick his pre-cum. "No. You can come on my tits."

"And at dinner? You think I should come on your tits then?"

I smile, taking him back into my mouth for one long suck before letting him go again. "I'll swallow then, but you should know it's not my favorite thing to do."

Something I say inspires Owen to stop what we're doing, reach down and lift me into his arms, carry me into the bedroom, and place me on the bed. He's like a man possessed with the way he does this so fast.

When he's got me under him, he places his hands to the bed on either side of me and kisses me. When he ends the kiss, he looks down at me and says, "I want to know all your favorites, Charlize. Every filthy, dirty thing you like and want me to do to you." He removes my bra and spends a great deal of time kissing my breasts before moving down my body to my panties.

Looking at me, he runs his finger over the fabric of my underwear. "I want to watch you come in every restaurant we eat at. I've never seen anything hotter."

Oh. God.

"We might be banned from every restaurant if we do that, Owen. I was a hot mess of trying not to moan and cause a scene."

He bends so he can kiss my panties, taking hold of my hips when I try to push my pussy closer to his mouth. "No, you were fucking beautiful. My only regret was that it was my fingers inside you instead of my tongue."

I'm so wet right now.

I'm beginning to think I'm destined to live in a perpetual state of being turned on.

Owen slides my panties down and takes hold of my thighs to spread them before giving me his tongue.

He licks the length of my pussy, ending with his mouth on my clit. He dedicates good time to my clit, sucking, kissing, and licking it. Just when I think he's about to move lower, he lifts his head and says, "I want you on my face."

Oh. Yes.

"For future reference," I say as he positions me where he wants me, "this is one of those filthy favorites of mine. Any time you want me to ride your face, I am there."

He grips my thighs either side of him and makes more indecent sounds as he uses his lips, tongue, and face to kiss, lick, slide, and rub me. I slowly roll my hips back and forth, and around in circles, loving the feel of his beard against my skin.

Leaning forward, I place my hands to the headboard as Owen gives me more pleasure than I think I can take. Something he's skilled at. "I feel like you should do this blindfolded next time."

His fingers dig into my thighs at that suggestion, and he pulls me closer to his face.

I squeeze my eyes closed and lean harder against the headboard.

Owen is ensuring every nerve ending of mine is alive.

Blazing alive.

And then, he makes a deep sound as he buries his face in my pussy, and the vibrations of that explode through me until my body is quivering from the orgasm he delivers.

As I chant my way through the orgasm, Owen sits up, taking me with him. He positions me on my back with one leg up over his shoulder.

Eyes to mine, he thrusts inside me.

He pulls out and thrusts in again, his strong shoulders working hard and drawing my attention.

I grip his biceps and hold on while he fucks me.

It's rough. Hard. Unrelenting as he takes what he needs.

It's the best damn sex I've ever had.

I come again, right before he thrusts deeply one last time and orgasms.

After he collapses onto the bed next to me, he pulls

me into his arms. I settle there with my head on his chest while we both recover.

When I've caught my breath, I look up at him. "I'm on birth control."

He curses softly before saying, "Sorry about that. I got caught up in the moment."

I smile. "I'm okay with that. I just wanted you to know we're good."

He bends his face so he can brush his lips over mine. He then pulls me tighter against him and lies silently with me.

After a few minutes of silence, in which I get lost in his necklace, I say, "You didn't get to come on my tits."

He looks down at me. "Now that you're not limiting me to twelve months, we've got plenty of time for me to come on your tits."

"Let the record show, I'm here for that happening sooner rather than later."

"Fuck," he rasps, kissing me again. "How many of those hourly thoughts that you have are filthy?"

I grin up at him. "Oh, you have no idea, Mr. North."

With that, he pulls me on top of him and kisses the hell out of me.

He then tells me to get in the shower so he can work harder on making it so I can't walk tomorrow.

I tell him I am also here for that.

"In fact," I say as I stare down into those blue eyes of his, "it turns out that there's not much I'm not here for if it involves you."

Owen *really* likes that, and I find it hard to make him stop showing me just how much.

I WAKE JUST after one a.m.

I passed out about an hour ago after Owen fucked me two more times. He's not in the bed with me, so I go in search of him.

I'm a little cool and put the first thing on that I find: his suit jacket.

When I find him on the sofa, he runs his gaze over the jacket, approval flaring in his eyes. "That's now yours. I want to see you in it every time I fuck you."

I pad over to him and curl up in his lap when he pulls me onto it. "I already have one of your jackets. I don't need another."

"In my experience, you can't have too many jackets." He kisses my neck. "Fuck, you smell good."

"Speaking of items of clothing that we each have of the other's, I'm going to need my red thong back."

He shakes his head. "No, I'm keeping that. In case I ever want to strangle you."

I run my hand down his cheek, searching his eyes. "I really like that you have this playful side. I think it's one of my favorite things about you."

We turn silent for a few moments until his phone buzzes with what feels like a million texts.

"Holy whoa," I say, glancing at his phone on the side table. "Is the world ending?"

He reaches for it. "It's Jill. Work stuff." He reads the messages before placing the phone back down and giving me all his attention again.

"She still loves you." I decided that she doesn't message me incessantly about Owen because she thinks either of us are fucking idiots. I think she does it because she still loves him.

He's not surprised by what I say. "No."

"She's messaged me a *lot* while we've been here, Owen. Not just about work things, but about you. She wanted me to ensure you ate well, slept well, had everything you needed. She even explained to me how you can get grumpy when you're tired, and that I shouldn't take it personally." I pause. "She throws things in her office when you upset her because she still loves you."

"No, she *thinks* she still loves me," he says thoughtfully. "But she doesn't. She's in that space where she's struggling to move on. Half her heart's in, half's out. There's a difference, and it's a fuck of a difference, but she doesn't still love me. Jill stopped loving me a long time ago."

I frown. "What do you mean 'a fuck of a difference?'"

He thinks about that for a moment. "Do you remember how we discussed the lines that loving well carves into our heart?"

"Yes." It was the night we met. A conversation I loved.

"Jill's struggling with those lines. She's mistaking the good ones for love that isn't there anymore. The difference between love with your whole heart in and only half in is the bad lines. When they're deep enough, you can't go back. Jill still has to come to terms with the fact our bad lines are too deep to ever go back. And from my experience, existing in that space is worse than the getting there in the first place. It's filled with confusion, and regret, and grief. You cling for fucking life until you're bleeding out."

I put my hand to his chest and feel the steady rhythm

of his heart. "This is why you didn't want her to know about us at work, isn't it?" I say softly. "You didn't want to make this harder for her."

"Yes. I didn't realize that at first, but it's the main reason. There are others, though. I'm no saint, Charlize. Jill could ruin an opportunity for me if she discovers what I've done and uses it against me."

I kiss him, putting my arms around his neck. "None of us are saints." I give him a playful smile. "I mean, you *do* have stalker tendencies as far as I'm aware. So, I'm keeping an eye on that. And I'm the world's messiest messer of life, so you should know that about me."

He runs his hand up my back and tangles his fingers through my hair. "I've taken note of this about you."

I fake shock. "Take that back. I've tried to be very tidy while we've been here."

"You did well until you showered for dinner. After that, all bets were off, and you were the world's messiest messer of life."

I wiggle on his lap, settling in for this discussion. "No, I think we need to be honest here and acknowledge that all bets were off when you insisted on waking up with a hard-on that you then insisted on teasing my ass with. I deserve full credit for making it through almost an entire day without throwing all my good habits out the window and showing you my true self."

He chuckles and pulls my mouth to his so he can kiss me. "I want to always see your true self."

"Oh, you should be careful what you wish for. That mess wasn't even close to my messiest mess of life."

"I have no doubt," he says before standing. Taking me with him, he walks into the bedroom and places me on the bed. At my questioning look—because, hello, if he thinks I'm up for more sex, he's dreaming—he says, "It's time for sleep."

After he removes his jacket from me, he pulls me close, and I curl into him. I put my arm across his chest and say, "How are we going to play this when we get back to work?"

"I'm going to tell Jill," he says, and I realize this isn't even remotely close to what I assumed he would say.

"Wait." I push up on an elbow and look down at him. "Why?"

"I don't ever want you to feel like I'm hiding you away, Charlize. I'll find time tomorrow to speak with Jill."

"I don't need you to tell her for my sake. What's the opportunity she could ruin for you?"

"I've been nominated for the Bluestone Award."

Oh, wow. I've had previous bosses who won that. The Bluestone is one of the most prestigious business awards in the world.

"Owen, we knew each other and slept together before I worked for you. Let's just pretend this didn't happen, wait another week, and then go from there."

"I don't want to wait another week," he says with determination.

"Okay," I say slowly, liking how his determination makes me feel. "We won't wait, but I'll stay away from you at work. Don't tell Jill. There's no need."

He thinks about that, and I sense his unease over my suggestion, but in the end, he says, "I'll tell her if it becomes necessary."

I lie back down. "It won't become necessary."

My last thought before I fall asleep is about the kind of man Owen is.

I was right: he's a values kind of guy.

He's the most values kind of values guy I've ever known.

Even if he did pocket my red thong and is insisting on keeping it in case he wants to strangle me one day.

21

Charlize

The flight home to New York is long. Mostly because I'm tired after a busy few days, but also because we didn't get much sleep last night and I have a lot of work to get through on the flight. We arrive in New York just before lunch. Owen drops me off at Dylan's place before he goes into the office. I try to convince him to take the afternoon off, but he doesn't even consider it. I didn't really expect him to, but I tried. The man needs sleep.

Poppy bombards my phone with texts as I'm walking into my bedroom.

Poppy: ONE MORE SLEEP AND I GET TO SEE YOU.

Charlize: What time do you arrive tomorrow?

Poppy: I should be home by the time you finish

work. There will be anarchy if I don't see you. I was thinking cocktails after work.

Charlize: I'm in.

Poppy: I have a new cocktail for us to try that I found in Rome. The Rossini. It's a whole lot of strawberries. You'll love it.

Poppy: Are you home from London?

Charlize: I just got in. I'm about to start the sleep of all sleeps. If I didn't have to work tomorrow, I would just sleep all the way through to our cocktails. Managing Owen is exhausting.

Poppy: Ooh, I like this new code word. It seems apt. I have to manage Seth a LOT.

I begin typing another text to her when a message comes in from my mother.

Mom: Is it David Cross?

I switch back to Poppy.

Charlize: OMG my mother is doing exactly what I knew she would and is trying to figure out who I'm seeing. She just asked me if it's David Cross!!!!

Poppy: Oh, God, the toxic masculinity he exudes would be enough for me to kidnap you away from men for life if you thought dating him was the way to go. Would you like me to educate Aunt Joan about David?

Charlize: LOL. I'd love to witness that conversation. I honestly think she'd talk around you and educate you back on how much she doesn't care because marrying a Cohen to a Cross would help her reach a life goal.

Poppy: You're right. It would be a waste of my breath.

Poppy: Oh, I have to go.

Charlize: Is Seth giving you the eye again?

Poppy: You joke, but when you are a married woman, Charles, you will speak like this xx

I send my mother a text.

Charlize: This is a fun game.

Mom: It's not one I care for, Charlize.

Mom: Can you please come an hour earlier for dinner on Sunday so we can discuss the gala?

I flop down onto my bed and commence my first pity party of the season.

Charlize: Will it really take an hour?

Mom: Charlize, you are the one who inserted yourself into this. Please don't let me down now. The committee liked a number of your suggestions, so I'd like to get started on them and ensure you can make them happen.

And just like that, my mother makes it so I will be there for that hour and for any other planning sessions she wants to have.

Of course, I can make these suggestions happen.

Charlize: I'll be there.

I SLEEP ALL AFTERNOON, waking when Owen calls me at six p.m.

"Hey, you," I say sleepily, rolling onto my side.

"Did I wake you?"

"Kind of. Are you still at work?"

"Yes. I've got a few more hours here."

I really want to tell him he needs sleep, but he's a grown man and can figure that out for himself. "At the risk of sounding like I'm trying to manage you, what are you planning for dinner?"

I hear his smile when he says, "You know I like your style of management. I haven't thought about dinner yet. I'll probably order takeout."

I sit up and move off the bed. "Can I bring you something to eat? Would that be okay?"

"You never need to ask me if you can bring me something, Charlize. My answer would never be a no."

I like the way those words settle in me. I've been told no too many times in my life in similar situations. "What time would you like to eat?"

"I've got a call to take at seven thirty. I should be finished with that by eight, so any time after that."

"Okay, I'll see you then. Oh, wait, what did you call for?"

"Just to hear your voice. I'm sorry I woke you."

No one has ever told me they called just to hear my voice. I don't know how I made it this far in life without knowing how good it feels for someone to just want to hear my voice. "You know how we're starting that list of every filthy, dirty thing I want you to do to me? Well, I'm also starting a clean list, and you calling just to hear my voice is now on it."

"I've already started that list. I'll add this to it."

He's trying to kill me here.

Spoiler alert: it's working.

Consider me dead, slayed, breathless.

Why did I not know men who start lists like this exist?

"You really are an overachiever, Owen. Starting lists all by yourself."

"It's for purely selfish reasons."

"You're just trying to score pussy, right?"

"And that filthy, filthy mouth of yours."

"That mouth is dying to suck your dick again."

"Fuck," he growls, and that word alone causes a throb of need deep inside me.

"I think that's my signal to let you get back to work because while I'd love nothing more than to have phone sex with you right now, I really want you to go home at a respectable hour tonight so you can get some sleep."

"Don't wear panties tonight."

Oh, holy stalker of stalkers.

Yes.

I COOK Chicken and Snow Pea Fried Rice for dinner and arrive at Owen's office at 8:15 p.m. to eat with him. It's quiet in the office; there's no one else here.

He glances up from his work and spots me walking toward his office, a sexy smile spreading across his face like I'm the best thing he's seen all day. I don't think I could ever get enough of those kinds of smiles from him.

"For future reference," he says when I meet him in his office, "wearing this kind of dress won't ensure I get much sleep." His eyes are all over my bun, my neck, and my red dress that I thought wasn't even that sexy. I decide right this very minute that I am more than good with Owen gluing his eyes to my body. Like, let's just sign a contract for that now: *I, Charlize Cohen, approve Owen North to sexualize me all hours of the day. Please and thank you. Signed, Charlize.*

I hit him with a sexy smile even though he probably

won't notice it. See: eyes glued to my body. "You should see what's not underneath it."

Before I know what's happening, Owen's reaching for a remote on his desk so he can close his office blinds. Then, he's taking our dinner from me and placing it on the other end of his desk. Then, he's got hold of my hip and is bending me over the desk with a firm hand to my back.

I was already turned on just coming here. Now, I'm ten levels beyond turned on. Owen could fuck me right now without one second of foreplay.

He presses his dick against my ass.

He's just as turned on as me.

Dropping his mouth to the nape of my neck, he kisses me there while bringing both his hands to my ass. He runs them over my cheeks, slowly bunching my dress up to reveal my naked bottom.

When his mouth leaves my neck, I turn my face and find him looking at my ass.

He meets my gaze and leans in to kiss me roughly.

He devours me with this kiss.

His tongue forces mine to tangle, his lips crush mine, he takes every breath I have and keeps it for himself.

When he finally tears his mouth from mine, he growls, "Good girl."

Those two words are fast becoming my kryptonite.

Owen North's Good Girl.

I'll take the stickers, the mug, *and* the T-shirt thanks.

It's shameful what I would do to have him call me that.

Gripping the edge of the desk, I push my ass back and

grind it against his hard dick. "Tell me what else I can do to be your good girl."

Owen's hands curve around to my hips and his fingers dig into my skin as he helps me grind into him. "You can get on your knees and suck my dick."

Good Girls Suck Dick.

I'll take that T-shirt too.

I turn and reach for his trouser button all while keeping my eyes firmly on his. Owen manages to maintain eye contact until I wrap my hand around his dick. As I stroke him, his gaze drops to my chest, and he reaches for the hem of my dress. It lands on the floor a moment later and his mouth comes to my breasts, and *holy God*, he gives me a taste of the pleasure that's to come.

I moan loudly.

Too loudly for the office, even if we are alone.

Fucking Owen in his office has now been added permanently to the *Filthy Dirty Things I Like* list. In fact, I'm going to add a recurring appointment to his calendar after this.

"I really want to get on my knees," I say, arching my back and looking down at his head buried in my breasts, "but I want you to suck my tits for a long time."

He sucks my nipple and gives me just the right amount of teeth before lifting his face. Taking his dick from me, he strokes himself as he brings his other hand to my chin. Gripping it, he directs me to look down at his cock. "Good girls do what they're told, Charlize."

I look down at his hard dick.

At his hand wrapped around it.

And I let the need I hear in every syllable he just uttered work its way through me.

I slowly get on my knees, not taking my eyes off Owen's for even one second.

I allow him to put his dick in my mouth.

And I show him just how good I can be.

Owen pulls out just before orgasming, bending me over his desk again, and slamming inside me.

I take every hard thrust, every indelicate touch, every impolite word out of his mouth.

I submit to all of it.

Being fucked by Owen is like finding the right key for the door after searching for it forever.

I come right before he does.

I make a lot of noise.

He doesn't pull out after we catch our breath. He stays in me, circling his arm around my waist, and kissing my shoulder. "I want you in my bed tonight."

"How many pillows do you have?"

I feel his smile against my skin. "What's an acceptable number? I'll make sure I meet your expectations."

"Ten."

He moves to my other shoulder and kisses it. "I don't recall seeing ten pillows on your bed."

"It's my minimum requirement, Owen. Take it or leave it."

He gives me one last kiss before pulling out and turning me to face him. His arms come around me and he settles his hands on my ass. "Consider it done."

"You'll just magically have pillows multiply?"

"Yes."

My breathing speeds up as an unfamiliar sensation flutters in my stomach. I can't quite put my finger on it, but it feels like hesitation. Uncertainty. Like maybe I need to pause a moment here.

I put my hand to his chest. "No, you don't need to do that. I was just getting frisky with you."

Owen's eyes fill with determination and his hold on me tightens. "I want to do that."

I stare at him. "I don't expect it."

"You should always expect me to want to stretch, Charlize."

It's in this moment I realize that although I told Owen I'm a high-expectations kind of girl, I've given up on expecting even the littlest things from men. And while I don't think expecting a man to suddenly produce ten pillows is an acceptable demand, I want him to. I want him to go to the ends of the earth to bring me those pillows.

I lean forward and kiss him.

It's a slow, deep kiss, and I hope it shows him just what this means to me.

When I end it, I let my lips linger, not wanting to part from him yet. I tangle my fingers into his hair at the back of his neck. "I like you a little too much, I think."

This earns me a look I'd like to capture in print. "Good."

With that, we dress, and I use his bathroom to clean up. When I come out, he's on the phone. I take the dinner I brought into the break room to serve it up, hearing the word *pillows* as I slip out of his office.

I'm not certain, but I think I just fell a little further.

For a girl who only wanted sex for a year, I'm fast falling my way to so much more.

22

Charlize

"So, when's the next wedding?" I ask Seth when he joins Poppy and me for a drink. She and I started two hours ago and have spent that time mixing these strawberry cocktails she discovered in Italy, drinking a few too many of them, and catching up on every single thing we've both done over the past two weeks since her wedding. And when I say "every single thing", I mean every.single.thing. Poppy and I don't ever skip details. That's why Seth wasn't here when I arrived. He's sat through enough Zooms with us to know of our love for details, a love he doesn't share.

He glances at his wife before looking back at me. "To who?"

Poppy smacks him. "To me. Seriously, if you think you're ever marrying anyone else, you're dreaming.

Charles and I will unalive her, cut her up, and bury her before I'll ever allow you to do that."

He's amused. "Unalive?"

I grin. "Yes, that's how married women speak, Seth. They speak differently to the rest of us."

"Right," he says to Poppy. "I'm impressed with your dedication to ensuring she never takes another breath, but cutting her up seems extreme, sweetheart."

"Never," I declare, taking a sip of my Rossini. "A girl can't ever be too careful when it comes to these things."

Seth laughs and Poppy eyes him with an arched brow. "I'm being deadly serious, darling. The only weddings of yours in your future are to me. And our next one is in six months. Start thinking about where our honeymoon will be."

A text comes through on my phone and when I attempt to pick it up, I drop it. Then, when I bend to retrieve it, I hit my head on the table on the way up.

"How many of those cocktails have you girls had?" Seth asks while I swipe at my phone to unlock it after seeing Owen's name on the screen.

"Not enough," Poppy says.

"Oh my God," I mutter as my swipes are unsuccessful. "Definitely not enough, but also"—I look up at him—"maybe too many. Either that, or my phone is being difficult and trying to keep this message from Owen from me."

I swipe some more and finally unlock it.

I can't open Owen's text fast enough. I haven't seen him since I left his condo this morning because he was out of the office all day. We've texted a few times, and holy hot sexting, who knew texts could be so dirty? Not me.

He wanted to cook dinner for me tonight, but I told him I never abandon my friends for a guy. Seeing Poppy tonight was my priority even if my vagina is mad at me for that decision. I really like that Owen didn't try to convince me otherwise.

I'm not sure if I'm disappointed his text now isn't filthy. A girl could do with some good foreplay before her late-night date with her vibrator.

Owen: We haven't talked about the weekend yet. Are you free tomorrow for a hike?

I look up at Poppy. "Do you think 'hiking' could be code for sex?"

Seth laughs and Poppy says, "Charles, everything is code for sex when it comes to a man. *'Pancakes for breakfast, sweetheart?'* Sex in the kitchen. *'I'm doing laundry today.'* Sex on the washing machine. *'Let's play chess.'* You can ride my dick while I figure out my next move."

"Right," I say. "I'm taking it chess is another one of those married women things."

I go back to my text.

Charlize: If 'hike' is code for sex, yes. If it isn't, maybe.

Owen: What are the maybe conditions?

Charlize: Three hours max. I am not a hike-all-day kind of girl, Owen. And after, I'm going to need to fill that huge bath of yours with bubbles, and you're going to have to bring me food.

Owen: Done. I'll pick you up at six.

Charlize: I wasn't finished with my conditions. This body is only available for hiking after seven a.m.

Owen: I'll pick you up at seven.

Charlize: It's a shame you aren't drinking cocktails with me right now. I would do obscene things to you if you were.

Owen: I'm already planning the obscene things you'll do to me tomorrow.

Charlize: See, this is why I like you.

Owen: I hope it's not the only reason.

Charlize: Stop being so good at this.

Owen: At what?

Charlize: At convincing me that I want so much more than just filthy sex with you.

Owen: I'm not stopping.

"Charles," Poppy says, drawing my attention. "You should go. Get some 'hiking' in tonight. You look like you're in heat."

I place my phone down. "No. Sorry, I didn't mean to ignore you." I reach for my cocktail. "We haven't finished discussing your honeymoon."

"Okay, so when I say that you look like you're in heat, you do, but also, Seth just gave me the eye, so you need to go."

I laugh as I look at Seth who is now in their kitchen with his head in the fridge. "He's got his head in the fridge, Pop. I think you're confusing his search for food for wanting sex."

She gives me a pointed look. "Did I or did I not just explain these things to you? *Honey, what do we have to eat?*' translates to *'Babe, come sit on my face.'* Honestly, we need to schedule in some lessons. You have a lot to learn about men."

I slide off my stool. It's truly shocking how easy I am to persuade to go and see Owen.

I say goodbye to Seth, hug Poppy, and find my way to a taxi after Seth insists I don't walk to Owen's in my inebriated state. They don't live far from him, but I do agree that I'm perhaps a little too tipsy to walk.

I don't let Owen know I'm coming, so I hope he's home, and that he's not busy. He told me earlier that he was planning a quiet night in, but plans can change.

The great news is that he *is* home.

The bad news is that I stumble when I step out of his elevator into his foyer and show him just how intoxicated I am.

He catches me, concern etched into his face. "Did you walk here from Seth's?"

I grip his shirt, my eyes zeroing in on all those buttons that aren't done up. We have a new record tonight. There must be at least four buttons undone. "No, he wouldn't let me walk." I narrow my eyes at the tanned skin on his chest before bringing my hands to the next button that needs to taste freedom.

Owen chuckles, placing his hand over mine. "I hate to break it to you, but we're going to have to take a rain check. Bradford is here."

I pout. "Remind me to have words with him for ruining all my fun." I let him go so I can get back in the elevator. "Maybe you should pick me up later than seven tomorrow. I may need to sleep these cocktails off."

He takes hold of my hand. "You're not leaving. Come and eat with us."

Without waiting for my response, he guides me into

his kitchen where Bradford is sitting on a stool at the marble island.

Owen's kitchen is gorgeous. It's large and open, decorated in white, gray, and black with hints of gold throughout. The color scheme along with the marble creates a striking and elegant space. And while I don't often spend a lot of time cooking, I would cook in this kitchen.

"Charlize," Bradford says after he takes a sip of the whiskey he's holding. "This is an unexpected pleasure."

I slide onto the stool next to him, my movements not graceful at all thanks to the alcohol I've consumed. "The pleasure is not mine, Bradford. I'd be hiking with Owen right now if you weren't here."

Bradford lifts a brow. "Hiking, huh?"

I give him a very serious look. "Yes. Hiking."

He studies me for a moment like he's getting great enjoyment from this conversation before eyeing Owen. "I don't recall you ever dating anyone who liked hiking on a Friday night."

Owen looks at us from across the island where he begins cutting steak. "That was a mistake."

"I have to agree," Bradford says before looking back at me. "Would you like a drink?"

"I like that you're not a man who makes a decision for a woman, but I think we can both agree that I do not need another drink," I say as his phone sounds with a text.

He glances down at the phone sitting on the countertop in front of him and mutters, "Fuck, she just doesn't know when to leave well enough alone."

Owen eyes him. "What's she done now?"

Bradford taps out a reply before looking at Owen.

"She's arranged a fucking interview for us with *YR Magazine*."

"She means business," Owen says.

"She's about to learn what happens when she pushes me," Bradford says darkly.

"Who are we talking about?" I ask, not even caring that my question is maybe a little rude since I don't know Bradford and am forcing my way into their conversation.

"The woman destined to ruin my life." Bradford throws some more whiskey down this throat.

I frown. "How? Is this someone you're in business with?"

"I would say no to that, but that's exactly how she would describe it."

I keep frowning. "Okay, so because I've had one too many cocktails... You *are* in business with her? Or you aren't?"

"It's his fiancé," Owen says.

"She's not my fiancé," Bradford says emphatically.

"You're as good as married," Owen says.

"Okay, stop," I say. "My brain is far too slow for this tonight. If I've understood correctly, you're not engaged to this woman, but you will be soon, and then she's going to ruin your life?"

"Yes," Bradford says.

I stare at him. "Is this like some kind of arranged marriage deal?"

"From the dark ages?" Bradford says dryly. "Yes. Although my future bride would have my balls for telling you that. She's fucking intent on the world thinking we're the real deal. I'm not sure how anyone in their right mind will ever look at Cecelia Aniston and me together and think there's passion between us."

I lean in close to him as my intoxicated thoughts chase around after each other. "You said Cecelia Aniston?"

He nods. "Yes."

My voice drops to a whisper as I say, "You know she's gay, right?"

Bradford barks out a laugh while looking at me like he thinks I'm the best fucking thing of life right now. "Yes, Charlize, I know she's gay."

I rest my elbow on the island so I can then rest my face in my hand and contemplate the puzzle of all this. "Right, so as far as the world will think, your dick is the dick of all dicks and turned Cecelia straight. That's the story you'll stick with?"

Bradford lifts his glass of whiskey and toasts me. "That is the story I am now running with. If you ever decide to work in PR, call me. I could do with a good spin doctor."

I'm about to ask him why he needs a spin doctor when he receives a text that causes him to snatch his cell up and leave the kitchen to make a call.

I look at Owen, watching for a moment as he prepares dinner. He moves around his kitchen with ease, like it's a completely natural thing for him to do. I don't think I know anyone who seems as comfortable in a kitchen.

"You look good in the kitchen," I say.

He stops what he's doing and gives me all his attention, smiling as he says, "You look happy. How was Poppy?"

"She gave me a lesson in understanding men."

"Was it useful?"

"Apparently not. She thinks I need more lessons." My gaze drops to his chest. "I don't like buttons. I mean, who designed them and why? They're ugly little things that serve absolutely no purpose." I look back at his face and find a whole lot of heat there. "I really want to negotiate your preference for wearing clothes with them."

Amusement joins that heat in his eyes. "What would you suggest I wear instead?"

"It's a no-brainer really. Why wear a shirt when you can wear nothing?" I shrug. "Or just wear a tie and jacket. I could get behind that. Although, I have picked up on your preference for no ties, and I'm good with that too."

Bradford strides back into the kitchen. Looking regretful, he says, "Something's come up. I have to go." He glances at me. "Hiking is now an option for you. Nothing too strenuous, though. Owen and I are golfing on Sunday, and I need him at the top of his game."

"You've obviously never hiked with Owen. He prefers strenuous activity."

Bradford smiles. It's not a full smile but I'm not sure I can imagine a full smile on this man. I've met him twice now and both times he appeared intense like he doesn't have a lot of time for fun in his life. Like maybe he doesn't find many reasons to let loose and laugh. "The pleasure was all mine, Charlize," he says before leaving.

"How long have you known Bradford?" I ask Owen once we're alone.

"Since we were five."

"Did you go to school together?"

"Yes."

"And you two golf?"

He chuckles. "You say that like golf is a bad thing."

"Well, doesn't it get a little boring? There's so much walking, which I'm usually okay with, but there has to be scenery or else it's just one long stroll of nothingness. How long does a game take?"

"It depends how many are playing and whether you walk or use a cart. Our games take roughly three to four hours."

"Don't ever ask me to play golf with you. That's four hours I'll never get back in my life."

"What would you prefer I ask you to do with me?"

"I'm good with hiking. Real hiking, I mean. I love the beach and anything that involves water. I really am a mermaid, just FYI, even if I can't confirm their actual existence. If you ever want to take an art class, I'm your girl. And visiting art galleries, I'm here for that. Live music too. And watching movies with the worst reviews of life. I'm all over that. Oh! And dancing. I already know you do that very well, so let the record show I would like to do more of that with you."

"You like to watch movies that have bad reviews?"

"Why are you looking at me like that? I mean, you're the one who likes to play golf. That's worse than watching bad movies."

"I would argue that."

"And I would argue right back at you."

His eyes sparkle. "I'll watch a bad movie with you if you play a game of golf with me."

"That is a horrific suggestion."

More of that sparkle. "It's the best way to settle this."

"It's the best way to settle that *I'm* right."

"I'm willing to take that gamble."

"I feel like you're taking advantage of me while I'm intoxicated."

"If I was taking advantage of you, Charlize, you would be on your knees."

Holy mother of *good girls suck dick*.

I squeeze my legs together.

"Okay, one bad movie in exchange for one bad game of golf. I'm choosing the movie."

"What is it you like about bad movies?"

"Well, sometimes they make you laugh, which is always good. But they're not all bad, and that's the thing. Reviews are personal and subjective. I've found some great movies that were on other people's bad list. I don't know, I'm not a fan of judging things as good or bad. Or of always looking for perfection. We can find beauty in the flaws, right?"

Owen listens intently in the way he always does. He turns all of that over in his mind and then he nods slowly. "I like the way you look at things."

He finishes preparing dinner while I share many disconnected, inebriated thoughts with him after he asks me about my mermaid tendencies. Well, my thoughts aren't disconnected to me. Everything connects in my brain. It makes perfect sense to me to go from telling him about my love of the beach, to my love of sitting in the sun, to my love of bath bombs, to my inability to meditate, to my question over whether I want to ever smoke weed again, to my love of outdoor music festivals. And full points to Owen because he keeps up with my conversation with ease.

He cooks the best Steak au Poivre and roasted vegetables I've ever tasted.

We sit at his dining table and eat.

I ask him a million questions about which bands he loves, what books he reads, his favorite movies, and whether he thinks Elvis really is dead. He does. I'm not so convinced.

He asks me a million in return, including why I think romantic comedies are life. I spend a good fifteen minutes educating him on why they far outrank the action flicks he prefers. I'm not sure we come to any agreement on this, so I make a note to myself to revisit this discussion at some point.

After dinner, we clean up together.

It turns out that cleaning up after dinner is code for *I want to eat you on the dining table.* Poppy was right: I need more lessons because I was not aware of this.

Owen then takes me to bed. With all those pillows he procured for me last night.

When he gets a little strenuous with me, I try hard to tell him not to. I want to help Bradford out with his golf game on Sunday, but really, that's a lie. What I really want is for Owen to keep giving me the best orgasms of life.

He does, and then he pulls me close, puts his arm around me, and makes it so I don't need to count my way to sleep.

I think about that. About how I'm spending a lot less time counting since I met Owen.

And I do my best not to think about how fast all of this is happening.

23

Owen

I walk into my ensuite just after eight a.m. on Saturday morning to encourage Charlize to finish her shower. She's been in here for fifteen minutes and while I wouldn't usually care how long someone showers, we were supposed to leave over an hour ago for our hike.

Music blares from her phone which is sitting on the vanity with Spotify open. If I'm not mistaken, it's a Taylor Swift song Charlize is singing along to.

When she spots me, she says, "I'm nearly finished. I promise."

I rest my ass against the vanity and watch her clean herself. It's taking everything in me not to get in the shower with her, but I know we'll never make it to our hike if I do. "Do you always play music while you shower?"

"Of course. I'm not sure why everyone doesn't. Wait, you don't?"

"I can't say I ever have."

"Oh, Owen, your poor, sad life. It's a good thing you met me so I can help you with that."

She turns the shower off and pushes the glass door separating us open. I'm helpless but to look at her body as she comes my way. Charlize is all soft curves and beautiful hollows my mouth wants to spend hours in. Today is no exception, so I pick up the towel I put out for her and wrap her in it when she reaches me.

She eyes my hiking pants and shirt. "It's a pity hiking requires so much skin to be covered up."

I don't want to get into this discussion because it won't lead to anything but sex with all the sexual energy between us this morning, so I push off the vanity and say, "We're leaving in ten minutes."

"I'm sensing a lot of bossiness in you right now and I'd just like to point out that I am not the reason we're running late. I do believe you're the one who demanded I let you put your dick in my mouth this morning."

Fuck.

Even just the word "dick" anywhere near Charlize's mouth gets me hard.

"You are the reason for everything, Charlize." I brush my lips across hers before saying with some determination, "Ten minutes." With that, I stride out of the bathroom so I can put some space between her and my need for her.

A call comes in from Julian as I exit the bedroom and

I head into my office to take it. We discuss stocks for almost ten minutes, making a plan to talk more about this later. After I end the call, I go in search of Charlize.

I don't find her in the bedroom or bathroom, but I do find her in the living room.

She's on her hands and knees under the dining table. My mother is also in the living room, watching Charlize. The way Charlize is muttering to herself tells me she has no idea she's not alone.

As I round the corner into the room, Charlize mutters, "I'm not letting him put his dick in my mouth anymore. Or anywhere for that matter. These were my favorite earrings and now they're lost, and it's all his dick's fault."

My lips twitch and I come to a stop, interested to see what happens next.

"Well," my mother says, moving closer to Charlize, "I, for one, am glad he's putting his dick somewhere. I was beginning to think he'd never put it anywhere ever again."

Charlize's head snaps up and she quickly crawls backward, out from under the table. "Oh my God," she exclaims, the words rushing out of her mouth as she clambers to her feet, mortification written all over her. "You must be Owen's mom. I can't believe you just heard me say all that. I promise you I am not usually that crude. I would never have said that if I knew you were standing there." Her eyes shift to me when she realizes I'm watching. They plead with me to save her before she looks back at Mom. "Please forgive me." Her pleading eyes come back to me, widening as if to say, "If you ever want your dick in my mouth again, you will get your ass over here *now*."

"My dear girl," Mom says, "I've only ever seen one other woman in Owen's private space before, so this tells me you mean something to him. I'm more interested in that than anything crude you might say."

I walk toward them. "Mom. I wasn't aware I'd be seeing you today." It's unusual for my mother to drop by unannounced.

She turns and looks at me. "When a son of mine stops taking my calls, I take it very seriously, Owen."

Fuck, I meant to return her calls this week but got distracted by work.

"I haven't stopped taking your calls. I was in London this week."

"That may be the case, but I'd appreciate it if you returned at least one of them." She glances at Charlize. "And perhaps you could introduce me to your friend."

Charlize's expression tells me she wishes the floor would open up and swallow her whole. But she's pasted a smile on her face for my mother. I appreciate that smile because I suspect there's a whole lot of anxiety swirling deeply inside her right now.

I introduce them, moving next to Charlize and sliding my arm around her waist.

"It's lovely to meet you, Mary," Charlize says.

"Likewise," Mom says before looking at me. "Your brother will be in town tomorrow night. I'd like you to come to dinner with us." She shifts her attention to Charlize. "You're welcome to join us, Charlize."

Charlize smooths her dress as she stares at Mom. "Thank you," she says. "But I have a family dinner of my own to go to, and while I'd love to come to yours, I've already told my mother I'll be at ours."

Mom looks at her like she's assessing her. She then nods and says, "Next time."

"I'll be there," I say. My brother doesn't get to New York often, and when he does, I always make it a point to spend time with him.

"Good," Mom says. "Also, is everything going well with Jill as far as the Bluestone Award is concerned?"

"Yes."

"Good to hear. Surely you can keep her in line for five more weeks."

My mother is nothing if not focused when there's a goal to be met.

She eyes Charlize. "It was good to meet you, Charlize. We must plan a dinner soon so we can begin getting to know each other."

Mom turns to leave, and Charlize looks at me questioningly.

"I'll see Mom out. You finish getting ready," I say, leaving her to walk Mom out.

I talk with Mom for five minutes while she catches me up on her latest news. She also tells me she's impressed I've found a woman who values family. I don't miss her jab at Jill who would never have put her parents first for a dinner. I then make my way into the bedroom where Charlize is rummaging in her purse, pulling items out and dumping them on my bed.

"So, that might just be my worst *meeting the mother of the man I'm sleeping with* moment of life," she says.

"I thought it went well."

Her eyes widen. "That's because you're a man and

have no clue on the workings of a woman's mind."

"I'm well-versed in the workings of my mother's mind. Trust me when I tell you it went well."

She drags a bottle of perfume and some other beauty product out of her purse and places them on the bed. "All I can hope is she doesn't hold today against me."

"She wants to have dinner with you, Charlize. My mother doesn't have dinner with people she doesn't like."

She pulls wet wipes out of her purse, looks at them, and then puts them back in. She then drags a nail file out and spends a few moments contemplating it.

"What are you doing?" I ask.

"I'm figuring out what I can get away with not taking today."

I eye her purse and recall the night we met. "In your emergency kit?"

"Yes. I'm lightening the load for the hike."

"You don't need to take any of it. I've got everything we'll need in my backpack."

She looks at me like I'm a clueless male. "I highly doubt that, Owen."

"So, you're planning on taking your purse on the hike?"

More of that clueless male look. "Of course. We'll put it in your backpack." She finishes rummaging in the purse, picks it up, and shoves it at me. "Now, I know you wanted to leave hours ago, but after meeting your mother and vomiting dicks all over her I need caffeine, and you're going to make it for me. The coffee war starts today."

I look down at the purse I'm now holding, mentally figuring out how to fit it in my backpack that's already full. Then, meeting Charlize's gaze again, I say, "I do believe I've already given you my sample of coffee."

"We need to start from scratch. I was under the Owen sex spell that day."

"If you're not under it today we need to skip this hike so I can fix that."

She moves to me and places her hand to my stomach. "I'm always under it, but the fact I've misplaced my earrings thanks to all that sex you insisted on means it's dulled enough for me to be objective about your coffee." She gently smacks my stomach. "Let's go. Oh, and just so you're prepared, we may need to stop on the way to get a snack for me. I've got a lot to process after the events of this morning and I always do that best with snacks."

I'd stop ten times for ten different snacks if that's what Charlize wanted, and that isn't something I've ever done for anyone.

I'm the guy who makes plans and sticks to them.

I don't like being late.

I don't like unexpected things delaying me.

I don't like stopping on road trips.

All those things are out the window now.

And I am more than okay with all of this.

"I DON'T THINK I can ever trust you to plan a hike again," Charlize says fifteen minutes into our drive home from Breakneck Ridge.

I take my eye off the road for a moment and look at her. She's fucking sexy in her hiking gear, especially after having hiked. I love her hair when it's a flyaway mess, and her face when it's free of make-up and flushed. "Why?"

"Well, for one, I have never had to scramble like that before. I am not a rock climber, Owen. If the golf you play is extreme golfing like your extreme hiking, I'm out for that."

"We were hardly rock climbing today." Before choosing the hike, I established that she'd be able to manage the scrambling, and she did great. I would never have put her in harm's way.

"It was hardly just walking, though, either."

I frown, wondering if I misread her when we discussed the hikes she's done in the past. "Were you not okay with today's hike?"

She releases a breath and angles her body to face me. "I was a little unprepared for it mentally, that's all."

"Would you do it again?"

"Yes. Now that I've done it once, I know what to expect."

I make a mental note about this. I never want Charlize to feel anxious over something when I can help her prepare for it.

I glance at her again. "I apologize. I forget that not everyone's like me."

"You like the thrill of the unexpected?"

"Not always, but generally. And I'm good with risk. But I'll remember you prefer to know what's coming."

"Thank you." A text sounds on her phone and as she reads it, she exclaims, "Oh my God! Harry Styles is performing at The Rooftop at Pier 17 next month! We have to go."

"He's the One Direction guy?"

"Have you not listened to his music since then?"

"No."

"You work too much. Harry has moved past One Direction. You're going to love him."

"When is it?"

She rattles off a date at which point I say, "I'll check my calendar and let you know. If I don't have anything on, I'm in."

The smile she gives me is another one of those smiles I'd do anything to receive. "I totally get it if you're already busy, but I hope you're free."

We fill the rest of the drive home with a conversation about the bad movie she's chosen for us to watch tonight after I cook her dinner, her confusion over why Bon Jovi isn't higher on my list of favorite bands, the next hike we'll take, our favorite places we've visited in Europe, and another discussion about whether Elvis really is dead.

After she's finished trying to convince me he isn't dead, she shifts in her seat and groans about how stiff her body is. "I'm going to need a long, hot bath when we get back to your place." She looks at me questioningly. "Are you a bath fan?"

"I can't recall the last time I had a bath. I would have been a child."

She appears shocked. "Are you being serious right now? You have that massive bath in your bathroom."

"It came with the place."

"How long have you lived there?"

"Eight months."

"Oh, my goodness, Owen, we are taking a bath this afternoon. I can't believe you've lived with that beautiful bath for that long and never enjoyed it."

My phone vibrates with a text message. It's the fourth one that's come in during the drive. The fourth one I haven't checked.

I've never not checked my messages as soon as they arrive, but right now I don't care what any of them say.

The only thing I care about is spending every second of this day fully present with the woman sitting next to me.

The one capturing my attention, my hours, my heart.

24

———

Charlize

Owen and I spend an exorbitant amount of time in his bath.

He dedicates himself to the experience in the same way he appears to dedicate himself to everything he thinks is important in life.

We talk for a long time about his summer vacations with his grandparents. About the hours he and his brother spent sailing with their grandfather. Owen has so many good memories of his summers and I love hearing about all of them. When he gets to his teen years and talks about the parties on the beach and the girls, I only get a little bit jealous that I didn't know Owen back then. I think I would have liked teenage Owen.

We talk about my adventures in Australia when I was twenty. I tell him I escaped there after Timothy Shining broke my heart. When he asks me if an Aussie guy helped me forget my heartbreak, I tell him that they have some of the hottest lifeguards of ever in that country, and that yes, one of them helped me forget Timothy. He kisses me a little possessively and tells me he's making a mental note to keep me away from lifeguards in future. I tell him that might be a little hard since I'm an actual mermaid.

Owen gives me two orgasms in the bath, and I tell him this was my best bath moment of life.

After our bath, I put on the pajama pants I packed into a bag when Owen took me home this morning to change for our hike. When I join him in the kitchen, he eyes the pants and says, "These would be an acceptable choice over dresses like the ones you wore in London."

I rest my hip against the island. "You like demure dresses." It's not a question but rather a statement of something my brain has just puzzled out. Both the dresses I wore in London that he lost his mind over were carefully selected for what I considered their lack of sexiness.

He moves into me, his hand coming to my hip. "I like all dresses on you, but yes, I'm more affected by modesty."

"And you like buns." I cock my head. "I'm beginning to wonder if you might have a sexy librarian kink."

He brings his other hand to my neck, curving his fingers around it and rubbing his thumb over my throat. "I'm developing all sorts of kinks for you, Charlize."

I'm about to show him what I think of that when his butler announces guests.

Jameson and Adeline have arrived unexpectedly.

"I just need half an hour," Jameson says when he and Adeline meet us in the living room.

Owen leads Jameson down the hall to his office while Adeline eyes my pants and says, "Girl, I love these! Where can I get a pair?"

"I picked them up in Italy. I can't remember where, sorry." My phone rings and when I see it's my mother calling, I ignore the call. I'll phone her back after Adeline leaves.

"I'm definitely going to search for a pair. They look so comfortable. I'd wear them everywhere."

"I do. And I don't even care that they're pajama pants."

She grins. "I knew I liked you the moment I met you. Have you tried that coffee shop yet? The one I recommended."

"Not yet. I haven't had time, but it's on my list for sure."

"I tried one of their new Nutella Sea Salt Cookies yesterday. It was so good." She stops talking for a second as her eyes light up. "We need a breakfast date on Monday! You, me, and a whole lot of Nutella before work. Please say yes."

"A breakfast date! Hell yes! Ohmigod, are breakfast dates a thing for you? You have no idea how much I love breakfast!" It's like Adeline just said all my magic words in one go: breakfast date, Nutella, cookies.

I ignore my ringing phone again as she laughs. "Breakfast dates are the best kinds of dates in my opinion." She reaches into her purse for her phone and hands it to me. "Put your number in. I'll text you later to plan it."

I key my number in and pass her phone back. When

my mom calls me again, I grimace. "I'm sorry, I need to quickly take this call. It's my mother and I think she's just going to keep calling until I answer."

Adeline waves me off. "Take your time."

"Thank you." I answer the call and say, "Hey, Mom."

"Charlize, thank goodness you finally answered." She sounds unnerved. "We've just had an extremely disappointing turn of events for the gala, and I don't know how we're going to fix it at this late notice."

"What's happened?"

"The emcee has pulled out, and since his presence has been instrumental in attracting attendees, the committee is in a state over this."

She's right that losing a top Hollywood actor as the emcee is extremely disappointing, but I'm unsure why she's telling me this. It's not like I can just wave a wand and produce another actor for her. "I'm sorry, Mom, but surely you'll find someone who can step into his shoes." I look at Adeline and mouth "Sorry" to which she shakes her head and mouths back "It's all good."

"Charlize," my mother snaps, and it's at this point that I realize she's more than unnerved. She's actually completely frazzled, which isn't a state I've ever seen my mother in. "These aren't shoes that can just be *stepped into*. Without the exact right replacement, our entire night is at risk."

Wow.

Okay.

My mother needs me to step up here. She needs someone to help calm her. To reassure her that she and her committee can pull this off.

If there's one thing I'm good at, it's taking charge and

managing situations that need managing. See: Owen. But also, see: all my previous EA jobs. This is what I do, so I can do it for my mom.

"I know I'm not a committee member, Mom, but I can help you find someone."

"No, I didn't call for that. I just got a little sidetracked there. It's quite stressful having to worry over something like this. What I called you for was to see how you're doing with getting in touch with the fund's past scholarship recipients. We'd like to finalize that portion of the night and know it at least is arranged."

One of my suggestions to the committee was to invite past recipients to attend the gala. The recipients who have gone on to success. Having the chance to speak with them might help the donors connect more deeply with the work the fund is doing and see how their donations make an impact.

"I've been in touch with the five recipients I mentioned. So far, four have agreed to attend. I'm just waiting to hear back from the last one. I'll follow up with her tonight and let you know ASAP."

"Thank you, Charlize." I hear her exhale a breath. "The committee will be very happy to hear this."

"Mom, I know people. I can find you someone to emcee." *People* might be exaggerating. I know Poppy and I know Dylan. I hope to God they know the kinds of people I think they do.

She's silent for a moment before finally saying, "Okay, we would appreciate your help. Please work fast. We don't have a lot of time."

When I end the call, I stare at Adeline. "Right, so I just told my mother I could do something that I'm not sure I can actually do. I may need a strong drink. And then I need to get to work because failing my mother on this is something I cannot do."

"I could hear your mother. She sounds stressed."

"She is." I tell her all about the gala and how I managed to get myself involved in it. I then tell her about the emcee pulling out, and about how I've never known my mother to experience stress like this. "So, now I have to be a good gala girl and figure out how to go *poof* and magically make a new emcee appear."

"I know people who might be able to help."

"Oh God, no, I didn't just tell you all that so you would help me."

She smiles. "I know. But seriously, I have a large network. Let me put some feelers out for you."

It's not often I meet women like Adeline. Women I feel comfortable with so fast. I return her smile. "Thank you. I would really appreciate that."

We move to the sofa and curl up there for the next hour. Jameson takes longer than his half hour with Owen but neither of us care. We're too engrossed in a conversation about our favorite restaurants in New York and London which veers into a conversation about art galleries and our favorite artists. When I tell Adeline that one of my favorite artists is Ione, she tells me that Jameson commissioned an erotic abstract of her done by Ione. I'm only a little jealous over that. I mean, one, I would die to meet Ione, let alone be painted by her. And two, I would die for a man I loved to commission that painting and hang it on his wall.

When she and Jameson leave, Adeline promises to text me about our breakfast date once she checks her schedule for Monday. She also promises to get onto her network tonight and find me the best emcee out there.

"I really like Adeline," I say to Owen as we walk into the kitchen so we can cook dinner. He gave his chef the night off again and I'm looking forward to spending time in the kitchen with him after seeing how relaxed he is in here.

"She's great. And she's been great for Jameson." He reaches into the fridge for some of the ingredients he needs.

"In what way?" I eye the onions on the countertop. "Do you want me to cut these up?"

"Yeah." He finds me a knife and chopping board.

While we work together, he tells me all about Jameson and how marrying Adeline has softened him a little and made him happier.

I think about that and about happiness.

And I think about how happy I've felt since meeting Owen.

I like spending time with him.

I like our big talk, our banter, our sex.

I like his thoughtfulness, his confidence, his natural leadership.

I like more things about Owen than I've ever liked about any man.

But most of all, I like *us*.

OWEN DROPS me at my place early Sunday morning on his way to golf with Bradford. I think we're both disappointed not to be spending the day together, but I decide it's probably for the best.

I tend to throw myself into a new guy, spending every spare minute with him. I think maybe I lose myself a little in the process. After taking the last year to figure out who I am without a man, and doing okay at figuring that out, I don't want to go backward. So, spending today with Dylan and then going to dinner at my parents will be good.

Dylan and I go out for lunch and catch up. We have a few drinks in the sun and I love getting this time with him. He's in one of his art-making phases, and when Dylan is making art, he's at his happiest.

After we have lunch and some drinks, we come home, and he plants himself on the sofa to watch a documentary while I sit at the table and work on some gala stuff for mom. Just after four p.m., I receive a text from Adeline.

Adeline: Can you do breakfast at six thirty tomorrow morning?

Charlize: Yes! Perfect.

Adeline: Also, do you mind if I bring a friend? I think you'll love her.

Charlize: I don't mind at all.

Adeline: Great. And can you send me the gala date and info? I've got a few people who might be able to do it if it works in with their schedule.

Charlize: Will do!! You are a godsend <3

"Who was that?" Dylan asks.

"Adeline." I told him all about her earlier when I also asked him if he knew anyone who might agree to emcee the gala. "She might have some people who can emcee."

He pauses the documentary and comes to sit with me. "Babe, you know if you can't find an emcee for your mom, it won't be the end of the world, right?"

I smile at the concern I see in his eyes and hear in his voice. "You love me, Dyl." This is the thing I say to him often. I sometimes wonder if I'm reminding myself that men can come into my life, and love me, and stay.

"You know I do, Char." He's looking at me so seriously, like he really wants me to hear whatever it is he has to say. "Just like I know how much your mom's approval means to you."

He's bringing the elephant in the room out. The one I try really hard to avoid.

I allocate a good amount of energy to telling anyone who will listen, including myself, that I don't need my mother's approval. It's not true. I'm not sure if there's any girl alive who, at some point in her life, didn't crave her mother's approval.

I swallow the feelings coming up over what he said. At least, I try to. "I'm never going to get it," I say softly, almost like I'm willing those words not to be right.

"Does it matter if you don't?"

I think about that for a long moment. "I think so." God, I wish *that* wasn't right.

His eyes search mine. "One of these days, you'll see what I see when I look at you. I can't fucking wait for that day." He leans back in his seat and crosses his arms. "I sent some texts to people who might be able to help you find an emcee. Between us all, we'll find your mom someone great."

"I love you, too, Dyl."

"Yeah," he says, like he has an infinite well of confidence. "I know."

MONDAY MORNING COMES FAST, but not fast enough.

After spending the day with Dylan yesterday, I spent a few hours at my parent's home last night for gala planning and our family dinner. Mom and I talked at length about the gala, going over every tiny detail. She's still stressed over the emcee situation. She's also concerned about an argument that has erupted between two of the women on the planning committee. I got the impression it all feels a little apocalyptic for her. I did my best to keep her focused and I feel like I was successful with that.

I'm on my way to my breakfast date with Adeline and her friend when Owen texts me.

Owen: Are you free for dinner tonight?

Charlize: I might be. I'll have to check my schedule and get back to you, Mr. North.

He calls almost as soon as I've sent the text.

"Aren't you supposed to be working?" I answer the call. It is 6:20 a.m. after all, Owen's prime working time.

"I'd be doing that if I wasn't sitting here thinking of ways to convince you to say yes to dinner tonight."

"Does this mean that work has been knocked off the top of your list of the four things you think about?"

"Charlize."

Oh, holy hot Monday morning growls.

"I'm free for dinner. And I promise I'll be your good girl."

"Fuck."

"Did you just run your fingers through your hair?"

"What?"

"When you swore, were your fingers in your hair? I've noticed you do that sometimes when I get you all bothered. It's hot and I think I'm adding it to my list of goals in life. I want to inspire you to mess your hair up more often."

I hear Julian's voice in the background, and Owen turns silent like he's listening to whatever Julian's saying.

Then, he comes back to me. "I have to go. I'll pick you up at seven tonight."

"Should I wear panties?"

"Jesus." Monday growls are fast becoming a new favorite of mine. "No."

"I like the way you think, Mr. North."

I end the call with a huge smile on my face. Who knew Mondays could be so good?

I carry on toward the coffee shop where I'm meeting Adeline, arriving eight minutes later. She's already here, sitting in the back with a blonde woman. They appear to be deep in discussion over something.

"Charlize," she greets me warmly when she spots me.

I take the seat across from them. "Do you know what I love?" I say as I get comfortable. "Early morning flirting. Is it not the best thing?"

Adeline laughs, and the blonde woman smiles as she says, "Oh, I love you already. And I agree, it's such a great way to begin a day."

"Right?!" I say.

"Charlize," Adeline says, "meet Jenna. Jenna, meet Charlize." She looks at me. "Jenna's my business partner, but we've also become good friends."

"It's lovely to meet you," I say to Jenna.

"Adeline has told me all about you," Jenna says. "I'm so excited that Owen's met you."

"You know Owen too?" I ask her.

"Yes, through my husband, Beckett."

"So," Adeline says, "Beckett and Jameson are in business together with another guy, Ashton. The three of them are currently working on a hotel development. Owen does some investment consulting for them. That's how we're all connected."

"Thank you for that," I say, liking that I can now connect it all in my mind.

Adeline eyes the counter. "I am so ready for Nutella. There was no flirting going on in my life this morning, so I need a chocolate hit."

"Why no flirting?" Jenna asks.

"Jameson was being his bossy self a little too well this morning. Let's just say that he'll have to work hard tonight if he wants his hands on me."

Jenna laughs. "I think we both know that's not true."

"Seriously," Adeline says, "why can't men pick up on our cues more often? I give him enough." She pushes her chair back and stands. "If I order five cookies, you now know why."

Jenna and I follow her to the counter, and I order one of the cookies Adeline told me about and one of the Nutella slices she mentioned at dinner.

We then spend the next hour eating the most amazing Nutella goodness, drinking coffee, and talking. Adeline and Jenna tell me all about the business they're building. They ask me about my work. We share stories about how we met the men in our lives. And we discuss the gala.

"I've spoken with Diana Black," Adeline says. "I think she may be able to emcee the gala for your mom. She's going to confirm with me today. I'll let you know as soon as I do."

Holy hell, my mother will be speechless if I get Diana Black for her.

Eyes wide, I say, "You are the absolute bomb, and I will owe you so much for this."

She waves me off. "It's nothing. This is why we have networks, Charlize. To get good things done in the world."

This sits with me all day.

Long after I say goodbye to Adeline and Jenna, I'm still thinking about this.

I've always looked down on my mother's network. I've judged them for wanting to climb the social ladder. For being what I saw as superficial.

They also do a lot of good work for the world.

Owen said that to me.

And now Adeline has mentioned it too.

Maybe I've been wrong.

Maybe there's a whole lot more to being a gala girl.

25

Charlize

Adeline: Okay, bad news. Diana Black can't emcee the gala. But all is not lost. I have more feelers out. Jett Vaughn may be able to do it! I'll keep you updated.

Charlize: Oh wow, I love his band!

Adeline: And he's a great guy too. He does a lot of charity work. He said he'd love to be involved in this if he can.

Adeline: Also, I have to cancel yoga tonight, sorry. Jameson has sprung a dinner party on me at the last minute.

Charlize: My body will thank you, I'm sure.

Adeline: LOL. Let's plan for another class soon!

Adeline and Jenna lured me into yoga at breakfast on Monday. I attended my first class with them last night. I'm not telling anyone yet that I think I liked it. I need to attend another class to make sure before broadcasting that kind of information.

"Charlize," Jill says as I read Adeline's last message. "How are you going with those reports?"

I glance up at her as she comes out of her office, looking at me expectantly. "I'll have them finished in about ten minutes."

I've worked hard to get these done for Jill today because I suspect she's having a bad day. She looked like she wanted to throw things in her office again this morning while muttering something about the article in *The New York Times*. I heard something like "Of course, they only mention me once."

She looks relieved when I tell her I'm almost finished with her reports. "Thank you. That's great." She pauses, smiling at me. "I've enjoyed working with you over the last few weeks, and I know Owen was impressed with your work in London. I wasn't sure if you were looking for more permanent work or not, but I checked to see if we have anything available or coming up. We don't, unfortunately, but a friend of mine knows someone looking for an executive assistant. Would you like me to pass your details on?"

"I am looking for full-time work. That would be great, thanks Jill."

All I can wonder as she leaves me to go back into her office is whether she'd be so quick to recommend me if she knew I fucked her ex-husband in his office this morning.

A cat.

My next life.

It's happening.

I finish up for the day and send Owen a text as I'm leaving.

Charlize: I never did get back to you about tonight. Dinner at 7?

Owen: I made the assumption I'd see you at 7.

Charlize: One should never assume.

Owen: One should never keep a man waiting all day.

I grin as my stomach somersaults all over itself.

Charlize: I'll see you at 7.

I'm home, showered, and dressed for dinner when I receive an email from the friend Jill passed my details onto. I read it three times before sitting on my bed and releasing a long breath.

The job sounds amazing.

The pay is fucking amazing.

And it starts in just over three weeks.

But I'll have to move to California for the job.

I stare at the four outfits hanging in my room. The outfits I'm considering for the concert Owen's taking me to.

He has no idea what this concert means to me.

I love live music but every boyfriend I've ever had has refused to go to a concert with me. I went to concerts with them, to their choice of bands, but whenever it came to my choice of music, they all said no.

Owen didn't even blink when I asked him to go with me to see Harry Styles. He checked his calendar as soon as we got home from that hike when I asked him and then told me he'd get the tickets.

I have the tickets.

I have the outfits.

I have the man who is doing everything he can to show me how much he wants me.

I don't know if I can move to California.

A text comes through from my mom as I'm contemplating all this.

Mom: Is it Owen North?

Charlize: Who told you that?

Mom: So, it is?

Charlize: Yes, but you can't tell anyone.

Mom: It's hardly a secret, Charlize. You were seen with him at Poppy's wedding.

Charlize: Okay, but please don't tell anyone. Not until we do.

Mom: I want you to bring him to dinner.

Charlize: Not yet. It's still early.

Mom: Well, soon.

Charlize: Yes, soon.

Mom: Any news on an emcee yet?

Charlize: I'm still working on it, but yes, we'll have one soon!!!

I add all those exclamation marks because they feel as jittery as I do right now.

A job in California.

A mother who wants to meet the man I'm seeing so she can try to persuade him to marry me.

An emcee I still haven't found.

It's all a little too much.

The cat life is looking better every hour.

∾

MY LAST DAY at North Management is uneventful.

That is, until four p.m. rolls around and Owen decides to really shake things up.

I'm on my way to my desk after just having come back up in the elevator from getting a coffee downstairs. I'm minding my own business, when a strong hand comes around my waist and pulls me into the boardroom.

I'm so startled that I almost spill coffee all over myself.

Owen saves it, though, taking it from me and placing it on the boardroom table. That's right before he puts his hands all over me, taking hold of my hips, and directing *me* to the table.

"I've been thinking about you all day," he rasps, his hands making their way down my dress, bunching it up as he goes.

"Owen," I say, but he silences me with a kiss before I can complete that sentence.

Holy mother of Friday afternoon quickies.

Owen is turned on, and when I say turned on, it should be spelled *hard as fuck*.

He kisses me like he *has* been thinking about me all day.

Like he can't get enough of me.

And while he's kissing me, his hands are pushing my dress up and tearing my panties off.

Like, ripping them off.

Into pieces.

"Fuck," he growls, his lips leaving mine for only a second to utter that word while his fingers slide through my pussy.

And then, he's lifting me onto the table and dragging

NINA LEVINE

his mouth from mine so he can kiss his way down my neck.

I arch my back and thread my fingers through his hair.

I grind myself into his hand, into his fingers.

"Fuck," I moan, wrapping my legs around his body.

And then, a loud noise comes from the other side of the door, and I'm reminded we're in the boardroom. And I don't think the door is locked.

"Owen," I say, but he doesn't respond.

He's moved on from kissing my neck to kissing all the way down my body to my pussy.

Laughter sounds from outside the door.

Owen buries his face in me while his hands slide under my ass so he can press me even harder against his face.

Dear God.

I want to just lie back and let him eat me.

But. We're. In. The. Boardroom.

I grip his hair so hard he can't ignore me.

When he gives me his eyes, I widen mine and ask, "Is the door locked?"

"No." With that, he goes back to what he was doing.

He sucks my clit and circles his tongue around it.

He licks every inch of my lips.

He presses his tongue inside me.

And all the while, a group of staff members stand outside the boardroom talking and laughing.

The thrill of getting caught proves to be the biggest turn on of life.

When Owen finally lifts his face from my pussy and

brings his mouth back to mine, I kiss him harder than I've ever kissed him.

I taste myself.

I feel myself on his beard.

I think about someone walking in on him fucking me.

And. I. Can't. Get. Enough.

He pulls his mouth from me and unzips himself.

He keeps his eyes firmly on mine as he lifts a finger to his mouth in a silencing motion.

When my lips lift into a smile, he leans in close and says, "I'm going to have to keep you quiet, aren't I?"

I take hold of his neck with both hands and smile into a kiss before saying, "Yes, Mr. North, you are."

"Jesus, Charlize, I can't fucking get enough of you," he says right before pulling me to the edge of the table, hooking one of my legs around him, placing one of his hands over my mouth tightly, and slamming inside me.

I cling to him while he fucks me.

The group outside keep talking.

And Owen silences all my noise while making me come hard.

When we're done, we both go into the bathroom that joins the boardroom and clean up.

As I'm fixing my hair in the mirror, Owen moves behind me. "I'm going to miss having you here."

"That's only because you'll miss being able to boss me into doing inappropriate things here. Who knew office sex could be so hot?"

"Not me," he says before kissing my neck.

"Wait." I frown. "You've never had sex in the office?"

"No." His eyes meet mine in the mirror again.

"But you and Jill worked together for years."

"We never had sex here."

I stare at him like I don't understand a word coming out of his mouth.

"Why not?" I mean, this isn't weird at all, discussing his sex life with his ex-wife, but I can't wrap my head around the thought of it.

"Jill always complained I worked too much. The truth was, I did."

I turn to face him. "Well, I'd just like to say, for the record, that I quite like doing inappropriate things with you, Mr. North." I stand on my toes and kiss him. "But now, I have to go and drink my coffee while completing the three million jobs Jill has asked me to complete before I finish today."

"You're breaking your *no caffeine after two p.m.* rule."

I really like that he remembers the things I tell him. "It's Friday and I can sleep in tomorrow. Plus, I think a man I know might keep me up all night, so I can probably do with the caffeine."

With that, I let him give me one more kiss, I rescue my coffee, and I go back to my desk to finish out my time at North Management.

~

POPPY: I'm having a cocktail to celebrate the end of your work at Owen's company.

Charlize: I'm about to celebrate in other ways. If I was married, I'd say Owen's giving me the eye.

Poppy: My mother asked me today if you're seeing Owen. I have to commend you on keeping a secret from the Winters sisters for three weeks, Charles. That's a secret-keeping record for you.

Charlize: I'm excelling at life these days. Queen Secret Keeper, Queen Gala Girl, Queen Good Girl. Just give me a crown and be done with it.

Poppy: Have you got an emcee yet?

Charlize: I think so! Jett Vaughn seems ready to confirm.

Charlize: I do have something we need to discuss, though. I got a job offer.

Poppy: You don't sound excited.

Charlize: I'm not. It's in California.

Poppy: I forbid you, under any circumstance, to take that job. Thank you, but next.

Charlize: I don't know. I need some Poppy time to talk about it.

Poppy: Tomorrow afternoon?

Charlize: Yes <3

I put my phone down and go in search of Owen who's actually not giving me the eye. It's almost nine p.m. and he brought me home to his place to cook me dinner and spend the night with me. Instead, he received a phone call from Julian as we walked out of the elevator, and he's been working ever since. I cooked dinner which he ate with me, but then he went straight back to work.

He glances up from his desk when I enter his office. Cursing softly, he stops typing and leans back in his seat. "I lost track of time, sorry," he says.

I go to him and curl up on his lap. "It's okay. I get it." I kiss him. "How much more have you got to do?"

He lets out a breath. "Probably about an hour."

I run my hand down his chest, resting it on his stomach. "Okay."

He kisses me again, taking hold of my neck. "Thank you for understanding."

I leave him and go into his bathroom to take a bath.

I have a long bath, hoping Owen will come and join me.

Spoiler alert: he doesn't.

However, he does wander into the bathroom as I'm drying myself.

Coming to me, he reaches for the towel. "You don't need this."

With that, he takes me to his bed and spends the next couple of hours giving me his full attention.

He's extremely strenuous about it all.

It's a good thing he's not golfing with Bradford this weekend.

The last thing I say to him before I pass out from all that strenuous activity is, "I know it's my turn in the coffee war tomorrow morning, but I really think you're going to have to take one for the team. I think you killed my legs tonight."

I fall asleep with Owen's arms around me, a kiss pressed to my forehead, and his deep voice saying, "Goodnight, beautiful."

There are only four thoughts in my head as I drift off.

One: My legs really are dead.

Two: I'm really glad I have Owen to myself all weekend.

Three: Can I really see myself moving to the other side of the country, away from him?

And four: This really is happening very fast.

26

Owen

"Y ou've been stretching your neck like you want to stretch it right off your head," Charlize says after I finish brushing my teeth. "I feel like you need yoga in your life."

I chuckle and pull her into my arms. "Look how far you've fallen. A week ago, you told me Adeline and Jenna lured you into yoga. Now, *you're* trying to lure *me* in."

She grins and presses her lips to mine. After she kisses me, she says, "I know, I know, but seriously, Owen, it really helps your back. You can't deny you've been grumbling about your back for the last few days, and now your neck is out. Come to tonight's yoga class with me."

"What time is it?"

"Six p.m. or seven thirty. I'm easy for either time."

Since Charlize finished working for North Management last week, she's back searching for a job. She picked up a temp job on Monday, but had yesterday off, and doesn't have anything for today or the rest of the week so far.

"Okay, maybe the seven thirty class. It'll just depend how today goes. I've got a meeting at five thirty which may run late."

"I'll book us in, and we can just cancel your spot if you can't make it."

A text comes through for her and she reads it.

"Holy shit," she breathes, eyes wide. "Adeline got Jack Kingsley for the gala. I was beginning to think I'd have to force you to get up there and do it, but Jack has said yes."

"I thought Jett Vaughn was doing it?"

"He was, but something happened yesterday that meant he had to cancel."

I frown. "You didn't mention it last night."

"You were distracted by work." She smiles. "But all is good now, and Mom can stop losing her mind over all this."

She's right. I was distracted by work last night. Julian and I have been working long hours going over our current strategies. I've also been having lunches with various industry people in my efforts to win the Bluestone Award, which means I often have work to catch up on at night.

"She's been losing her mind?"

"A little. To be honest, though, she seems to have calmed down and put this in my hands. She sent me the nicest text yesterday thanking me for all the work I've put into the gala."

I note the pride on Charlize's face. Her mother's

approval means a lot to her, which isn't something that surprises me after the things she's shared with me over the last month.

"She'll be happy with Jack Kingsley," I say. He's one of the world's biggest movie stars.

She cocks her head. "Have you met him? I got the impression that Adeline knows him?"

"Jack's married to Ashton's COO, so I've met him once through her. I think Adeline knows him through her work, but I've never gotten the impression they're close friends."

"Well, I don't know much about him, but I suddenly adore him."

I tighten my arms around her. "If you watched action films rather than those romances you keep trying to force on me, you'd know Jack." Charlize has introduced me to her love of watching movies late at night in bed. I've taken to working in bed next to her, occasionally glancing up and catching some of whatever romantic comedy she's got playing.

"One of these days, you are going to give one of my romantic comedies your undivided attention, and you will see why they should be on your list of movies to watch."

I brush my lips over hers before letting her go and checking the time on my phone. "Fuck, I have to go." It's almost seven. I wanted to be at work two hours ago.

Charlize grasps my shirt and blesses me with a smile. "I loved our morning, Owen," she says softly, and any regret I had over going to work later than I wanted is erased.

"Me too." I slide my fingers into her hair and pull her

mouth to mine for one last kiss. I take my time with this one, and when I finally let her go, she's as breathless as I am. "I'll be at that yoga class tonight. And then we'll have a late dinner together."

IT's a long day of meetings, and of Jill.

She arrives in my office a couple of minutes after I do and proceeds to unleash her thoughts on the new strategies Julian and I have been mapping out. I sent them to her late last night for her consideration and she's not happy with them.

"I don't understand why I wasn't involved in this," she says, her eyes flashing with anger. "I'm the COO, Owen. God knows why, though, when it's clear you'd rather have Julian by your side."

I loosen my tie. "You're involved in it now, Jill. And I'd appreciate your thoughts on it."

She stares at me. "Do you ever listen to me? I'm standing here telling you I want to have a discussion about who you want as your COO, and you're standing there not even addressing that."

"You didn't say you wanted to discuss that. You simply stated that you are the COO."

"Yes! And I said I don't understand why!"

Fuck.

This argument will go round and round, and not achieve a damn thing if I let it continue. Jill has a way of not saying what she means, and I have a way of misunderstanding almost everything she wants me to hear.

"Okay." I push out a breath. "Would you like to

discuss your COO role?" Fuck knows, I don't have the time for this today, but something tells me I need to make the time for it.

"Yes, but not right now. Can we talk tonight?"

"I can't tonight. I can come in early tomorrow morning or stay back tomorrow night. Or you tell me when is good for you."

"Tonight is better for me, but I can rearrange things and do it tomorrow morning at ten."

I nod. "Done."

Julian passes her on her way out. She doesn't say a word to him, and I can't see her face, but I assume she doesn't give him a smile.

"She doesn't look friendly today," he says as I sit at my desk.

"No, and I suspect tomorrow's not going to be any better."

I fill him in on my conversation with her, suggesting we put our new strategy ideas on hold until I speak with her tomorrow.

I see Jill three more times during the day. She snaps and snarls at me each time over whatever issue she brings up.

As the day goes on, I wonder what will become of our talk tomorrow. She's right that I would prefer Julian as my COO, but only because my working relationship with her has become almost too difficult to be effective. The simple fact of the matter is that if Jill wasn't my ex-wife, and I didn't have all the emotional baggage I have with her, I wouldn't keep her on as COO. I've reached the point where I can't ignore that any longer.

"Did you love it?" Adeline asks as we pack up our mats from the yoga class we've just done.

"I learned that my ankles are stiff and I'm inflexible," I say.

Charlize laughs. "But did you love it?"

I eye her yoga pants and the tank she's wearing. I can't say I loved the class, but I can say I enjoyed being with Charlize. I spent a great deal of time glancing at her so I could understand the sequence and positions. She understood my struggle and gave me the cues I needed. I enjoyed that connection, not to mention watching her move her body.

"I'd come to another class."

"Good." She smiles.

We say goodbye to Adeline and then Charlize says, "I was thinking we could order takeout from the place where you got those lobster noodles from. And that we could sleep at my place tonight."

"Are you missing your bed?" We've spent most of our nights together at my condo.

"I'm missing Dylan and he said he'd be home tonight."

I've briefly met her friend once when we were at her place, and I'd like the opportunity to spend time with him. I also don't want Charlize missing her people or her own space. "He could have dinner with us."

Her eyes light up. "I'll text him to see if he's eaten yet."

She confirms he hasn't had dinner and that he'd like to eat with us. I order food on the way to her condo and once I've placed the order, she moves closer to me in the back of the car. "Thank you."

"For ordering dinner?"

"No, for tonight. For coming to yoga with me, for having dinner with Dylan, for staying at my place. I know you're busy with work, so I appreciate you taking the time for all this."

"These aren't things you thank me for doing, Charlize. These are things people do when they want to be with someone."

"I know, and I agree, but I also think it's important to acknowledge that I appreciate your choices. I always want you to know I'm not taking you for granted."

What she says triggers something in my brain, but I can't quite grasp it. It was something someone said to me recently, I think.

I let it go when she brings up the yoga class with me again. We fill the rest of the drive to her place with this conversation.

We talk about my yoga experience, her love of the classes she's taken so far, the classes she wants to take, the yoga retreats she's found to attend, the yoga pants she's thinking of buying, and how great her body feels thanks to the yoga.

"You're a fanatic after one week," I say as we walk into her bedroom. "Is this a yoga thing or should I prepare for your fanaticism over many things?"

"Well," she grins, "based on my fanaticism for your dick, it may be a problematic trait of mine. You should absolutely prepare yourself for this being a part of your future."

I pull her close and kiss her. "Consider me prepared."

She blinks. "Just like that?"

I keep my eyes firmly on hers. "Just like that."

She stares at me. "Is this a problematic trait of *yours*? Like, do you always just accept women who obsess over things, and who think about things far too much, and who talk your ear off about these things? I mean, I know you have your stalker tendencies, Owen, but maybe you might want to be more selective with who you choose to stalk."

"I'm being extremely selective, Charlize. Trust me on that."

She must hear something in my voice that she connects with, or perhaps it's what I said, because she loops her hands around my neck, and says, "I would do so many inappropriate things to you right now if Dylan wasn't about to arrive home." She pauses before softly adding, "Also, I can't believe I ever thought using you for sex for a year would be enough."

She kisses me and then leaves to go into the bathroom.

I glance around her bedroom, noting the scattered clothes, the open books piled beside her bed, the make-up crowding her bureau, the shoes kicked off in random places, and the three outfits hanging in one corner.

I wouldn't have Charlize any other way.

And if she ever thought I was only going to allow her to use me for sex for one year, she was very mistaken.

The last thing that catches my eye is the hotel key card from London sitting on her bureau.

I wasn't aware she'd kept it.

Charlize was in deep denial over the one year of sex.

She's been keeping memories of me since our first night together.

I ARRIVE at the office at five a.m. the next day. I've come in early to run on the treadmill while going over my fund's current positions. I've also come in to prepare for my meeting with Jill.

At seven-thirty, Ron walks in.

"We need to talk," he says, and I know deep in my gut what the outcome of this conversation is going to be.

"You're pulling your money."

"Yes. I'm giving you my notice of withdrawal. I'm out next quarter."

I've crunched the numbers enough times over the last few weeks to know we can survive without Ron. I was wrong when I told Jill there weren't ten more Rons to be found. That was my fear talking, and I've come to see that. But still, there's an ugly feeling that comes with losing your biggest investor. With failing to convince him your company is worth investing in. With failing to carry on the North name like my father expected.

I could ask him to give me twenty-four hours. To have my conversation with Jill about her COO position. Because that's what he wanted; he wanted her gone. But I'm not going to ask for that time because I don't know what decision Jill and I will come to today. And also, I refuse to compromise my principles for him.

I nod, my chest growing tighter. "I wish you well wherever you go."

"That's it, Owen? You're not even going to fucking fight for me?"

I work my jaw. *Fight for him?* What the fuck does he think I've been doing all these years with him? "I fought for you every day, Ron. That's what I do. I give my all, day-in, day-out for my investors. I make sure you get what's promised, and I make sure you get that above and beyond. I'm in the fucking ring fighting hard every second of every day for you." I step closer to him, my entire body rigid. "What I won't *ever* do is compromise my values to gain. I won't walk all over someone or walk away from them. If I'm not the kind of man you can believe in, you can take your money today. I won't make you wait another quarter."

His lip pulls up in a snarl. "She's not worth this."

I square my shoulders. "I might not be married to her anymore, but I care about her more than you care about your own wife. Yes, she made a mistake, but if all we ever looked for in people was perfection, we'd be looking a long fucking time. And as far as money goes, I like making it, but I also like knowing I can sleep at night because I didn't fuck someone over to do that." Julian joins us as I say, "Now get the fuck out of my office, Ron. And don't ever come back."

"You're a fucking idiot, Owen," Ron sneers, contempt plastered across his face. "She'll ruin you if you let her."

I'm about to reiterate that I want him out of here when Jill storms in, yelling, "I knew it!" Her wild eyes come to me, and she jabs a finger my way. "I knew you were trying to push me out!"

"Fuck." I yank at my tie to loosen it. "Jill, calm down, this—"

"Don't tell me to calm down, Owen! God help you if you ever say those words to me again!"

Ron looks at me like his point has just been proven. "Good fucking luck with this. You're going to need it."

Jill stares after him as he strides out of the office.

Julian takes this moment to get a word in. "I'll leave you two to this."

Jill's head whips around and she focuses her attention on him. "No! If you two are planning to get rid of me, I want to know."

"There's no plan, Jill," Julian says.

"I don't believe that." I've never seen her so enraged. "You two have been slowly pushing me out for a year. Ron sent me a text an hour ago telling me he hoped I wouldn't miss my office too much after you fired me today, so I know you're going to use this as your opportunity to get rid of me."

Jesus.

Jill continues giving Julian a piece of her mind, including every angry thought I think she's had this year before turning to me and yelling, "And *you're* seeing someone and falling in love, and it'll only be a matter of time before I mean even less to you than I already do! I refuse to give up everything I've worked so hard for, Owen. I made so many choices for you, gave up so much, and let you take me for granted for too long. I'll be damned if I don't make all of that worth it. And—"

"Ron is out!" I yell, needing to gain her attention somehow. "You're not going anywhere."

Her mouth slams closed, and she stares at me. "What did you just say?"

I wrench my tie off and throw it on my desk. "I told him he can take his money today. We're done with him."

She continues staring at me, speechless for the first time in a long time.

"That's my cue to leave," Julian says.

I nod before stalking to the window and gazing out over Manhattan.

My body is filled with a roaring energy.

It's turbulence like I've never known.

My thoughts are all fucked up and I don't know where to begin with them.

Silence fills the office while Jill and I gather ourselves.

Finally, she comes to stand next to me. "I remember the day we moved into these offices. I was so proud of you. Of everything you'd achieved."

I remember that day too but for different reasons to Jill.

I was twenty-six and felt so far behind the game already. If my father had still been alive, I was sure he would have told me that.

I worked for nineteen hours in this office that first day. I then worked sixteen-hour days for years after that. I was determined to get ahead of the game.

I look at Jill. "I'm sorry I wasn't present in our marriage."

Shock covers her face.

I'm not surprised. I've never apologized for this.

In all the therapy we did, all the yelling, all the conversations, I accepted blame for many things, but I never once told her I was sorry for not showing up like I should have.

"You sacrificed a lot for me, Jill, and I want you to know I saw it all even if I didn't acknowledge it."

"Thank you for saying that," she says softly.

"You will always mean something to me. I want you to know that. But you have to accept our marriage is over."

She takes her time responding to that, her voice wavering when she does. "I know it's over, Owen. I'm just having trouble letting go because even though I know deep in my heart that we were never compatible, I loved you with everything I had." She gives me a small smile. "You were my first everything. It's hard to let go of your first. And I'm learning it's even harder to watch him fall for his next."

"You know about Charlize?"

She nods. "Yes, I didn't know who until this morning when I saw a photo of you with her at a yoga class last night on a celebrity Instagram post, but I've been seeing the signs for weeks. A woman knows when her ex-husband is falling in love because she was once the girl who made him act like that."

I look back out over the city, thinking about when we first met and how we spent so many of our days helping each other study. "Do you ever think about working in law?" Jill got her law degree just before we opened these offices. She always planned on using that degree but working here took over and she never spoke of it again.

"Yes."

I hear so much in that one word.

Regret.

Sadness.

Hope.

"I think you should consider it."

"I have been," she says. "I think I've known since our divorce that my place isn't really here. Letting go is hard all the way around."

I look down at her. "It's one of the hardest things I've ever had to do."

She takes her time running her gaze over my face before saying. "Thank you for taking my back with Ron."

"Always."

We turn silent for a while until she gently bumps her shoulder against me. "You would never have gone to yoga with me."

I watch her walk out of my office and I know I'll be watching her walk out of my life soon. We're done carving bad lines into each other's heart. Now, it's time for us both to let someone new carve good ones.

27

Charlize

Poppy: I respectfully must turn down your request for me to attend your yoga class tonight.

Charlize: You are the worst cousin of life.

Poppy: Charles, you have to be a good gala girl tomorrow. I'm unsure why you're even going to yoga tonight. Don't you have last minute jobs before the gala?

Charlize: It's a good thing I have a boyfriend who is willing to take one for the team and come to yoga.

Poppy: Take that back!

Poppy: Also, do you realize you just called him your boyfriend? Does this mean you've FINALLY turned that job in California down?

Charlize: There is such a thing as a long-distance relationship, you know.

Poppy: Pfft. No one wants one of those. And don't think I haven't noticed your avoidance of two things: the fact you're now referring to Owen as your boyfriend, and your refusal to turn that job down. Surely they won't wait much longer for your answer.

Charlize: Ugh, they convinced the girl currently doing the job to stay on for a bit longer. I have to tell them by the end of this weekend.

Poppy: Have you told Owen?

Charlize: No.

Poppy: Good. That tells me you don't plan on taking it, which makes me very happy. As you were.

"Charlize," my mother says, drawing my attention from Poppy. "I'd like us to go over the program for tomorrow night one more time. I'd especially like to discuss how we will allocate the volunteers."

Mom and I are with the committee at the venue where the gala will be held. We're going over every little detail for tomorrow one last time. The fascinating thing for me is just how much my mother is seeking my input on everything.

"Absolutely," I agree.

We're ten minutes into this when one of the committee members interrupts and says, "Jack Kingsley is here." She points at the doorway where I see a dark-haired man standing with a shorter dark-haired woman. "Can you break for a minute to talk with him about tomorrow night?"

"You go," Mom says. "I'll keep working on this. We've got a lot of volunteers to sort through."

I smile. "Okay. I won't be too long."

I make my way to Jack who is deep in conversation with the woman.

"Hi," I say when I reach them. "I'm Charlize."

Jack shakes my hand, his mouth spreading out into a smile I bet millions of women around the world would die to see up close. "Charlize. It's great to meet you. I'm Jack and"—he looks down at the dark-haired woman—"this is Jessica, my wife."

Jessica smiles at me. "Hi Charlize. You're in luck today." Their Australian accents are giving me life.

"Okay?" I have no idea what she means.

"I kept him alive just for you today." She gives Jack the kind of look a wife gives her husband when she's exasperated with him. "I even abstained from bringing my fishing spear with me. You're welcome."

I laugh and glance between them. Jessica still has that same look on her face while Jack is grinning down at her with the kind of adoration every woman wants a man to look at her with.

He meets my gaze. "In my defense, I was not aware that when a woman opens multiple tabs on a computer, she might still want them a week later."

My eyes widen while I fake gasp, "You *didn't*?"

Jessica's eyes widen back at me. "He *did*."

"I'd just like to point out those tabs had been open for one week," Jack says. "Not one hour, not one day, but a whole *week*."

I hook my arm through Jessica's. "Oh, Jack, I'm not sure you can be our emcee after all. I think maybe we'll get Jessica to do it." With that, I guide her to the front of the room while saying, "Honestly, computers need to come with a warning for all men: *Leave our tabs alone.*"

"I could not agree more," she says.

"I don't know what a fishing spear is, but I feel like one could come in handy."

"I do like to threaten Jack with it often."

Jack's voice comes from behind us. "If you two don't need me, I'm more than happy to find a game of golf somewhere."

I stop walking and turn to him. "Really? Golf? I thought so highly of you until this very second."

He grins. "Fuck, you and Jessica are going to get on too well."

"The attire," Jessica says with a shudder. "It's so wanky."

I laugh. "That might be my new favorite word."

Jessica looks at me. "You don't use it?"

"I never have, but it will be all I say from now on."

"You have to agree, though? About the clothing golfers wear," she says.

"I haven't seen my man in his golfing attire yet. We've got a date for a game of golf on Sunday, so I can report back after that."

She looks horrified. "Don't do it, Charlize. Chasing a ball around with a stick for hours? You will live to regret it."

"I'd love to hear your report," Jack says. "And don't listen to my wife. She's still to agree to a game with me. She doesn't know what she's missing."

Jessica shakes her head at him. "I recall playing a game with you when we first met." She looks at me.

"Men. They think they remember everything, but they don't."

Jack gives her another one of his loved-up gazes before saying to me, "Right, tell me about tomorrow night."

We spend half an hour going over the gala program. For all his playfulness, Jack is serious while I need him to be, which I appreciate.

When we're finished, I say, "I can't thank you enough for agreeing to do this."

He smiles and it's a genuinely warm smile. "It just so happened that we were going to be in New York this week. And I looked up the Scholarship Fund. They're doing important work. I'm more than happy to help."

Mom joins us and I introduce her to Jack and Jessica. When they leave ten minutes later, she says, "I'm so proud of you, Charlize."

I would fall off my chair if I was sitting on it. "Because I got Jack to emcee?"

She smiles. "No, because you've done an amazing job helping the committee turn what was a good gala into a great one. I hope you'll consider helping us again next year."

Hearing these words from my mother feels like basking in the sun. Warmth and happiness float through me. *I* feel like I'm floating. I must surely be glowing from the inside out.

And then, while I revel in my mother's approval, I realize she's right. And it doesn't matter whether she thinks it or not, I *have* done an amazing job helping with the gala. On top of that, I've enjoyed it and am enjoying seeing it come together.

I pull out my phone and text Owen.

Charlize: I just realized something a little disturbing.

Owen: What?

Charlize: I'm a gala girl.

Owen: And you're a damn good one.

Charlize: I may need many snacks tonight to process this.

Owen: I'll ensure I have what you need at my place in case we stay there tonight.

Charlize: How will you know what I need?

Owen: Trust me, I know your favorites.

Charlize: I forgot, you're a stalker.

Charlize: Are you having a good day?

Owen: I'm behind on a million things. You?

Charlize: I just met Jessica Kingsley. My day is at one hundred.

Owen: Did you meet Jack too?

Charlize: Oh, yes, he was here too.

Charlize: My mother is motioning at me like she either has constipation or she needs my help. I'm hoping it's not constipation she needs my help with. I better go. I'll see you at yoga tonight.

It's only later, when I think about this text conversation, that I realize I texted Owen about my gala girl epiphany. Usually, I would text that kind of thing to Poppy or Dylan.

MOM and I work through the afternoon, finishing up at four p.m. I go home after that, shower, and get ready for the yoga class Owen and I are taking at seven thirty. I hang out with Dylan for a while, catching up on the art he's made this week and the travel he's got coming up to show his art. He and I are in the middle of a discussion over his work plans for next year when Owen calls.

"Hey, you," I answer, smiling as I think of him.

"Hi," he says, and I instantly hear his stress.

"What's wrong?"

"Two things. I can't make it to yoga tonight, sorry. Something's come up here and I have to work late with Julian to fix it."

"It's okay. I get it."

"I hate canceling on you. Particularly when I also have to cancel the Harry Styles concert."

"Oh, okay," I say slowly. I'm absolutely more disappointed about the concert than the yoga class.

"I got a call from the Bluestone Award people today. They've invited me to a dinner that's on that night. Only one person gets the call for this dinner, and that's the person who always goes on to win the award. If I don't attend, I won't have any chance of winning." He pauses. "I'm sorry, Charlize."

"I understand, Owen. You don't need to apologize for this. I know that award is important to you."

"Going to the concert was also important to me," he says, his voice revealing the honesty in what he's saying. "I hope you know that."

"I do."

"Okay, I have to go. I'll call you later."

After we end the call, I stare at my phone for a long time, lost in thought.

I understand why Owen can't come to the concert, but

disappointment isn't something you can just wipe away. I'm really disappointed about this. I'd even narrowed my outfits down and selected *the one*.

Next time.

There'll be many more concerts for us to attend when he's not busy with work.

I WAKE EARLY on Saturday morning, the day of the gala. I'm meeting Mom and the committee at the venue at seven a.m. to begin the long day of setting up for tonight.

I send Owen a text, checking to see how he is after a long night at work.

Charlize: Hey, sexy man. I'm on my way out the door. How are you today? How late did you work last night?

Owen: I got home around two.

I call him. "Tell me you're actually asleep and I'm communicating with your clone. There's no way you've had enough sleep."

"Fuck, I missed waking up with you today." God, he sounds exhausted.

"I missed that too. But seriously, Owen, I know I'm not telling you anything you don't already know; you need sleep." I only just manage to stop myself from telling him he works too much. I don't want to nag him about this.

"I've still got some work to do today and then I'll take tomorrow off."

"Maybe we should postpone our golf game tomorrow so you can rest all day."

"Golf *is* resting to me. We're not canceling that. Not when I've had to work hard to get you to agree to it."

He won't budge on this. I'm learning that while Owen can be easygoing, he likes to stick to his plans. "Okay."

"I've got that meeting at four this afternoon and then I'll come and help you with any last-minute jobs."

"Thank you. Okay, go. The sooner you get through your work, the sooner you can go home and rest."

"Was that Owen?" Dylan asks, joining me in the kitchen as I slip my phone in my purse.

"Yes."

"Are we still on for drinks before he woos your mother at dinner on Sunday?"

It took my mother only two weeks to break me down and agree to bring Owen to a family dinner. *Two weeks.* I'm off my game.

I nod. "I thought we could go to that new bar you love."

"Yeah, if Owen's cool with that."

"Owen's cool with anything." I smile. "He just wants to get to know you."

"I like him, Char. But more importantly, I like him for you."

My chest does the weird fluttery thing it does when I'm nervous. "It's all happening really fast, though, isn't it?"

"Stop overthinking this, babe. It's happening as fast as it should."

"Sometimes I feel swept up in it, like I'm going to lose myself all over again after just beginning to find myself, you know?"

Dylan's gaze is serious, strong like he's resolved about

whatever he's about to say. "Owen is not Benjamin. I can pick a Benjamin from a fucking mile away, and Owen doesn't even come close."

I swallow down my nerves and my fears. "I know you're right. I guess I just need a reminder every now and then."

"I'll remind you whenever you need me to." He checks his watch. "Okay, we better go, or your mother is going to have my balls for getting you there late."

I roll my eyes. "My mother loves you too much to ever hurt your precious balls." It's true. She once had ideas about marrying me off to Dylan, she loved him that much. We had to sit her down and explain that if we lived together long term, we'd stab each other to death. Dylan and I love each other, but not in an *I want to live with you forever* kind of way.

He drives me into Manhattan and drops me off with a promise to be on time for the gala.

Mom is already at the venue, in full Joan Cohen bossy control, and soon has me busy helping with the room decorations.

The day flies by.

Mom and I manage to have only eleven disagreements.

I'm taking that as success because it means I kept my mouth shut at least twenty times.

Everything is going well until the caterers cause mass stress at DEFCON 1 level.

At five p.m.

One hour before the gala starts.

One. Freaking. Hour.

"Charlize," Mom says sharply when she finds me

hiding in a corner. Well, I wasn't actually hiding, but if I'd thought of doing that, I would have. "Please tell me you've got this under control."

"Yes," I squawk. I really do sound like a bird right now. I can't even deny it.

Mom's eyes almost hit her eyebrows. "Why don't I believe you?"

Deep breaths.

In. Out.

In. Out.

I can do this.

Just because the catering manager quit and stormed out fifteen minutes ago, taking ten of his staff with him, including his Michelin-trained chefs, doesn't mean this night can't still be a success.

We may just need to redefine *success*.

Composing myself, I stand tall and fake a whole lot of confidence I'm not currently feeling. "Please believe me, Mom. I'm finding people to replace the staff that left. They will be here as soon as possible, and the dinner will go ahead as planned. You go and do your thing and leave this with me."

I must sound convincing because she exhales a breath and says, "Thank you, Charlize. Please keep me updated."

With that, she leaves me to get back to redefining success.

I'm five minutes into that when Jack and Jessica arrive. The committee member who greets them directs them to me because I've been their point of contact all along.

"Why do you look so pale?" Jessica frowns.

"Because my mother insisted on bringing in our own catering team rather than using the team here, and our catering manager just quit and took ten of his staff with him. Trying to find replacement staff at this late notice is proving difficult." I suck air in. "I'm not sure why I ever thought it was a good idea to become a gala girl."

Jessica laughs. "A gala girl?"

"It's what I've always called my mother and her girls who run these galas. To be honest, it came from a mean place. I thought they were just trying to climb the social ladder. I've learned there's so much more to being a gala girl."

"Right, so gala girls are good?"

I smile. Just talking with her has helped take my mind off my stress for a few moments, and sometimes that's what my anxiety needs. A moment of reprieve. "Yes."

"Okay," she says, and suddenly she sounds all boss babe. "Let's get to work."

I frown while Jack grins. Glancing between them, I say, "Get to work?"

"My wife just put her bossy pants on," Jack says. "I haven't let her wear them today, so she's itching to get them out. I'll leave you girls to it."

As he turns to leave, I say, "Wait, Jack. Do you have everything you need for tonight?" My brain races through everything, trying to remember if there's anything I forgot to tell him.

He looks at me. "I just have to get up there and talk for a bit. You've given me all I need. I've got this."

Jessica swings into action as her husband walks away from us. "I used to be an executive assistant, so I can help you with this. Let's take the list of people you're calling and break it in half and work our way through it. If worse comes to worst, I'll roll my sleeves up and help your caterers myself."

I want to ask her if she's even a real person.

I also want to ask her to be my new best friend.

Well, maybe not that. I'm far too loyal to the bestie I already have.

But seriously.

"Thank you," I gush, releasing a weight of tension from my body.

I share my list with her, and we make quick work of it.

Fifteen minutes later, we've got enough staff on their way to ensure the dinner will go ahead as planned.

"I can't thank you enough," I say to Jessica.

She waves me off. "You would have handled it on your own if I wasn't here."

"Yes, but having you here helped me focus, so I appreciate that."

"Right, I'm going to go and rescue whoever my husband is talking to. That man has a way of talking people's ears off. If you need help with anything else, please come find me. I'm your girl."

I find Mom after Jessica leaves and let her know the catering situation is no longer at DEFCON 1 level. The look of pure gratitude she gives me is one I want to bottle and keep forever. It quickly disappears, though, replaced by her strict mothering look while she directs me to the next task she has for me.

At six p.m., attendees begin making their way into the ballroom.

My job is behind-the-scenes, so I only catch a quick

glimpse of all the beautiful gowns before getting back to work

Poppy and Seth arrive. She's been texting me throughout the day, making sure I haven't killed my mother yet. She texts me when she's at her table.

Poppy: I just met Jessica Kingsley. I think she's a mermaid just like you.

Charlize: LOL. Why?

Poppy: She seems fiercely independent and head-strong. I like her, but then we both know I have a soft spot for mermaids.

Charlize: Is Owen here? I haven't heard from him.

Poppy: Can't see him. Will let you know when I do.

"Charlize." I look up to find a committee member coming my way, worry etched onto his face. "We've got a situation and need your help."

I'm learning that when it comes to a gala, the words "a situation" never mean anything good.

This situation turns out to be the fact that one of the gala attendees just knocked a candelabra over, meaning we now have a table that requires fixing after the fire ruined the tablecloth and decorations.

I refrain from finding my mother and telling her I was right about the candelabras. I told her I could only see trouble ahead with them. She refused to listen and now, here we are.

At 6:30 p.m., while I'm in the middle of the cande-labra debacle, I receive a text from Owen.

Owen: I'm running late. I'm sorry I didn't make it in time to help you.

I don't have time to reply to his message. I'm too busy

managing decorations and people who need a table to sit at.

After I finish with that table, I glance around the room and take a moment to catch my breath. My eyes land on Adeline who is waving at me to come over.

I've filled a table with Owen's and my friends. Adeline, Jameson, Jenna, Beckett, Jack, Jessica, Poppy, Seth, Bradford, Cecelia, Dylan, and his date are seated at the table Owen and I will also sit at.

They're happily chatting when I join them.

"This is amazing," Adeline says, eyeing the room. "It's all so beautiful, Charlize. Congratulations."

"Thank you. Although, the candelabras are a danger. Don't let anyone near yours."

"Oh, I saw the fire. I've already told our people not to get too boisterous."

Our people.

I like that.

A lot.

"Charlize," Jenna says, motioning for me to come to her. "I want you to meet my husband."

She introduces me to the man sitting next to her and I swear I'm looking into Chris Hemsworth's eyes.

"It's a pleasure to meet you," he says as he rests his arm on the back of his wife's chair and leans into her. "Jenna tells me we're all heading out to the Hamptons next weekend."

Jenna's smile blazes from her eyes as much as her mouth. "I can't wait. Girls' weekend with the boys along for the ride."

Jenna invited Owen and me, along with Adeline and Jameson to hers and Beckett's Hampton's home next weekend. I'm as excited as she is. "We're having a spa day on Saturday, right?"

"Of course," she says. "The boys can golf to their heart's content."

Bradford, who's sitting next to Jenna, leans across. "Did I just hear something about golfing?"

"Ooh," Jenna says, "You and Cecelia should come for the weekend too. It's a couple's weekend in the Hamptons."

"I'll pass," he says.

I meet his gaze, and after noting that Cecelia is deep in conversation with Seth who is on her other side, I say quietly, "You should come on your own. It'll be fun."

He considers that before saying, "Maybe."

I grin. "I promise not to let Owen get too strenuous with our hiking beforehand. He'll be at the top of his game for golf with you."

"You and Owen hike during the week?" Jenna asks. "I would have thought Owen worked too much to find time during the week for that."

Bradford arches a brow as he lifts his glass of whiskey. "These two hike like bunnies."

Jessica joins in on the conversation from across the table. "Really?"

I shake my head at Bradford who is very amused with the conversation now. I then look at Jessica. "No, not really. Bradford is full of shit."

Adeline nods her agreement. "It's why he'll make a great politician one day."

I look down at Bradford and glance at Cecelia by his side, everything falling into place in my brain. That's the reason for his dark-ages marriage.

"Where's Owen?" Bradford asks. "It's unusual for him to run late."

"Oh, shit." I pull out my phone to reply to Owen's text. "He had a meeting. I guess it ran over."

I tap out a text.

Charlize: I hope everything is going well with your meeting. I've already dealt with a thousand emergencies and am ready for my gala girl days to be over.

Owen: We ran into some problems. I'll get there as soon as I can.

"Charles," Poppy says. "A minute please."

I spend five minutes with my cousin who has a question about her stocks. I then make my way to my mother who waved me over with a look on her face that says "I desperately need you to solve another problem for me."

I always thought my mother was calm and unruffled when it came to her galas. She has planned so many of them over the years and is well-known for smoothly run events. It turns out Joan Cohen gets in as much of a flap as the rest of us do in life.

I help her with the new situation and after that, I help her with at least five other situations.

I was wrong about gala girls in so many ways.

They're not about social climbing.

They're about taking charge and getting shit done.

At eight p.m., Mom looks at me questioningly. "Where is Owen? I haven't seen him yet."

"He's stuck in a work meeting."

"Oh, that makes sense," she says, like out of all the things I could have said, this is the one thing she would have expected me to say.

I guess it *does* make sense. Because that's the experience she's always had with my father.

I glance at the table my father and brother should be seated at currently. Neither has arrived yet. And if I know anything, my father probably won't turn up. My brother may, but he's increasingly started to follow in our father's footsteps when it comes to family functions. And while this isn't a family function, I don't think he should promise her he'll attend something if he doesn't care about honoring that promise.

I'm not mad at Owen for working tonight, but this conversation is stirring up a lot of feelings for me. Growing up without seeing very much of my father still sits deeply in me, and not in a good way. When I have children, it will be with a man who better manages his time between his work and his family.

I'm disappointed for Mom that her husband doesn't show up for her, but I don't say anything to her. This is how it's always been, and she's obviously made peace with it.

My brother arrives just before 9:00 p.m. and I run into him as he makes his way to the bar. Unfortunately for him, I've spent the last hour thinking about the fact my father rarely makes it to Mom's galas. And about the fact her son is now treating her the same way. This means I approach him in a slightly antagonistic mood.

"It's lovely of you to show your face, Nate."

He comes to a stop. "Am I detecting some animosity here?"

"Let's just say it would have been nice for you to make it on time to a gala you know is important to your mother."

He lifts his brows. "Since when do you say things like that? And since when do you care so much about galas?"

"Since today. I never knew the work that went into these events before. Mom works hard on them, and I think she'd appreciate it if you and Dad cared enough to turn up on time. That's all. Just show up when you say you will." I might have grumbled about coming to Mom's galas in the past, but at least I attended them.

"Don't take your issues with Dad out on me."

"I'm not."

"Bullshit."

"It's not bullshit."

"You've always thought he worked too much."

"Yes, and I recall you feeling the same way when we were growing up."

"Well, we're adults now, and in case you didn't know, adults have to fucking work."

"Fuck you, Nate. I work."

"I never said you don't, but you do seem to like to run away to other countries a lot rather than staying and building a career. The rest of us don't have that luxury, Charlize."

"I've never asked you or anyone to pay for my life. I work as much as I need to afford my travel."

"Yeah, but what about your future? Or are you planning to rely on a man to pay for it like Mom wants you to? You need to grow up and figure your shit out."

I glare at my brother. "You can be a real asshole, Nate."

"No, I'm just saying what you don't want to hear. You're my sister and I love you, but you live with your head in the clouds sometimes." He eyes the bar. "I'm going to get a drink."

He stalks to the bar, and I stalk toward the door. I need some air after that.

I'm in the middle of a million thoughts over what Nate said, all angry, and all madly plotting ways to prove him wrong, when I run into Owen who's entering the gala.

"Hey," he says, concern filling his eyes as he takes in my angry state. "What's happened?"

"My brother happened!" I blow out a harsh breath. "I'm so fucking angry with him right now." I release more angry energy. "I need to go outside for a bit."

Owen changes course and walks with me back toward the door he just came through. We're almost through it when a committee member calls out to me, waving me over.

I wish I could ignore her so I could go outside and have a moment to calm myself down. However, I won't because I know she needs me. I look at Owen. "You go and find everyone. They're at a table near the front. I'll come over once I'm done with this."

He places his hand on my hip, slowing me down. "Take a breath."

I know he's trying to care for me, but I'm in no mood to be cared for. "I don't have time to take a breath."

I stride away from him feeling all kinds of knots inside.

My brother.

My father.

My mother.

Owen.

It's all a tangled mess in my head.

And. I. Don't. Have. Time. To. Untangle. It. Right. Now.

I spend the next hour before the gala finishes run off my feet with tasks from my mother. I catch sight of Owen a few times, talking and laughing with our friends. His eyes meet mine as often as mine find his. He's concerned about me. I can see that much. And I appreciate that concern, but I have no time to go to him and ease it.

He comes to me as the room is emptying. "What can I do to help?"

Before I can answer, Mom joins us, a highly focused expression on her face. She rattles off a list of jobs for me before looking at Owen. "It's good to see you, Owen. I'm looking forward to dinner on Sunday."

"Likewise," he says. "How can I help you clean up?"

She shakes her head. "No, you go home. We've all got our jobs. You'll just get in the way." Then, to me, she bosses, "Charlize, please don't waste time. I'd like to leave before midnight."

If I wasn't so tired, I'd have something to say about that. I'm not wasting time. I haven't wasted even a second tonight. But I let it go and eye Owen. "Thank you, but she's right. You should go home."

His eyes search mine, and I'm sure he's trying to figure out how to help me, regardless of having been told there's nothing he can do. Finally, he bends to brush his lips over mine. "You'll sleep at my place tonight?"

"It'll be late by the time we're done here."

"I missed you last night, Charlize."

I missed him too. "Okay, but that should not mean

you don't try to get some sleep before I come over. You're exhausted."

He kisses me again. "I'll see you later."

I don't watch him walk out. I've got too much to do for that.

I see Jack and Jessica on my way through the room, and quickly stop them. "Thank you for being the best emcee of ever," I say to Jack. He did a fantastic job.

He blasts that million-dollar smile of his my way. "We had a wonderful night."

Jessica also gives me a smile. "Any time you want a gala girl by your side, call me."

I really want to hug her, but I don't. That might be a little too much. We hardly know each other. Instead, I say, "You may live to regret that."

"I doubt it," she says before taking her husband's hand and looking up at him. "Let's go. You owe me a foot massage, Mr. Kingsley."

Jack puts his arms around her shoulders, and after saying goodbye to me, he walks her out.

I'm so glad our original emcee quit. Meeting the Kingsleys has been a highlight of this gala for me.

It takes a couple of hours to clean up.

The great news is that Mom's stress levels have calmed down.

The bad news is that my anger over the things my brother said hasn't.

I'm also angry with my father for not showing up tonight. The fact my mother just takes this in her stride, like she has every other time he's not shown up for her, only angers me more.

By the time I get to Owen's home after midnight, my knots of anger are tight.

Too tight.

He meets me in the foyer, still dressed in his tuxedo he wore to the gala. His white dress shirt is half undone and his bow tie is hanging around his neck.

I frown as he pulls me close to kiss me. Putting my hands to his chest, I stop the kiss. "I thought you were going to try to get some sleep?"

"No, I still had some work to do."

I continue frowning at him. "I don't understand how you can survive with such little sleep, Owen. You're up at four most mornings and you're in bed late. You work around the clock. I'm worried you're going to collapse of fatigue any day now."

He lets me go and runs a hand down his face. "I'm sorry I didn't make it to the gala until late tonight. It was unavoidable."

"I'm not saying this to you because of that. I'm saying it because I'm genuinely concerned about you."

He watches me closely. "I want you to know that canceling plans with you isn't something I take lightly."

"I won't deny I'm disappointed about the concert, but I know what that award means to you." The knots in my chest strangle each other and I force breath out, trying to loosen them. "I know you do your best to show up when you say you will, unlike my father and brother who fail at that all the time."

Still watching me intently, he asks, "What happened with your brother tonight?"

"We had a disagreement about men who work too

much. I told him it's disappointing he and Dad always let Mom down when they choose work over her."

"They do that often?"

"I can't remember a gala or party that Dad was on time to."

"I imagine being a partner at his law firm must be demanding."

I stare at him. "Yes, but don't you think it'd be nice if he put his family first at least every now and then?"

"I agree, but I know the pressure he's under."

"I know the pressure he's under too." The words snap out of me. The knots inside me move painfully closer to snapping too. "But I'm tired of making excuses for him. I'm tired of accepting less than he should be willing to give the people he loves."

"Unfortunately, some firms make it hard for a person to walk away from work at the end of the day."

"I know, but that's a choice they make."

"What, between the job and the family?"

"Yes."

"It's not always that easy, Charlize. Not when it's your career you're talking about."

"I'm not saying it's easy. I'm saying figure out how to be better at managing your priorities. And if they clash all the time, think about whether they really are your priorities. I get it, Dad can't make it to everything. But making it to nothing says a lot, don't you think?"

If I thought he was watching me closely before, he's really watching me closely now. "I know what you're saying, but I've also seen this from the other side. I know the weight that's felt to perform and to achieve. It's not as easy as you're saying."

"So, what you're saying is you agree with Nate and my father?"

"Fuck. No, that's not—"

"It sounds a lot like that's exactly what you're saying."

My knots have frayed so badly there's no salvaging them now.

My anger breathes all around us.

My inability to hear anything he has to say has roared to life.

When he places his hand on my arm and says, "Let's take a minute," I yank my arm out of his grip, and say, "No."

"No?" He frowns.

"No. I'm not taking a minute." I turn to the elevator. "I'm going home." I stab at the elevator button.

"Charlize." He reaches for me again.

I refuse to let him take hold of me. "No, Owen, I'm tired and I'm angry, and I'm going home."

"It's late. Stay here and go to bed. We'll talk in the morning."

I stare at the elevator doors. "I don't want to talk to you about this anymore."

I know I'm being unreasonable, but I can't stop myself.

Not even if I tried.

One of my deepest cuts has been ripped open tonight.

My very first cut.

The one my father made.

The one so many men before Owen have carved into too.

I know he has no way of knowing this, but I. Can't. Look. At. Him. Right. Now.

I can't explain all of this to him right now.

He curses. "Okay, let me drive you home then."

I hold my purse tighter to me. "No."

The elevator arrives and the doors open.

Owen's hand curls around my bicep as I take a step toward the elevator. In the firmest voice he's ever used, he says, "It's late. I'm driving you."

My heart beats faster than it ever has.

My chest feels every thump, every thrash, every tremor.

I look at Owen, finally.

I see so much in those blue eyes.

Misgiving.

Worry.

Uncertainty.

But mostly care.

So much care.

Tears threaten at the back of my eyes.

I swallow every emotion crowding me and nod.

I don't say anything because I know I'll start crying if I do.

Anger always makes me cry.

But more than that, I hate that after finding so many rights between us, we've found a very big wrong.

28

Charlize

I sleep horribly.

I think I get at most two hours. It's disjointed and filled with dreams I know were terrible and am glad I can't quite remember.

I drag myself into the kitchen at seven a.m. and find Dylan sitting at the island. He's watching me with concern, which makes sense since I cried half the night and look terrible.

"Why am I looking at you?" he asks as I move to the coffee machine. "I thought you were sleeping at Owen's last night."

With that, I burst into tears.

"Fuck, Char." Dylan's arms are around me a moment later and I bury my face in his chest while clinging to him. "What happened?"

"I had a fight with Owen. Well, not so much a fight as a disagreement. One I walked out on," I say in between sobs and a whole lot of snot.

I go back to planting my face in his chest.

Dylan lets me cry for a long time.

I've cried in his arms a lot in my lifetime, but this may be the hardest I've ever cried over a guy.

When I finally lift my face to his, he says, "Tell me what happened."

I sit with him on the sofa and give him a blow-by-blow of everything from the conversation with my mother, to my argument with Nate, to what happened with Owen.

Dylan listens intently to everything.

When I finish speaking, I wipe my tears and blow my nose. "I don't think we're as compatible as I thought we were."

"You need to have a long conversation with him about this, babe. He needs all the facts here. All the ways your father let you down over the years. All the ways you watched him let your mom down. And all the ways other guys did the same thing to you."

"I get that, but none of it changes the fact Owen is who he is. He's a guy who sees things differently than me when it comes to this."

"You also need to give him the opportunity to give you all his facts. And then you need to talk about whether what you have together is something you both might want to compromise things for. You're never going to find a relationship where you both automatically get what you want."

"I don't think he's going to change, Dyl. He's driven.

Focused. His work is important to him. And I never want to be that person who expects her partner to change for her."

"No, but do you want to be that person who doesn't even give him the chance to choose her?" He pauses, his eyes boring into mine. "You're scared. I know you are. But give him a chance here."

My chest is tight. Fluttery, and not in a good way. In a super anxious way.

"I think I have to take this job in California," I say.

I watch Dylan while he processes that.

I think I'm going to vomit, but then, everything inside me is twisted so tightly together than I don't think even vomit could get through.

"Why?" he asks.

"Because I need it."

"Something will come up here."

"What if it doesn't?"

"What if it does?"

I really am going to vomit.

"Nate's right. I need a plan for my life. This is a great job with the kind of income I've never had before. I should take the job."

"So, you'll do the long-distance relationship thing with Owen, then?"

"I don't know if that's the best idea."

"You're talking yourself out of this relationship, Char," he says softly. "Don't do that."

"You don't know Owen. *I* don't know him. It's hasn't even been two months for us yet. We're probably not even that well suited. It's probably just all the good sex that's made us get along so well."

Dylan gives me a look. It's *the* look. The one that says I'm telling myself lies. It's the look he reserves exclusively for me when I get myself in a muddle of too many thoughts and not enough good sense. I'm not sure why he's giving it to me now. I'm thinking straight about my career for once. "Only you can make this decision," he says. "And we both know that you know deep in your gut who Owen is."

My phone sounds with a text and when I don't get up to check it, Dylan moves off the sofa and brings my phone to me. "Don't ignore him. That's a shitty thing to do to a guy." He looks at his watch. "Fuck, I have to go. I'm meeting with an art dealer this morning."

I wave him away. "Go. I'm okay." I give him a smile. "And thank you."

I check the text after he gives me one last look and leaves.

Owen: Are you awake?

Dylan's right. Ignoring him is a shitty thing to do. But there is no way I'm ready for this conversation yet.

Charlize: Yes, but I need some space to think, Owen.

He calls. "We need to talk, Charlize." I hear his lack of sleep in his voice, and memories of him driving me home last night flood my mind. We didn't speak on the drive, but there was so much noise. And the look of anguish in his eyes as I left his car. I will never forget that look.

"I agree," I say, "but I need to process my thoughts first."

"What thoughts? Talk to me."

"All my thoughts over what we said last night."

"We need to have a do-over of that conversation."

I grip my phone harder. "I don't know if that will achieve anything different."

"I think it will." Owen's determination blazes fiercely, even through the phone.

"Owen—"

"I'm coming over."

Shit.

No.

I'm not ready for that.

I need time.

"No, don't come over."

"I'll be there soon."

The call disconnects and I stare at my phone.

I am not ready for him.

Nothing good is going to come of this conversation.

I have a quick shower and get dressed.

I make the strongest coffee known to humankind.

And I send an SOS to Poppy.

Charlize: I think I'm about to break up with Owen. I need you.

She calls straight away. "Charles, what is going on over there? You know I don't do well with distress calls like that."

I burst into tears again and tell her everything.

"Okay," she says, in her take-charge voice. "I've told Seth to stop giving me the eye. I'm coming over. Do not, I repeat, *do not*, break up with Owen. Tell him you need more time and that he'll just have to give that to you. We need an intervention before you start running."

"I'm not running, Pop."

"Oh, my darling, that's exactly what you're preparing to do."

We end the call and I burst into tears again.

I hate crying.

Like, why does it even have to be a thing?

Why can't we just sit and stare at the wall and experience the same kind of emotional release? I'd be okay with that.

By the time Owen arrives thirty minutes later, I'm a wreck. A puffy-face ruin. And I hate that he sees me like this.

Cursing softly, he steps into Dylan's kitchen and slides his arm around my waist to pull me close.

I try to stop him.

I try to push him away.

I try not to let him in close.

But he won't have any of it.

Pulling me into his arms, he brings one hand to the back of my head and presses a kiss to my forehead while I start crying. *Again*.

"Stop being you," I grumble into his chest as my tears fall.

"I'm not stopping."

My arms slide around him for a long time.

For too long.

I could live in this chest just as much as I could live in his neck.

I try to memorize it.

The feel of his hardness.

Of his muscles.

Of his *soul*.

When I unwrap my arms and try to move out of his hold, he hesitates. He doesn't want to let me go.

"I took a job in California."

He drops his arms and allows me to step away from him. "Okay. But that doesn't have anything to do with what we need to talk about."

"It negates the need for that conversation."

"No, it doesn't."

"It does. I'm moving across the country."

"So, we'll be separated by a six-hour flight."

"I'm not interested in a long-distance relationship."

"Neither am I, but I'll do it for you."

"Forever?"

His eyes bore into mine. "No."

"Right. So there's your answer. This relationship has an end date."

His eyes keep boring into mine. "It doesn't. I'll move if you decide to stay in California."

My eyes widen.

My heart races.

What is he saying?

"No. I wouldn't let you give up everything here for me."

"I'd do it in a heartbeat, Charlize."

What is he saying?

Why would he do that?

"No."

"I can work from anywhere," he says.

"No, you can't.... You shouldn't have to.... No."

He watches me with such a steady gaze that all I can feel is a sense of safety. Of dependability. Like I can trust what he's saying and feeling. "The night we met, you told me you look for men willing to make a strong, emotional commitment. You found one. Let me make that commitment to you."

I can't.

I just can't.

Men don't just promise to uproot their lives for me.

And they certainly don't keep their promises.

They lie to me.

They break their promises.

They do not stick around and make a life with me.

I shake my head. "No, Owen. I don't want this. I tried to tell you that when we met. I told you I just wanted sex."

"And then you kept memories of me, took me to yoga, started a coffee war with me, introduced me to bad movies and romantic comedies, almost convinced me Elvis is still alive, charmed my mother, and agreed to golf with me even though you don't want to play golf. You made me fall in love with you, Charlize, and I never want to be anything but in love with you. I want all of those things with you every day of my life. And you can't tell me you don't feel the same way. I've seen it in your eyes, felt it in your touch, known it from your kiss. You do want this."

He's in love with me?

What is it about our brains that causes them to feed us so many conflicting thoughts?

I'm looking at everything I think I want.

I'm listening to him say all the right things.

And yet, I can't believe it.

I can't believe he'll come through for me.

I take a step back, my heart breaking as I take it. "I don't want this. I'm moving to California and you're staying here."

He listens to me.

He processes what I say.

"When do you leave?"

"Tomorrow."

His eyes trace the lines of my face for a long time. "When I told you I was deliberately going out of my way to make you mine, I meant it." He then moves into me before I can stop him and slides his fingers through my hair. He claims a kiss I won't ever forget. And when he finally comes up for air, he says, "This isn't finished."

Every inch of my body and soul feels this kiss.

Deeply.

It steals breath.

It steals thoughts.

It steals my heart all over again.

I know I'll feel it forever.

But Owen is wrong: this *is* finished between us.

29

Owen

"Get the jet ready," I say to Tahlia over the phone as I drive home from Charlize's.

"Where are you going?" Her confusion is clear.

"California. I'll send you the exact location once I confirm it."

"Okay," she says slowly. "You're leaving today?"

"As soon as the jet is ready."

"For how long?"

"For an indefinite amount of time."

She takes a moment with this information. "I hate to be the bearer of bad news, Owen, but you've got a lot of important meetings next week. Not to mention the Bluestone Award dinner. What are your plans there?"

"Cancel everything I can't do over Zoom."

She's silent for a moment again. "Is everything okay?"

"It will be."

"Okay. Right." She's perplexed, and I don't blame her. I rarely cancel anything. I certainly never cancel *everything*. "I'm not sure you'll be able to do that Bluestone dinner over Zoom. Or your lunch meetings."

"Cancel everything connected to the award. It's no longer a priority."

"Oh. Okay."

"I'll email the information you'll need for the flight and to book a hotel and car for me."

I end the call and then phone Poppy.

She answers immediately. "Where are you?"

"I just left Charlize."

"Shit, if you've left already, that means bad things, right? I'm about five minutes away from her. I got caught in traffic."

I smile. Thank God Charlize has Poppy. "She told me about the job in California. I'm going to fly out there, but I need to know where she'll be. Since I'm certain she won't tell me, I need you to."

"She's taking the job?"

That confirms many things for me.

Charlize only just decided to take that job.

"Yes. She's leaving tomorrow."

"The job is in LA. I'll text you the details once I get them all from her."

"Thank you."

We end the call and I contemplate my future.

I wasn't lying to Charlize when I told her I'd pack my life up for her. My roots have all been with my business for seven years. I've felt them shifting for a while now. They've been restless. Searching for more.

I didn't know what that *more* was until last night.

I think it was love at first sight for me with Charlize.

If anyone had told me I'd fall in love at first sight, I would have laughed in their face.

But the moment I saw her in that bathroom, and she started bossing me around, I was captivated. The moment she wanted to know something about me that no one else knew was the moment I fell in love with her. When we shared all that big talk, I knew no other woman would ever earn my attention again.

Having to drive her home last night when she shut down on me was the hardest thing I've had to do in a long time. I spent a sleepless night thinking about our conversation, about the mistakes I made in my marriage, about the conversation I had with Charlize regarding the expectations my father had of me.

I thought about what she said last night: *I'm saying figure out how to be better at managing your priorities. And if they clash all the time, think about whether they really are your priorities.*

Charlize told me that she knows what the Bluestone Award means to me. The thing I came to understand last night is that the award doesn't mean what I thought it did.

I was chasing it because I was nominated and that felt good. It felt like all the long hours and years I've put into my company were worth it. That I finally would have met my father's expectations if he'd been alive.

I don't give a fuck about the award.

I only ever cared about those expectations.

But that was before I found something I care about more.

Someone I care about more than any of that bullshit.

My priorities have been clashing, and last night I realized it was time to think about whether they really are my priorities.

The Bluestone Award isn't important.

Playing the game isn't important.

Working my ass off so I can just keep getting up to continue working it off isn't important.

I'm in love with Charlize and she is my priority now.

30

Charlize

Poppy: Are you in LA yet?

Charlize: I just got to my hotel.

Poppy: Have you heard when you start work?

Charlize: Next week, which is good. It'll give me time to find a place to move into this week.

Poppy: Just a heads up. Aunt Joan is in a flap. She's talking about flying out to see you.

Charlize: OMG really? I know she doesn't think I should have taken the job but flying out to see me is a little much.

Poppy: Well, not really. You moving across the country with a day's notice is a little much. Us worrying about you isn't. I'm surprised Dylan isn't also on his way to you.

Charlize: I'm fine, Pop. This is what I wanted.

Poppy: This is NOT what you wanted, but we can pretend for a few more days. I might even give you a week before I start calling your bullshit, so make the most of it, 'k?

Charlize: I love you, but I have to go.

Poppy: You have to wash your hair? Cut your toenails? I mean, you're all alone, Charles. What could you possibly have to go and do so urgently?

Charlize: Don't be mean to me, Pop. I'm already sad enough.

Poppy: Well, COME HOME. I'll hug you instead of being mean.

Charlize: I think Seth's giving you the eye. Bye xx

My first tear for this afternoon falls as soon as I type that last *x*. The only reason it's my first tear for the afternoon is because I've just spent hours on a plane, and I was determined not to cry on that flight. But now, I can't stop the tears.

I allow myself to wallow in my heartbreak for an hour. Then, I go in search of food.

I find some greasy pizza to wallow in.

Yes, I'm all about the wallowing.

I even started a new playlist on Spotify.

So far, I've added fifty-three sad songs to it.

See: Queen Wallower

I eat far too much pizza before heading back to the hotel just after seven p.m.

The hotel is busy tonight with a large group of people checking in as well as many groups of people chatting on the couches in the retro-inspired lobby. The hotel bar is full. Noisy too. I weave my way through the group checking in, past the couches, and am almost past the bar on my way to the elevators when I spot him.

Owen.

He's sitting in an armchair in an alcove near the bar and he's got his eyes firmly on me.

My feet slow as my heart speeds.

What is he doing here?

My brain begins trying to work so fast it feels like it's pedaling in there.

Pedaling backward, forward, sideways, every which way.

He can't be here.

I frown.

It's the only thing my face can think to do.

It's the only thing that makes sense to do.

Why is he here?

He stands and walks my way.

I take in his blue jeans, navy button-down shirt, and white sneakers.

I've never seen Owen in such a casual outfit on a workday.

Well, except for that time in the gym and when he's come to some yoga classes with me.

His sleeves are rolled up so imperfectly I could fall in love with them.

"Why are you here?" I ask when he reaches me.

"I told you this isn't finished." He takes his time with my face. Like he's missed it, which is crazy because he saw it yesterday. But still, that's how it feels when he looks at me.

"Are you staying here?"

"Yes."

"Owen," I say, still frowning, "coming here and staying in the same hotel isn't going to make me change my mind."

"What are you afraid of, Charlize? Tell me so I can tell you why you don't need to be afraid."

"I'm not afraid of anything." It's a good thing I'm still not Catholic.

"You are. You wouldn't be here if you weren't. But we can find our way there slowly if that's what you need. I'm not going anywhere."

I stare at him. "What do you mean you're not going anywhere? You have work. You have the Bluestone Award dinner. Owen, you have a lot on this week. I know you do."

He smiles and I swoon so much I want to peel that smile from him and keep it. "If you didn't love me, you wouldn't know all that, and you wouldn't care that I'm missing those things."

I keep staring. Until I get all flummoxed and start giving him all my thoughts. "You should not give up work for me. I didn't tell you those things about my father because I think you should stop going to work. Oh my God, Owen, get back on your jet and go home and go to work. You have absolutely misunderstood me. This casual look does not look good on you. Put your suit back on." At that point, I slam my mouth shut before opening it again to add, "One of us needs to leave this hotel and it needs to be you."

With that, I practically scurry to the elevators.

I do not look back at him.

I do not imagine dragging him into the elevator with me.

I do not wish I could take all those words back.

But oh, my goodness.

He came to Los Angeles for me.

I'M in the middle of bawling my eyes out while watching *The Notebook* at 9:34 p.m. when Owen texts me.

Owen: I hate playing chess.

I spend an exorbitant amount of time re-reading that text.

They are four little words that I am sure will determine my fate.

My fingers are dying to get busy sending him a reply, but my heart is torn.

What are you afraid of, Charlize?

Poppy spent a great deal of yesterday telling me that I have big feelings that I'm afraid of. And I've spent a lot of today thinking about that.

Benjamin didn't just break my heart. He smashed it to pieces.

Our relationship started out great, but after we got engaged, he changed. He started working a lot, which I was okay with. But the more he worked, and the more he pushed himself, the shorter his temper became, the more promises he broke, and the more lies he told. He became a mean bully and broke me emotionally.

The men I dated before him weren't much better.

I worked through all that, but I admitted to Poppy yesterday that deep down I know I'm letting that hurt get in the way of Owen and me. I also told her that I don't know if I have it in me to let him in.

"Oh, my darling," she'd said, "you've already let him in. I've never seen you as happy. Now, all you have to do is keep going. Together. One step at a time."

I read Owen's text again.

One step at a time.

Charlize: Why?

The blue dots start instantly.

Owen: My father forced me to play it.

Charlize: Did you have a chess tutor?

Owen: Yes. My father.

Charlize: And not in a good way, huh?

Owen: In the worst possible way. He made me play for hours at a time.

Charlize: I bet you're a great chess player.

Owen: Yes.

Charlize: I hate playing Monopoly. It was the one game my father played with us, and I never won. I mean, I'm not saying a parent should always let their children win, but he was so ruthless. Nate and I never had a chance of winning.

Owen: Do you want children?

I pause at that question, but only for a moment.

Owen and I skipped all the small talk right from the beginning. Why would we start now?

Charlize: Yes. Do you?

Owen: Yes. How many?

Charlize: Well, that's up to fate.

Owen: You believe in fate?

Charlize: Of course. Wait, do you not?

Owen: No.

Charlize: Oh my God, Owen. How is this even possible? What do you believe in if not fate?

Owen: I believe that we have the ability to create our own reality. I believe our actions determine our lives, and that what we think of as destiny is the result of our past actions.

Charlize: Okay, I get all that, but tell me, would we have met if not for fate?

Owen: Yes. You were in that bathroom screaming on your deathbed. I was walking past. My action to go into the bathroom meant I met you.

Charlize: But it wasn't your action that ensured I was in that bathroom.

Owen: That was good timing. I believe in timing.

Charlize: It was fate!

Owen: So, you're saying we were predetermined by a greater power? I could get behind that.

Charlize: I see what you just did.

Owen: What are you doing for breakfast?

I stop breathing for a second while I read his text and re-read it.

Charlize: I have a room service date for breakfast.

Owen: If you decide you'd like company for that date, I'm free.

Charlize: Goodnight, Owen.

Owen: Goodnight, beautiful.

I go back to *The Notebook*, but I can't continue watching it.

I can't focus.

Not when all I can think about is the man who is deliberately going out of his way to make me his.

The man who always seems to know what I need.

The man who owns my heart.

31

Charlize

I wake to a knock on my door at 7:00 a.m. and find Owen standing on the other side. He's dressed casually again and is holding two coffees.

"I thought you were happy to take this slow," I say.

"I am, but to do that we need to spend time together."

"I'm busy today, Owen. I have to find somewhere to live."

"I have a car and a driver. I can take you anywhere you need to go."

I look at the coffees in his hand, demanding, "Which one is mine?" I take the one he offers. "And just so you're aware, you're being very bossy today."

He leans in close. "This isn't anywhere near bossy, Charlize, but I can make that happen if you'd like." With that, he finds his way into my hotel room and to one of the chairs.

I stay where I am near the door.

I sip some coffee.

I try not to look at the top two buttons of his button-down that are undone.

Spoiler alert: I fail.

"You're playing hardball," I accuse.

"I always do." He drinks some of his coffee. "Have you had breakfast yet?"

"No, I was still asleep when you knocked on my door."

He doesn't even have the decency to look regretful about that. "Good. I took the liberty to order breakfast. It will be here in twenty minutes."

If he's trying to rearrange all my thoughts and get them out of a straight line, he's succeeding. "I'm not hungry."

"You're always hungry."

"I'm not."

"At this time of day, you are."

"What if I take all day searching for somewhere to live? Will your driver be able to work all day?"

Owen never falters, never fails me. He always keeps up with my train of thoughts, even when I redirect our conversation like I just have. "He's yours for as long as you need him."

"What if I decide I want to live in LA forever?"

"We'll live in LA."

"What if I decide I want five children?"

"We'll negotiate that number."

"What if I take up a shopping addiction and spend all your money?"

"I'll make more."

"What if I eat my way into fifty more pounds?"

"I'll love every curve."

I stare at him.

Why must he be so good at being the man I need?

I take a gulp of coffee. "I'm taking a shower."

I take my coffee and practically run to the bathroom.

I then proceed to spend a very long time in the bathroom.

Owen has muddled every thought I was in the middle of, and that means I'm in a mess.

A big, fat, hot mess.

Except I'm not.

I have one thought that not even Owen can jumble, shuffle or tangle.

When Benjamin asked me to marry him, I said yes, but I later googled "how to tell if you're in love". Still feeling confused, I googled "what does being in love feel like?". And then I googled "how do you know if you have a deep connection with someone?"

I had so many tabs open on my computer with what felt like a million variations of those questions and still, I didn't have the answer I was looking for.

I *did* have the answer, though.

I just didn't want to accept it.

When you're in love, *you know*.

And it doesn't matter if it's been a year or a minute.

I fell in love with Owen in one night.

Being in love feels like magic.

It's enchantment.

It's being cherished.

It's him paying attention to the tiny details of you.

It's him knowing how to ease your nerves, learning how you like to be touched, doing your favorite things with you.

It's him wanting to stretch for you.

It's you wanting to stop running and start trusting.

I finish my shower and wrap the towel around me before going back to Owen.

I expect to find him either on a call or checking emails on his phone.

I don't find him doing either of those things.

I find him sitting in that seat, drinking coffee, doing nothing but waiting for me.

He watches me walk to him, his eyes never leaving mine.

God, those eyes.

I will never get enough of them.

When I reach him, I straddle him, resting my knees on the chair on either side of his legs. I loop my hands around his neck while his hands come around my waist.

"You keep your word," I say.

His eyes search mine. "I do."

"You show up."

He nods. "Yes."

"And you get naked with me."

"I'm presuming you're not talking about literal nakedness."

I smile. "I'm not, although if you ever stop doing that, I'll have a conniption."

That amuses him. "Good to know."

I bring my hands around to his face. "I love you,

Owen. I've loved you from our first night together because even then, when you barely knew me, you *knew* me. And ever since then, you've been showing up exactly how I needed you to. I do want this with you. I want all of this with you, and I want it forever."

Every ounce of restraint I know he's been using since the moment I told him I didn't want this disappears and his lips crash down onto mine. His tongue finds mine and he kisses me like it's the only thing he wants in the entire world. Like *I'm* the only thing he wants in the entire world.

When he ends the kiss, he cups my cheek and says, "I don't care where we live, Charlize, so long as we're there together. Three nights without you was three nights too long. Don't ever make me do that again."

"Never," I promise. "I will never run from you again. My home is wherever you are.

EPILOGUE

Charlize
6 Months Later

Poppy: Seth's giving me the eye. I may disappear for a while.

Charlize: Is that code for *we won't see you again tonight*?

Adeline: You know it is, Charles.

Lorelei: I thought Ashton demanded a lot of sex. He's got nothing on Seth.

Jessica: Get it, girl. I'm thinking of dragging Jack somewhere fun for some vibe action.

Charlize: Ooh, yes! Owen needs some Motley Crue in his life tonight.

Jenna: Did I miss something here? Motley Crue?

Poppy: Charles has a Motley Crue vibe. She likes to tease Owen with it as often as possible.

Adeline: She randomly texts and emails him images and stories about Motley Crue.

Charlize: I just texted him.

Lorelei: Where are the guys?

Jessica: The last I saw them they were at the Black-jack table.

We're in Vegas with our husbands for the weekend. It's something that's becoming a tradition for us. This is our third weekend together.

I'm in the middle of tapping out another text when Owen's arms come around me and his lips brush my neck. "Whoever thought we could wait another four months to get married was dreaming."

I smile and turn in his arms. "This is the first and last time we ever give our mothers any say in any decision we make."

"This is the last time *I* give you any say in when I'll marry you."

Owen proposed to me a month after he made me his and moved me into his New York condo. I never wanted to live in LA anyway. We talked about getting married straight away, but our mothers were horrified. They had a little get together, unbeknownst to us, and presented us with a date in April that worked well for them. Owen wanted to say no. A nine-month wait was too long for him. It was me who said yes, we'd give them this. I blame Owen's sex spell. I was clearly not of right mind that day. I blame that spell for anything and everything.

"What do you mean it's the last time you give me any say?"

"I just decided I'm marrying you tonight."

I blink. "Really?"

"Yes. I found you an Elvis I think you're going to love. He's so old he might even be the real Elvis."

"Smartass."

He grins and kisses me.

He tastes like whiskey and love.

Bradford joins us. "I believe this casino is a hiking-free zone."

I look at him. "You wish you were hiking."

Jenna's sister, Kristen, leans in as she walks past and catches some of our conversation. Eyeing Bradford, she says, "Cecelia is so frigid I doubt he even remembers what hiking is."

This is the first time Kristen has joined our group in Vegas, but she's quickly picked up on our hiking reference which everyone is now aware of.

Bradford looks at her. "Says the woman who's on the prowl. If you need tips for what men are actually looking for, hit me up."

Kristen shoots daggers at him. "You would be the last man I would ever ask for help. I doubt you even know how to find a clit, let alone what to do with one."

"Sweetheart, I'm not convinced you *have* a clit. You're so fucking sexually repressed, I imagine it is too."

"Jesus, Brad," Owen says as Kristen glowers at Bradford and walks away. "That was low."

Bradford is glaring after Kristen. "She pushes all my fucking buttons." He looks at Owen. "And don't think she doesn't give as good as she gets."

"Does she know Cecelia?" I ask. I don't know Kristen well. Jenna dragged her along this weekend to help her get over a breakup.

"I'm not aware of all my fiancé's friendships, but I

suspect Kristen must at least know of Cecelia," Bradford says.

"Aren't you on a crash course at the moment?" I ask. Bradford's wedding is in a month. The last I heard, Cecelia had forced him to learn everything there is to know about her.

"I refused. I know enough to get by."

Ashton joins us. "Have you seen Lorelei?"

I met Ashton and Lorelei a month after I moved in with Owen. It was during our first Vegas weekend with the group. They only confirmed my love of Australians.

"I think she's with Jessica, but I don't know where," I say to Ashton.

We arrived in Vegas yesterday for two nights. Today was spa day for us girls while the men played golf. I swear the year-round golfing in Vegas is the real reason for our trips here.

Also, spoiler alert: I don't agree with Jessica that golfing attire is wanky. But probably see: the Owen sex spell.

My phone sounds with texts as our girl group chat lights up.

Poppy: Charles, I just saw that Harry Styles is playing here next month. You and Owen can add to your Styles addiction.

Lorelei: What's their Styles addiction?

Poppy: Charles drags Owen to Harry as often as she can. They've been to no less than six of his concerts in seven months.

Charlize: Owen already emailed me tickets for his concert here next month.

Poppy: Jesus, that man is pussy whipped.

Charlize: Lorelei, Ashton is looking for you.

Lorelei: He just saw me and is coming my way. I think we're heading up to our room. If we don't make it to breakfast tomorrow, thanks for the best weekend, girls!

Charlize: Owen and I definitely won't be at breakfast. He's found Elvis for me and we're getting married. I'll be on my honeymoon.

Poppy: WHAT???????????

Charlize: Tomorrow, Pop, I shall commence speaking like a married woman.

Adeline: Are you serious? You guys are really getting married, tonight?

Charlize: Apparently. I'll text you as soon as I start speaking differently.

Poppy: You kid, but it's a real thing, my darling.

Jessica: Okay my beautiful gala girls, I've finally located my husband and have slipped my vibe in his hand, and we're calling it a night. We won't be at breakfast either, so we'll see you in a few months.

Jenna: Wait! Is our next gala meeting next week, Charlize? I can't remember what was decided.

Charlize: Yes, next week. I'll text the info.

Two weeks after I moved into Owen's condo, I got a call from the Scholarship Fund who I helped plan the gala for. They were looking for an Event Manager to coordinate their galas and other fundraising events. My mother recommended me for the job. And my girls use their network to help me do so much good work in the world. Jessica dubbed us the Gala Girls. I loved that she remembered that little detail from one of our first conversations.

Jenna: OK, great! Beckett and I are heading up to our room now too. I loved our weekend xx

Adeline: I'm already in my room and there's no way I'm allowing Jameson out of my sight for breakfast in the morning. I think we need three nights next time. Two is never enough with you girls xx

Charlize: I love you all xx

"We've got a date with Elvis," Owen says, taking my hand after Bradford leaves us to go to the bar.

I look up at him. "It's a good thing I wore a red ribbon for you tonight."

He eyes the ribbon around my waist. "Why?"

I smile. "I can't marry you while not wearing a red ribbon. It just wouldn't be right."

He catches my lips in a kiss, his hands all over me in so many inappropriate ways. He kisses me so thoroughly I'm concerned he's going to try to get friskier with me than he should in public. When he finally comes up for air, he says, "I'm almost tempted to skip Elvis."

"Why?"

"Because I want you on your knees."

Holy mother of *good girls suck dick in Vegas*.

I grip his hand. "Right, Mr. North, one of us has to take me to my Elvis and make it so you can call me Mrs. North the next time you tell me to be a good girl, and it has to be you."

Owen takes me to Elvis.

I think he's right: I think this is *the real* Elvis. He's that old.

Owen purchases the "Burning Love" package which gets us one song from Elvis.

I tell him he's stingy for not buying the package that includes extra songs and Elvis-inspired sunglasses.

He tells me he's saving cash for when I take up my shopping addiction.

I only tear up once while we say "I Do". I think I don't cry more because of Elvis and the fun Owen and I have getting married with him.

After, Owen carries me into the elevator on our way up to our suite.

He then places me down, pulls me close, and kisses my neck. "I love you Mrs. North."

I don't think I was even nearly prepared for how good those words sound.

I press myself against him and kiss him. When the elevator stops three floors up, Owen drags his mouth from mine and turns me in his arms, pulling my back against his chest.

I look at the couple of who get in the elevator. The woman runs her eyes over me with judgment. I'm unsure if she's judging my dress or Owen's hands that are all over me.

"Darling," I say, running my hands down over his arms, bringing my hands to his and threading our fingers together. "You really need to stop trying to fuck me in elevators. We might miss our floor."

Owen's lips graze my ear as he chuckles and murmurs, "Trouble."

I turn in his hold and look up into his blue eyes. "Your favorite kind."

He smiles down at me with so much love. "Yes, Mrs. North, my favorite kind."

The elevator stops and the other couple exit before it continues up to our floor.

A text comes through on my phone, and since it reminds me that I promised my girls to text them once I was married, I check it.

Poppy: OMG did you girls see this????

She links us to an Instagram post.

@THETEA_GASP

OMG GIRLFRIENDS, do we have some juicy tea for you tonight?! Gather round. @bradfordblack our favorite sexy future Presidential candidate (we hope!) just got married and NOT to his fiancé #gasp We can officially confirm he married @kristenblaise tonight in Vegas. No official statement from either party has been released but look at the happy couple in that photo #swoon We all knew Bradford and @thececeliaaniston lacked something, and now that we've seen this photo of him with his new wife, we can see what that was - #passion. Stay tuned for more soon because you just know there's going to be so.much.more from this couple.

I SHOW Owen who frowns and shakes his head. "That has to be bullshit."

"I don't follow this gossip account, but Poppy does and says it doesn't post anything that isn't true."

He pulls me close and kisses me again. "Put your

phone away, Mrs. North. We're almost at our floor and you have your first job as my wife to do."

"Wait." I laughingly push him away. "I have to text my girls."

He keeps trying to pull me into his arms. "Why? Can't it wait?"

I look at him very seriously. "No. I have to tell them that I am now your wife. It's the happiest day of my life and my girls need to share in that with me."

His expression turns serious. "It's the happiest day of my life too, Charlize."

I reach for his face and kiss him.

This kiss is slow, and we lose ourselves in it.

I will never love another person as much as I love Owen.

When he pulls his mouth from mine, I say, "For our third wedding, I want the top package with three songs and the sunglasses."

He grins. "Our third?"

"Well, you do realize we're still going to have to have our April wedding for our mothers, right?"

"Fuck. I was hoping we could skip that."

"If you think we have any chance of Joan Cohen and Mary North letting us skip that wedding, you are dreaming. Our mothers have trained for that day their entire lives."

I send the text to my girls.

Charlize: You can officially call me Mrs. North now. And Pop, he's giving me the eye, so I must go.

I then place my hand in my husband's and begin our married life.

Deciding not to run from Owen, and to trust that he

would keep showing up, continue keeping his word, and never stop giving me every piece of himself was the best decision I ever made.

I have loved all of our dating moments, but I think our married moments are going to be the best moments of my life.

Thank you so much for reading Owen's & Charlize's story.
I hope you loved it as much as I do!

Want more?
Download their Bonus Epilogue here:
https://ninalevinebooks.com/bradford-black

The next book is...

Accidentally, Scandalously Yours

Bradford & Kristen's story
an accidental marriage romance
https://ninalevinebooks.com/bradford-black

ALSO BY NINA LEVINE

Escape With a Billionaire Series

Ashton Scott

Jack Kingsley

Beckett Pearce

Jameson Fox

Owen North

Storm MC Series

Storm (Storm MC #1)

Fierce (Storm MC #2)

Blaze (Storm MC #3)

Revive (Storm MC #4)

Slay (Storm MC #5)

Sassy Christmas (Storm MC #5.5)

Illusive (Storm MC #6)

Command (Storm MC #7)

Havoc (Storm MC #8)

Gunnar (Storm MC #9)

Wilder (Storm MC #10)

Colt (Storm MC #11)

Sydney Storm MC Series

Relent (#1)

Nitro's Torment (#2)

Devil's Vengeance (#3)

Hyde's Absolution (#4)

King's Wrath (#5)

King's Reign (#6)

King: The Epilogue (#7)

Storm MC Reloaded Series

Hurricane Hearts (#1)

War of Hearts (#2)

Christmas Hearts (#3)

Battle Hearts (#4)

The Hardy Family Series

Steal My Breath (single dad romance)

Crave Series

Be The One (rockstar romance)

www.ninalevinebooks.com

ABOUT THE AUTHOR

Nina Levine

Nina Levine is a *USA Today* and *Wall Street Journal* bestselling author of over twenty books, including the Escape With A Billionaire series and the bestselling Storm MC series. She's known for bossy alphas and women who don't hand their hearts over easily.

She lives in Australia and when she isn't creating with words, she's busy being a Pilates goddess, a Peloton Queen, or drinking one too many cocktails with friends. Often though, she can be found curled up in the sun with a good book and some chocolate.

www.ninalevinebooks.com

ACKNOWLEDGMENTS

Jodie, I seriously could not do this without you. I don't think you have any idea just how much you lift me when I think I can't go on. Owen's book would not be finished right now if not for you. Jameson almost ended me, but I don't think I actually considered giving up like I did on Owen at times during the end there. I am so thankful to have you in my life, to have your support, your love, and your belief in me. I don't know how any girl gets through life without a Jodie xx

To my author friends who checked in on me. You know who you are and I love you dearly. Thank you <3

To my family and friends who allow me the space to write. You always let me disappear for weeks on end to get my books done and I am so grateful for your support and love.

Lisa Fox, you check in on me often and your texts all mean a lot to me. I never imagined being your friend that first day we met, but you've become such an important part of my life now and I am so grateful.

Rose, thank you for being you. I appreciate your last-minute work and all the suggestions you make. You tweak my sentences perfectly and show me how even just one different word can make such a difference. I am grateful to have you on my team.

To my beautiful readers, thank you for loving my characters and stories, for sharing my books with your friends, for helping me get the word out about my books, for your support. I am so grateful every time you choose to read one of my books. Some of you read the first version of Owen & Charlize's story years ago. You waited so patiently for the rest of it. And I changed it on you. I reworked what I'd already written, tweaking the plot just a little. I made the characters a lot deeper but I kept their essence, the reason you fell in love with them in the first place. I hope you loved their story. And I thank you so much for waiting so long for this book.

To my freaking amazing reviewers and bloggers! You are the fucking bomb and I thank you so much for reading, reviewing, and sharing my books. It means the world to me that you give up your time and choose my book when there are so many books out there you could choose instead to review and talk about. Thank you <3

To Wander & Letitia, another stunning cover that I am so grateful for!! Owen might just be my favourite cover of this series. Thank you for your stunning work!

PLAYLIST

"Enchanted" by Taylor Swift
"Little Bit of You" by Chase Bryant
"Horses" by Keith Urban
"Woke up Like This" by Chris Young
"I Do" by Morgan Evans
"Change Your Name" by Chase Bryant
"Leave Her Wild" by Tyler Rich
"Dive Into You"by Loving Caliber
"Can I Get It" by Adele
"Something Just Like This" by Coldplay, The
Chainsmokers
"Just The Way You Are"by Bruno Mars
"Night Like This"by LP
"Fallin'" by Jessica Mauboy
"I Think He Knows" by Taylor Swift
"Welcome to New York" by Taylor Swift
"You Are in Love" by Taylor Swift
"Do It Again" by Pia Mia, Chris Brown ,Tyga

"Close" by Nick Jonas
"On My Way (Marry Me)" by Jennifer Lopez

Made in the USA
Las Vegas, NV
15 August 2022

53350837R00236